STUNNED

SARAH NOFFKE

Preston,
Thank you for
your support! It means
a ton!
Best,
Sarah Noffke

One-Twenty-Six Press.
Stunned
Sarah Noffke

Published in the United States by One-Twenty-Six Press
ISBN: 978-0-9862080-2-7

Praise for Works:

"There are so many layers, so many twists and turns, betrayals and reveals. Loves and losses. And they are orchestrated beautifully, coming when you least expected and yet in just the right place. Leaving you a little breathless and a lot anxious. There were quite a few moments throughout where I found myself thinking that was not what I was expecting at all. And loving that."
-Mike, Amazon

"The writing in this story was some of the best I've read in a long time because the story was so well-crafted, all the little pieces fitting together perfectly."
-The Tale Temptress

"There are no words. Like literally. NO WORDS.
This book killed me and then revived me and then killed me some more. But in the end I was born anew, better."
-Catalina, Goodreads

"Love this series! Perfect ending to an incredible series! The author has done this series right."
-Kelly at Nerd Girl

"What has really made these books stand out is how much emotion they evoke from me as a reader, and I love how it comes from a combination of both characters and plot together. Everything is so intricately woven that I have to commend Sarah Noffke on her skills as a writer."
-Anna at Enchanted by YA

For Lydia.
May all your dreams come true.

Chapter One

Sixty-five days. That's how much longer I'm obligated to physically remain at the Lucidite Institute. I'm thinking of starting to count in hours. For now my consciousness is passing time at a café in Prague.

The rain makes a pitter-patter song on the canopy outside the window. People run into the café, searching for relief from the constant drizzle. They stop once they find refuge, shaking out their water-soaked coats and hats. The barista keeps eyeing each new arrival like they're a nuisance. No doubt they're the staff responsible for cleaning the floor later. Watching people is fun, especially when they can't see me, and especially when I don't know them—their flaws, their demons, their lies, their injustices.

A guy is chatting up a girl in the corner. She's being polite, but keeps tucking her nose back in her book. He isn't getting the hint. He also doesn't get that he's too old for her. My guess is he's married. Probably runs a sham of a business selling forged art to tourists. Cheats on his taxes. Beats his cat.

Even when I don't know the people, I still find their faults. Or invent them.

I need a vacation. I laugh. At least I still have my stellar sense of humor. Oh, and my modesty.

Absentmindedly, I twirl the frequency adjuster between my fingers.

Baffled. That's how I felt when it wasn't George, but rather Aiden who begged me to wear the adjuster again.

"Why? Why do you care?" I replied when a week ago he asked me to put the frequency adjuster back on.

"Because he can't concentrate and tune into emotions if you're not wearing it," the Head Scientist said. He was all business. No flirtatious looks or heated glances. Just his agenda.

"Well, I'll be gone soon enough and then I won't interfere."

1

He shook his head. I didn't know if he was shaking off my plans to escape the Institute or my resistance to comply. "But we need you to wear it *now*," Aiden pleaded.

"We? Why?" I said, trying to stand my ground.

"Because we're working on something, and George needs his ability to read emotions to perform adequately," he said, staring not at me but off in the distance.

"You two are working on something? Together?" I asked in disbelief. "What is it?"

Aiden averted his eyes. I sighed. More secrets. Hooray…

"Look, I can't tell you," he said. "It's confidential. But…Roya, you can trust me."

I somehow doubt that.

I dissected him with my eyes for a long time. It's hard to like someone so much and also feel intensely frustrated by them. I love the way Aiden made me feel when we danced at the party. I love when he speaks excitedly about his newest inventions. His passion pulls me to him like a vacuum. But it isn't enough, because at the end of it all I know he can't commit to me. He's always straddling some fence between his career and me. I want to have faith in him, but heartbreakingly…I don't. Aiden loves his secrets, and sadly I've become one of them.

"I'm actually kind of surprised by your behavior," Aiden said, disappointed. "You know that George suffers a great deal when you're not wearing the frequency adjuster. It's torture on him."

"That was kind of the point," I said dully.

"Well, your point has been made. Give him a break now."

"Do you even know why I took off the adjuster in the first place?" I asked, my hands on my hips.

"He said you two had a fight. Whatever the disagreement, don't hold your power over him. It isn't fair."

I was so close to telling him that George had made an ultimatum. One that involved Aiden. I wanted to make him see that I was right and George was wrong. But if I did, then everything would become even more complicated. There was no way to tell Aiden that George professed his love to me without making things uncomfortable.

I'm actually surprised that George agreed to work with Aiden at all. He was pushing me to disclose my true emotions that night

2

because he didn't know whether I was falling for him or Aiden. The truth is I didn't know either. I wanted them both, for different reasons. Now I'm furious at both of them. I can't get a break.

"Please, Roya. Will you do this for me?" Aiden asked, persuasion spiking his voice.

The frequency adjuster sat lonely on a nearby table. Just looking at it made George's calculating eyes swim into my vision. I had no idea what Aiden and George were up to. Somehow I was interfering. To try to rid myself of some of this drama, I picked up the adjuster and tied it around my neck. A smile spread across Aiden's face.

"Fine," I said, tying the necklace in a double knot.

"Roya, you're always—"

"Save it, Aiden. You got what you wanted," I said, frustration laden in my tone.

"Well, thank you."

My eyes drifted to the monitor hanging overhead. Its cascading graphics were morphing in perfect choreography to a Frou Frou song.

"Is there anything else? Any *other* reasons you called me down to your lab?" I asked, hoping my tone didn't sound too expectant.

A smile tugged on his mouth. "Unfortunately, no. Right now I've got to get caught up on some work."

A curt nod. "Right. See you around."

That was the last time I'd seen Aiden. A week ago. Too long. Apparently, he had *a lot* of work to catch up on.

My mind shifts back to my current surroundings, shaking off my irritation at Aiden. The tax-evading, animal-abusing adulterer has gotten up to order a few more coffees from the barista. His smug attitude oozes off him and is more repelling than his cologne. I have half a mind to push out a chair suddenly to trip him when he waltzes past my table. If it wasn't for the Lucidites' damn laws against such things then I would—with no guilt. The girl is already engrossed back in her book. She's got to be thinking about how she's going to handle this guy when he returns, ready to make his next move. Maybe she's not. Maybe she's like me—reactionary under romantic tensions.

When I had torn off the adjuster, George disappeared, no doubt dealing with the torture my frequency caused him. On the day I once

3

again tied it around my neck, he plopped down next to me at lunch. His nonchalant attitude was enough to make me want to tear off the adjuster again and throw it in his mashed potatoes. However, when I met his eager gaze, I lost my resolve. It was hard to be furious with him since I knew he was reading my angry emotions and deciding to act friendly despite them. He was obviously trying to mend relations, but I'm North Korea. I don't want to get along with the rest of the free world. Mostly, I want to be left alone. Fat chance that will happen though.

"Hey," he said to me, taking a sip of water.

I cut my eyes at him.

"Thanks for putting the frequency adjuster back on," he said.

Again I didn't respond verbally. Instead I shot all my disappointment at him. Everything had been intensely emotional since my fight with Zhuang. George was a huge part of that fight. In a way I felt closer to him than I did to Aiden because we were in battle together. Had shared those horrors. However, he pushed me at my weakest moment and demanded more than I was willing to give. If Aiden would have done this then I would have understood, because he was always ignoring boundaries. But George had the ability to recognize my emotional states and therefore know when to back off. We *had* potential, but George couldn't live in the moment. He had to assert pressure on a relationship which was going along just fine. He had to ruin everything.

The way he chewed his lip made me certain he'd read my emotions. I pushed my plate away, having lost my appetite. "What's this project that you're working on with Aiden?" I asked him.

"It's confidential," he said in a mechanical voice.

So I had heard.

"I think we both know I can be trusted with confidential information," I said. "I never leaked a bit of the emotional data you confided in me during our training, did I?"

"No, but this is different. Trey has asked—"

I rolled my eyes. "Oh, never mind then. If Trey said to keep it a secret, then I won't know unless he's the one who chooses to tell me. My own brother didn't even rebel against the Head Official the last time he made a demand like that." I turned to Samara, who was doing a lousy job of pretending not to listen. "Speaking of Joseph, have you seen him around lately?"

4

"Hardly," she admitted.

"Yeah, me either." I sighed. I really needed his counsel, but he hadn't been coming by my room in the evenings like he normally did. At meal times he was mostly absent or rushed. Strange that he's the one who begged me to stay at the Institute and he was missing most of the time. "What about you, Trent? Have you seen Joseph?"

"Girl," Trent said, tucking a dreadlock behind his ear, "I'm lucky to see my own image in the mirror as of late. I've been working too much to keep up with anyone."

Trent had been recruited by Ren to work in his department. Although I thought Ren's full time job was being a middle-aged, red-headed jerk with a chip on his shoulder, he apparently was pretty successful as the Head Strategist for the Lucidite Institute.

"I know what you mean," Samara said, turning to Trent. "The news reporting orientation is pretty time consuming." She stood up from the table. "Hey, maybe Trey has Joseph working on a project too."

"Yeah, maybe," I said.

"Well, speaking of work, I've got to run," Samara said.

"Me too," Trent said, and followed Samara out.

Since I didn't want to be alone with George, I made up an excuse about having something to do and left the main hall. The truth was I didn't have a single thing to do. Everyone from my team had a project to keep them busy during the day. Not me. This left me hours to idle around my room and read books. When I couldn't stand it any longer I'd throw on my sneakers, grab the iPod Aiden gave me, and go for a run. Other than these activities I didn't have any way to occupy my time at the Institute. The only relief I had was when night approached and I traveled to whatever place and time on earth I chose. Most of my dream travel was spent searching the past for interesting times in history. This is apparently what most new Dream Travelers spend their time doing.

"Everyone is always obsessed with the past," Shuman informed me one day during lunch. "Nothing is as real as the past. It is that surreal aspect that draws people to it repeatedly," she said in her airy tone. "However, a time will come when you realize the past holds fewer answers than the present. Those who live in the moment are the most powerful."

For a while, I hardly spent any of my time dream traveling in the present. Apparently I wasn't after answers as much as distraction. There were so many times in history I wanted to see with my own eyes. In a little over a week of dream traveling I'd witnessed everything from Lincoln's assassination to the coronation of Queen Elizabeth II. My nights were a history book of education. However, I did learn that I had to limit my time travels. It was more draining than present time dream traveling. It was difficult too. Going back too far, for too long cost energy and required me to return to my body where I was forced to fall into mindless sleep. Luckily, my night spent with Bruce Lee, when I learned kung fu, had worked because it wasn't too far into the past and didn't take too much out of me.

Currently I was distracting myself by brushing up on present-day sociology. Right now, Eastern Europe was on my curriculum list. Cafes like this one in Prague offer richness that can't be found in museums. For hours I listen to conversations, watch interactions, and study the human condition. And as a bonus, I'm learning Czech.

Still, the people watching isn't enough. Exploring the major points in history isn't enough. My dream travels have failed to take my mind off my loneliness. A few weeks ago I didn't want to die because I'd lose all the people I'd come to love. Now I'm miserable because I'm alive and very much alone.

The older gentleman sets down his coffee cup and slips the girl his phone number. She politely accepts it, but I'm guessing she'll only use it as a bookmark. People are so unbelievably convoluted. Soon I'll forget all the complicated people and emotions inside this tin box where I'm forced to physically reside. Soon I'll be living with Bob and Steve, who aren't difficult at all, but rather simple. From their place I'm going to soak up normalcy. Right now I'm craving that more than nineteenth-century poetry.

Chapter Two

No one speaks to me at breakfast the next morning. They're all too busy shoveling food into their mouths so they can get to work. George looks like he wants to say something, but doesn't dare.

If it wasn't for Patrick, the Institute's courier, then I would have taken a vow of silence for the day—just for the hell of it. He stops me in the hallway. "How you liking your stay at the Institute thus far, sweetheart?" he says, tipping his baseball cap at me.

"Fine." I sort of shrug. "I could use a window in my room though."

"Couldn't we all." His chuckle makes his mustache twitch. "Sweetheart, you need to badger your admirers to send you more gifts, that way I have an excuse to grace you with my presence."

"I'll get right on that. Actually, I wanted to send a letter this morning."

"Well then, I'm your man. You got it with you?"

"No, haven't written it yet. I was wondering, though, does the Institute have internet?"

"Well, sure," he says with a laugh. "We're underwater, not in the dark ages."

"Oh good. I was thinking that for letters and stuff I could send emails. That would save you the trouble."

He frowns. "Whoever said it was trouble?"

"Well…I…just…"

He dismisses me with a wave of his hand. "Oh stop now. You send your emails. I'll find a way to see your pretty face, even if I have to write letters to you myself."

I laugh. "Patrick, you're a charmer, aren't you?"

"I've been called many things, but that's not one of them," he says.

After getting directions from Patrick I take off for the computer lab. I find it on the third level. Of course, email! Why hadn't I considered that before? Must have been that whole fear of being murdered thing that overwhelmed my practical nature.

The rest of the day I spend reading Stephen Crane's *The Open Boat*. This classic is one I was waiting to devour on a lonely day, just like this one. Strange emotions arise as I read. Passages are completed in my mind before my eyes finish them. The entire book is like a long-lost best friend—or twin brother. It's like I've already read this book, although I haven't. Something in this particular fiction speaks to me and I can't shake the feeling. And I also don't understand it. Crane wrote, "When it occurs to a man that nature does not regard him as important . . . he at first wishes to throw bricks at the temple, and he hates deeply the fact that there are no bricks and no temples . . . ."

If I'm truly delving into my psyche, as George would have me do, then I admit that on a subtle level this passage makes me wonder if we're truly all alone. I wonder this more lately with all my solitary hours. If God reigned in this world, would Zhuang have been capable of doing what he did? But what people did to stop a man like Zhuang was an inspiration. And I've read enough to have an idea of where most great writers believe inspiration comes from—a holy source. Still, the passage keeps me wondering, not just about God, but also about whether we're always grasping at straws that aren't really there. That's what keeps me up most nights. Those damn straws.

I close the book, then my eyes. I have an important appointment to keep. The silver tunnel is smooth and long, full of turns. I enjoy the wind on my face and the adrenaline which always accompanies my dream travels. This time it's also accompanied by a sense of joy.

It feels good to see their faces—Bob's round one, Steve's long. Hard to believe it's been a month since the last time I was in their company.

Bob studies me. "Roya, you've changed." His tone doesn't carry a bit of criticism, only wonder.

"I'm not any taller, if that's what you mean."

He snickers. "No, and your days of growing may be over, but you do look stronger—like you could beat Steve in an arm wrestling contest."

There's no doubt about that. "I'm still the same Roya though, just more seasoned."

"Yes," Steve says, "and you still have that defiant look in your eyes. Don't ever lose that."

"No worries. It's inborn," I say.

8

They both wear skeptical expressions as they scan the surroundings. Our ghostly figures stand in tall, damp grass by the lake. Even though it's dark, I can see Bob and Steve's house isn't built yet. The field where the house will stand one day is open except for a few pecan trees. The lake beats on the shore of an unprotected beach.

"All right, Roya," Steve says at last. "What gives? Why we'd meet here? I don't mind, but…"

Bob's at Steve's shoulder. He looks like he's wondering the same thing.

"Well," I begin, "I probably could have come up with a better location, but I knew this one would be perfect for my purposes." They both exchange curious glances. "And besides, I wanted to return to you guys' place. I've missed it. It's just I forgot the house wouldn't be built yet," I say. What I don't say is I've also missed the lake. It's where I grew up and the only part of my childhood I can still fully experience.

"Why November 17, 1966, though?" Bob asks.

"I figured it would be great to have a show to watch while we catch up," I say.

"Show? What kind of show?" Steve asks.

I point to the sky, allowing the grin I'd been suppressing to escape. "Only the largest meteor shower ever."

Satisfied expressions unfold on both their faces.

"If my research is correct," I continue, "then we have approximately three minutes to find a nice place to sit before the show starts."

We settle down on a sturdy log along the beach. The first stars fall right on cue. With each passing second, the volume of meteors increases until they're sprinkling down all around us. We're speechless for a few minutes watching the best fireworks show in the world. It's impossible to count the meteors streaking from every possible place in the vastness. According to what I read, on this night the meteors fell at a rate of approximately sixty per second. When I read that I could hardly believe what a display of that magnitude would look like. Now I know. *Unearthly.*

I recede into my thoughts and pretend I'm on a distant planet and this is the show I watch every night before I go to sleep in my antigravity chamber. These stars are a part of evolution and their falling means that more stars are being created to take their place. Bigger ones. Better ones. But one day they will fall too.

I gaze across the lake. The house I grew up in hasn't been built yet either. As if sensing my thoughts, or maybe following my line of vision, Bob says, "You think about the family you grew up with often?"

"Only when I feel like torturing myself, so yes," I say.

"I'm certain they feel a loss, not having you in their lives anymore," Bob says.

"I wouldn't bet on it," I say.

"Even though their minds have been reprogrammed, their hearts have not. That would be impossible," Steve says.

I shrug. I don't feel like telling them that I know for certain my absence has gone unnoticed by my fake family. Shortly after the battle with Zhuang I returned to the home where I was raised. Joseph had been the one to suggest it. *Closure.* That's what he'd called it. That night he traveled to the pig farm where his father made his life hell after his mother died. I returned to the lake house to spy on the people who raised me. It felt weird to call them my parents now. I realize now the modifier, which the Institute had used to manipulate them to accept me as their child, had begun to wear off a couple of years ago. That's the reason numerous times they acted as if I didn't exist—or at least I believed they were acting. Now I know that for them, I didn't truly exist in their reality. It was only once Aiden had perfected the technology that the device worked more fluidly, but it still was no match for Zhuang. He was the one to undo all its programming. He was the one who set me on a new course by getting me thrown out of my fake family's home. Zhuang thought he was sending me in his direction, but he was wrong.

My fake brother's space in the garage hadn't changed a bit. The same lumpy couch sat in front of a nearly burnt out TV. Even his dirty laundry was piled in different corners of the room. My phony family was still coming to terms with his passing. Shiloh might have been an established loser, but he was also a beloved member of that family and the community. People liked his easy grin and carefree attitude. Turns out those are the same traits that made one effortless prey to Zhuang. That's the reason Shiloh was the first to succumb to the brainwashing. He was barely functioning the last time I saw him, which is why he didn't survive the blast that we suppose happened when Zhuang's consciousness imploded or exploded or whatever it did.

The people I'd known as my parents for the first sixteen years of my life were lying on the couch, curled up in each other's arms and watching a reality TV program when I visited. They seemed subdued as they chatted about their favorite characters during the commercials. There was absolutely nothing new or different about them. The modifier's failure had proved useful in this situation at least. There didn't seem to be any indication that I ever existed in that household. Trey explained they'd probably disposed of my stuff when in the hallucinator phase of Zhuang's attack.

Who knew what the school or town thought? Honestly, I was one of those people who didn't make much of an impact. It wouldn't surprise me in the least if my disappearance went unnoticed.

What bothered me the most about that visit was that I felt no hurt at being obliterated from these people's lives. The point that these things rarely upset me is the most bothersome part. Most people feel. They care. Maybe that's the reason I'm on the verge of living a new, unmemorable life at the Institute. Obviously, I'm trying to manipulate myself into doing something about my emotional numbness, but so far it isn't working.

Conversely the people in Joseph's life had great difficulty forgetting him. They apparently thought he'd been in an accident or kidnapped. His paranoid father believed Joseph was hiding on the farm somewhere, waiting to attack when the old man fell into one of his usual drunken stupors. However, the townspeople organized a search party, scouring the fields and forests for weeks trying to track him down. Joseph recounted his findings to me with great pride. I knew how the town felt, because I missed Joseph too.

Now, my fake family, Joseph's fake father, and all the people who had ever known us before we came to the Institute have been "reprogrammed." Their memories of us have receded. They'd never remember us in their lives. We are footprints on the shore and the modifier is the ocean, erasing all marks. Trey explained this was for the best, but I hated the idea that the modifier was once again used on Middlings to manipulate their thoughts. Yet I also knew I couldn't go back to the place I grew up. And I didn't want to one day see my face on a missing person's report. I acquiesced to the use of the modifier—but only in this one instance.

Meteors still rain down from the sky when I turn to Bob and Steve. "So how's business?" I ask in an effort to take my mind off my troubles.

"Well, gold is up, which is always good for us," Steve says.

"And I've managed to find a few new resources," Bob adds.

"So we won't starve anytime soon." Steve chuckles.

I know for certain they deal in rare antiques because it's fascinating and not because it's extremely lucrative. It's one of the things I love most about them—they're intrinsically motivated. More than that, I love that with Bob and Steve there's no pressure. They don't appear to want anything from me. Part of me used to wonder why they were so nice to me—buying my clothes and offering to let me live with them. However, my education in people watching has started to pay off. There are two types of humans in this world: those who function so they can get something and those who function so they can give something. The former are the majority. The latter are Bob and Steve. They're innately driven by some power of benevolence. Maybe still in their giant hearts they pity me, see me as a charitable pet project, but I don't really give a damn. If their aim is to fix me then I'll hand them the tool box. I can't think of two people I'd trust more with that job. They're the only Lucidites who have never lied to me.

"What about you, Roya?" Steve asks. "How are you keeping busy?"

"I'm not," I say and explain how unproductive I've been lately.

"Have you considered," Bob says, not taking his eyes off the sky, "that maybe you should ask Trey to put you on a project? It might help you if you weren't so idle."

I shake my head. "Well, I wanted to, but then I wondered why he hadn't approached me like he did with everyone else," I say.

"Maybe he thought you'd had enough responsibility for a while and needed a break," Steve offers.

"Yeah, maybe," I say, watching the tail of a star trace across the sky. "I don't even know what I'd do for the Institute."

"There's plenty of stuff they could use you for." Steve pats me on the back.

I close my eyes and make a wish that he's right.

Chapter Three

I decide to take Bob and Steve's advice. The only problem is I don't know how to find Trey. He's another one I rarely see. Since Flynn's death, he's taken over as the Head of the Institute and I think the new stress and responsibility has been more than overwhelming to him. The only time I see him is by accident in the hallway, or the one time when he came to debrief after the fight with Zhuang.

I'd been pretty closed off during that conversation and didn't get as much out of it as I should have. Trey explained what I'd expect to find at my fake family home. He welcomed me to stay at the Institute as long as I liked. Then he offered to answer any questions. I had a million questions about my life, Dream Travelers, the Lucidites, and the Institute. However, I still resented that Trey had lied to me about Joseph, had the Institute keep this secret from me, and manipulated my life since the beginning. So when Trey gave me a chance to ask him anything, I just stared at the bare conference room wall and said, "Why don't we have more artwork in the Institute?"

Trey looked disappointed, like I lacked imagination. He said if I needed anything I could always come and find him. The problem now is I don't know where to look. I know where Ren and Shuman's offices are, and his isn't in that vicinity. Most people probably would ask someone for this information. I'm obviously not most people.

My search for Trey takes me to the second level, where the residential corridor and a bunch of meeting rooms are located. There are also a few large classrooms, storage areas, and a door on one long single hallway. It's unmarked and locked.

I move my search to the third level. More locked doors, the kung fu studios, and offices with people who look annoyed when I happen into their space. Defeated, I turn, ready to abandon my mission. A voice halts me. Not only do I recognize it, but it's uncharacteristically high. I listen, hiding my presence behind the corner.

"I really enjoyed seeing you last night." A giggle. "Thanks so much for joining me," Amber, Aiden's assistant, says in a voice unlike her usual clinical one.

"Yeah, it was fun. Thanks for the invite," Aiden says.

What!?

"We should do it again soon, Aiden," Amber says.

Do what!?

"Actually, should I call you Dr. Livingston now? Since you've completed your PhD?" she says in a voice that's making my skin cringe.

"Aiden is fine," he says. I imagine he shrugs and blushes.

"Look, I'm glad I ran into you because I'm having a tough time understanding the coding for the upgraded GAD-Cs. Do you think you could run me through it one more time?" Amber sounds like a lost puppy. I loathe dogs.

"Oh, definitely," Aiden says with his typical enthusiasm. "It really is quite simple, but not until you understand a few principles."

"Well, I've read through your notes, but something isn't clicking in my head," Amber says with an exasperated sigh. "I do so much better with one-on-one instruction."

"Cool, well, why don't you buzz down to my lab this afternoon? I'll sort you out."

"Oh, that would be really wonderful," she says. I feel like gagging at the oh-so-bright eagerness in her voice.

"K, until then."

Footsteps retreat to the elevator. Another set patter in the opposite direction. I slide up against the wall and watch Amber's brown ponytail trot down the hallway to the left. The urge to reach out and yank it courses through me.

Once the door to her office slides closed, I throw my head back until it hits the brushed stainless steel wall. A sharp pain echoes through my body. I welcome it.

Is this really happening? Is Aiden putting the moves on Amber now? How long has it been since we kissed? Not even two weeks.

I throw my head back again, ramming it loudly into the wall. The ache is now dull, but as intended, numbs my emotional frustration. I storm off to the elevator. I'll go to the fourth level, but no farther. I don't care if Trey's office is on the fifth level, that's where Aiden's lab is and I'm not setting foot there for as long as I possibly can.

The fourth level's aquamarine carpet under my feet doesn't greet me the same way as the treadmill, but it still feels good to run. I jog past doors, not even stopping to inspect them. I've completely abandoned my mission now. Each step I take is another one away from Aiden. His games. His secrets. Maybe I should have seen this coming. But I never see anything, it seems, until it's right in front of me.

Racing around a corner I slam into Shuman. Her amethyst eyes bore into me, irritation heavy in her gaze. A normal person might have been pushed over by my assault, but Shuman doesn't even waver.

"You all right, Roya?" she asks, flattening her leather vest and staring at me hesitantly.

"Yeah, I'm fine," I say, still startled. "I'm sorry. I just…"

Shuman raises an eyebrow at me. "Are you looking for someone?"

Yes.

"No, I'm just exploring," I say.

"Hmm," Shuman says, skepticism loaded in her tone. "Well, since I have you here, I want to ask you a question."

I straighten. Prepare myself. "Yes?"

Shuman's hair is tightly pinned in its usual braid. The hairstyle makes her appear young and innocent, which is the opposite impression her demeanor gives off. I wouldn't say she's older than thirty, but she has an air of maturity—or maybe it's entitlement. Whatever it is, Shuman commands a level of respect, which I've only threatened once.

"Roya," she says in an airy voice, "I could use your help in my department. I am not sure if you would be interested, but if you wanted to explore the possibility then I would welcome you."

"Really? Me?" I ask.

"I can always use the help of a clairvoyant. With practice I think your insights could give us access to significant events in the immediate future. You and your brother together would be an impressive force, but by yourself you are an asset."

15

Me as a News Reporter? They're such an elite group, revered by most Lucidites. They're also a complete mystery. *Hell, yes, I'm interested.*

"Sure, I'll check out the opportunity," I say, trying to sound indifferent.

"Good," Shuman says softly. "My department is on the fifth level in the Panther room. Meet me there tomorrow morning. I will give you a tour, then we will see if you are interested in participating."

Damn it! The fifth level? I feign a smile. "Sure, I'll be there. Thanks." I turn and head to the elevator.

"Roya," Shuman says, not having moved.

Turning, I face her.

"Before, when you ran into me, I had the impression you were upset."

Always the observant one, isn't she?

"I'm just feeling a little lost," I say, averting my eyes.

"That is not such a bad place to be," she says, looking characteristically stoic.

I think about Aiden and how much I want to slap him right now. "Yeah, well, I'd settle for a hundred other *places* right now."

"I understand that, but also consider that the way to love anything is to realize that it might be *lost*."

Nodding, I turn back around. I have absolutely no idea what she's talking about. This is so typical of Shuman that I don't even question it anymore. Hell, the day she starts making sense is when I've officially lost my mind. Might be tomorrow.

♦

For the rest of the day I lie low in the workout facility, listening to music that tugs on my heart like ropes on a sail. I guess I shouldn't be surprised when George shows up.

"Oh, you're in here? I had no idea," he says in an unconvincing voice. Slinging a towel over his shoulder, he sets off for the treadmill beside mine.

"Right," I mouth.

I know my emotions are intense. If they were a three-year-old they would have spattered paint all over the room and thrown a

16

tantrum up and down the hallway. For a moment I consider yanking off the adjuster and having some privacy. I decide that at the current moment I don't care enough. George and I are so far gone at this point and apparently Aiden and I are too. It really doesn't matter who knows how I feel right now. Besides, George can pick up on emotions, but he doesn't always know the reasons behind them.

"I couldn't help but notice you've only run seven miles," George says, starting up his treadmill. "Slow day?"

I stop my iPod, slow my treadmill, and stare at him with contempt as my feet hit roughly on the conveyer belt. "Yes, it's been a slow day. I set up a lemonade stand on the first level and hardly anyone came to buy anything. I'm just so upset about my failure," I say, glancing at my heart rate. 184.

"Sugar," he says revving up his machine until he's running.

"What?"

"Did you try putting sugar in your lemonade?" he asks.

"Ha. Nah, I'll try that next time. I thought people would give me a handout for my efforts and winning smile." I stop my treadmill and stumble off, my legs wobbly from the sudden stop of motion.

"Oh, that's too bad," he says between breaths. "If I knew you were there I would have patronized your stand."

"Yeah, that's funny, because you knew I was here and you showed up." I eye him suspiciously.

"Roya," George says, slowing his treadmill, "I can feel emotions, but I don't always know whose they are."

"You're going to tell me you don't recognize *my* emotions when you feel them?" I snap at him, my anger rising to the surface for the first time all week.

George takes his towel and wipes it over his dry brow. He hasn't run long or hard enough to sweat yet.

"Look," he finally says, "if you need someone to talk to then I could be that person."

"Really, George? Because I don't think you're the most qualified person for me to disclose myself to. The last time I checked you were on the hunt for information, and if I had my choice then you'd know a whole lot less than you already do."

He focuses on the adjuster hanging loosely around my neck. His eyes drift up to mine. "You have to give me another chance."

"Not right now I don't."

17

"How much longer are you going to be mad at me?"

"I haven't decided yet."

"Well, will you let me know when you do?"

"Unfortunately, I won't have to do that. You'll know," I say and stride off.

Chapter Four

The stainless steel door is cold under my knuckles when I knock. Nervous tension constricts my chest. I eye the hallway, hoping Aiden doesn't materialize with his glasses and smile. Lucky for me, and probably Aiden too, Shuman answers after a few seconds. "Follow me," she says and strides down a hallway.

Good morning to you too.

I follow Shuman through a dark corridor. The walls are lined with wires and ports. I track them the best I can, but they twist away before I can figure out where they lead. Shuman guides me past a main conference room with a table. A few strangers glance up at me with curious expressions.

The next room resembles a darkened dentist's office. A dozen or so stations are arranged with reclining chairs. In each of the seats, leaning back and looking quite relaxed, is a person—eyes closed, ears covered.

"These are news reporters," Shuman says as we walk along the row of chairs. "They are seeking newsworthy stories." A light over their heads bathes them in blue. "This set-up—chair, light, and audio—is all crafted to foster a higher state of awareness. This is one of the many strategies we employ to make reporters universal observers."

I nod, pretending this all makes perfect sense.

"When they gather information of use to us," Shuman continues, "it is recorded at one of the computer stations nearby. Then the information is checked against other reports for contradictions, and once deemed accurate it is posted onto the Lucidites' internet feed."

"So, do these reporters just lie down and hope to find some event of interest?" I ask.

Shuman spins, facing me abruptly. "That would be a clumsy approach at best. Hope is never a part of the equation. Faith maybe, but that is a discussion of semantics. These news reporters are disciplined in the art of focus." She folds her arms tightly across her chest. "There is much training that takes place before someone can become a news reporter. They have to know how to focus, upon

19

what to focus, and if something is newsworthy. I have spent decades perfecting the strategy for training our news reporters."

Decades? Shuman doesn't look old enough to have worked here for decades.

She pivots and strides away. I follow. We enter a hallway again, with windows looking into dark purplish rooms. I peer through to find women and men lying on cots and seemingly in hypnotic states. Samara is one of the initiates in the room. A peaceful expression coats her face. Her long, whitish blonde hair sprays out along the cot.

"Here these participants are in the final stages of investigative reporting orientation," Shuman continues. "We expect our investigative reporters to focus on specific stories to uncover more details about newsworthy events. If they awake with information of use then they pass this part of orientation."

"But I thought that news reporters picked up on events," I state blankly.

"These people are not clairvoyant, therefore they are investigative reporters. I rely on individuals with skills like yours to discover new reports. Other types are expected to investigate them for authenticity."

She strides down the hallway to another window. Three women lie on cots. They're bathed in the blue, purplish light which illuminates most of the department.

"These are news reporters. Here we ask the trainee to find something of usefulness to the Institute and record it. This is the last task that a news reporter must pass before moving to the floor." She points to the area that resembles the dentist office.

"If these participants rouse with information that is of use to the Institute or a Lucidite then they will continue with us." Shuman stares through the glass, her hands clasped behind her back.

"So, you want me to start training?" I ask, turning to Shuman.

With a quick shake of her head, Shuman leads me through a door at the end of the hallway. I squint from the sudden bright light in this new area. It's another conference-type room, but the light has a gold tone to it. Shuman takes a seat at the table and indicates I should sit opposite of her.

"I could never ask the person who challenged Zhuang to go through my training practices," Shuman says, her hands steepled in front of her. "This would be an insult. You have already been tested in multiple respects and proven yourself in extraordinary ways. Furthermore, it would be an insult to the Institute that chose you for the challenge."

"I don't think it would be an insult. Wouldn't the news reporters be offended if I worked alongside them without having to pass any tests?"

"You sacrificed yourself to protect every person in this Institute. So no, I do not think any of them would be the least bit offended."

"I appreciate what you're saying, but I don't want special treatment."

"Then stay in your room."

I blink, startled.

"It is no good for me to delude you into thinking that you are average or that you are going to assimilate into this culture the same as everyone else," Shuman says, her tone rough. "You did not enter this Institute under normal circumstances and the ones that kept you here mark an incredible event in the Lucidites' past. The battle between you and Zhuang is the single most frequented event in our history."

My mouth drops. "What? How do you know that?"

She tilts her head. "It is my job to know that."

The idea that Lucidites have dream traveled to watch Zhuang pummel me to bits is jarring. I never thought that our battle would be like a trending video on YouTube.

"O-kay. Soooo, you don't want me to pass a test, I get that. But I don't know *how* to news report. I *do* need to be trained."

Shuman shakes her head. "No, you do not."

I open my mouth to argue, but she holds up her hand, silencing me. "I believe you possess the skill and intuition to successfully news report. What you lack is confidence. What you need is to prove to yourself that you are worthy of the position."

Reading Faulkner right now sounds a million times better than what I've just gotten myself into. Tension constricts my thoughts as I await Shuman's next words. She's appraising me, making me self-conscious of my every nonverbal behavior.

"In a minute I am going to leave you alone in this room. This will give you the opportunity to use your clairvoyance to pick up on

21

one newsworthy event. It must be important, unreported, and verifiable. If you do not have something to report to me within the hour then we can agree that news reporting is not the right fit for you. If you do succeed in this challenge, then I will expect you to start work on the floor with the other news reporters tomorrow morning." She stands, looking down at me, her cheekbones even more pronounced from the gold light overhead. "If this is agreeable to you then stay here. If not then show yourself out." Shuman strides away. At the doorway, she flips a switch and the gold light is replaced with the bluish purple. "Call me at any time to make your report and I will return," she says, and leaves.

What in the messed up world that is the Institute have I gotten myself into? This is my chance to prove myself. To take on a new challenge, one that will distract me from my sad love life. But I have absolutely no idea what I'm supposed to do.

Defeated, I lay my head on my hands resting on the table and try to breathe deeply. It isn't so bad if I fail this test and nothing comes of it. I can always go back to sitting in my room. There's also the chance I can find Trey and ask him to assign me to a project. I have to admit, though, that I was relieved when Shuman offered me this opportunity. Truthfully, seeking Trey out was never something I wanted to do. It had to do with my ego, which feels like it's currently being caged and shocked with a cattle prod.

My anxiety is no good to me, so I push it to the corner of my mind, just how Shuman taught me to do. I clear the blackboard of my mind and allow myself to float in and out of consciousness. This lucid meditation has become second nature for me at this point. And I know that the benefits I've garnered from it are worth every second of focus. The practice has kept me sane when I was losing it, guided me when I was lost, and given me courage when I thought I'd die.

In my mind's eye I see a flash of red, so bright, so unsettling. Blood. It trickles down a man's chin. He flicks it away with an arrogant jerk. My vision suddenly blurs, but I still hear everything perfectly, even the unsteady breathing of the battered man. "Is that all you've got?" he says.

A cackle answers his taunt. "Umm…More?" a girl says, her voice high-pitched, sing-song, cloaked in a French accent. "Is 'at what you vant?"

"What I want is to be left alone. Could you manage that?" the man answers.

"It appears I cannot," the girl says, like she's kissing each word. "I'm certain I can't be happy unlez you're dead. And I really do deserve to be happy, don't you zink? You still vant me to be happy, don't you?" she says, in one big, flowing breath. The cackle again. It hurts my ears.

Then all noise fades and my vision returns. The blade racing to the man's chest is already stained with blood. His blood. But he won't escape this assault. I know it. I know it with such certainty. The same as I know the man. I'd never forget that voice. That accent.

My eyes bolt open. "It's Ren!" I scream. "It's Ren! He's in trouble! She's going to kill him! You've got to help him!" I hear myself say. I can't believe the words are coming from my mouth.

I hear movement right before Shuman enters. One-way glass sits to the right of the door. I was being watched.

Shuman strides over to me. "What did you see?"

"I saw Ren. He's been attacked. Tortured. By a girl...with a French accent." Each word sounds wrong in my mouth. But I know what I saw; I stand by it. My breath has escaped me now. I pause to catch it, to understand what I've witnessed. "I'm not sure what's going on with him. I didn't see his attacker. I only heard her."

Shuman nods her head once and exits, leaving me to sit enveloped by my own confusion. Maybe all those solitary hours have caused me to lose my mind. I've always had a crazy imagination and now my own lust for Ren's demise has literally gone to my head. What's going to happen when Shuman comes back and tells me that I'm dead wrong about my premonition? One thing is for sure, my ego will be branded with the word "LOSER."

And still it gets me that in this flash I saw Ren—my nemesis at the Institute. He's the last person on earth I would save if I had a chance. If the vision was real, then whatever was happening was undoubtedly something he deserved, had brought on himself. If that girl is real, then he'd probably done something corrupt to her. I don't even want to imagine the awful torment the people in Ren's personal life suffer.

Ten nerve-wracking minutes later the door to the room slides open and Shuman materializes again. She takes hurried strides in my direction and settles into the chair across from me. Her eyes meet

23

mine with hesitation, then focus back on the table. My nerves hum with a dangerous capacity.

"Everyone at the Institute owes you a huge debt of gratitude for this report, especially Ren," Shuman says. "You have saved his life. Without a doubt he would have been dead, if it was not for what you just saw. The strange thing is that none of my news reporters picked up on this event. You were expected to see something new to pass the test, but not something of *this* magnitude." There's a pause while she gives me a cautious glance. "The news reporters really *should* have seen this, but they did not…you did."

I stare at her for a long time trying to register what she's said. "Wait," I say, leaning forward. "Ren was actually in trouble? I interpreted what I thought I saw accurately? And no one else saw this? Why?"

Shuman settles back in her chair. "Yes, you saved Ren's life. Thanks to you, Lucidites were able to rescue him and bring him back to the Institute."

Wow! That was fast.

"Who attacked Ren?"

"That is not of importance at the moment," Shuman says at once.

I know from her previous answers to these questions that this means she knows the answer but isn't going to tell me. If she didn't know the answer then that's what she'd say, instead of deferring the conversation.

"I am not sure why you saw this when no one else did. However, numerous events are missed every day and that is why I am always looking for different news reporters to add to the group. More eyes mean we can know more."

Of course that makes sense. I take a skeptical glance at Shuman. There's something else. Something she isn't saying. I sense it. But she doesn't speak.

Silence sits between us for a while. It makes me think. Think about what she said. About my confidence. About me having to prove it to myself.

For a long moment I think over this situation. There's definitely something about the Panther room that enhances my clairvoyance. Shuman's right that if Joseph were here I'd probably be even stronger. I can feel that power coursing through my veins now. I

24

close my eyes and let it vibrate in me, enjoying the feeling. I don't even care that Shuman is staring at me with my eyes closed. When I open them my head is already shaking. I'm hooked on this feeling and want to do this again.

I swallow and look up at her. "I'd be happy to start tomorrow," I say.

Her hands are clasped on the table. Except for a tiny squeeze of her fingers, there are no other indications of satisfaction. Not a smile or an expression in her eyes. "Okay," she says finally.

Chapter Five

"I passed!" Samara squeals when I sit down at dinner.

"Oh, that's wonderful!"

Relieved and excited for Samara, I tell her I also accepted a position as a news reporter, which I wasn't going to disclose if she'd failed. Another enthusiastic yelp of delight follows.

"Usually testing and training takes between six months and a year," Samara says, stirring her soup. "It's unheard of for someone to start with the news reporters after only a couple of weeks, or a day, in your case."

"Yeah, it's good to know there's some perks associated with risking our lives to fight Zhuang." I laugh morbidly.

Although I'm probably breaching some confidentiality agreement, I share my vision of Ren with her. Sue me. "When Shuman confirmed it was actually Ren and I'd saved his life, I'd never experienced a bigger rush," I explain, feeling the excitement all over again.

"Really? Even when you defeated Zhuang? You didn't get a huge rush then?" she questions.

"For starters, we don't know I *did* defeat Zhuang. And secondly, I was kind of dying at the time. That kind of thing kills any rush."

She laughs. "So you don't know what exactly happened to Ren?" she asks under her breath.

I shake my head. "No, Shuman wouldn't tell me anything. And I don't know how much of the vision came to pass. He might not have even been assaulted when they rescued him. It's so hard for me to know since the timing of my visions is either a few seconds or several minutes before something is going to actually occur. I just know he was in imminent danger."

"That's really bizarre. I mean, Ren is supposedly pretty powerful. What kind of person could take him down? And why? It's scary to think something is out there attacking people like Ren. Makes me nervous."

I hadn't really thought about that yet. Who exactly *did* attack Ren? Was it someone connected to Zhuang? Should I be worried about my dream travels? Someone would have told me if I was in danger, right?

Samara glances around. "Something else is worrying me too. It's Joseph. He's been acting different. Do you know why? Or what he's up to?"

His absence hasn't worried me. It's been downright irritating. "Beats me," I say with a huff. "He's never around anymore. I don't know what he's doing. At least I know he's not working with Shuman. She said that much."

"Yeah," Samara says. "And he's not working with Ren. I already asked Trent."

"Well, he's probably doing something with Aiden. The Head Scientist has a way of recruiting people," I say. I can tell Samara notices the bitterness in my voice but I really don't care.

I feel a hook slip into my mind and gracefully pull on a thread. It's brief but I know the sensation well enough to tell Samara has just popped into my brain for a thought. She stares at me guiltily.

"Sorry," she says, looking down at her hands. "Sometimes my desire is stronger than my will."

I narrow my eyes but can't keep the smile off my face. "What'd you get?"

"You're really pissed off at Aiden for flirting with Amber, working with George on some secret project, and possibly taking your brother away..." she says, a little doubt in her tone.

"Damn." I sigh. "That's a lot of information for a little snag, which is what it felt like."

"Well, in my defense, your thoughts are sitting on the top of your brain right now. You're still processing them, so they're in the main stream, which makes for easy picking."

"Hmmm, I'll try and process faster."

"Don't worry about Amber," Samara says. "She's just after Aiden to get a promotion."

My jaw drops. "Are you kidding me?" I whisper. "How do you know that?"

She winks. "You're not the only one processing stuff."

"But still, she's buttering him up and it sounds like it's working," I say with an edge.

27

Samara doesn't protest this, just gives a sympathetic shrug. "But I don't think Joseph is working with Aiden. It doesn't seem right."

"Have you seen anything about him in your training?" I ask her.

She shakes her head. "I wished I would have. I'm starting to worry about him. I wonder what he's up to."

"Yeah, me too," I finally admit. "He told me I could work with him on this project, but he's obviously changed his mind."

"Maybe," she says. "And what about George?"

"What about him?" I say, scanning the nearby area to ensure he's not spying.

"Well, I noticed the other day that you two had some tension going on between you."

"Oh, you mean when you were eavesdropping on our conversation?"

A bemused expression falls on her face.

"Come off it," I say. "And you had to have noticed I wasn't wearing the adjuster for a few days."

She nods. "All right, I might have heard you giving him a hard time the other day. So what's the deal? Why'd you take off the adjuster?"

"It's complicated. I might tell you later." Then I add, "Of my own accord, so stay out of my head, would you?"

She gives a guilty smile. "Sure, since we're friends and all."

"Yeah, why don't you spend more of your time spying on Amber," I say. "Wait, on second thought, don't. I don't want to know what's going with her and the Head Scientist. Oh, and anything you know about Aiden and me will you please forget and not share with anyone. It's complicated."

"Sounds like you've got a lot of complicated stuff going on."

"That's how I roll."

A premonition flashes over my vision. Clearly I see Samara in her room, her face expectant. Joseph leans into her and trails feather kisses down her cheek. I clench my eyes shut. It's weird to see this, and I force myself to maintain composure.

Samara and Joseph? Damn it, when was she or he going to tell me? Not that it's any of my business, but I'd rather not learn these things through a flash. And I'd really prefer not to see their intimate relations. Gag.

My eyes peel open. "Hey," I say nonchalantly, "if you see Joseph tonight would you pass a message for me?"

Like a bunny rabbit, Samara wiggles her nose. I've learned it's one of her microexpressions. It means she's about to lie. "I doubt I will. And I don't know why I would," she says too fast.

"Well, if you do, tell him I really miss him and could use his help with something."

She smiles and pats me on the shoulder. "I'm here to help if you need me."

"Thanks."

Chapter Six

The next morning I stare at the door to the Panther room for a solid minute.

Do I knock again? Or can I push the button and walk into the department? Indecision freezes me in place until Aiden's bright eyes, full of life and lies, come around the corner. Immediately I slap the button. He's just caught a glimpse of me and holds up his hand to get my attention. I step onto the other side of the door and will it to shut before he catches up to me. The last thing I want to do is talk to him right now. The door closes, and I stare at the other side of it for another minute. I know he's standing in front of it and wondering why I ran off. Maybe he'll hit the button and confront me. At that thought I quickly back away and into the news reporting department.

Shuman is hunched over a table in the conference room, looking at a blueprint of some kind. "I was wondering when you would be done with that," she says as if speaking to the table.

There's no one else in the room. *What does she mean?* I'm sure I don't want to know. Tightly I close my eyes, waiting for the embarrassment to fade.

"I'm here and ready to work," I finally say evenly.

"Good," she says without looking at me. "Follow me and I will set you up at a station."

She leads me to the right. I take in the strangeness all around me as we walk past reclining chairs and their relaxed inhabitants. When we reach the end of a row she stops abruptly and I run into her. She turns, gives me an irritated expression. Not going well so far.

"Here is your station. Lie down when you feel ready. Cover your ears with the headphones and focus. When you gain information then you will rise and report to the closest computer station." She points to one about six feet away, catty cornered to the chair. "Once you have logged one report then your job is done for the day. If you have any questions come find me."

Then she's gone. *How's that the extent of the instructions?* News reporters train for months. Shouldn't I at least get a reference manual or best practices guide? And why only one report a day if, as Shuman admitted, so many events are missed? I stand rigid. What have I gotten myself into? Why am I doing this again? Oh yeah, this is how I've chosen to spend my free time until I get back to Bob and Steve's house. Right. Well, the next time I have an idea I should go back to sleep until I get a better one.

A stream of blue light rains down on the chair. I have to admit that it's already having a calming effect on me. Lying back in the recliner I nuzzle deeper into the cushion, resting my head comfortably and enjoying the sensation of warmth on my face. Easily I find the headphones resting next to me and clap them on. My head fills with white noise. A tangible comfort streams through my blood, instantly softens my core. The sensation satisfies something primitive inside me. A security I've rarely known. It makes it easy to slip into a meditative state and tune into the ethereal.

When the spaces between my breaths is long and slow I focus on my heart chakra. This chakra, also known as Anahata, houses and governs clairvoyance. People often think this power comes from their mind. However, Shuman taught us the mind is the interpreter and that's why it receives the praise for the work the heart actually does. It's through the heart that the vibrations of spirit actually enter, allowing us insights. When we recognize the presence of these vibrations then we take them to the next level of the mind and process what we feel.

Most of this process is automatic, but still I love the words and traditions used to honor this power. I'm more than a body with a mind. I'm an interconnected system. Though, always the question tugs on my mind—what am I connected to? Where does my clairvoyance come from?

After four or five minutes something shimmers to the surface of my consciousness, drawing my attention to it. Like a watercolor painting grows darker as it dries, my vision slowly becomes recognizable. A girl about my age stands in a corner, hate radiating in her dark doll-like eyes. She's speaking to someone I can't see. "I vill have it. If he desires it, I vill have it." Her hostility-coated words scratch at my skin. With absolute certainty I know her voice is the one I heard speaking to Ren in my vision yesterday. Her high-pitched cackle and French accent are distinct. "Ve vill steal it. And zen he vill reward me, vonce and for all."

The evilness in the girl's eyes fills me with the urge to fight her, to stamp her out right there in order to rid the world of all the destruction I know she's capable. Long, black hair drapes around her shoulders. She projects a façade of innocence as she twirls her hair around in a playful manner. However, there's nothing innocent about her. She's dangerous.

A loud intrusion. A voice. A male's. "*Les Lucidites sont vous espionne. Ne voyez-vous pas?*"

A high-pitched cackle. "*Oui. Je fais maintenant,*" she says. Her black hair, like a cape, swings around and she casts her evil, dark eyes—on me! "You're naughty. No more spying for you." With a vengeful smile, she pulls her hand back and throws a knife directly at me.

I awake with a start, heart pounding with fear. The blue light bathes me in comforting warmth. I'm safe and the French girl is nowhere.

This whole thing is too strange and contrived. I wonder if this is the kind of thing the other news reporters see when they focus. Maybe this isn't real and just my warped imagination. Regardless, the girl's words are already seeping from my memory. I shove myself off the chair and start for the computer station. The keys are smooth under my fingertips as I type my report. When I'm done I hit the "submit" button.

The system processes for a minute. I stare blankly at the hourglass on the screen. A window pops up. It reads, "Information unverifiable."

Chapter Seven

The hallway light is harsh compared to the soft glow in the Panther room. My head swims with images of the evil girl. It rattles my insides with terror, makes my skin cringe. I want to run or shower or do whatever it takes to rid myself of the negativity. This is completely the opposite of how I felt yesterday after having the premonition that saved Ren. Consumed by my thoughts and unanswered questions, I don't even notice him stalking me until I'm at the elevators.

"Roya, are you seriously going to ignore me again?" Aiden's voice is full of frustration.

"What?" I swing around and focus on him properly, then avert my gaze to the floor. "Oh, right, what do you want?"

Aiden takes a couple quick strides until he's right in front of me. He's seeking my eyes, but I'm focused on the blue carpet under my feet. "Hey, what's your deal? Are you still mad at me for asking you to wear the adjuster?"

Suddenly I have no problem shaking off the vision I just witnessed. I feel a renewed sense of frustration pulsing through me. My mind flashes on the memory of Amber flirting with Aiden.

"Oh, no," I say, pulling my eyes to his. "I've got new reasons now." I stare at him without flinching. His dark blue eyes try to read me and decipher what I'm really talking about.

He shakes his head like he's attempting to ward off some evil spirit. "Well, I've been trying to locate you for a while now. You aren't easy to track down." He glances at the Panther room. "Are you news reporting?"

I don't answer.

His expression shifts into one of heedless passion. It sends a warning light off in my head. *Caution!* my instinct urges. I'm never good when he adorns that look. It obliterates my willpower. Makes me cave in to whatever he asks. "Why have you been avoiding me?" he says, sounding faintly amused.

I stare at him and shake my head, repulsed. Hurt. Disappointed. A long moment passes where he searches my eyes. After a tense minute he finally says, "Look, whatever it is you know about my project, you need to also know that I'm only working under Trey's orders."

That doesn't make any sense. Trey ordered him to flirt with Amber? Why? "What?" I say.

Aiden draws in a step closer. "I can totally explain everything if you give me a chance. *And*"—he says the word with a brilliant smile—"I have something I'm dying to show you." He reaches for my hand. I could have pulled away before he grabbed it, but I didn't. A sensual shock pulses through me when our fingers meet. He gives me a fierce grin. "Come on," he urges, pulling me down the hallway.

I allow myself to be led to his lab because I do deserve an explanation. My hope is there's a justified reason for his interaction with Amber. There has to be a chance that I've misinterpreted the whole thing. That's what I want, anyway.

"I need your iPod," he says as we walk.

"What?" Sincere dread courses through me. Is he going to give it to Amber? Is this the whole ruse? "Are you taking it back?" I say, trying not to sound as injured as I feel.

He laughs. "I wouldn't dream of it." His easy laughter opens up the space around me like a light. I wonder if he knows he has that effect on me. I hope not.

"Then why do you want it back?" I ask.

"It's just so I can update it with more music," he says, striding in front of me and twirling me around in an impromptu dance. "We have to keep your education in music going, right?"

I'm startled by his casual, romantic nature. It makes me feel I'm the only girl he spins in these hallways, but am I? With a jerk I yank my hand from his. He stops, tilts his head sideways at me, confused disappointment written on his face. Ignoring him, I stride into his lab.

"I'll be right back," he says in a promising voice.

I make excuses to myself for why I should be there. These are then followed by a round of insults from another part of me.

You're weak. A fool. Leave and don't look back.

I'm about to push forward on the balls of my toes and rush away when Aiden's voice sings to me from the back of his lab. "I can't think of anyone I'm more excited to share this new technology with."

34

A pocket of air sticks in my throat. I can't push it out or swallow it. I'm frozen, torn.

A minute later Aiden strides from the back of his lab carrying a large box. Swallowing the uncomfortable feeling in my throat, I focus on the box, on his hands, on anything but his eyes. He pulls a silver helmet from the cardboard box. It's molded like a head, compact and sleek. "This is my newest invention," Aiden says, wearing a cunning smile. "It sends a signal to the prefrontal lateral cortex, preventing the wearer from being able to dream travel. In the past it's been impossible to imprison evildoers like Zhuang because they could always dream travel away, thwarting our attempts at justice. But with this, we can finally capture whoever we need to. It's called a dream blocker. Pretty neat, huh?"

"Is this what you've been working on with George?"

Aiden deflates. "No," he says promptly. Slowly, as if brought on by a realization, a sly smile spreads across his face. "So you think this is what we've been..." He hesitates, head sideways. "Never mind, no, this isn't it."

"Wait. What are you talking about? What's the project you're working on with George?" I ask, confused.

"I thought you already knew."

"I don't."

"Well then, what are you mad about?" He puts the dream blocker down and looks at me with his arms crossed.

"You first. Tell me what the project is with George."

"If you don't know then I can't be the one to tell you. Trey has been very clear that it's to remain confidential. I'm sorry."

"That's ridiculous," I mumble.

"Don't even concern yourself with it. It's an ancillary project." His eyes light up again. "So what do you think about the dream blocker?"

My mind is all over the place now. I can't focus. "Is Joseph working on this ancillary project with you guys?"

"Errrrgh....No," he says with a frustrated growl. Somehow we've gotten miles away from music and romance. "No," he repeats. "Joseph isn't involved. But that's not what we're talking about. I was asking about the dream blocker. What do you think?"

Confusion muddles my thoughts. It doesn't make any sense that this project with George is so secretive. And now I'm really wondering what Joseph is up to.

Footsteps interrupt the little bit of focus I have remaining. In unison we turn our heads to the entrance. "Oh, Aiden, where are you, Aiden? Where's my favorite per—" Amber's broad smile drops the moment she rounds the corner and sees the two of us standing and looking at her, bewildered. "I didn't know you had company. My apologies," she says to me with a nod of her head, her silver earrings gently swaying with the movement. "Good to see you, Roya," she says.

"Is it?" I say. I've never been good at pretenses.

She recoils a bit. Her eyes dart to the dream blocker, then to me and then to Aiden. "Were you showing her the dream blocker?" she asks, a hint of concern in her voice.

"I was," Aiden says, looking straight at me.

Amber turns to me. "It's pretty incredible, don't you think? Aiden is sooooo brilliant."

I don't look at her or answer; instead I stay focused on Aiden. He looks like his shoes are suddenly too tight.

"Well, it's advanced technology, so it may be a bit difficult for non-scientists to understand," she says, condescension laden in her tone.

I swivel around to face Amber. "Surprisingly, I was able to understand the concept fairly well without my head exploding."

She gives me a snobbish smirk and turns to address Aiden. "I was really hoping to discuss something with you. At your earliest convenience would you please come by my office?"

"Yeah, sure," Aiden says in a clipped voice.

"Oh good," she says, rubbing her neck. "I'm so sorry if I've interrupted you two."

"No worries. I'll come and see you in a little while."

"Thanks," she says, her voice sounding pained as she massages her neck with more vigor. "Ow, my neck. I'm so sore from being hunched over, doing all those reports that you asked for, Aiden."

"I'm sorry to hear that, but it's necessary. Those reports are crucial."

"I know you're right. You're always right. I'll get it done for you. And maybe you can help me out again with another massage," she says, and then to my horror she winks at him. Blatantly, f-ing winks. "The last time you did, it was really helpful."

The color drains from Aiden's face. I draw a long breath in through my nostrils, trying not to let my jealously become apparent.

"Well, see you later, Roya," Amber says, tossing her ponytail over her shoulder as she prances out of the lab.

Whirling in Aiden's direction, I lower my chin and shoot an accusatory stare at him. If he didn't know why I was mad before, he knows now. Unable to stomach looking at him any longer I start for the door.

He catches my wrist, spinning me around. "Look, Roya, I don't know what you think is going on."

Swiftly I break clean of his grasp. "I think it's pretty clear."

"Not to me," he says.

"Well, you're an idiot." That's for sure the first time he's ever been called that.

"I've never given her a massage. I swear to it."

"Why would your employee say such a thing?!"

"I don't have a clue."

"You don't have a clue, or you don't want to tell me?"

"I don't know, Roya. Seriously. I don't know. You have to believe me. She's lying. I've never touched her."

"Why would she lie? In front of me?"

He shakes his head. "I sincerely don't know." I have to give him credit, he does look the part—completely puzzled.

"So you didn't meet her the other night? You didn't take her up on her invite and have 'fun'?" I say, my arms tightly crossed in front of me.

If he ever had a case it's gone now. Sunk to the bottom of the ocean. I see it in his face. And it deflates any hopes I had too.

"I thought the whole team was supposed to be there. I didn't know it would just be the two of us. I didn't know..." He stops, having read the look in my eyes. It says what my mouth doesn't: *I don't believe you.*

"Do we really have to be discreet because of your position? Or is it so you can play me? And Amber? And who else?"

"No, Roya. It's not like that."

"Really? I can't get more than a few minutes with you. And you're off..." I close my eyes, feeling the heartbreak finally set in.

Such a fool to ever believe him. Such a fool. Opening my eyes I find Aiden staring at me regretfully. He's on the edge of saying something; his mouth is about to open and make excuses. Excuses I'll believe. He'll make this all go away. Then he'll do it again. I won't be made a fool though. I turn and stalk off before he has a chance to manipulate me the way he always does.

"Please don't do this," he calls as I approach the exit. I continue my march. "Don't storm off like this," he insists, but I remain focused on my path. "Let's work this out between us."

I halt. Turn. Find his blue eyes. I want to ensure he understands what I say and doesn't question it. I will not be made into a fool, not by him or anyone. "Aiden, there is no 'us.'"

Chapter Eight

The treadmill takes my abuse without complaint. Each stride hisses with anger. Each beat of my feet drums with hostility. I am so furious with Aiden that I don't even use the iPod he gave me. I just run and try to find solace in the sound of my feet pounding against the treadmill. If George senses me down here enraged, then he's decided to give me some space. I'm glad for that.

After dinner, I decide I've let off enough steam that I'm willing to be somewhat sociable. Samara and I lie on the floor of her room exchanging details of our reports.

"I investigated this elderly man. I'm not sure why he was of importance though. He'd been kicked out of his run-down little house by some guy with an accent. I followed the old man around for half an hour and listened to his thoughts," Samara says as she braids a strand of her hair. "Then he was thinking about all sorts of unrelated stuff that I'm certain wasn't important. I probably should have disconnected at that point, but I was afraid I'd miss something."

"Who was the old man? And who was the guy with the accent?" I ask, intrigued.

"Haven't got a clue," Samara says, finishing the braid. "Truthfully, I love investigative reporting, but I wish I could news report like you. Discovering reports has to be so much cooler."

"Yeah, well, different doubts go along with my line of work. So far the only report I've logged said it was unverifiable. Who knows if I'm picking up on anything of use. My wild imagination is probably making it all up."

"I wouldn't worry about it so much. My guess is your reports will be authenticated…maybe by me."

"I was wondering, and you might know, why do we only log one report a day? Why not try to find as many newsworthy events as we can?" I say.

"I'm guessing it's because it's draining and risky. However, as an investigative reporter I'm given a few stories each day."

"Oh, really."

I share with Samara what I saw. She listens intently and flinches when I tell her about the French girl throwing a knife at me.

"Oh my god, that's totally gruesome," she shrieks when I'm done. "What do you think that's all about?"

"I haven't got a clue. This whole thing is so new to me. But I'm wondering if in time I'll pick up a pattern," I say.

"What do you mean?" she asks, frowning.

"Well, it's the second time I've seen the girl, so I suspect I'm seeing events that are connected."

"That does make sense," she muses. "Sooooo, to change the subject." Her voice is hesitant.

"Yes?" I ask with dread.

"Well, I know it's a secret and all, and you can always blame it on my telepathy if you need to. Anyway, I'm dying to know what's going on with Aiden."

"He's toast as far as I'm concerned," I say. I tell her about our fight and Amber, and how I really wish he'd drop off the face of the Institute.

"It sounds like she was trying to make you jealous. Do you think she knows about you and him?"

"I doubt it. He made it pretty clear that no one should know. His precious reputation could be harmed."

She gives me a regretful frown. "He was obviously looking for some praise on his new device."

"Yeah, I know," I say.

"But you've got too much going on to know you need to stroke his ego," she says.

I bristle at what almost sounds like an insult. "Hey, whose side are you on?" I ask. Then I chew on my lip. "He drives me crazy. How can he make me feel incredibly drawn and repulsed to him at the same time? And his act is so freaking convincing. I really thought he…" The heartache cuts off my sentence prematurely. "I'm not going to allow him to make me a fool, that's all."

"I know how you feel," she says, staring off at the far wall, a strong emotion in her words.

My guess is my flash was accurate and Joseph visited her last night. I'm not sure why he's visiting her and ignoring me. I'm actually more irritated than hurt.

"Did you by chance see Joseph last night?"

40

She wiggles her nose. "Nope."

I'm not certain why she's lying to me about this, but I suspect Joseph has put her up to it. I also suspect that he's got her completely wrapped around his finger. He's pretty convincing like that, but not on me.

"So are you going to tell me about the 'complicated' situation with George?" Samara asks, using air quotes.

I really don't see why I should share anything with her about my personal life if she won't even tell me she's dating my brother. However, some people are governed by the law of reciprocation. I'm hoping Samara is one of them. And besides, I could use some advice.

"As you know, George kind of likes me and—"

Abrupt laughter erupts from Samara. "Roya, he's completely enamored by you. You do know that, right?"

I sigh.

"Let me set you straight, if you don't know. George is captivated by you," she says.

"I thought you read thoughts, not emotions," I say.

"Yes, and you're all he really thinks about."

I draw in a long breath, feeling suddenly heavy.

"Yeah, well, it's more complicated than him just *liking* me."

She rolls her eyes.

"George knows how to give me exactly what I want most of the time. He's so acquainted with my emotions and we share an unmatched intimacy because of that. However, I can't offer him the same. I don't know what he wants. And I feel like I'm going to disappoint him, either because I'm such a moron when it comes to love or because I'm terrified when it comes to relationships."

"And to make things even more complicated, there's the whole Aiden factor."

I cut my eyes at her. "Aiden is not a factor." *Not anymore.*

Samara stares off at the ceiling, seeming deep in thought. "You know, you should really—" A knock at the door cuts her off. She shoots into a sitting position, her eyes wide. "Stay here," she commands. I have absolutely no intention of doing that.

In an instant she's on her feet, racing to the door. She hits the button and the door slides back. My knees almost lose the strength to hold me up. The image of my brother makes me think I'll crumble. Disbelief is the only thing keeping me upright. Pain roars through me and I know it's his pain. Weakness overwhelms me and I know it's his weakness. But his thoughts are shrouded in a cloud. Lost to me.

"Joseph," I say in a scared hush. I push Samara out of the way and search his hollow expression. His skin is pale. Dark circles hang around bloodshot eyes. A leather jacket hangs loosely on his sunken shoulders.

"Oh, hey, sis," he says with an empty expression.

I worry he'll pass out right here. He's too frail. All the spark that makes him Joseph is gone. Although he's moving and interacting I know it's only through instinct. Joseph isn't fully in his body and I want to rattle him until he rises to the surface.

I drag him into Samara's room. He tries to resist, giving me a petrified look, but he's too weak to overpower me. "My God, Samara, why didn't you tell me he was like this?"

"I didn't know," she says, wiggling her nose.

"That's a lie."

She darts her eyes to the floor. "He told me not to. He said you wouldn't understand, that it would only make you worry unnecessarily."

"Look at him." I wave my hand at a barely present Joseph. He's slumped on the bed, staring off in a daze. "Shouldn't I be worried? Aren't you?"

"Yes, but he wasn't like this last night. Not this bad. I promise," she says in a pained voice. She's right. He didn't look like this in my vision.

"What you girls talking 'bout," Joseph says in a hoarse voice. "I'm fine."

Is he drunk? On drugs? Sleepwalking? No real clues support any of these assumptions.

"Give us a minute or two. I need to talk to him," I say to Samara, not taking my eyes off my brother.

"Yeah," she says. "I'll be outside."

When the door slides closed I cautiously approach Joseph. He's gone somehow. Had he even witnessed the last few minutes? I can't be sure. I sit beside him, curling my feet underneath me.

"Please tell me what's going on," I plead.

With a thud he lies back on the bed. "Oh, nothing much, sis," he says, looking at the ceiling. "What's goin' on with you?"

"Well, my life is falling apart and on top of that now I'm super worried about you," I say. Joseph's eyes shoot wildly around the room, like they're watching a fly buzz in the air.

"Oh man, that sounds tough, Stark," he sings with a whistle. "How 'bouts you sleep on it and we'll discuss it something fierce tomorrow?"

"Yeah, I'm thinking now works better for me."

"I'm kinda feeling out of sorts right now though." He wraps his arms on either side of his head like he's trying to block out a sharp noise.

I go to reach for him, but pause, afraid I'll disturb him even more. "Joseph, what's wrong? You're making me nervous."

"Shhhh…do have to be so loud?" he says, an ache in his voice.

I'm not even yelling. Not yet, but I feel a frustration building in my chest. Still I manage to bring my tone down a degree. "You know the only reason I stayed at the Institute is because of you. You asked me to stay and I did. I thought you needed me. You said I could work a project with you. But you've disappeared and now look at you. What are you doing?"

With a great effort Joseph turns over on his stomach and rests his chin on his hands. "I don't need help with the project. Thought I did, but you can't be involved."

"Why not? What is it? Who you working for? And what kind of 'project' has this kind of effect on someone?"

"It's a surprise," he says in raspy voice.

"I don't like surprises."

"You're gonna like this one."

For some reason I don't believe him. "And why in the hell are you coming to see Samara, when I've hardly seen you in almost a week?"

"'Cause I knew you'd ask me about the project and I can't tell you," he says.

"What? You're really not going to tell me what you're doing?" I ask, hurt, frustrated.

"Yeah," he says, looking at the bed. His short blond hair is matted to his head. "I can't tell you yet, but you have to believe in me."

"Believe in you? How can I do that when you won't be honest with me? How can I believe in you when you look deathly ill?"

"Well, that's kinda disappointing." Joseph turns to face me for the first time since he arrived.

"If you think that's disappointing then you're really about to be upset." I lock onto his cold, dark eyes. "I'm leaving the Institute. I don't know what you're doing, but I'm not going to watch you kill yourself, which is what it looks like you're about to do." I shove off the bed and stand up, shaking.

"No, you can't do that!" Joseph exclaims, pushing himself up to an awkward standing position. He staggers a bit. "You promised."

"If you're going to sneak around and refuse to tell me why you look like a heroin addict, then I have no problem breaking my promise to you."

"I need you though," he says, lunging forward.

"You don't need me." I slip easily from his feeble attempt to detain me. "All you need is my energy and I'm not giving you any more unless you tell me what you're doing."

He sinks down on his knees, his eyes wide as he begs. "I can't. I just can't. Please, you gotta believe me. Please don't leave. Please."

The Joseph I know would never beg. He'd never reduce himself to look so pitiful. Whatever Joseph is mixed up in, it's stripping him of his integrity, along with everything else.

"If you can't tell me what you're working on then I can't stay here. That's the deal. No negotiations."

He shakes his head, a look of horror on his face. "Please. Please."

"No," I say firmly and stride out of the room before he can say another word.

Samara sits beside the door braiding her hair. "Good luck," I say over my shoulder. "He's a goner. I wouldn't kiss him tonight; he's vampire status at this point."

Only once I'm safe on the other side of my door do I breathe properly. The only thing good that has come of the last twenty-four hours is that I'm absolutely certain of one thing: I'm getting out of here.

Chapter Nine

Changed My Mind
___

Roya Stark <roya.stark713@gmail.com>
to bobandsteve

Hey Bob and Steve,

My brother and I don't need as much time together as I thought. Also the Institute is starting to creep me out. I think they need to rename this place the Secret Institute. Everyone here is lying about something. I'm really tired of getting tangled up in all the drama that ensues from the treachery. I'm looking forward to returning to the land of the living, where people walk in real sunshine. Will you please pick me up at the GAD-C in Oklahoma on June 27th. I'll totally wash all your windows, repaint your house, mow your lawn, hell I'll even clean the gutters— just say you'll take me in.

Love,
Ms. Completely-Over-This-Place

I hit the send key with a silent prayer. If they don't take me in then maybe I'll join the circus. No, that's just trading one band of freaks for another.

♦

Hemingway once said, "I love sleep. My life has the tendency to fall apart when I'm awake, you know?" *Yes, old friend, I do know.* That night sleep doesn't come though. No matter how hard I try I can't get the constant babbling in my brain to shush. I'm thinking of naming my inner voice Chatty Kathy. Or Katherine Chatterson. Or Chatty McChatterson. Having a name would at least give me a way to address her.

Hey, Ms. Chatterson, shut up already.

When I couldn't take it anymore I dream traveled to some of my favorite places, but they all seemed lame right now. The hipsters in Portland were especially irritating. A nasty green moss kept washing up on the shores of the Florida coast. And the locals in my most loved Istanbul coffee shop weren't flirting, fighting, or doing anything of particular interest. Most of them read their newspapers and sipped their coffees like they were intentionally trying to be boring. Again and again my mind returned to my troubles, without any suitable distraction. Morning brings a small bit of relief. At least another night has passed and I'm that much closer to leaving.

◆

The familiar rap at my door sounds as I'm pulling my brand new racerback tank—another present from Bob and Steve—over my head. I answer the door, looking forward to seeing that white mustache and the man on the other side of it.

"Hey, Patrick," I say with a small forced smile.

"Hey, sweetheart." He smiles and plays his air guitar with a letter in his hand. "I've got a note for you."

"Oh, really?" I ask, surprised. Bob and Steve and I've been exchanging emails, not letters anymore.

"It's a good thing you're still getting hard copy correspondence, otherwise I'd never have the pleasure of bugging you."

"You aren't bugging me."

"Of course I'm not." He waves his hand at me. "Everyone likes the mailman. Hopefully today I've brought you good news." He lays the letter in my hand.

"Thanks," I smile.

"Well, sweetie, duty calls." He tips his hat and trots away.

My stomach flip-flops when I realize who the letter is from.

Dear Roya,

You won't listen to me if I'm standing in front of you. Maybe you'll listen to me now. I told you before that our situation was complicated. I fear that because we have to be discreet about our relationship you doubt how much I really care about you. Please come by my lab today so we can talk about this.

Yours (and I mean it),
Aiden

I wad up his note and throw it in the trash. We don't need to talk. Aiden and I need space. I'm thinking a few thousand miles should do the trick.

♦

At the breakfast table I find George eyeing me with a sensitive compassion, which is quickly threatening my firmness. He doesn't say a word. Instead his eyes roam over me, like he's trying to mend the emotional bruises with his gaze. My shield is down and I know he feels the dull ache in my heart. The disappointment. The sadness. The loss. And all I see in him is the same, like he's mirroring my emotions. I almost want to feel this pain so I can allow him to fix me, which is what I think he's offering, with his quiet stares.

"Do you want to talk now, Roya?" he says, pushing away the food he never touched. "If so, I'm here…but you already knew that, didn't you?"

I shake my head. "Thanks, George. There's nothing we can say that will make me feel any better, so no. I don't want to talk."

"We don't have to talk about what's bothering you," he says, letting the obvious truth be known. "Maybe something else, something that takes your mind off of things."

I release a long exasperated sigh. That's what I spent my entire night trying to do: take my mind off my worries. "I'm game for anything at this point," I say, mashing my peas with my fork.

"When I was a kid, and I heard people say they had a *sixth* sense, I thought they said *sick* sense," he says, staring off, recalling the long-ago memory. "After that I actually wanted to get sick.

There was a long period where I didn't wash my hands. Luckily I didn't contract a fatal disease. Pretty ridiculous, huh?"

"That's adorable actually. How old were you when you thought that?" I ask.

"Last year."

We laugh.

"Actually, I wasn't more than eight-years-old. Then a couple years later my empathesis developed, and I actually thought I was sick. I thought I was going crazy. Schizophrenic. I couldn't understand how all of a sudden I felt so much around me. It took a little while for me to realize it was other people's emotions I was feeling."

His intimate admission jolts me. George rarely talks and when he does it's not like this. He eyes me again like before. And I realize he's trying, really trying, like there's something major riding on this moment. He's pulling out all the stops, trying to repair things between us. And if he could read my mind, he'd know it's working.

"It's interesting that you wanted to have a sixth sense so badly and you ended up with one," I say, thinking of all the kids who wish for special powers and grow up to be accountants.

"Yes, surprising to say the least," he says, a satisfied expression in his eyes.

"The first clairvoyant flash I saw was of an owl," I say.

George raises a curious eyebrow at me.

"I saw it in a tree, then a few seconds later it flew into the same tree from my vision. This was followed by a flash of a leaf falling off the exact same branch where the owl was perched. Then the leaf fell, just like in my vision. Like you, I always wanted a special gift. I was pretty disappointed to discover that my power was so lame." I laugh, remembering the memory clearly.

"That's ironic, actually," George muses.

"How so?" I ask.

"You're the most powerful person I know."

"You need to get out more then," I say.

He chews his lip. "You have more power than you realize."

I clasp the frequency adjuster, feeling suddenly heavy from its weight.

With a deliberate shake of his head, he says, "Not only in that way." His voice is tormented.

Tense silence fills the space.

"Roya, your power isn't solely in your clairvoyance. I can't even tell you what it is though. I just feel it."

Nerves clamp my throat shut.

"Maybe you know what this hidden gift is within you," he continues. "But my guess is you don't. My guess is that it's waiting to be revealed. And when that happens I think you'll feel more confident than you do now."

How do I respond to that? All my words sound cheap in response to his heavy insights. Finally I meet his quiet eyes and say, "Thanks for trying to make me feel better."

"That's not why I told you this."

Why did he tell me I had some veiled gift? Is this a game? A way to keep me intrigued? George doesn't play games though. I never have to doubt his words. Question his integrity. "Yeah, I know," I finally say, my voice awkward.

♦

"I've made up my mind to leave the Institute on the twenty-seventh," I say to an impassive Shuman. "But I'd like to work here until then, if that's all right."

She gives me a cold stare. "Your reports are interesting. You have been picking up something new. That is why it is unverifiable. I have been able to confirm them though. They are authentic events."

"The French girl, you mean? And the man?"

"Yes, although I do not know the significance yet. But you are picking up on these events for a reason and I believe it to be important."

"The girl's the one who was going to kill Ren, right?"

"Yes."

"Maybe he knows the significance," I offer.

"He has been consulted."

"Oh. So do I need to focus on finding more events linked to these people?"

"No, let your intuition guide you. It will always deliver the event of most importance to you and the Institute."

"But you said before that sometimes reporters are asked to find specific events, right? And if you think these are important then maybe—"

"I did, but in this instance that is a job for investigative reporters. Your job is to pick up on original stories or whatever comes to you naturally. Is that clear?"

Why does Shuman make me feel like an eight-year-old child? I swear I sense pigtails I'm not wearing swing beside my head when I nod.

"I will be disappointed to lose your talent," she continues. "And yes, I would like you to continue to report until you leave." She points at the chair. "Your station is open." With a quick pivot she trudges away.

I sink into the chair. When I'm in position I clap the headphones on and focus. The process is becoming second nature, automatic—like driving a car. A few seconds later something flashes in my vision. The gasp that falls out of my mouth is audible over the static filling my ears. An image of Joseph in his room crying fills my mind. He's clawing at his bed sheets like there's something underneath them that might provide sustenance. I watch this for a few seconds, but it tears my chest into little aching pieces. It hurts worse than anything I've felt recently and that's saying a lot. The image of my brother drenched in tears and sweat is too much to bear. I force myself to wake up. At the computer terminal I type two words: no report.

There's no answer at Joseph's door. I consider breaking and entering, but decide against it. Feeling lonely and disappointed I hide in my room for the rest of the day, skipping all meals. I spend my time reading the books that Bob and Steve had sent. Most of them I've already read, but even still their messages are deep and can use a second reading. I do everything I can to distract myself from the pain I know Joseph is experiencing. I don't know what to do for him. I'm so lost and he's further gone than I thought. I know most twin sisters would be twisted by the pain I witnessed. Hell, wouldn't most people be distraught by the heart-wrenching letter from Aiden or the sweet attempts from George? But I'm the girl in the center of the country, the one who's already so far away from here. The one they're talking about in the past tense. The one who defeated Zhuang, or didn't, however the story is written, and I'm in there somewhere. I've already visualized myself as the girl who isn't here anymore, because more than anything that's who I need to be.

Chapter Ten

The next day when my alarm tells me the sun has risen I awake. I slap on clothes and go to breakfast like a zombie would, if they did such formal things instead of eating brains.

"I'm leaving the Institute," I say, not making eye contact with anyone at the table.

"Why?" Samara asks, dropping her fork. "You can't!"

"I think my time here is at an end," I say, feeling George's penetrating stare. He's already plunged into my emotions and explored them layer by layer. I push my oatmeal around with a spoon.

"But," Samara argues, "there's so much more to do. Your news reporting, aren't you going to miss it?"

"Of course, and I'll miss you all too, but I can't stay here right now."

"Girl, I guess I've been ignoring you," Trent says, batting his long black eyelashes at me. "If you need me to give you a bit more attention in order to stay then all you need to do is dress provocatively."

I laugh. "Whose attention I could have really used was Joseph's. Will you please keep an eye on him? I'm worried."

Samara lays her hand on mine. A gentle squeeze. "Yes, of course."

"Thanks," I say, sounding exactly how I feel. Wounded.

"When?" George's voice is rough. "When are you leaving?"

I look at him directly. He's mirroring my emotions again and it's enough to almost make me fall apart. "The twenty-seventh," I say, shoving tears to the bottom of my being. "I've got to get to work," I lie and rush off from the table.

♦

The Panther room is the only place that holds a real mission for me these days. A new apprehension creeps into my thoughts as I settle in at my station. I brace myself to see something devastating, something about Joseph, or something about someone else I know. However, what I actually see is ordinary and not at all disturbing. It's a scene of a man in a black knit cap playing chess with another gentleman. The entire exchange is neither terrifying nor of obvious importance to my life, unlike my recent visions. For that I'm grateful. Other than a few oddities, what I witness appears to be a typical game of chess between two people.

After several minutes the man with the black knit cap moves a chess piece across the board and smiles at his opponent. *"Échec et mat,"* he says. I don't speak French, but I'm pretty sure he's just won the game. Then he swivels and looks directly at me, where my "camera lens" is anyway. His wrinkled face arranges itself into something between a smirk and a scowl. "Are you enzertained? No?" the man says, looking too pleased with himself. A laugh like a car's rattling engine. "You von't get anyzing from me. So off vitz you."

I stiffen with sudden dread. This man knows I'm there spying, just like that awful girl in the previous vision, but how?

I awake from this report feeling exhausted and a complete failure. After I input this information I'm not the least bit surprised when the results say, "Information unverifiable."

My mind combs over the report I just logged. *Who are these French people? What do they have to do with the Institute? They seem so familiar and yet also a complete mystery.* I sink deeper into these curious thoughts trying to find a pattern, a clue I've missed. *Do the French people have anything to do with me? What's their connection to Ren?* Nervously I tap the elevator button a dozen more times than is necessary. *What's the connection? Why do I get the impression these people are more than just deranged? They're fatally dangerous.*

The elevator doors are almost closed when a hand reaches in and forces them back open. Aiden steps in, but doesn't give me the slightest look. I straighten with dread. Once the elevator begins to ascend he steps forward, scans his key card, and presses a few buttons. The elevator halts swiftly. Stuck. Aiden turns and faces me, his sapphire eyes intense. Breath hitches in my throat.

"You can't leave," he says, arms crossed.

"I can and I will," I say, regaining my composure.

"This is ridiculous. You belong here," he argues.

"How do you know where I belong?"

"The Institute needs you."

"No it doesn't."

He searches me, looking injured. I can't believe he even has the audacity to speak to me.

"And since when did you care? You've got your projects."

"I've always cared," he says, pushing his dark brown hair out of his eyes. The air grows stiff in the tight space. "Don't do this," he urges. "You're trying to push me away. You're running."

"You know," I say, taking a sip of air, "this might be a surprise, but this isn't about you. I've got other reasons, better than you, for wanting to leave this corrupt place."

Scorn flashes on his usually happy face. I'm being cruel. And I want to take it back, but my pride won't let me.

"Look, I really need to get out of here," I say, panic creeping into my head, creating dizziness. "Now," I add.

"George said you were staying until the twenty-seventh, that's four days away."

"No." I roll my eyes. "I need to get out of here." I point to the floor to indicate the elevator.

He looks at me earnestly. "Roya, please reconsider this whole—"

"No." I shake my head, cutting him off. "I've made up my mind."

His blue eyes, his face pleading—they're threatening my resolve. I wish everything was as simple as he tries to make it. "Why do you have to make me so crazy?" I ask in desperation.

He smirks, but still holds his arms across his chest. "What you're feeling is completely mutual, if it makes you feel any better."

"Good," I say, hostility saddling my tone.

He glares at me.

"Why are you trapping me in this elevator?" I say, enunciating each word through clenched teeth.

He draws in a breath and loosens his arms. "Because you ignored my note. You're so stubborn and I love that about you, but damn it," he says with a growl low in his throat.

I'm starting to feel lightheaded. *Please don't pass out here. Please.* The walls are closing in on me. I wish he'd start the elevator back up. I never thought I was claustrophobic, but in this tight compartment, overflowing with all our emotions, I am.

"We need to talk," he says.

"No. I don't want to, not after that whole Amber fiasco."

"I fired her."

The words strike me with coarse surprise. I expected a dozen different responses, but not this one. "What?" I say in a hush.

"You were right," he says, softening. "Her intentions weren't professional, and I learned that much when I confronted her. I wanted to know why she lied about the massage."

"Oh," I say, floored. "So you really didn't give her a massage?"

"Of course not. I may be a guy governed by certain urges, but I'm truly not an *idiot*."

Guilt courses through me at the mention of that word, at the memory of insulting him with it. "Aiden, when I called you that I thought—"

"I know what you thought and completely understand why. Roya, if the roles had been reversed, I'd have been beyond jealous." He hesitates, on the verge of saying more. My heart beats slowly, hanging on his every word. Beating by it. Living for it. "I would have been enraged to think anyone had their hands on you in that way," Aiden says, a bitterness in his voice. "It would have driven me crazy."

"So you fired her?" I ask, still in frozen disbelief.

"Yes. She has seventy-two hours to pack up and get out of the Institute."

"Wow, that seems harsh," I say, locking my eyes on the floor.

"Roya," Aiden begins, "she's a liar, and making advances toward her superior is not even the top reason I terminated her. I don't know exactly why she lied. Maybe she was hoping to get me in trouble with the Institute. All I know is what she did hurt you and I won't stand for that."

My eyes eagerly find his. In this oxygen-deprived elevator his desire is tangible, like an electrical current pulsing through a wire. Aiden grips my elbow and I don't resist when he tugs me closer. He tilts his head and seems to marvel at me, like I hold some truth to life's mysteries. And for a moment his expression startles me, but in this stuffy elevator that's all I see. His affection engulfs the space. I feel his loyalty in every touch, every breath. And I can't believe I questioned it.

Aiden's passion, which I've craved, is finally unleashed when he kisses me. A gasp escapes my lips. My stomach lurches forward as if trying to grasp onto something. I'm breathless, but not from being stuck in the elevator. The space isn't too small; instead the space between us now feels too vast. He softly pulls away, leaving me intoxicated. The combination of his eyes and smile weakens me. However, I yank him closer, asking for more, knowing it will split me forever, but unabashedly I dive head first. I never stand a chance of truly resisting him, but he can never know that.

He snakes his arms around me and wrenches me into him tightly. "Roya, can I tell you a secret?"

"Umm...sure." My voice cracks.

"I could have done without all this drama, but I'm grateful I had an opportunity to show you how much I care."

"Oh yeah? So are you going to fire someone every time I get mad at you?"

"Whatever it takes," he teases.

"I think we can come up with other ways of resolving our conflicts," I say, zipping up the last bit of space between us.

"I like resolving conflicts with you," he says, regarding me with a primal intensity.

"Me too," I admit. "But shouldn't we think about getting out of here? People are going to start wondering why the elevator is out of commission."

"Always the practical one, aren't you?"

"Oh, I don't know about that. I'm having some especially impractical thoughts right now," I say, threading my hands in his hair.

A fierce smile spreads on his lips. "You never cease to surprise me." Aiden backs away, never taking his hungry eyes off me as he fires up the elevator. Once we arrive at level five he turns and plants a soft kiss on my cheek. "Please don't go."

Aiden steps out of the elevator, giving me one last licentious look. My life is a massive ball of uncertainty right now, but there's one thing I know. I'm absolutely, forever in love with that guy.

Chapter Eleven

The knock thuds at my door. Actually it sounds more like something collided with it. I tap the button and a second later my heart deflates. Joseph leans against the doorway, his eyes closed, head resting on his arm. Is he sleeping? He's paler than the last time I saw him, although I didn't think that was possible. I prod his arm and his eyes flutter. He jerks, appearing disoriented, lost.

"Joseph?" My voice doesn't sound like my own. "Are you all right?"

"Stark." He waves a finger at me. "You. Can't. Leave," he slurs.

"Are you drunk?"

"Course not."

"Then what's wrong with you?"

"Tired, that's all."

My mind flips to the vision I'd seen of Joseph tormented in his bed, suffering from a night terror of some kind.

"You can't leave," he repeats.

"Tell me what you're working on."

"I-I-I can't."

"Then I'm leaving." Everyone's got a breaking point. If I hold out, I'll find Joseph's. If it means bringing him back from this desolate state then I'll stay, but I have to know what he's doing so I can help him.

"Please, Stark." He grabs both of my shoulders. Shakes me. His breath smells like dirty lake water. "Please don't do this. I beg you. You don't understand. I know I can't do this without you and it's so, so, so important. Please. Don't. Go."

Through clenched teeth I say, "What are you working on, Joseph?"

"It's so great and you're gonna love it. But it's a surprise. I need you to wait until it's ready." The bloodshot red in his eyes makes the green of his irises more intense. "Just stay here, please, and I'll show you what I've been working on soon. It's so worth the wait," he says with his hands clasped together.

"No. Tell me what you're working on or I'm leaving," I say, a strict firmness in my voice.

"Stark, I'll never forgive you if you leave. You'll ruin everything!" Spit flies, landing on my face.

Disgusted, I wipe it away. "That's your threat to me? You're going to hold some grudge? You can do better than that."

"I don't have anything else I can do to make you stay."

"Oh, but you do. If you tell me what you're working on then I'll stay. It's that simple."

"I CAN'T! Why don't you understand that?!"

"Joseph, have you looked in the mirror lately? There's something truly wrong with you. You're sick or on drugs, and I can't figure it out. And it's scaring me."

"There's nothin' wrong with me," he snarls. "And I'm not on drugs."

"Let me help you." I reach out to grab his arm.

"No!" He yanks away from me.

Tyrannical tears threaten at the corners of my eyes from his rejection. "Fine," I say in a hush. "Then I'm going to ensure someone else helps you; protects you from yourself."

Joseph's eyes grow wide. "No, Stark. No."

"I'm going to Trey. I'm telling him you're working on something that appears to be killing you."

"You can't do that!" His forehead wrinkles. Every feature on his face is etched with terror. He's got to be close to breaking now.

"Why not? Siblings are supposed to tattle on each other, didn't you know?"

His eyes burn with anger. The scowl on his face actually scares me. "Go ahead and leave the Institute. I don't give a damn anymore," he says in a hoarse voice. "I'll complete the project without you and you'll be sorry. Sorry you ever doubted me."

"Let's hope you're right. Let's hope I'm not the one who's sorry this secret project kills you."

His jaw flexes. "You think you're better than me, don't you? Everyone else here may bow down to you and never doubt your judgment, but I do. You're wrong on this. I'm right."

"Tell me what you're working on." My words come out in a rush, desperation replacing my confidence. "I'll help you. I won't tell anyone. I promise."

"NO," he says, his tone much more strict than mine had been moments prior.

I shake my head, at a loss. "Fine, Joseph," I say, surrendering. I don't know what else to do at this point; my heart can't take one more evil look from him. "Don't tell me. And I won't rat you out to Trey. But please be careful."

"Does this mean you'll stay?" he says, hope in his voice.

"No, you know the deal. If you change your mind then let me know. And if you choose not to forgive me for leaving then so be it, but no matter what I love you."

Chapter Twelve

A soft rap jerks my attention away from the book I'm reading, *Zen and the Art of Motorcycle Maintenance.* As I yawn into a standing position, the blood starts to pump more vigorously in my legs after being curled up for too long. I'm not sure why Bob and Steve would send me any packages since I'll be seeing them in only a few days.

The door slides back with its usual *shush.* I'm surprised not to find Patrick idling, holding a package for me. No one stands at my door. The hallway is empty. I step back with a shrug and barely catch out of the corner of my eye the glint of red on the blue carpet. The random object looks out of place on my doorstep. A playing card. Specifically, a queen of hearts. I sneak another look around and when I don't spy anyone I lean over and pluck the card from its spot. It appears ordinary enough, but I know it's not. For one thing there's a weight to it, much heavier than a normal playing card. Flipping it over I find neatly printed text. It reads:

A queen of hearts can get in anywhere.

I frown. *What is this? A riddle?* I despise riddles. Why can't people speak in plain English in this place?

I want to believe this isn't meant for me, that someone left it at my door by mistake. However, I don't buy it. I tap the button beside my door and it shuts behind me with a sucking noise. A full minute passes where I stand perplexed in the middle of the hallway with a strange playing card in my hand. Where exactly will this queen of hearts get me? I take a tentative step and eye the card. I'm not sure what I'm expecting, maybe a brilliant insight to materialize.

The corridor of the administrative lodging is one big rectangle with the hallway to the elevators at the north end. My room, Z, is located next to this hallway. I stalk past the elevators and round the corner. I've never ventured down this other corridor. The idea to turn back seizes me just before a pulse surges between my fingers. I freeze. With a cautious look down, I eye the card pressed between my fingertips. *Why did it do that?* Is it about to explode, like this has all been a trap? The card looks harmless clenched between my thumb and pointer finger.

Sighing, I take another step forward. Again the pulse. Again I stop. Take a step backward. Nothing happens. What exactly does this possessed card want me to do? Obviously not to go backwards. Another step forward and as I expect the card vibrates, encouraging me to continue. Five more steps and with each the queen of hearts sings its praises by pulsating between my tightly clamped fingers. My insides jangle with both anticipation and trepidation. Is this a treasure hunt or a trick? What am I searching for and who put me up to it?

This corridor is different than mine. The hallway where my room is only has doorways on the exterior wall. But here, in this hallway, a solitary door sits in the middle of the interior wall. Several doors cover the opposite exterior wall, all marked in alphabetical order.

The card keeps up a continuous buzz as I stroll with curiosity to the lonesome door. Beside it isn't a letter, like every other one in the administrative lodging wing. Instead there's a key card scanner. Dozens of doors like this occupy the Institute. I never give them much thought. It's strange to find one here, but no stranger than anything else in this place.

With a shrug I pass the door. The card goes suddenly still. After a few paces I stop and take one deliberate step backward. This action is greeted by a pulse from the queen of hearts again. With hurried steps I walk until the vibrations discontinue. It's at exactly the point that I move past the door with the key card scanner. Suspiciously I eye the door. So is this where I'm supposed to go?

I tap the button under the scanner, thinking that maybe it's unlocked. It's not. I growl at the door. Maybe I should chuck the card on the ground and retreat to my room. If someone really needs me to find something then they should give me a real map. Still, curiosity snakes around my insides, willing me to figure out this riddle. I turn the card over again:

A queen of hearts can get in anywhere.

Tentatively, I peer around to make sure no one's watching. With nervous anticipation, I hold the card up to the scanner. It buzzes once. The door slides back, disappearing into the wall. Triumphant joy resounds in my chest until I spy another hallway with more doors. *Ugh.* At least this one is short. I take a hesitant step forward, expecting the card to buzz again. It doesn't. Instead the door slides shut behind me. Then the card lights up. Actually a single dot illuminates on the bottom of the card.

Several steps bring me to the first set of doors. Door A sits on my right. E on my left. The card now has three lights illuminated at the bottom. I peer down the dead-end corridor. Two doors sit across from each other. One more flanks the end of the hallway. I continue to take tentative steps, watching the card for any indications. It remains quiet, but the three lights stay illuminated until I reach the next set of doors. B and D. Now there are four lights at the bottom. I wonder if I'm supposed to go to the doorway at the end. I take one curious step toward it and the card's lights fade away. One swift step backward brings me even with the other doors. The four lights shine bright again. *So now what am I supposed to do?* Pivoting, I face the door marked B. Nothing happens. Baffled, I swing around to the door marked D. The card zings with the most intense vibration I've felt from it yet. The heart next to the queen illuminates. I peer down the hallway where I came from and consider retreating, feeling like a nut standing here. Do I knock on some potential stranger's door? The red heart continues to shine bright. I shake off my cowardice and rap on the door. *Here goes nothing.*

It slides back immediately.

Chapter Thirteen

"You found me," Aiden sings, impeccably framed in the doorway and wearing a brazen smile. It's the first time in a while I can remember seeing him not wearing his lab coat. The black button-up shirt fits perfectly over frayed jeans. I glance down at the card, then to his excited expression, putting all the pieces together.

"You?" I accuse.

"Yes me," he says, seizing my wrist and tugging me into his room. He shuts the door once I'm inside. I squirm with unease as I search him, then the place he calls home.

"Dr. Livingston, did you lure me to your room?" I say in pretend outrage.

"Indeed I did." He tips forward on his toes, then back to his heels.

"I'm not sure it's prudent that I remain behind a closed door with you. I dare say my honor might be in question."

Aiden smirks. "Well, if you harbor a single hesitation then I encourage you to gather your petticoat and march out of here. Please do spare me with your forgiveness though for my presumptuous nature." He plucks the card still pinned between my fingertips and slides it into his back pocket.

I blush and break into an easy laugh. "All right, Aiden, what's up your sleeve? Why the game?"

"You enjoyed trying to find me, right?" he asks.

I level my gaze at him, but don't answer.

He shrugs. "All right, I know this isn't the most romantic place, but it's quiet and private and the perfect spot for what I thought could be our first date." He steps aside to reveal a table arranged with candles, flowers, a tea kettle, a bowl of fruit, and a deck of cards.

My eyes drift back and forth between him and the table.

"But…" I lose my words easily.

"You don't have to stay, of course…"

I wave him off. "What about the other Head Officials? What if they saw me come in here? Or how about when I leave?"

A dazzling smile unfolds on his face. "They're all at a budget meeting, and those last ages."

"Shouldn't you be at that meeting?"

"Absolutely not. I never attend those bore fests. I always send my vote by proxy with the excuse that I have work to do."

"And don't you have work to do right now?"

"Always," he says at once. "But it will have to wait."

"Because I'm leaving," I say and regret it immediately. I don't want to ruin this, but it's true. I've wanted his undivided attention for so long and all he can ever offer is a few minutes in his lab.

"Yes and no. Yes, because if I'm not going to get another chance like this, then I want to seize the moment. And no, because I've wanted to spend time alone with you, uninterrupted. We're overdue, don't you think?"

My heart suddenly beats faster. I take a few deep breaths to steady it. "But why all this? Why couldn't we just dream travel and meet up?"

He shrugs again, but this time it holds regret. "I wanted to spend time with you in the flesh. It's so much more personal." I stare at him, trying to gauge his sincerity. "And, I have to be honest with you." He hesitates and it's enough that I suck in a breath and hold it. "I do my best work during dream travel. I rarely ever take that time to go anywhere but my lab. And I'm currently working on a big project so…that's simply what I have to do right now." His hand brushes against my cheek. I love when he does that. "But I have this time devoted to you and only you right now. I hope that's enough."

It's enough! One hundred percent yes! It's enough! "All right," I say indifferently. "That will suffice for now. What did you have planned for us tonight?"

Aiden holds my chin in his hand and I think he's about to kiss me. "I'm so very glad you asked that." He turns and presents the table that sits a few feet away. "I'm going to school you in a game of spades. Have you ever played?"

I shake my head.

Aiden rubs his hands together. "Then I vote we wager something on this first game."

I laugh. He pulls the sturdy, wooden chair out for me. His room is easily double the size of mine with a private bathroom and study. Honestly, the room looks way too tidy to belong to Aiden, but I'm

64

guessing he cleaned up for our date. The floor still has stacks of books punctuating the area.

He takes the seat next to mine, giving me a flirtatious look. I'm all nerves and anticipation.

"How do I get you to do *that* more often?" he asks.

"What?"

"Smile. You don't do it as much as you should."

I hadn't realized that I was smiling but of course this whole surprise date has lifted my mood considerably.

"So how do we play this game?"

Aiden shuffles the deck. "It's very simple. The object is to have the most spades when the game is over, hence the name. I'll deal us both out some cards, and there's also a center stack. I'll go first because I'm the oldest. Then—"

"Wait, that doesn't seem fair."

"Please don't interrupt your elder," he scolds with a smile. "Anyway, you can pick up from the card that's upturned or pull from the pile, but you must always discard."

I nod. Sounds a bit like gin rummy.

"Now when someone lays down five or more spades then the other person has to pick up the discard pile. That is, unless it's your birthday month then you have one free pass. And if you don't have five spades then you can throw down three and make your opponent pick up three from the discard pile. Oh, and if you want to pick up a few extra from either the deck or the upturned cards then all you have to do is have a straight flush of any other suit. Then you're—"

"Do you have any idea how to actually play this game?" I suppress the urge to laugh, although I'm losing my resolve.

Dealing out some cards, he smirks. "I read the rules. They're lame…so I added some of my own."

After the last card is thrown out he says, "All right you have thirteen cards and I have twelve because I'm the dealer."

I scowl at him, fanning the multitude of cards out in front of my face.

Aiden takes a card from the deck and discards. "So, Roya, what are your plans once you leave the Institute?"

I take a card and throw away a two of diamonds. "I'm going to do the reality TV circuit."

"Oh, is that all?"

I nod.

"And after you grow bored of that, as I'm sure you will? What are your plans?"

I sigh. "I crave some normalcy, so I'm going to bathe in that until I grow tired of it. Then I'll apply to college. I'm looking into a degree in comparative literature. Stanford has an exceptional program. I'm hoping Trey can write me a reference letter; maybe say something about my role in freeing the population's consciousness from Zhuang's greedy hands."

"Oh, that would get you in without ever having to take the entrance exams."

"Hmmm…Really?"

"Yes, really."

"Aiden?"

"Yes." He looks at me expectantly.

I throw down five spades. "Time for you to add some cards to your hand."

He rolls his eyes. "Your plans all sound great and all…"

"But…"

"But, couldn't you do them here?"

"What am I supposed to do, dream travel to class? I'm certain my professors won't go for that. 'Yes, I'll be there even if you don't see me. Trust me.'"

He smirks. "I'm just saying, couldn't you find a way to do what you want and also stay here?"

"This coming from the guy who puts his career at the forefront of everything, and never compromises anything for it?"

He takes a frustrated breath, then throws down three cards.

"Is that all you got?" I tease.

"Oh, just you wait."

The air between us grows quiet, interrupted only by the slapping of our cards as we lay them on the table or pick them up.

"Aiden, this place is suffocating me right now. I have to get away. You understand that, right?"

He stops. Puts down his cards and stares at me across the table. There's such earnestness in his beautiful blue eyes.

"I don't even know who I am anymore," I continue, my nerves humming in my chest. "The people who raised me aren't my real family. They're all I've ever known. It feels like everything is

66

wrong. My whole life has been a lie. I have so many questions and every time I try to dissect them I get nowhere. I thought Joseph could help me, but he's…lost. I need to figure out who I am. Please tell me you can understand that."

He swallows. A rawness fills the space between us. "Yes, of course," he says. Regret coats his words and I don't believe for a minute that he understands, or maybe I don't want him to. Maybe I want him to make me stay, make me need to stay.

"Oops," he chirps a moment later. "I forgot the music. I'll be back momentarily."

Under the bowl of grapes and cherries is a stack of books. I set the fruit to the side and pick up the book on top right as a gentle drum beat echoes from the speakers. It's soon met by the soft plucking of a guitar. The rhythm is enchanting, calming. The voice that accompanies the instruments is deep, perfectly smooth, and overflowing with soul. I close my eyes and let the chords of the piano wash over me. It feels like I've heard this melody a thousand times, but I know this is the first. Opening my eyes I smile as Aiden strolls back in my direction. He returns the smile, eyes bright.

"Gregory Alan Isakov," he says, answering the question I was about to ask. "I never tire of listening to his music. It has depth."

I tap the book I took from the stack. "*Entanglement, The Greatest Mystery in Physics,*" I read from the cover of the book. "Light reading to help you drift off at night?"

A relaxed grin spreads along his mouth. Instantly he's in one hundred percent Head Scientist mode, passion lighting his eyes, and a thrill in his tone. "Actually, it's very easy stuff to understand." He takes a seat on the sofa that sits in the study area on the opposite wall. It's ensconced with shelves of books and objects. "Come here and I'll show you a diagram that will make it crystal clear."

"I seriously doubt that," I say to mask my hesitation as I take the seat next to him on the dark leather couch.

He flips expertly through the book, like he has all 300 pages memorized.

"Ever heard about the double slit experiment?"

I shake my head.

"How about Schrodinger's cat?"

Another shake.

"Particle theory?" There's an edge of doubt in his voice.

"Nope," I say.

Aiden rubs his hands together, eyes eager. "That means I have the very privileged honor of blowing your mind with quantum physics. Yes!"

You'd think he just won the lottery, with so much giddy excitement oozing out of him.

"I'm ready to have my mind blown," I say.

Provocatively he narrows his eyes. "Well," he draws out the word. "Let's start with entanglement. It's what I centered my dissertation on. Simply put, the theory states that when two particles have an interaction then they become intertwined. The result to this is whatever happens to one particle will have an effect on the other. And it doesn't matter how far the particles are separated from one another. They are forever entangled."

A chill runs down my spine. I'm at a loss as to why, but it's similar to the way I feel after déjà vu. "That's crazy. How's that possible?"

"The quantum world makes all sorts of impossible things possible," he says enthusiastically.

"You truly love what you do, don't you?"

"I do."

"Have you always been this way? Passionate about science? Bordering on obsessed?"

A smile tugs on his perfect mouth. "Yes."

"Why?" I ask.

"Science, my work, is like music. I feel like an artist driven to create. And I fear that if I don't push myself then I might die with something really great inside me. That would be the worst possible thing to ever happen."

I gulp. That makes sense. Perfect sense. Yet it's heartbreaking for some reason. How can you ever know if you were done, if you'd created your legacy or if you died before you finished?

"Hasn't there ever been anything else? A hobby? A sport?"

He shakes his head. Maybe this complex guy really is simple after all.

"Even when you were growing up?" I ask.

He shakes his head again, still looking at me intently like he's having a different conversation in his mind, something secret about me.

"Where *did* you grow up?"

"Here," he says, shutting the book.

My eyes widen with surprise. "What? I thought that wasn't possible. Trey said..." I trail off, trying to make sense of that idea.

"I was a special case," Aiden says.

"Obviously." I'm hoping he'll elaborate, but he doesn't. "So you really spend all your time working?" I ask again, still disbelieving that this handsome, extraordinarily suave guy doesn't hang out at clubs every weekend.

"I do. I never let anything distract me...until now." He looks down at me under hooded eyes.

"What about your family?" I ask. "Don't you spend time with them?"

He shakes his head, this time sharply. It's a slight movement, but it means something powerful.

Is he like me? A transplant? An orphan?

"Did the Lucidites take you away from your parents too?"

"No. I grew up with them."

"Here?"

"Yes." There's a pause. "They're dead."

My face probably says exactly what I'm feeling. Aiden shakes his head again. He doesn't want my pity. Doesn't need it. Maybe he's more like me than I give him credit for. Maybe he's not all smiles. He opens the book again and flips to another page. He's reading, trying to find a certain passage or page, but I'm reading him. I feel him desperately trying to avoid the topic we've approached. It's his weak spot, and I gather he doesn't have many of those. Right now in this space, I feel a brand new pull to him. I've always been drawn to his features, his brilliance, his laughter, his passion. But right now I'm attracted to his pain. It makes him human. It makes him real. It makes him something he hardly ever is to me: accessible.

I touch his hand as it thumbs through the book, drawing his attention to me, away from his thoughts. He hasn't composed himself after our conversation and traces of the pain still lurk in his eyes. We're frozen in time for a moment, watching each other. I want to pull him to me, but I just stay gripped on his hand, his eyes.

Aiden runs his bottom lip under his top teeth. There's a shift in the air. His grip slips from mine as he leans forward; the book

69

clatters to the floor. A warm hand slides along my neck until he cups the back of my head. I rush into his lips, wishing he'd kissed me earlier, so ecstatic to kiss him now. My lips part under his hungry pressure. I push back on the couch, letting him direct the space we occupy. Together. His other hand finds mine, entangles in my fingers and guides it to the cushion lying behind my head. Hovering above me, he strokes my neck and glides his lips along mine. Maybe it's the sensitivity of the conversation that launched us into this moment, but I suddenly feel wild. Bewitched. By him. By what we are when we're together.

Aiden eases back, separating us. He hovers over me looking intense, almost frazzled as he whispers, "Tell me…please tell me you feel this too."

There's no question to what he's referring. Never in my life have I felt something so pure. So dynamic. It has color and texture. Like a volt of electricity. It's the charge I feel when his lips touch mine. I bite my lip and nod. "Yes," I whisper.

Satisfaction flickers across his eyes. "Good." He dips down and kisses me again, but this time gently, brandishing his lips so lightly against mine, each touch accompanied by a tiny spark. Having been electrocuted before I never thought electricity could feel good, but this current between us is amazing. Intriguing. Stimulating. He slides back enough that I see the blue of his eyes again.

"Roya, I really do understand why you're leaving. I do." Fingers brush the hair back from my face. "I'm being selfish for wanting you to stay, but I almost lost you once and I can't imagine it happening again. I'm not going to complicate things by asking you to stay, but I also want you to know where I stand. Whatever you do I support you one hundred percent."

"Will you dream travel to meet me?" My question is loaded with hope. "At least every now and then," I add.

Disappointment falls on his face before he recovers. "Of course."

"Good."

My free hand knots in his shirt, yanking him back to me— urgent to feel his lips again. Heat rushes down my body as he trails hungry kisses along my chin and neck. My heavy breaths catch in his ear. Hands I forgot I possessed tug against his waistband, pulling him closer into me, zipping up all space between us. A satisfied grunt reverberates against my neck. I've never wanted anything more than what comes next in this moment. I'm starving for it.

He breaks away, a crazed look in his heated eyes. "Although budget meetings feel like they last an eternity, they really don't," he says, panting. "You should go very soon."

I pout and press into him.

Aiden growls in my ear. Nibbles my lobe. I respond by ever so gently trailing my fingertips up his lean back. He shivers. I'm about to press my lips to his again when he grabs my free hand and locks it above my head with the other one, a wolfish grin plastered on his face.

"Ms. Stark, are you trying to seduce me?"

"Is it working?"

"You don't even need to try, but the point that you are is making it increasingly difficult to resist you."

I peer up at my restrained hands above my head. "Is this you resisting me? Because it looks like you're trying to make me resist you."

Aiden leans in closer and howls quietly, his breath stroking my cheek. One single kiss graces my lips before he rocks back, taking a seat on the far side of the couch. "I still have to work here even after you've gone skipping off to Texas. So against my every desire I have to insist you leave."

"You don't *have* to work here," I suggest. "There are other, non-corrupt, places you could find employment."

He gives me a tempting smile. "We both know I'm not suited for the real world."

Chapter Fourteen

To my astonishment, the Institute is actually paying me for my news reports. I thought it was charity work or my exchange for room and board. A bank account has already been set up for me and the Institute is depositing $400 into it for each of my reports. Being paid to news report actually puts a new pressure on the job. It was easier to deliver stories when I thought I was giving away information. Now it's weird knowing whatever I report equates to cash. Still, that anxiety doesn't deter me. I love news reporting and will miss it like crazy when I leave. I've never had a job. Hell, as a kid I didn't have a clue what I wanted to be when I grew up. Now I'm a member of an elite department and making more in a week than my fake father makes in a month.

The Panther room always smells of sweet grass, with a soft undertone of gardenia. It's the only place in the Institute with such a complex aroma. Not even the main hall at dinner time is that intoxicating. A constant buzzing sound emanates from the computer stations and the bluish light overhead gives off a gentle hum.

The fondness I've grown for this space in such a short time leaves me in a new state of vulnerability. The idea that I've become attached to the job is disconcerting and completely out of character. Maybe my apathetic nature is eroding. Aiden is probably partly to blame for this. And still, I know leaving is the right thing to do. It's not like I'm a Middling, bound to a single place and time. Everyone's acting like I'm going to a different planet. I get that Texas is pretty much Mars, but I still have dream travel. Samara and I'll spend our nights hanging out in Phoenix and New York. When Joseph comes around we'll find our own special places to haunt. And every now and then Aiden will grace me with his presence in Egypt or Budapest or wherever he likes to go when he's not in his lab. Of course, I know being in the flesh is always better, but still. I made the expectation clear to Joseph and I can't go back on it. If I did then he'd never take me seriously. And still I think he'll change his mind at the eleventh hour. Concede what he's working on. And if he doesn't then maybe by leaving I'll stop him from further work on this demonstrative project by taking my energy reserves from him. Because there's only one thing more important than my friends, my work news reporting, and my love for Aiden: Joseph.

I settle myself in my familiar station, trying to put my attachments out of mind and focus on the present moment. My breath slowly softens. I invite serenity into every inch of my body. This is a gradual process, one that can't be rushed. But today, I sink into stillness quicker than usual. A large room flashes into my vision. Multiple tables fill the space, their surfaces crowded with electronics. Cabinets streak the walls. A song plays in the background. Aiden's lab. My heart leaps when I see him sitting at a nearby workstation screwing something into a device. Guilty tension surges through me for spying on him like this. But it's not like I meant to. And isn't that what news reporting is all about?

His dark hair, currently not governed by product, falls into his eyes when he leans forward. Distracted, he pushes it away from his face. I wish his unruly hair would flop back on his forehead, just so I could watch him do it again. When he looks up, there isn't that same expression of wanting he usually has when he looks at me. His gaze is speculative. "I'm almost ready to take another round of readings." He drums his fingers on his lips. It's an adorable gesture that he does when something is momentarily stumping him. "I've got to figure out what we missed the last time."

The vision retracts until I see the person Aiden's talking to. Nervousness cocoons my being. George's eyes are closed. He's chewing on his lip. His eyes open to reveal his deep brown eyes. "What *you* missed," George says, tone clipped.

Distracted by his thoughts, Aiden glances at George. "Pardon?"

"I'm only the lab rat. You're the scientist."

"Right," the Head Scientist says, scratching his head. "And you say lab rat like it's a bad thing. Numerous discoveries may not have occurred if it wasn't for those four-legged creatures. Besides, I'm not running tests on you, but rather studying how your empathesis works. That puts you in a very special league of lab rats," he says with a laugh.

George gives him a mutinous expression. "Why wasn't the first round of readings enough?"

"I'm not sure. My guess is it didn't provide enough data to change the programming in the modifier. All I know for certain is with the new encoding the modifier still isn't successful at changing or erasing emotions." He shrugs. "This is all about trial and error, really. We'll keep trying until we get it right."

"Are you going to need me to be involved for each trial?" George says evenly.

"I'm afraid so. Each time it doesn't work then that means I have to take another set of readings on you. I'm trying to copy the structure of your empathesis, which is about like blueprinting your DNA. Does that make sense?"

"Not really," George says, squeezing his eyes shut and opening them with a sigh.

"Well," Aiden begins in his casual, yet professional tone, "I'm trying to determine the mechanics of how you read emotions. I suspect this information is critical to the emotional modifier's encoding. If I can define how your empathesis works, then it's possible I can rewire the modifier to function on emotions the same way it does with thoughts." He leans forward, giving George a conspiratorial look. "Honestly, I'm not entirely sure this strategy will be successful. Thoughts and emotions are two different beasts and just because we can program one with the modifier doesn't mean we can the other. I think this whole project is a long shot, but I also said the same thing about the consciousness screen I built on the GAD-Cs. So don't be deterred by my skepticism. It keeps me grounded." Aiden laughs. George doesn't. All color suddenly drains from his face. Eyes full of dread, George twists his head over his shoulder, a new tension knitting his brow.

Usually my subconscious indicates when the event I'm witnessing is done. Now is not one of those times. I've seen enough. I spiral until I'm back in the Panther room.

I don't make a report at the computer terminal. Instead I tromp past the station and down the hall. I'm not certain of the timing of the event with Aiden and George. All I know is the anger and betrayal I feel is jolting. It wraps around me, inciting a fast-burning rage. I allow this fire to fuel my actions. Right before I round the corner to Aiden's lab I press my eyelids together and draw in a heavy breath.

George knows I'm there immediately. Now I realize *I* was the cause of him going pale and turning tense. Aiden, on the other hand, looks rather startled. No one says a word as I stomp across the lab. I stop in front of them, pin my hands on my hips, and briefly center my thoughts. I'm not an activist and I have no platform. But I'm a human being and speak from a place that wants to protect what we were all given when we were born—the right to think and feel for ourselves. The breath within my body has grown hotter, less steady, but I'm not shaking and for that I'm grateful.

"Hey, Roya," Aiden says, sounding casual but wearing a nervous expression. "What brings the pleasure of your visit?"

I step forward and slam my hand down on the table. He flinches, inches back. George gives a worried stare.

"It's not enough to manipulate people's thoughts, now you're going after their emotions?!"

"No, no, no, no, no," Aiden says in a rush. "Whatever you've heard is wrong. Let me explain."

"I didn't hear about your project from anyone."

Startled, he shakes his head. "Then how do you know—"

"I'm a News Reporter. I know."

I level my gaze at him. There's a terror in his eyes that increases moment by moment as he realizes just how much I know and how far gone that makes *us*.

I turn, pointing at George. "I'm thoroughly shocked you've consented to be a part of this! You know better than anyone this is a violation."

George shamefully looks off to the right, nodding his head. "I know," he says in a frustrated whisper.

I believe him. He appears genuinely remorseful. In a lower voice I say, "By consenting to be a part of this you're abusing your power."

He rubs his hand over his face. "Yeah," he says, then nothing else. I stare at him for a minute. His eyes are red and full of an inescapable self-loathing. How did he get roped into this?

My accusatory stare turns on Aiden. I feel his treachery scrape at my insides as I bore into his intense blue eyes. "And you," I scold, backing away, knowing I can't be next to him or otherwise he'll instantly try and right his wrong. Although I want to yell at him, insult him, make him feel as heartbroken as I do, I just stare across the five long feet that divide us. Shaking my head I force the sudden ache out with my words. "You are not who I thought you were. You're evil." Aiden stands suddenly, rushing over to me. I throw up a hand, blocking him. "Don't come near me...ever again." He responds with a pleading expression and I can't afford to look at him for one second longer. I turn and stalk off, not looking back at the two guys who individually owned pieces of my heart and sent them up in a bushfire.

Chapter Fifteen

Like the autumn leaves of an oak tree, the reasons to get away from the Institute keep piling up. Maybe those jerks are actually doing me a favor by making it easier to leave. My brother's a zombie. Aiden's working on a demonic device like he's God. And George is allowing himself to be a pawn in another deceptive game, a game that Trey is no doubt behind. I was right all along to leave this place. This time tomorrow, I'll be gone. That's my only bit of consolation.

I spend the rest of the day packing my belongings. Each garment reminds me of a memory I've had within the walls of the Institute. Steady fingers make every fold with precision and neatly arrange the items inside the many boxes scattered around my room. My mind meditates on releasing these memories, abandoning them here. Leaving the Institute is about creating a fresh start, since the life I've lived thus far has been a bunch of lies.

When my room is just a stack of boxes, I head for the computer lab. My heart feels shallow as I send a quick email to Bob and Steve to confirm the pickup time for tomorrow. They must be online because their reply arrives within minutes. *At least I can count on them.*

That night I sleep, but my dreams are full of scary images. My subconscious is trying to express itself, but I don't want to hear its messages. When I awake I shake off the dreams of Aiden's head on a chess piece and Joseph praying at an altar. These dreams make me doubt my decision, which is the last thing I should do. All I need is to get through the next few hours. That's easy. I can do that.

My last meal at the Institute and unsurprisingly I'm not hungry. Apparently neither is George. He takes the seat next to me without his usual omelet. "Can we talk? Please."

"No," I answer too fast. "Not right now," I say, my tone softer this time. "Not today."

He nods with understanding. "Okay, then I just want to say I'm sorry." The humility in his expression has a disarming effect on me. I'm just about to say more to him, but right then something takes me by utter surprise. Joseph sits down on the opposite side of the table.

I haven't seen him in the main hall for too long. His appearance hasn't changed; if anything he looks skinnier.

He gives me a cold expression, one that alienates me. "I came to see you off."

"That's big of you. Why don't you eat something while you're here," I suggest.

"I'm not hungry."

All eyes around the table lock on us. Usually I crave my privacy, but what's the point in hiding this feud.

"I wouldn't be trying if I didn't take this last opportunity to ask you to stay," he says across the long space that separates us. Everyone turns to me, awaiting my reply.

"Oh, so you didn't really come to see me off, did you?"

"I did," he says through clenched teeth.

"No, this is all about you and what you want."

"It's about us, Stark. It's about us sticking together."

"I'm all for that. Tell me, where were you last week? Or this week? I've been here, but you haven't been *sticking* around much at all, have you?" I accuse.

The volley is in his court. Everyone's heads turn to Joseph, awaiting his rebuttal.

A layer of bitterness settles over his dull expression. "Why wouldn't you want to stay here with your friends?" He makes a sweeping motion at the table.

"Because I can't be here. The Institute is full of lies and secrets. I can't put up with it anymore. I don't trust this place. And I especially don't trust *that* man." I point to Trey, who's just taken center stage in the main hall.

A hush falls on the crowd. Trey's actions are rushed, coated in stress. He taps the microphone twice but we're already looking at him. "I need everyone's attention." Running his hands through his overworked hair he says, "Dr. Livingston, the Head Scientist for the Institute, is missing. We believe he's been abducted."

No! The word is short but deliberate in my mind. Disbelief leaks into me like toxic gas into a room, leaving no breathable air. Startled gasps echo around the room, but not from me. Trey's words can't be real. *Can't be real. Can't be real.* All realness has slipped out of my life in one giant breath. Trey's words can't mean what I think they do. He's joking. I wait for Aiden's eyes to materialize in the doorway. His smile to unfurl. For Trey to laugh and say it's all a joke. But he doesn't. *He doesn't. He doesn't.* And with each passing second this becomes real. My reality. My nightmare.

"We are on full lockdown," Trey continues, his voice strict, urgent. "No one is to dream travel out of the Institute until further notice. Lastly, if you see Amber Morten then alert a Head Official immediately. We'll give you more information as we have it." With hurried steps Trey walks off the stage and out of the room.

The main hall is a sudden commotion of voices and movements. I remain frozen, eyes locked on nothing. My heart sinks beneath my knees, to a place lower than I thought it could ever go. Everyone speaks and moves all around me, but I just stare at the table feeling myself recede further and further. I dive down into that hollow part of me until I feel the ache take over and my head begins to throb. How could Aiden be missing? Why would someone abduct him? How could someone do that? Worry is a wild horse inside me, charging, scattering dust, marking everything with its hoof prints. Every time a new worry runs across my mind I feel it reverberate and echo in the depths of my stomach.

A hand touches my shoulder. In one movement I turn, throwing a hard block, sending the hand away. Samara's eyes widen. I look at her, frozen. "I'm sorry," I say in a hoarse whisper. It's almost impossible to force words through my aching throat. "I just…and that caught me off guard."

"Don't apologize," she says, pulling her hand to her chest like it's injured. "Are you all right?"

I realize I haven't been breathing properly when my head becomes suddenly light. Everyone at the table is looking at me. Did they all know? Did they know how *much* I cared for Aiden? Did they know that this hurt? When I see Trent's consoling expression I realize that everyone probably knew something. His look is enough to make me realize I can't face George. His expression will surely break me in two. My eyes flick up to find Joseph's, then away. It hurts worse to see him and know he knows I'm upset. He doesn't look away but instead says, "I guess you can't leave now." His words are cold, unkind. I want to punch him, but instead I let the statement in his words take full control of my being.

"No, I have to go. I have to get out of here." My voice shakes. *More now than ever, I have to get out of here.* Instinctively I know if I get away from this place then the piercing pain will subside. Aiden, wherever he is, will be found. He has to be. And I can't help him anyway. All I can do here in this stainless steel box is worry and ache, and I'm at my threshold with that. I have to get out of here, very soon, or otherwise I'll combust.

I race through the first level trying to determine where I can find Trey now. Would he be in his office and if so, where is that? I'm searching like never before, hitting every button next to every door. When I don't find anything on the first level I move my search down to the second. It doesn't take long for me to determine that his office isn't there. I descend to level three. The brushed stainless steel walls are extra cold right now. My heart races in my chest. I round a corner and pass the computer lab. After I turn again I realize that I'm in new territory. Passing through a long hallway I finally come to a door. When I'm just about to hit the button I see above it a label: "Head Official." I stop just before my fingers touch the button and knock.

There's a sudden shuffling. The door slides back and disappears. Trey stands looking anxious, tired. When I was searching for his office I kept rehearsing the insults I would say to him in order to get my way. My resolve dissipates as I take in his turquoise eyes, red and heavy. Now I feel stupid for bringing my pitiful, selfish wants to him when he's in the midst of something awful. I shake this off and chew on my lip momentarily. "Trey, I'm sorry to disturb you, but—"

"No, it's fine." He steps aside, welcoming me into his office. "Please come in."

His hospitable manner surprises me. I step past him and into the large office. It distinctly reminds me of Bob and Steve's inviting library, with books lining the walls, strange artifacts punctuating different areas, and beautiful tapestries hanging here and there. A large wooden desk sits in the middle of the room. On it is a stained glass lamp that gives off a brilliant array of colors and lights. Trey pulls himself up to his desk. He indicates the leather armchair opposite him. The chair is firm and the leather cool under my skin.

Trey stares straight at me with his hands folded on his desk. His expression is playing at sincerity, but I don't buy it. One doesn't master the art of manipulation without garnering trust. "You have something you want to ask me?"

"Yes," I say, trying to catch my breath, feeling a bit surprised that it escaped me suddenly. "I know you said that we're not supposed to dream travel, but I've made plans to leave the Institute. I'm going to live with Bob and Steve and—"

"Wait, what? When?" Trey leans forward, frowning.

"I've been trying to find you, but you haven't really been around. I'm scheduled to leave today," I say, mustering confidence even though I feel submissive and weak.

"I know I have been absent. I'm working on something," Trey says, spreading his hands out on his desk.

"Well, that's no matter at this point." I try to take charge of the conversation, thinking this will work in my favor after my request. "Anyway, I'm here because I know you said we can't dream travel right now, but I need to in order to leave. All I'm going to do is travel to the central GAD-C, generate, and then I'll be safe in Bob and Steve's protection."

Trey's shaking his head at me before I'm even done talking. "No, you're not going."

"But that's not fair! I'll be fine," I say. "It's not too dangerous."

"Roya, this isn't about fairness."

"Look, I'm sorry that Aiden is missing." My breath hitches in my throat. Seeps from my being. My face must be an awful shade of burgundy at this point. Trey can't know how I feel. He can't. "It's awful that something has happened to him, but that doesn't negate the fact that I'm leaving the Institute."

"You're not leaving," Trey says rather calmly.

"It isn't too dangerous." I continue to argue with him even though I'm not saying anything new. "I can make it and I'll be fine."

"I'm not saying you're not going because it's too dangerous, although it is," Trey says, sitting back in his chair. "You're not going because we need you." He pauses, tucks his chin, and looks at me intently. "We need you to bring Aiden back."

81

Chapter Sixteen

Stunned. There's no other word for it. This is not the answer I expected. At all. I anticipated Trey to tell me no, or dismiss me, or even not to grace me with his time and attention during this demanding period. I never expected that he needed me to rescue Aiden. My stomach turns over twice before I find my voice.

"What?"

"Specifically, we need you to lead the rescue mission, but I'll explain everything to you in twenty minutes. I was about to send a note requesting that you and the team meet me in room 222." He stands and strides to the door, opening it for me. "Please be there and I'll fill you in on the whole situation."

My legs stand without a command from my brain. Footsteps carry me over the threshold. I'm truly on autopilot at the moment. My brain registers the sound of Trey's door sliding closed behind me and the sight of the empty hallway, but I have zero idea what's going on in my head and my heart. Those parts have retreated to a storm shelter. Vaulted away, unable to properly deal with the idea that Aiden is gone and his safety depends on me. The part of me currently controlling my body is all instinct—my autonomic nervous system. This portion of me which for all of my life has controlled my breathing, heartbeat, and blinking is now taking on the extra burden of putting each foot in front of the other again and again and again.

◆

Fifteen minutes later I awake on the floor of my room. I don't remember going there. I don't know how I ended up on the floor. All I know is I have five minutes to put myself together before I'm expected in room 222. I haven't the slightest idea how to avoid going to this meeting or accepting the role Trey has volunteered me for. It doesn't make any sense that he's chosen me over Ren or Shuman or a dozen other people. What's going to happen to Aiden if I'm in charge of his fate? A dull throbbing takes residence in my chest. Aiden. Where is he? Who has him? Why? Is he all right? Could he be dead?

Dead.

The word, and its possible connection to Aiden, assaults my chest. My heart has been encased in a box too small for it. Each beat is accompanied by aching pressure as my heart tries to contract, but can't fully.

If I'm going to be forced to stay at the Institute during this tumultuous time, then I'll only survive this by distracting myself from this pain. Maybe there's no better way to do that than to be thrown into this mission. But first I need answers. A lot of them.

♦

When I arrive in room 222, Ren, Shuman, and George are already present. Sitting. Not talking. These are not people to make small talk. Right now I like this about them.

My eyes seize a painting taking up the far wall. An abstract composition of blues and greens reminding me of the ocean. It definitely wasn't there the last time I was in here.

"Hey," George says, pulling out the chair next to him. I take the seat, gauging his expression. It doesn't give anything away. Neither does Shuman's. Both have sullen expressions, which is pretty typical for them. Ren, on the other hand, looks quite out of the ordinary. For one, he has a greenish bruise around his eye, a two-inch cut along his check, and his hands are battered. He isn't looking at anyone, but rather staring at the table. Usually he'd be flaunting his arrogance around, making snide remarks accompanied by hateful sneers. Instead he looks humbled. Hopefully this new demeanor will stick around for a while.

Joseph and Samara arrive looking uncomfortably subdued. They slip into the chairs on the other side of me. I have the urge to reach out and hug Joseph. Partly because I need the comfort and also because it looks as though he does too. He appears lonely sitting in his leather jacket and looking at his hands like they aren't his own. Hard to believe only a few weeks ago he was full of life. Not just full of life; he provided so much of the energy around this place. Now that he's become a zombie, the Institute is colder than ever before. Joseph looks up at my spying eyes and nods his chin. His expression is a mix between sympathy and concern.

He leans down low so only I can hear him. "You wanna talk later?"

"To you?"

"Well, that's better than to yourself, which you do too much already." It's a joke, but neither of us laughs or breaks our stony expressions.

"Let's just figure out why we're here," I say, wishing I had something I could do with my hands.

He nods and leans away.

A short girl with soft brown hair rushes into the room seeming lost. She stops and stares around the table, then takes a seat at the far end. I've never seen her before. She's rail thin, with tiny wrists and arms which are covered in freckles.

My attention is withdrawn from her when Trent enters talking animatedly to the white coat I'd met more than a month ago. James. He has wild, curly brown hair and pronounced canines. If a Viking and teddy bear mated, he'd be the result. Trent says something and James responds with a nervous laugh. Ren flicks his eyes up, giving them both a punishing look. James takes a seat and the room falls deadly silent.

The silence is about to drive me mad when Trey walks in, shutting the door behind him. His face is drawn, strict. "Thank you for joining me here." The Head Official picks up a dry erase marker and writes one word on the board:

Voyageurs

With a brutal look in his eyes he taps the marker on the board. "The Voyageurs, that's who took Aiden. Before I brief you on the abduction, I'll share the history with you. Without the background you might be confused and it's best if we start off this mission with everyone focused and clear on all details." Trey clears his throat. Everything he does is robotic. "Flynn founded the Institute, but shortly afterward he recruited Pierre, his research partner. They worked together, traveled together, and both had a vision of protecting Dream Travelers and Middlings. Flynn's focus was technology, and Pierre's, abilities. Under their leadership the

Institute gained momentum and more and more Lucidites joined and found solace within these walls.

"However, an irreconcilable dispute ensued between the two men, and they parted ways. Flynn naturally held onto the Institute and Pierre founded his own place in France—the Grotte."

He runs his fingers through his silver hair, examining each face in the room. "The Voyageurs spend the majority of their focus honing abilities. Whereas we focus on abilities, science, *and* strategic ops. Although dream travel investigation only revealed *how* Aiden was abducted, I suspect *why* the Voyageurs took him is because they're deficient in scientific advances. Before, they relished that they didn't rely on the technologies that we prided ourselves on, but now I think they've realized their shortcomings. Currently they're not guarded by shields or protective charms of any type. Furthermore, they have no devices, with the exception of one GAD-C. For too long they have boasted about not needing technology, but times are changing and Dream Travelers must protect themselves from all sources of conflict or we'll pay the price. Pierre knows this and has acted in order to protect his people."

Trey gives a heavy sigh. "Actually, let me make a correction. I speculate Pierre's actions are a result of fear and vengeance. I'm working hard to prove this, but no matter his reason it doesn't change the circumstances. Once Aiden has been returned we will learn the Voyageur's pure motives—which I suspect to be selfish, as well as dishonorable." There's acid in his tone, which is new. Even when Trey spoke about Zhuang his voice didn't carry *this* anger.

"They've been planning this attack for a while. It isn't just a strategic move, but also one based on a long-running vendetta." Anger burns on every feature of Trey's face. "Could they have recruited their own scientist? Yes. But they took ours. Now I'm the first to admit that Aiden is among the best, but still this is not the act of people who operate under diplomacy. Amber has been spying for them and she's the one responsible for executing Aiden's abduction."

Amber! She's responsible for this? Heart pounding, I lean forward, perched on the edge of my chair.

"She drugged him and escaped through the dry-dock. It was this breech that first alerted our attention to the problem. What complicates matters is that Aiden recently invented a new piece of technology known as the dream blocker. The device prevents the wearer from dream traveling. It has been impossible to abduct a Dream Traveler in the past because this technology didn't exist. If captured, a person could always dream travel and regenerate their body. This has always been our biggest challenge when tracking Zhuang. Anyway, Aiden's technology has now made this a new reality and I'm sorry to say he's the first person to suffer because of it. The dream blocker has been stolen and I'm certain it will prevent him from returning."

Trey draws in a long breath. "Whatever it is the Voyageurs require of Aiden, I suspect he will not be compliant to their demands. His parents were murdered by these people."

Murdered? When Aiden said his family was dead, I never considered that they were murdered.

"Whatever Pierre asks of Aiden will be met with resistance. I'm certain of that. This is the utmost reason we have to act fast if we want to rescue Aiden before he's killed."

I close my eyes and try to erase the last words I heard from my memory. Things like this shouldn't be a part of my reality. A person I care about can't be facing such a dismal fate. It's wrong. And it twists my insides, sickening me.

"You all are the team I've assembled to rescue Aiden." Trey begins walking around the table slowly. "The Voyageurs have battled us many times. Although we've never wanted to harm them, they've always reacted with violent force when we've come into contact. They've fought Ren, Shuman, and myself too many times to count. Due to the way their present security works, which is based on mental abilities, they're too attuned to us. None of the Head Officials can get anywhere close to the Grotte, or Aiden, without setting off a hundred alarms. For this reason, I've decided that the team who fought Zhuang, which has the most current level of experience and practice, will rescue Aiden, because time is of the essence."

Trey completes the long circle around the room and stands staring directly at me. "I'm asking you, Roya, to please lead this team. I know this is a lot of responsibility, but you're the right person for the job. You're my first choice." He swallows hard. "Do you accept?"

So this is what being put on the spot feels like. I'm fairly certain the entire room can hear my heart thumping in my chest. I don't really have a choice but to agree. However, if I did have a choice, what would I do? Thinking clearly isn't really an option with everyone staring at me. I pull my vision out of the current place and retreat into my mind. It only takes a second but suddenly I'm in Aiden's room staring into his excited eyes. His laugh opens places in me I didn't know existed, places with depth—and his affection fills those spaces. I spiral back to the present time. The anger and betrayal I felt for Aiden has all but faded to tiny distant emotions. Now fear for his safety is center stage. The last words I spoke to him ricochet around my head. "You're evil. Don't come near me…ever again." I can't let those be my last words to him. Can't.

Everyone's eyes still stare at me, awaiting my answer. When I reply I only see one pair of eyes—Aiden's. "Yes, I'll do it."

"Good," Trey says without enthusiasm. "Samara, Trent, George, and Joseph, you will all be in your same respective roles as before. That is, if you also decide to be a part of this mission. The decision is yours." He stops, eyeing each of them. I'm relieved the focus is off me for a little while. Each member nods, almost in a daze.

"Good. This time, though, you'll be traveling together to the Grotte. Roya will not be alone."

A new emotion enters the room and I feel it first from Joseph, who straightens, looking eager rather than worried. Trey runs his hands through his hair. I knew he was about to do that. I can almost guess what mannerism he'll do between sentences. I wonder if he knows he's so predictable.

"Now I'd like to introduce a new member of the team." He points to the tiny girl sitting next to Ren. "Please welcome Pearl. She will be your healer."

A pang of remorse courses through me—for Whitney. She was my friend. I loved her. When Zhuang brutally murdered her, my heart broke for the first time, really broke, like I'd never be whole again. The pain is still too fresh and I'm unable to look at Pearl directly. Thankfully Trey is already directing our attention to the white coat who entered with Trent. "James will be working with you on technology. I trust that he has enough experience to get you into the Grotte. And again you'll practice with Shuman for abilities and

Ren for strategy. We have to do this and do it fast. I want you to train hard." He rubs his fist into the palm of his hand. "I happen to be intimately acquainted with the Voyageurs' interrogation strategies. Aiden has roughly ten days before the tactics they use kill him. This mission needs to be executed one week from today. Understood?"

I don't nod. Thankfully, everyone else does. There isn't enough air in the room. This feels like a really stupid dream, and there's no waking up and no getting away from it. My head swims with everything Trey told us about these new people and all the risks and dangers. I can't even believe that an hour ago I thought I was headed home to rest easily on the porch for hours on end, and now I'm going to spend the next week training my ass off only to get killed by some French guy with a beret.

An epiphany occurs and once it does I realize it was overdue. My emotions must have delayed it from shimmering to the surface. I look at Shuman, half expecting her to be gazing at me with a knowing expression. She isn't. But what I'd seen while news reporting had been correct. There really was this strange and dangerous girl who wanted to steal something. That something, could it have been Aiden? And then there was the guy playing chess, had that been Pierre? My heart races faster as I piece all of this together. I'm anxious to get out of this room and away from all these people who make the space feel claustrophobic.

I find myself nodding in agreement to whatever Trey says. It's floating past me at this point. When I hear him clear his throat with finality, I push up from the chair and stride out of the room. Thankfully the meeting is over and I just look like I'm taking charge rather than being a coward, which is what I am. Trey's last words echo in my ears as I round the corner, "Your first training takes place at two o'clock today in the lecture hall."

Chapter Seventeen

I'm not sure what the rest of my team does for the hours allotted to us before training begins. Maybe they converse about the new mission. They probably all gather at lunch and poke at their food. Maybe they question my whereabouts, emotions, and mental state. All I know is what composes those hours for me.

Sullen, aching grief.

I fall into a new low and allow myself to wallow in it. I had convinced myself that I didn't care about Aiden because of what he was working on. But his abduction brings the raw truth to the surface. My fury at him is because I do care and I'm utterly heartbroken he made the choices he did. And I only know all that now because my heart constantly makes its complaints known due to his absence. No matter his choices, he owns a piece of me. Where is that piece now?

I lay in this pitiful mess of sorrow for a good hour. When I'm starting to push myself up from the pain I stick in the ear buds and crank up the music. Torment rips through me with a fresh intensity. Cary Brothers' voice and lyrics send me to an inescapable suffering.

> ♪ *I'll take your place when the world ends and you'll take mine*
> *I'll break us out of this jail and get you high*
> *'Cause when it all ends I want you to be free, free like you make me*
> *Free like you make me* ♪

I listen to his song a total of eleven times. Really, I would have liked it to be an even dozen, but I didn't want to be late to training. As intended I'm halfway through the first stage in a thirty-seven-step process of dealing with this grief. My breaths are heavy and unfulfilling, but I haven't cried and for that I'm relieved.

Just as I'm about to head into the lecture hall I realize I haven't sent a message to Bob and Steve. *How could I have forgotten to tell them?* They would have driven hours out to the GAD-C to pick me up. I rush off to the computer lab on the third level to send them an email. Once I log in I'm instantly relieved to find they have already sent me an email. Of course the Institute newsfeed has informed the society about what's going on. Their email explains they know I can't dream travel and will wait for more details. My fingers type hurriedly.

Trey's lost his mind

Roya Stark <roya.stark713@gmail.com>
to bobandsteve

Hey Bob and Steve,

Trey seems to think I'm the best person to lead Aiden's rescue mission. He has some valid reasons, but still… Although I had understandable hesitations, I decided to accept the role. So no more worries about me having too much time on my hands. Seriously though, I'm more than a bit intimidated by this challenge. You always give me such great advice. So please enclose all words of wisdom in the next email, as well as prayers that I don't lose my mind, get killed, or get a half a dozen other people murdered under my leadership.

Thanks for everything. Always.

Love,
Ms. Totally-Unprepared-For-This

P.S. Fighting Zhuang kind of seems easy right now…

Yes, I could have waited to send them an email, but it was more for me than them. My eyes flick to the clock, then dread follows. I'm late to training.

Ren narrows his eyes as I stealthily slip into the room. Everyone's seated and focused on him. He stalks me as I walk across the lecture hall and take a seat. I brace myself for his punishment, which will no doubt carry a round of insults regarding my competence and intelligence. To my astonishment he only shakes his head, repulsion written on his bruised face.

"The Grotte. It's French for cave," he says in a bad French accent. "This is where these *people*, and I'm using that word loosely, are holding Aiden. Their location is in the side of a massive confusion of rock in the south of France. We live in Buckingham Palace compared to their place. It's total rubbish. Actually it's pretty much the same digs our ancestors dwelled in when they discovered fire. The Voyageurs' headquarters isn't heated or cooled, nor does it have cable or Wi-Fi. And it most certainly isn't protected by any special technology like what we're accustomed to here."

Ren begins pacing, shoulders and back stiff. "The Voyageurs are primitive and savage people. I'm not saying this as a criticism as much as an observation. Here's my criticism of these people, so hear it and write it down, or whatever you prats need to do in order to get it straight: As long as these people don't know you then they can't find you. That's how their security works. They're experts at reading and recording an individual's energies. When they sense an approaching energy of an enemy the red flag goes up and the Neanderthals grab the nearest club. Before a Voyageur is familiar with your energy, it's like you don't exist for them. In this way they're naïve. We must always be on the prowl for new threats, not waiting around for unknown bullies to steal our milk money. An-y-ways"—Ren draws out the word, blinking back boredom—"the cave people's approach to security measures makes it terribly difficult to sneak up on them if you've fought them time and time again. However, if you're unknown to them, then breaching their walls is rather quite easy and for that reason, and only that one, you gits stand a chance."

I'm surprised when my hand rises in the air. Ren turns, tightens his eyes at me. I expect him to berate me with criticism, or at least say something snide. Instead he just gives me an impatient stare and says, "What?"

"When I was news reporting I spied on a French girl. A man informed her that she was being watched and she turned in my direction and caught me. And later a similar incident occurred. They don't know me so how were they able to pick up on my energy? And now if they've read my energy then maybe it's been recorded. Maybe I'm not the right person to head this mission," I say.

He flashes an evil smile, baring his sharp canines. There's the old Ren we all know and loathe. "Nice try, little Miss Muffet, but you're not getting out of this so fast. In your vision, you were caught by Pierre. He's a master at catching intrusions through news reporting. It's like a hobby of his and a quite lame one. Too bad they don't have a cricket field there at the Grotte. Who Pierre informed about your spying was his second in command, Allouette. Lucky for you they can't pick up your energy from a vision. They just know you were there. That's all."

As Ren intended I feel small and cowardly. I slide down an inch in my seat.

"If no one else wants to try and weasel out of this mission then I'll continue." Ren scans our faces. "Very well then. The Voyageurs have spent all their efforts honing their mental abilities. It's how they guide and guard themselves. For this reason it makes infiltrating their drab bearings too easy. However, if you find yourself face to face with one of them then you better cut your throat before they make you. They use their mental abilities for evil deeds and will spare no expense to make you bleed your last drop if they think you need to be punished." Ren sounds extra bitter. Between him and Trey I'm starting to notice a correlated pattern of hate toward the Voyageurs.

"You've already heard about the head honcho, Pierre. He wears a snotty expression on his face at all times. That's how you'll spot him. He'll spot you using his telepathy, which is stronger than the electricity powering all of London. If you're anywhere near him, he's going to bore into your brain like a saw. He'll know everything you've thought since you were old enough to construct anything of use. When you're finally looking into his eyes he'll already know the slightest thoughts you had when you were whimpering in the schoolyards hiding from bullies. No matter how insignificant, Pierre will know your thoughts, and he will use this insignificant knowledge to overpower, confuse, and destroy you."

Ren paces, looking at each one of us. He's walking with a limp. Allouette did a pretty bad job on him. Or a pretty good one depending on how I look at it. "The only strategy you can hope to use against Pierre," Ren continues, "is to shield yourself from his menacing probe of a brain. I taught you how to do this when facing Zhuang, but Pierre will be different. Furthermore, only Roya faced Zhuang, and I guess we can count Joseph too if getting briefly sliced counts. Telepathy is an extremely different beast when you're in close proximity to someone. Samara can attest to this. For this reason the shield is even more important. If you fail to guard yourself from Pierre, he will find your darkest and deepest thoughts and use them to knock you down, distract you, and then he'll send in his minions to finish you off."

I hate to admit it, but once again one of Ren's speeches has sent shivers through me. In my vision, the one where Pierre was playing chess, I remember thinking something was disturbingly off about him. At the time it was an interesting observation. Now that I know I'll have to face this guy, the observation is now chilling. The Head Officials expect us to break into the headquarters of a conniving, psychopathic genius. Something tells me we aren't going to just waltz into his lair and steal Aiden back.

Ren charges into the practical aspect of the lecture. I'm grateful for the distraction so I can bury these thoughts of worry, at least for the moment. We spend the rest of the time learning how to put up these shields and detect when Pierre, or anyone else, is trying to pull information out of our brains. As usual I jot down pages of notes, but when Ren shoots a glance at me I pretend to be bored. This is a hard act to keep up, but I know it's worth it.

Chapter Eighteen

I have no choice but to attend dinner since I skipped lunch. Although I'm not hungry I know I have to eat or suffer the consequences later. I'm shoving down some leafy greens when Joseph sits at the table. He glances at me, then shamefully looks away. *What's his deal?* At least he's showing up at meal time, which he hasn't done in a while. Still, it bothers me that I can't figure out what's going on with him. Since we're twins shouldn't I be able to pick up his activity? He always knows when I'm lying or what I've been doing. This is rarely the case for me, especially lately. Joseph wolfs down his sandwich and charges off looking angry.

I return to my swamp of a salad, which my heavy hand has drenched in too much dressing. The plate makes a screeching sound when I push it away. George is staring at me with a consoling expression, something he's been doing often, and it annoys me. I cut my eyes back to the table. He might think this whole catastrophe has erased his misdeeds, but he's wrong. All I want is Aiden back safely, but when he is it won't change how mad I am at the two of them for working on the emotional modifier.

♦

After dinner I go for a run. It's just about the only thing in the world that feels right at the current time. Each mile I'm weakened by new worries regarding Aiden: What's going on with him right now? Are they interrogating him? Starving him? Torturing him?

I don't run from these worries though. I invite each one into my heart and mind. At the doorstep of my emotional threshold I greet them like a perfect host. Each worry tracks mud into my home and dirties the furniture. I grit and bear my houseguests. Their time with me will be short-lived. Samara told me that processing thoughts was the way to remove them from the mainstream. I'm bent on processing these thoughts and emotions faster than ever. My worries can't be sitting on the top of my consciousness where someone can fish for them and realize how weak I am. I run. Sweat. Think. Feel.

At the six-mile mark I break through a wall. It feels like I'm starting to progress with this whole processing thing. Then Andrew Belle begins singing in my head. His haunting voice grabs me by the sternum and shakes. All of a sudden I'm sprinting. Shaking. Crying. The ache that was only in my belly now has taken over my chest. I'm a breath away from screaming. But I don't. I just run. Until I can't anymore.

After a terribly cold shower I pace my room, wondering why I'm not exhausted. A run that long and hard should make me want to sleep for days. I can't dream travel, and falling asleep right now is impossible. It feels like I'll never be tired. Fueled by frustration I throw myself on my neatly made bed and roll over. Something sharp pokes me in the back. The corner of the book I was reading last night. It's a collection of poetry from American writers. If anything is going to soothe me now it will be poetry. I thumb through it and randomly stop to read a page. It's a poem by Emily Dickinson. A rare poem of hers I've never read:

I never lost as much but twice,
And that was in the sod
Twice have I stood a beggar
Before the door of God!
Angels—twice descending
Reimbursed my store—
Burglar! Banker—Father!
I am poor once more!

I acutely relate to this poem. So much so that it brings back the sorrow all over again. I curse the poets, the songwriters, and anyone else whose job it is to make me feel.

This challenge to rescue Aiden will be my second one for the Lucidites. The first time I took on their challenge I felt like I lost everything: my home, my family, my identity. Here I am again, not even a month later, taking on another challenge for them. I stand on the edge of this rocky shore and peer down, realizing all I stand to lose *this* time: Aiden, Joseph, my friends, my life. The ache is brief this time and I'm glad for that. My eyelids have a sudden heavy pressure on them. Finally. I pull the covers over my head and force the current world out.

Sleep delivers me strange and awful dreams. Multiple times I try to pull out of the nightmares and back to my reality, but they hold me captive. Knives slash at my unclothed skin. Darkness surrounds me as I clutch for a wall, furniture, or anything to guide my way. And in all the dreams the constant ominous clunking thunders all around me. It's a clue, I think, but to what? In some dreams I try to find its origin and in others I run from it. And I'm always running—from something. Each corner brings a dread of finding that which wants to find me, end me. Facing fears is not something I aspire to right now.

Blissful dreams are of my highest aspiration, but they elude me. Again and again I'm held prisoner by my subconscious. It forces gory images into my mind. Confronts me with my insecurities. Takes me to terrible places. Too many of my dreams include Whitney. Over and over I've watched her die, arrived too late to save her. The blade had already done its damage by the time I showed up to find Whitney's apologetic eyes and Zhuang's triumphant grin. Whitney always wears an ashamed face, like it's her fault that she died. Her fault that I didn't react fast enough to save her.

When I'm not failing Whitney I'm fighting, blocking, defending myself against impossibly fast strikes and fists made of steel. I never win. Each attack pushes me further and further until I fall into a vat of hot, thick liquid—where I drown. Dream after dream I fail. I drown. I'm held against my will until my alarm clock screeches its usual wakeup call. I slap the button, never happier to hear the high-pitched wailing.

Twisted bed sheets sit in a heap on the floor. A crumpled pillow lies on the opposite side of the room. Sweat mats my hair to my head, soaks my shirt. I am dread and fear incarnate right now. Every part of me is a result of not wanting my current reality to be real. And I've had just about enough of it.

"No more," I say aloud to the empty room. My voice sounds shredded from the tears I've cried.

Terror races through me every time I think about the mission I'm leading. This is harder than facing Zhuang because my worry for Aiden constantly drains my reserves. Fear coats every strategic thought, disabling my mental faculties—which I need most to survive. As much as I've tried to resist the way I feel for him, my emotions run too deep. Nothing changes them, not even this situation. But this sorrow for Aiden and the dread of failing him will end us all. Every day I feel my love for him weakening me.

This path I'm on is getting me nowhere. I have to let go of the grief—and the love—because if I don't then I might as well stand down from this challenge now. I have a mission to do. And the only way to do it successfully is by disconnecting. Otherwise my dreams will be plagued by new nightmares, ones where I didn't save Aiden, was responsible for more people dying, failed again and again to overcome my fears.

If I don't become someone new, then I will forever be haunted by inevitable failures. If I don't isolate my emotions, then they'll get me and everyone else killed.

A switch flips in me and a robot takes over. I welcome its presence. The beat of my heart slows; its temperature drops a few degrees. For the first time in days I see everything in a linear fashion. Black and white. Suddenly I'm not a person with emotions and desires. I'm a machine with hardwiring and programming. Every machine has a purpose. Mine is to obtain what was stolen from the Lucidites. I will train. Focus. Complete mission. Move on.

And just like that I shut down a part of me, the part that made me love. The part that made me weak. No attachments.

Chapter Nineteen

Habitually I skip breakfast the next morning. The old Roya missed meals because of a lack of hunger. But the new Roya is more logical and knows that all good machines run on fuel. I detour by the main hall on the way to my first session and grab a protein bar.

Just as training with Shuman begins I manage to slide into the classroom. She's already standing at the front talking. "George," she says, pointing at him, "what am I feeling right now?"

"I don't know," he says after a long pause.

"Why?" she says, standing with her arms crossed.

"I don't know," he says after obvious deliberation.

"Try harder," she orders. The rattlesnake tattoo on her arm pulses when her muscles flex.

"I am," George says bitterly.

"Zhuang," Shuman says, turning her focus on the rest of us, "did not use this shielding because he did not care if you spied what was in his head or heart. To his fault he believed that even if you read his thoughts he would still defeat Roya. I believe he probably cared far less about the emotions in his heart. He was arrogant and saw no point in wasting energy on shielding."

Shuman raises her chin in the air, a self-assured look on her unyielding face. "The Lucidites do not practice shielding much because we are a trusting society," she says matter-of-factly. There's a pause and she adds, "This is my judgment anyway." Briefly our eyes meet before she focuses on the back wall. "Each of you must make this decision on your own, since trust is personal and based on private experiences. Still, none of you have dealt with any other Dream Traveler societies. We are a strong race of people and too often this power translates into a corrupt nature. The Voyageurs are neither arrogant nor trusting. They are experts at using shields and it is imperative that you know how to use them too. It is Ren's responsibility to teach you how to guard yourself against them. Mine is to teach you how to break through their shields." Shuman cracks her neck with a swift jerk. "And I have every hope you will do this without them perceiving your intrusion. Your fate rests upon this hope, so I encourage you to adopt it as well."

Shuman pivots, pointing at Samara. "What am I thinking?"

"I don't know," Samara says almost instantly.

"That is unacceptable. If you want to survive in the Grotte then you have to try harder, break through my shield—undetected."

I'm suddenly glad I don't have what Shuman calls an active power, like Samara's and George's. They actively go in and get information. My power is considered to be more passive and is delivered by a universal source. For this reason I don't have to worry about breaking these shields in order to use my power like George and Samara. Lucky for me my clairvoyance will work the same way it always has.

We spend the rest of the training session learning how to penetrate shields. It's energy-consuming work. I take a ton of notes although they don't specifically relate to me. Unfortunately, I'm to spend more of my shielding training working with Ren.

◆

My hardwiring instructs me to eat at lunch time. I do as it commands, filling up on tofu and vegetables. Each bite is followed by robotic chewing where I taste nothing. I only stop eating when a command from my system tells me I've had enough. Then I push up from the table, not seeing any of the people I spent the meal with. They could all be droids too for all I care. We have a mission. One I will complete with success. Then move on.

The team and I report to the lecture hall after lunch to train with James. He's standing behind a desk, teetering back and forth like he's trying to decide how to balance his weight between his legs. He's well over six foot tall, but appears harmless and kind, like a gigantic sloth. Curly brown hair springs up away from his head, giving the appearance so often associated with a mad scientist. James isn't mad when he speaks though, he's excited, eager. In that way, he reminds me of Aiden. The mention of Aiden's name in my mind brings no sudden heart palpitations or cold sweats, as I expected. It's accompanied by no more than data: stolen property, must return, keep unharmed. A satisfied smile spreads along my cold face.

"So," James begins slowly, "we're here to discuss the device that will guarantee your survival at the Grotte." A handkerchief rests over something on the desk in front of James. He picks up one end and yanks it away. "I present to you the modifier!"

My icy heart sinks to the farthest reaches of my chest. Even in machine mode it's difficult to compute this turn of events. Using this device is against all protocols. It's vastly against my nature. There's no overriding that. I know, inherently, that I can't do something that destroys my moral fiber.

The modifier is not what I expected. I envisioned it like a device similar to the first computer, which was about the size of walk-in closet. Compact and shiny, the modifier could easily fit in the palm of my hand. It's a small metal cube, with the same brushed stainless steel surface as the walls of the Institute. The modifier appears unassuming and insignificant. Appearances are deceiving, right? In this case they're downright life altering. It's hard to believe this device is responsible for shaping lives: mine, Joseph's, our fake families, as well as countless others—including all the government employees who originally inhabited the Institute.

I've tuned out James's long monologue, which no doubt is praising the many capabilities of the device. He's been at the front of the room squeaking for over ten minutes about the modifier like it's a god. I can't take this nonsense any longer. "What's the point? Why are we expected to use this demonic device?" I say, not camouflaging the resentment with a more proper emotion.

He stops, straightens, looking put off. "Because it's the most critical part of our plan to rescue Dr. Livingston."

Of course it is.

"The plan is that you'll travel to the Grotte, then generate your body. This part is easy. After that point you'll be a target for the Voyageurs. If they see you then you'll be dead and it will all be over. The modifier is your only chance at surviving long enough to find Dr. Livingston."

"You expect us to use *this* device? To change the thoughts of the Voyageurs?" I ask in utter disbelief.

"Specifically, as the team captain, I expect *you* to use it," he says like he's talking to a stubborn child.

Me? Of course me. If there's a God, then he's laughing at me right now. *Good one. You got me.*

"And yes," James continues. "You'll use it to program the Voyageurs to believe you belong there. This won't last long against their mental guards," James warns, looking sullen for the first time. "But it will buy you time. The key is to not do anything to draw too much attention. You see," he says, striding around the table looking excited, "the modifier will tell them that you all belong there, but not why. This will cause them to invent their own reasons for why you're there. If you do or say something that contradicts the reality they've told themselves then your cover will be blown."

"If"—Joseph says the word like it contains multiple syllables— "we can use this device on the Voyageurs, because they don't wear protective charms, then why can't we tell 'em to give Aiden back and be done with this whole thing?"

James shakes his head, a look of disappointed remorse on his face. "I'm afraid that wouldn't work. That's too big of a message. Their guards are strong and so any message that raises attention will be flagged, examined, and determined to be implanted. It would be easier to recede their minds about them ever abducting Dr. Livingston, but then you'd still have to get in there and rescue him. Our best bet is to use the modifier once for a broad message, one that will protect you all while you're there and allow you to find Dr. Livingston."

"If the modifier could draw attention to us, then maybe we're better off not using it at all," I argue, more out of desperation than logic.

"And what happens when a Voyageur stops you, asks you a question, and wonders why you don't speak French?" James responds like he's debating a philosophical point, rather than the greatest moral dilemma I've faced thus far.

"Any of you know French?" I ask, lacing my voice with hope.

No one nods.

James tilts his head, shrugs. "And this is just one of the main reasons to use the modifier. Others are that it will allow you to coast through the Grotte without having to invent a reason for your presence. Heck, I'm guessing that the Voyageurs might even go out of their way to help you, opening doors and such." He pauses, scrunching up his bushy eyebrows. "Actually, I'm not certain they have doors, but you get the point."

Unfortunately I do.

James continues explaining how to use the modifier and telling us different things to be observant of. I retreat into my mind, wondering how I've gotten into this hypocritical position. Wasn't I the person who just exploded on Aiden over this stupid device? It's what we always fought about. Well, and also Amber. A guilty shiver runs down my back.

Still, this device was the last thing I'd fought with Aiden about. And it had been the subject we'd steered away from, knowing we couldn't agree. Now they expect me to use it. If I don't then what would happen? Would I show up in the Grotte and be struck dead before I even had a chance? As I scroll down these questions I realize where the disconnect happens for me. It's in my judgment. I'd previously judged George and Aiden for their involvement with the device. If I hadn't judged them so harshly then I'd have no trouble using this device right now. In this circumstance, based on James's reasons, it makes sense. And these people have stolen what belongs to us. This logic brings with it a companion question: Was it wrong for the Institute to program my fake family to accept me if it kept me safe from Zhuang for all those years? The answer doesn't come. And still there are so many other things the modifier has been used for which I don't have time or energy to analyze.

The logical part of me accepts using the modifier under the current circumstances. But my heart cannot reconcile the past. It's the part of me having trouble coming to terms with this whole plan. I wish my heart would go back into hibernation. I had valid reasons for opposing the device's use in the past. But in this circumstance, it does seem logical to employ it, if it can guarantee our survival and help us rescue Aiden.

Is this what Aiden meant when he said the modifier was only employed to protect the greater good? I always thought qualifying that was arbitrary. Everyone always thinks their side is the one that represents good. Where does the greater good lie in this scenario? Putting a small message into the Voyageurs' heads so we can rescue Aiden before he's killed does seem like the right thing to do. It makes logical sense. Something about my new robotic nature is making me view the disagreement with Aiden from a black and white perspective, which unfortunately doesn't favor me in this situation. If this is the criteria for using the modifier, then it's a no-brainer.

My deliberation brings only one question to the forefront of my brain that I can't reason away. Arriving at this question leaves my ego battered. And the question assaults me with one more emotional injury as it runs through my mind: Can I overcome my pride if it means completing the mission, something I *must* do?

Bitterness coats my tongue. I dismiss myself to get a drink of water.

Chapter Twenty

The knock on my door startles me. It isn't Patrick's familiar rap. With an exaggerated sigh I flip over on my bed and continue leafing through my book. The knock comes again. This time it's longer, more insistent. I toss *The Golden Compass* off my bed and bury my head under a pillow. I'm not in the mood for another apology attempt from George. The cocoon of pillow around my head is surprisingly comforting. If George doesn't keep me up knocking, then I can probably fall asleep in this cozy darkness.

"What's that, Stark?" Joseph says too loudly. His voice rings through the solid door and my pillow-insulated head. "One of the last things Aiden said to you was 'when I kiss you it sends—'"

I rip the pillow off my head and bolt upright in one swift movement. My feet race to the door faster than should be humanly possible. The palm of my hand slams against the button, sending the door back into the recess. Joseph stands looking satisfied.

"Why?" I say through clenched teeth.

Joseph strolls around me into my room. "Because, sis, I wanted to see you. Plain and simple."

I narrow my eyes at him. "My God, Joseph, you're cruel."

Hitting the button, I charge up behind him and when he turns around I say, "Where did you come up with that ploy to get me to open the door?"

He picks up one of my locks of hair and tosses it over my shoulder. "Oh, all my material is based on true life experiences. Works better that way. I might have exaggerated a bit though. I was antsy to see you," he says, looking mischievous.

"That's low, Joseph. Really low."

He nods. "That's what you've come to expect from me. I'm just trying to meet your expectations. So you and the scientist, eh? Yeah, I saw that coming a million miles away."

"There's nothing going on with Aiden and me."

"Oh, I'm sure y'all will work out your disagreements once he's back."

"How do you know what's in my head? Why don't I know what's in yours?"

He smiles and sinks down onto my bed. "Let's call it luck."

"Damn it, Joseph!" I roar and stomp around my room. "Don't I have enough going on right now!? Do I really need you tormenting me!?"

Right there he returns. Suddenly from across the room I'm looking at him, the twin brother I love. It's brief, then I'm too acutely aware of the dark circles under his eyes, sunken face, and pale complexion. And yet, for a brief second I saw the guy I trusted—he's still there somewhere.

"I'm sorry," he says, lying on my bed. "I wish I could be good enough for you. I've lost it." I don't believe much of what he says anymore, but I believe this.

"What do you want?" I say, taking a seat on the floor.

"Don't criticize me for it, but I missed you," he finally says, staring at the ceiling blankly.

Criticize him? For missing me? I've missed him so much. How can he be so stupid?

"I won't and I'm glad," I say, devoid of real emotion.

A small smile surfaces on the corner of his mouth. "Been dreaming much, Stark?" he asks.

"Yeah, when Ms. Chatterson shuts her trap."

"Who?"

"Never mind," I say.

"You want my input on your dreams?"

"Nope. How about you?" I ask.

"No real dreams," he says, seemingly on another planet. "I don't sleep much anyway."

"Mmm," I say, wondering if it's possible he's become a hallucinator.

Just like that he cuts off my thoughts and says, "Don't worry, I'm not hallucinating."

"Damn it, Joseph! Stop it!"

He laughs and turns over on his stomach. "Sorry."

"No you're not," I say.

We're quiet for a few minutes. He doesn't say anything, but for some reason I get this impression that he feels sorry. I'm not sure if I'm imagining it, but it's like he's quietly apologizing to me for everything he's done and not done over the last two weeks. After a while I sit up and say, "So what about Samara?"

"What about her?" Joseph says, staring at the floor.

"When were you going to tell me that you two are seeing each other?"

"About the time that I told you I was seeing anyone else," he says with a rude laugh.

"What?" I jerk up, eyes wide with repulsion. "Are you playing her?"

"Look, Stark, she knows what's in my head if she wants to. I don't feel like I'm playing any games on her."

"You know she isn't invading your thoughts. She wouldn't do that and expect things to work out between you two."

"Who says things are supposed to work out between us?" Joseph says, sitting up.

"Have you always been such a dog?"

He stares off as though seriously considering the question. "As far back as I can remember," he says coolly.

"What if she finds out? And who else are you messing with?"

Joseph's eyes retreat. "Look, this is none of your business."

"Really?" I growl softly. "Why don't you remember that before you broadcast my private life to the entire Institute?"

His eyes turn distant. "I'm sorry. I know this is harder on you than anyone else. But to be fair, you're stronger than the rest of us."

"That's not fair," I say bitterly.

"Well, it's true," Joseph says.

"That's your opinion."

"Look, you think I abandoned you. And you distrust me for not telling you why. But you gotta believe me when I say I'm tryin', tryin' to make our life better."

I eye him suspiciously. "That's ironic, because you've made my life worse."

"Oh, stop playin' the victim. It doesn't suit you."

"I don't see myself as a victim," I say in a mechanical voice.

"No, I don't suppose you would," he says, like it's a canned answer and his thoughts are preoccupied on something else.

"Are you coming around to meals and by my room because you can't dream travel?" I ask, almost accuse.

"What I'm working on was quite consuming and took me away a lot."

"Are you working on it now?"

"In a way, but this mission needs my attention. And since you're leading it I know you need my attention too."

"Oh, is that why you came by?" I scold.

"Why you always got to think people's motives are dark?"

I give him a defiant look. "I just don't have much faith in people."

"Well, I got all my faith in you," he says in a sing-song voice.

"Stop it," I say, feeling extra irritable. I need to turn back into the robot before I do or say something emotional.

Joseph gives me an apologetic look. "I mean it, but I know why you don't believe me. I'll try and be a better brother."

"Fine," I say, indifferently. Why get my hopes up just to have Joseph disappoint me again?

"And why don't you work on lightening up a bit," he says.

"I'll see what I can do."

The space between us falls quiet again. Joseph taps his foot. I pace back and forth between my thoughts deciding what I want to say to him now that I have his sincere attention.

"Joseph." My voice is on the verge of sounding desperate. I steady it with a breath. "Do you see a vision where we get through this?"

He straightens and turns in my direction. A playful expression dances across his face. With his fist he gives me a pretend jab on the jaw. "Oh, come on, kid, you know as well as I do that knowing the future doesn't fix anything."

"Come on, Joseph, if you know something then tell me, prepare me."

With an embellished sigh he stands and yawns. "Gotta thank you for something, Stark. You made me tired. I haven't been tired in days."

"I tend to wear people out." I rise, folding my arms across my chest.

"That you do," he sings, striding for the door. He presses the button and turns and faces me. "Oh, okay, maybe you'll stop being so hostile at me if I tell you this much…"

I drop my arms, tilt forward, awaiting his words.

"I see a future where you're happy. Not just read-a-cute-little-story *happy*, or come-off-a-runner's-high *happy*, but one where

107

you've made a claim to the emotion. It's a beautiful thing, one that actually makes *me* truly happy."

"Really?" I breathe in surprise.

"Really," he says, a rare stillness in his eyes. After a moment he walks over the threshold, then turns around and looks at me directly again. "The thing is, that vision is so far away. So many choices that could make it or break it. I'm gonna try my darndest to ensure it happens, but you also have to work at it. We both know visions of the future are just potentials."

I give a heavy sigh. "If nothing else then at least there's a potential reality where I get what I want."

Joseph inclines his head. "Yeah, now you've just got to decide what that is."

His statement carries way more weight than I want to analyze.

"Good night, Joseph."

"'Night, sis."

Chapter Twenty-One

Ren storms into the lecture hall, takes a shallow breath, then twists around to face us. The bruise on his face is greenish, but the laceration is almost healed. His eyes are wild with hostility.

"Honestly, I don't fear Pierre. He's small potatoes in my opinion. I throw up a shield and I'm good against his attacks. However, one of his minions scares me to bloody hell. When it's dark at night she's my boogieman. She's what I'm afraid is hiding under my bed or in my closet. She's the closest thing to the devil I've ever seen and I've seen it all. She's Allouette."

Hate fleeces Ren's face. Usually he has a little bit of disdain in every expression, but talking about Allouette brings him to a new level of revulsion.

"While you girls," Ren says, sweeping his arms at all of us, "had posters of Justin Bieber pinned up in your room, Allouette chose to admire an exceedingly different kind of person. When she was a little girl, which was an awfully long time ago, she fancied none other than Zhuang. This brings up an important tidbit about this nasty little lady. While Dream Travelers age slower than Middlings, Allouette takes this to an extreme. When you're in the Grotte and you spot a girl who looks about sixteen with long black hair and evil, dark eyes then you've just met Allouette. And let's hope you're prepared to meet her, or she'll be the last person you see. She apparently has been using some of Zhuang's strategies to preserve her youth."

Focusing his attention on Trent, Ren continues, "If you're going to do your job in the Grotte, then you better start practicing. Allouette is telekinetic. Your ability to move Roya around is notable, but it's nothing compared to what Allouette can do. She makes you look like a kindergartener. I've seen her throw ten objects at once, turn over a cable car, and pull down a ship's mast. She has a motivation that none of you have." He stops, clenches his jaw. "She likes to watch people suffer. Nothing makes her happier than to inflict pain on another person."

Trent, who usually looks like he's just heard a joke, has a worried expression plastered across his face. Ren begins pacing.

"Your job, Trent, is to learn to intercept multiple fast-moving objects. Actually, let me be specific. You'll need to divert sharp objects that will no doubt be aimed straight at your heart. This little French maiden is known for throwing knives with her hands. The Voyageurs really have the lamest hobbies. Can't really expect much from people who dine on cave rats and mineral-heavy water. A diet of that sort no doubt robs them of their mental faculties.

"Allouette throws knives with incredible precision, and if you run then she uses her telekinesis to ensure it hits you." Ren stops pacing, looking winded but pretends to hide it by eyeing his fingernails casually. "Your best defense is to rely on the combination of Trent and Roya's abilities."

My stomach churns with anxiety.

"Roya." Ren doesn't look up at me, just continues picking at his nails. "If you can see an approaching attack then maybe this will give Trent enough opportunity to stop it. Communication between the two of you is key," he says in a monotone voice. "Honestly, your best bet is to hope Allouette is off sacrificing goats or whatever she spends her nights doing these days."

After this chilling monologue I wish I'd come down with some disease that rendered me useless in this battle. An awful thing to wish for, but facing these people sounds like a worse nightmare than Zhuang, and that's saying a lot.

We spend the rest of the time learning every single detail about Allouette that Ren thinks might be of importance. He's of the mind that knowing everything about your enemy isn't just wise, but also lifesaving. I'm not sure how knowing the assorted details of this deranged sociopath's life is going to help when six knives are chasing me through a cave, but I take notes anyway.

"One last thing before you all pop off for recess," Ren says in a hoarse voice. "The Voyageurs spend their energy training on offensive tactics. They're aggressive; I hope you prats have gathered that thus far." He gives that snide expression which is usually followed by a round of insults. Ren sighs heavily, looking momentarily defeated. "The Voyageurs don't observe our laws and they don't fight fair. Get over it. Expect it. They'll do something that Zhuang would never have done to anyone; they'll stab you in the back."

Chapter Twenty-Two

Needless to say, lunch is the most subdued one yet. Before, when I was challenging Zhuang, it was my head on the chopping block. Now everyone's facing what appears to be certain death. Maybe my team understands why I spent most of my free time alone.

Shuman begins our next training session by putting Trent to work right away intercepting objects being hurled at him. She and Pearl circle around him with a bag of squishy balls, throwing them as rapidly as they can. He has some luck with this, but if those balls were knives then his pretty little face would look much different now.

The rest of us pair up to practice shielding. There's no big surprise when Joseph immediately teams up with Samara, leaving me with George. This makes the most sense anyway, since they both have active skills and Joseph and I have passive powers. However, the last thing I want is to work with George one-on-one. We haven't really spoken since I blew up at him over the modifier.

"I don't think I need to practice with you," I say, not making eye contact.

He folds his arms and pulls his chin down. "Why's that?"

"We've already practiced enough when preparing for Zhuang."

He shakes his head. "No. That wasn't shielding we were practicing. Actually, we were working on bringing down your natural shield."

"Well, I think we both know if I want to I can keep you out of my emotions."

"Here's the thing, Roya. If in the past I've sensed your shield was up, I left you alone. But if I really needed to read your emotions then I'd try harder, the way the Voyageurs will."

I'm both humbled and outraged by his remark. "Aren't empaths rare? I doubt they will have anyone with your abilities."

He studies me with shrewd eyes. I know as well as he does that shielding is no different against a telepath or an empath, or whatever other creepy psychic abilities a Voyageur might have. "I'm not going to ask you to work with me if you don't want to," he says, his tone cold, "which is the impression you're giving off."

"It's true." I pause, fix my eyes on his. "You're the last person I want rummaging through my emotions."

"Then use that as a motivator to keep me out."

A frustrated sigh escapes my mouth. Where's the robot in me now? It's impossible to be my hardwired persona around George. Somehow his chemistry dismantles my mechanics, making me softer than I want to be.

"Roya, we're here to help each other. We're a team and we both need to practice. Do you want to do this together or not?"

My eyes search the ground. What I want to do and what I need to do are playing tug-of-war. Maybe I'm making this more difficult on myself than it needs to be. The mission comes first, right? "Fine," I acquiesce. "Give me a moment to get ready first." Steady breaths bring my focus inward. Around my body I envision an encasing. With deliberate force I push the barrier out a few inches until I feel it tightly cocooning the air around me too. I imagine the shield as green-tinted ballistic glass. With a confident nod at George I say, "I'm ready when you are."

If I felt awkward before, then it's multiplied by ten as I stare into George's bronze eyes while he tries to break through my shield. Now that I'm aware I sense him pushing against the barrier. It's like he's rubbing at it, trying to determine a weak spot. Then without much notice it becomes harder to keep it solid. Panic races through me. I search for the focus to maintain the strength of my shield. I search his probing eyes. My shield collapses like a deflating balloon and he races unbarred straight into my emotional center.

"Damn it!" I say reflexively.

"Breathing will actually help you," George says with a consoling smile. "It's strange but true."

"Thanks," I say sourly. "I'll keep that in mind."

"And try not to look at me the next time. I think I'm distracting you."

"Oh, do you? There's about a million distractions in my head right now."

"Still, until you've practiced more you might want to try it with your eyes closed. It helps with focus."

"What'd you read in me?" I demand.

George shakes his head. "That's irrelevant to the exercise."

A sudden undulant pressure takes residence in my chest. "I don't care if it's irrelevant, I want to know."

"Why, Roya? All of a sudden you care? You've been walking around this place unshielded all week. And you know that more than anyone your emotions bombard me with a unique intensity. So why do you all of sudden want to keep them protected?"

Fighting with George like this feels incredibly satisfying. The pressure builds, about to breach the surface, and I invite it. "Because, George, I've changed. I want to know what emotions are swimming around the surface so I can get rid of them. I don't want to be ruled by these..." I stop, stare off, searching for the right words. "By these weaknesses."

"Is that what you think your emotions are, a weakness? You've got it all wrong."

"I didn't ask for your unqualified opinion. I asked what you read in me."

"Nothing I didn't already know," he says with an impassive expression on his face.

"Thanks for the elaboration," I say, searching for something else to argue with him about. I want to yell. And strangely I want him to yell back. Nothing feels like a better idea right now than to fight with George. I'm intoxicated by the urge. "Why is it that you always get to ransack my emotions, but I never get to return the favor?"

He drops his head, nostrils flaring. "Stop it, Roya."

"Stop what?" I say with authority.

"I'm not doing this."

"Doing what!?" I say, fanning the flames of the argument.

"I know what you want and in this case, I'm not giving it to you."

Eyes burning, I say, "Because in all other cases when you read me you give me what I want? Is that right?"

"I would if you let me," George says, taking a step forward. I immediately take one back, keeping the space between us. "But right now, I won't fight with you. Don't you see what you're doing to yourself by cutting off your emotions? You may think you can be polarized, but it's impossible. All that will result is this." He motions at me like I'm an exhibit in his grand lecture. "You're a floodgate, about to break."

His words sting my insides, bringing aching tears to my throat. "All I'm trying to do, just like everyone else on this team, is stay focused."

"There are other ways," he says, his voice an urgent whisper.

Every word he's said is right and it makes me angry. Now the yearning to attack George is unbounded. If I can just hurt him, then I'll be absolved of the terror racing unleashed within me. It's unfair. Unfounded. But when you're split in two the irrational emotions gain a new power, no longer tethered between reason and love.

"Switch partners now," Shuman says, cutting through the tension.

I turn without a second glance at George and march away. Joseph wears an ugly look of frustration when I pass him.

"You know your brother is a real jerk?" Samara says, eyeing him with disdain from across the gymnasium.

I'm fairly certain I need to stay out of this. I'm in a losing position on this one. "Everyone has the capacity to be a jerk."

"You know better than anyone how insensitive and selfish he's been lately," she says, coaxing for my endorsement.

"Yes, Joseph isn't acting like himself right now," I agree, then redirect. "Did you by chance spy anything about the project he was working on?"

She shakes her head, eyes still boring into him. "No, Joseph's thoughts are not centered on his professional projects right now. They purely revolve around personal matters."

"Maybe we shouldn't practice right now?" I say.

"No, this is good. I need to be able to do this when I'm charged or distracted."

I'm not sure if it's because Samara is angry or because I've gotten better, but I'm successful at holding the shield. It feels good to keep my thoughts private. Now if I can just do the same with my emotions.

Chapter Twenty-Three

In a hilarious turn of events

Roya Stark <roya.stark713@gmail.com>
to bobandsteve

Hello Bob and Steve,

Depends on one's perspective whether my current state of affairs is considered hilarious. A stranger peering into my life would probably find it quite comical. I think it's tragically humiliating, to say the very least.

I'm expected to use the modifier to rescue Aiden. Yes, I know what you're saying. And yes, I'm referring to the exact same device which was used on my fake family. The same one I've been a strong opponent against. The one I've dreamed about destroying so that no more lives can be manipulated. And in a poetic turn of events, I'll go into unsuspecting (albeit evil) minds and implant my own message.
What has my world come to that this is my reality? What happened to watching reruns of I Love Lucy and eating too much ice cream on Sundays? Is it too late to ask the universe to redeal my hand?

Alright, I get that I'm sounding extra whiny right now, but I don't dare tell anyone else how ambivalent I am about the modifier. The Institute isn't forcing me to use it, but I don't really have a choice, do I? I have to use it if I want to survive and rescue Aiden. But why is it that the Lucidites always pretend I have a choice when in fact I don't?

You don't have to answer that. Actually you don't have to answer this email at all, although you always do. I just needed to vent, as I'm sure you've already gathered.

Love,
Ms. Apparently-I-have-no-real-moral-code-McGillicuddy

P.S. When I come to live with you, after I've sold my soul to the Lucidite Gods, can I have a cat...or two?

"Oh, hey there, Roya," Trey calls to me as I leave the computer lab. Since I'm in an "I hate the Lucidites" mood, it's probably the worst time to run into none other than the Head of the Institute. I have impeccable timing for this kind of stuff.

"Hey," I say, trying to mask my expression behind an acceptable one.

"Is everything all right?" Trey asks with concerned eyes.

"I suppose."

"Do you need to talk?"

Chewing on my pinky fingernail I shake my head.

"Okay, well, you know I'm here if you do need anything."

Somehow I doubt that. Trey keeps pretending to have this open door policy, but I don't buy it. It's a ruse to garner trust. He's mastered the art of politics: telling people what they want to hear, keeping pertinent details vague, and making appearances brief and rushed.

A quiet, awkward moment passes. Trey studies my face. I'm trying to decide how to end this whole small talk conversation.

"I'm sure the stress of the current mission is weighing on you greatly." He runs his fingers through his silver hair, a look of stress in his turquoise eyes. The Head of the Institute looks older than he did a month ago. "Thank you for taking the lead on this mission. You have to believe me when I say I don't want to put any more responsibility on you. But this project is too important and I wholeheartedly believe you're the right person to lead it."

"Why? Why do you 'wholeheartedly believe' this?" I ask bluntly. Trey thinks he can ask me to risk my life again and again using reasons that lack specifics.

He clears his throat. Looks around without seeing. "I have a multitude of reasons, actually. Primarily, you're powerful. So much so that Zhuang specifically wanted to acquire *your* consciousness. This power lends you extraordinary talents. The abilities that come naturally for you are effort for others. Honestly, I don't think you value these skills because you've never had to work for them."

Leave it to Trey to tell me I'm talented and seriously out of touch. And like I suspected, he's not telling me what I want to hear, but rather whatever it will take to convince me to sacrifice myself for the Lucidites. An impatient sigh falls out of my mouth. "Trey, I really—"

"I'm not finished," he cuts me off. "You asked and I'm prepared to explain why you were picked to lead this mission. You deserve to know and I'd like the opportunity to tell you. Will you allow that?"

"Yeah," I say, sensing an invasion in my thoughts or heart. What *is* Trey's ability? Is he telepathic? Does he know how much I hate him?

"Secondly," Trey continues, looking at me with a skeptical expression, "you're my choice not only because of your mental and physical agility, but also because you rely on your instincts. I can't even begin to tell you how important this is in the work we do here. It takes awareness and faith, both traits you possess."

His words sound too rehearsed, his voice too matter-of-fact. Is this whole speech printed in the secret Lucidite manual under "How to get others to do what you want"?

"And lastly, I picked you because of your integrity. I value the way you conduct yourself at the Institute. Even though you've had many reasons not to trust me or many of the people here you still treat us respectfully. I need the leader of this team to be someone who isn't corruptible, because you're about to meet people who value no one but themselves. If you were the least bit immoral then they'd break you down. But I have every reason to believe you're not."

Well, geez, thanks, coming from a bald-faced liar that really means a lot.

117

Trey studiously apprises me. "Those are my reasons for choosing you. I sincerely believe them, but I fear the more I try to convince you of that the more you think I'm manipulating you, which isn't the case."

Now it's my turn to examine him. Stone-faced, I study every single one of his microexpressions as I ask, "How would you know what I think?"

He draws in a long inhale. "I don't, but I have my suspicions."

If he wants me to trust him then he can start by telling me something personal. "What *is* your talent?"

Trey's left eye twitches. Only once, but I see it. Not certain what it could mean. Is he about to lie? "I have a few actually."

A few? Is that possible?

"Roya, I'm happy to satisfy your curiosity on this, but not right now. I'm late for a meeting."

Of course. Short office hours ensure the truth stays locked away and the lies keep circulating.

"Okay, well, thanks for sharing your reasons with me."

He nods, accepting my dingy bit of gratitude.

"I'll make time for us to talk again soon," Trey says, pinching his mouth together.

"Sounds good," I say, my voice artificially casual.

Chapter Twenty-Four

I have never been happier to walk into the combat studio. Hitting something sounds like a fantastic idea right now. Since everyone, except for Pearl, already has experience with kung fu this is the method we're practicing. Ren and Shuman both agree that it's most likely that any battle with a Voyageur will be wholly mental. However, we're being prepared for anything, even if that means a good ol' fistfight.

Before Joseph has a chance to pair up with someone else I recruit him as my sparring partner. He's the only person on the team who deserves my wrath. Right before we begin I picture that he's Amber.

"Damn, Stark, someone put Tabasco in your eggs this morning?!" Joseph says a minute later. He stumbles back, checking over his arms like they might already have bruises.

I smile. Then I remember his little stunt the night before when he was trying to get me to open my door. With my arms up in block position, I spin backwards on the ball of my front foot, tuck in my opposite leg, swing it around behind me and then forward. My foot slams into Joseph's chest, sending him to the ground instantly. I love spin kicks. Joseph remains planted on the mat, a stunned look on his face. "Are you freaking kidding me? Did that just happen?"

"It did," I reassure him, holding out my hand to help him up.

"What's your deal? You could have killed me," he says, eyeing my hand suspiciously.

"Oh, stop whining. I only used a fraction of my strength. But let this be a lesson to you. You may know what's in my head, but I can still kick your ass."

If I'm completely honest with myself then I have to admit the team is a pretty lousy bunch of fighters. Samara can throw a strong kick if she concentrates, but she isn't much good for anything else. Pearl appears to be about as dangerous as Whitney was, which means she leaves her attacker feeling warm and comforted after an altercation. The rest of the bunch is laughable at best. None of them really had to focus on fighting before because it had been up to me to hone my kung fu skills. Now that we're all facing mortal danger, they're going to need to be able to protect themselves if the situation becomes dire.

"Why can't we just carry guns?" Trent asks, rubbing his shoulder like he's in pain.

"Guns are for cowards," our sensei, Mario, says.

"Well, I'll take two." Trent laughs.

Mario shakes his head at Trent in disapproval. "I do agree that carrying a weapon is a good idea. Martial arts weaponry is all extremely useful in battle. Now, if you have a weapon on you when you dream travel to the Grotte then it should be with you once you generate. However, the only way to ensure this is to choose a weapon and make it yours."

He directs our attention to a rack of assorted weapons and tells us to practice. I spend the rest of the morning and early afternoon taking each weapon and trying out different moves. The nunchakus were at first my favorite because I like their balance and grace. However, the speed that's absolutely necessary to pull off a good nunchakus attack is intimidating. The bo staff also appeals to me greatly, but after about half an hour of practice I admit that I'm too petite to effectively manage such a large weapon. In the end I find the escrima sticks fit me perfectly and give that extra bit of power I'm looking for. They're about a little longer than my forearm and an inch and a half in diameter. In essence they're sticks, but when I show an interest in using them Mario demonstrates a dozen techniques. This includes everything from blocking, punching, and disarming. By the end I'm absolutely certain that I want to have these weapons by my side in battle.

"This afternoon you'll be fitted for your gear," Mario says. "Be sure to tell the seamstress that you want a compartment built into the shoulder area for holding these."

"Gear?" I ask.

"Trey wants you all outfitted in Kevlar suits," Mario explains. "The material is knife resistant. It may not prevent an injury, but it might lessen its severity."

♦

We're told we should dream travel that night, but only within the walls of the Institute. Dream traveling mixed with regular dreaming is the best way to maintain a balance. However, Trey still fears that it's too unsafe to dream travel outside the Institute with the Voyageurs on alert and ready to attack.

It's weird to think that we'll all be like ghosts meandering randomly around, haunting the Institute for six or eight hours tonight. I understand though. Dream travel is a talent that must be practiced regularly, like meditation. And there's a level of awareness that comes during dream traveling which is unique to that state.

I dream travel to my room and speed read through half a dozen books. Past the point of restlessness, I venture out into the hallway on a mission to explore. I float through the second level without so much as hearing a creak. Maybe I'm the only one who's decided to leave my room. The first level, which is usually the nosiest, is eerily quiet. I'm strolling at an even pace, enjoying the way the silence transforms the corridor. Putting one foot in front of the other at a measured pace, I feel a release start to expand in my body. In my mind I'm walking a labyrinth. With each step I let go of things I need to leave behind: worry about Aiden, fear of failure, concern for Joseph, fits of emotional numbness, and the anxiety that accompanies every thought in my head. My labyrinth's center, the place I'm not journeying to but will arrive at regardless, is the lobby. This is where I'll make my wish: to face this challenge as a whole person, one who uses all parts—mind, body, and spirit—to overcome obstacles. Then I'll return on my path, rewinding the labyrinth through the Institute. Since being a robot didn't work, I'm hoping this new approach does. I need something, something to assure me I can face the upcoming challenge.

I'm three feet from the lobby when I hear his voice. I freeze, listen.

"Girl, I don't know, I guess I never really thought 'bout it."

"Well…" The girl giggles. "If you could, would you go with me?"

"Yeah." Joseph gives a forced laugh. "Yeah, if it were possible to dream travel to the moon, I'd go with you."

That's the stupidest thing I've ever heard.

The tell-tale signs of kissing assault my ears, sending a creepy grossness over my skin. More giggling. More kissing. Heat rises in my head. Why is Joseph making out with some lame-ass girl in a public place? One where Samara could find him? Why is he acting so revolting? I want to strangle him—in the non–life threatening way.

Instead, I retreat. Feeling yet again frustrated with my brother I start down the hallway where I came. He used to be the sweetest person I knew, using his social skills to make others feel at ease. Now in just half a month's time he's become secretive, strange, and a two-timer. The harder I try to focus on what he's been hiding, the more it eludes me. I have no idea why I can't zero in on him and it's driving me bonkers.

I round the corner, infiltrated by these thoughts, and run into Samara. Her whitish blonde hair is draped in long pigtails. She smiles softly at me when we connect.

"Oh, hey there," she says. "I went by your room earlier, but you must have already been off. It's tough to find something to do for the whole night around this place."

"Yeah," I say, feeling suddenly nervous. "Why don't we go to the combat studio? We can practice blocks."

"Roya, do you ever take a break?"

"Of course, but not when a dangerous mission is hanging over my head. That kind of thing usually ruins any respite."

"Well, you should think about taking the night off. It can't be good for you to constantly train. You're going to wear yourself out," Samara says with a look of concern on her face.

"If I do and we all survive, then it will be worth it."

"All right, it sounds like there's no convincing you. But you're going to have to wear yourself out alone. I've got to find Joseph."

Her last statement makes my eyes bulge.

"Is everything all right?" Samara asks.

"Yeah, fine. I'm just peeved at him."

Samara looks at me, interest written on her face. "Because…?"

"He owes me money," I lie.

She laughs. "Well, when I find him I'll try and get it back for you."

"Good luck with that." I pull a piece of my hair into my fingers and begin twirling it. "Don't go that way looking for Joseph," I point in the direction I've just come from. "That is, unless you want to spend the rest of the night listening to Ren berate you about why you're so pathetic."

"Oh, no thanks." Samara laughs. "I get enough of that during the day." She motions to the hallway we're facing and says, "I'll just keep moving forward instead."

I smile and she passes, like a ghost.

With a huge wave of relief I let my head fall back and rest gently on the cold steel wall. I'm like this for only a few seconds when I hear footsteps. I don't open my eyes or move. Honestly, I don't really care who it is.

The person is only a few feet away. "Nice cover," he says.

I peel one eye open, then pull my head back to its normal position. "I wasn't covering for my brother for his sake. He's slime," I say.

"I know," George agrees.

"I was just trying to protect Samara. The last thing she needs is to witness that," I point toward the lobby. "It would break her heart to see Joseph making out with some giggling-astronaut-wannabe-girl."

"I know," George says again.

His dark blond hair always take on the color of champagne during dream travel. We all look lighter in this form, probably because we are.

"You know," George says, breaking the gentle silence. It's becoming easier to be quiet with him, without the usual need to talk unnecessarily. "The other day I read a poem I think you'd enjoy. It's by Archibald MacLeish." He stands so still in front of me. Not a fidget or nonverbal cue of any sort.

"I'll look it up later," I say.

"I have it in my room if you want to see it."

I shrug my shoulders and look off, staring at nothing in particular. "Why were you working on the emotional modifier? That doesn't seem your style."

George looks in the direction of my focus, then turns around, concentrating on me. "It isn't, but I did initially have a couple of good reasons." He pauses, chews tensely on his bottom lip. "After you found out, though, the reasons didn't feel good enough. I'm not sure where I stand on it now or if I want to be involved with the project."

"And these reasons…" I prompt.

"First off, Trey asked me to do it and I respect him. I know you have your reasons for disliking him, but he really does care about this place and the people in it. Actually he cares about all people, Lucidites and Middlings."

The last person I want to talk about is Trey. "What else persuaded you to work on it?"

"Well, I was happy to have a reason to stay. I don't have much of a life to return to. There's my mom, but she recently remarried and could probably use the privacy. She thinks I'm off at a summer camp." He gives a fake laugh. "I guess this place is kind of like camp, huh?"

"I wouldn't know," I say indifferently.

"Look, I believe Trey wanted the emotional modifier created to erase negative emotions. It would be easier to battle certain people, like Zhuang for instance, if they weren't overwhelmed by hate. Negative emotions color everything. They make it impossible for a person to reason clearly. All their decisions become tainted by these emotions."

"Modifiers don't work on Zhuang."

"I know, but it could work on other people, like the Voyageurs."

My eyes drift back to the distant focal point at the end of the hallway. "I guess."

"Roya, I need to say something." George's tone is softer, a tender need behind it. It's enough to beckon my full attention. "I'm sorry I hurt you and complicated everything the night of the party. It was unfair of me to demand to know how you feel. It was foolish. A mistake I won't make again if I haven't already ruined everything between us." He stands staring at me; a soft pleading expression marks his eyes.

Between us? He created friction that night, but does something still lie between us? If I'm going to start listening to this organ in my chest again then it's telling me there is. "No, I get it. I forgive you," I say.

Understated relief flicks across his face. There's something to be said for a man with such a subtle nature. Something good.

A sliver of a smile graces George's lips. Probably should have put a shield up before I went off having feelings about him.

"What you demanded was unfair. But I also realize that it's difficult for you to feel people's emotions and not always understand the thoughts that go behind them," I say, trying not to be flustered by his unrelenting gaze. "Have you thought of hooking up with Samara? You two would make a perfect pair."

George reaches out and grips my arm, tugging me toward him. "We both know I don't want Samara." He slides his arms around my shoulders, pulling me in closer. His warmth thaws my frozen insides. I hadn't even realized how cold I was until now. With a small squeeze the space between us doesn't exist anymore. My hands hold his sturdy back. Physical touch doesn't have the same intensity in dream travel form, but right now hugging George is beyond powerful. A dozen sensations run through my body as he strokes my hair. I press my face more firmly into his chest, breathing him in. Comfort resides in his arms. And it's what I needed, but didn't even know it. Suddenly I feel better than I have in days.

George pulls back, peering down at me, a look of empathy on his face. "Roya, no one knows like I do the amount of pressure on your shoulders right now. I also know how alone you feel, but you're not. Leaning on someone doesn't make you weak." He bends down and whispers into my ear, "I think you might find it gives you strength." A chill shivers through my spine. With my hands still wrapped around his waist I pull him back, burying my head in his chest. I don't want to leave the sanctuary of his arms, but it will all be ruined if someone sneaks up on us in this intimate moment. I ease back and say, "Show me that poem."

George's room is tidy and has an air of emptiness about it. It's not that it's lacking, but rather that it's impersonal. Other than a stack of books and a notebook on his desk there's nothing else personal in the room. Besides George himself, that is, who's currently lying on his bed, his eyes closed, abdomen rising and falling with each breath. It should be weird to see him in both his physical and dream traveler forms, but it's not. We've been through so much together already.

I take a seat at his desk. He picks up his notebook and removes a folded piece of paper from an inside folder.

"After the mission is over, are you still planning on leaving the Institute?" he asks, taking a seat in a nearby chair.

"I don't know. I can't think past the Grotte."

125

George nods, chewing on his lip. "I promise I'm not going to let anything happen to you. Not this time. Not now that I'll be with you."

I shake my head. "You can't promise that and you shouldn't. Also, I'm the leader and it's my job to ensure the safety of the team."

"And Aiden's." His words hang in the air. A tender knot rises in my throat. George looks subtly heartbroken. "Here's the poem," he finally says, handing me the paper.

Sweeping my eyes over the words I pretend to read it, but I can't focus. George warned me when we sat on the steps at the Sydney Opera House that his relationships never work out. He warned me that his empathesis usually causes him to be paranoid and jealous. I didn't want to believe him then. Now I do and I'm not sure if it changes how much I still find myself wanting what he can give me. In a million ways I feel torn, by him, by Aiden, and by another dismal event which threatens to leave me fractured. First I have to rescue Aiden. Then I have to make a decision, because I don't have the capacity to love them both—not the way they deserve.

"You're not reading," George says, breaking the silence.

"No, I'm not," I admit.

"You can have it. I copied it down because it reminded me of you."

I give him a pained smile. I wish I would have read it, rather than felt pitiful in front of him. "Thanks."

I return to my body feeling heavy and tired. Lying beside me is the iPod. I slip the buds in my ears, fire it up, and curl up in a tiny ball. Music lures me into restless sleep, where I dream of Aiden starving in a damp cave. I awake wanting to run to George's room where his arms will ease my pain, but I don't. This is all wrong. How can I need the comfort of one because the other is tragically missing? How can this all be possible? I push myself out of bed and do the only thing that feels right. I run.

Chapter Twenty-Five

The lights in the lecture hall are set on dim when I enter. I'm used to being the first one to every training session. Three steps into the hall and the automatic lights flicker on overhead illuminating the person sitting in the middle of the stage. Ren. Quickly I cover up my startled response. He must have been sitting still behind the desk for a while to make the lights go off. My presence isn't greeted by the slightest look; he just continues to stare at a pencil like he's trying to move it with his mind.

I slip into my normal seat and busy myself reviewing notes. I've already been over them twice this morning.

"Thanks," Ren says in a low hush.

My head jerks up. Ren's still-bruised face is looking at me. "What?" I say.

"Thanks," he says, refocusing on the pencil. "You saved my life with your news report. Thanks." There's a cold sincerity in his voice. Maybe Ren isn't the devil after all. He, just as much as the rest of us, feels the need to repay a good deed.

"You're welcome."

He shakes his head, like he's trying to dispel a frustrated thought. "Well, now that we've got that ugly mess out of the way, maybe we can return to normal."

"Because being nice to each other is somehow abnormal?"

"Nice isn't my style."

The normal dread that used to accompany his lectures had dissipated. I should have known it wouldn't last. The old, abusive Ren is back and has probably stored up an arsenal of insults. "Well, I apologize for thinking that saving your life would improve our working relationship."

"Hmmm," he ruminates, an evil toothy grin on his face. "'Fraid it doesn't work that way. I've saved your life plenty of times and you've been cross with me since the get-go."

"Need I remind you that when we met you stabbed me in the arm?"

"Oh, let the past die, would you?"

"Yeah, right. And what do you mean you've saved my life plenty of times?"

"I mean exactly what I said. It's really not my fault if you can't understand plain English."

Someone enters the lecture hall behind me. Within two paces I recognize the gait. George. With immense effort I pull my eyes from Ren's sharp gaze.

George takes the seat next to me. A glance in his direction fills me with both pleasure and anxiety. I give him a weak smile and he returns it. No words are spoken between us, but so much is said. It feels as though in one night we entered into a silent partnership, one with expectations and benefits and a whole host of things that make me uncomfortable. George scrutinizes me, then writes a few words on the paper in front of him:

Just lean. Stop worrying. I expect nothing of you.

I flick my eyes up to meet his. They're warm, full of sincerity. "Okay," I mouth.

He folds the paper in two and hands it to me. "Just in case you need to be reminded later."

"I've saved the very worst for last," Ren says a few minutes later when everyone is seated. He extends his arms triumphantly. "You're welcome." He begins striding between our desks, thumping the top of each as he passes. "Duck. Duck. Duck." Ren halts in front of Pearl's desk, smacks the top, and says, "Goose!" She flinches, but holds a look of determination. "You're it, little curly Sue. Tell me, what's the worst thing a person can do to you?"

Pearl looks straight to me, like the answer is written on my face. "Kill you?"

"In most all circumstance the most obvious answer isn't the correct one, and in this case that's also true." Ren strides forward, tapping desks again. "Duck. Duck. Goose!" He points a menacing finger at Trent. "Same question, what's the worst thing a person can do to you?"

"Torture you," Trent says, holding himself confidently.

"Well, well, well, you don't lack as much imagination as I thought. However, that's not exactly the answer I was looking for. Let's keep playing, shall we?"

Tap. "Duck."

Tap. "Duck."

Tap. "Goose!" Ren's pale hand slams down on the front of my desk. "Tell me, missy, what's your answer to this prized question?"

"The worst thing someone can do..." I pause, stare at him, and tap my fingers casually on my desktop. I wait until I see his eyes grow impatient. Tap. Tap. Tap. Then I wait a few seconds longer. Tap. Tap. Tap.

"Anytime now, missy," Ren says, bearing down on my desk.

"Freedom. If someone takes away my freedom, whether it's my ability to think or feel or choose. It's all the same really, but without it I'm tortured. That's the worst thing."

Ren retracts from my desktop, staring at me with a semblance of awe and irritation. He charges off toward the center of the room. "Well, that's a dreadfully good guess and although correct, it was still awfully executed."

He draws in a wheezy breath, then turns around and faces us. "Yes, freedom is the answer to the question, but how it can be assaulted is the ultimate riddle. The greatest adversary you'll face at the Grotte is someone who will not battle you for your freedom, but rather steal it from you when you're unsuspecting. And once he has it you'll want none other than the best for him, because that's what he'll intend."

Ren charges back to our desk and begins tapping them again. Now we all sit stoically, unaffected by his intimidation. "Truthfully, the ultimate answer to my question: what's the worst someone can do to you is...Chase." Tap. Tap. Tap. Ren slams his hand again on my desk and stares, his green eyes intense. "Chase is the worst Voyageur you'll ever meet. If you get past Pierre's probe, and Allouette's knives, then get ready for a real challenge. It will come from Chase. Of course, like me, he's a performer. He won't hurt you the way Allouette will, but what he'll do will warp you in ways you never thought imaginable. It will change how you view reality." Ren taps his head and says, "Mind control. That's what makes Chase a sideshow. And if you're in the audience to watch his act you might find yourself squawking like a chicken and trying to lay eggs, and that's if he likes you. For those he doesn't he'll have you pick up a knife and slit your own throat. What a way to go, huh?"

I gulp. My blood thickens. How's my spin kick supposed to measure up against someone like that?

"The guy who used to have Aiden's position," Ren says, casually rocking back and forth on his toes, "once found himself face-to-face with Chase unexpectedly. The next thing he knew he was standing in a busy market in Lebanon with explosives strapped to his chest. Needless to say, he didn't return to the Institute with a bag of oranges." His nostrils flare once before he continues. "Thankfully that was a long time ago and now we have our protective charms. These help guard against Chase's attacks, but don't think you're immune. He knows all too well all he has to do is get you to slip that charm off your body and then the party is on." Ren pauses, no doubt to add suspense. "Before you delude yourself with the notion that no one could persuade you to take off your most prized possession, know this: those smarter and more skilled than you have been fooled. I'm sorry that I can't bring them forward to offer a testimonial. They're dead. Once he separates you from your charm there's absolutely zero hope for you. And that's coming from me, the optimist." Ren gives an evil laugh.

"Chase is a master of illusions. He uses hypnosis, subliminal communications, and projections to weaken his prey. I dare say he is one of the best." He holds up one finger and smiles. "There's just one other living person who outperforms Chase in this arena." Ren winks and disappears.

In unison everyone leans forward, exchanging nervous glances. George's eyes widen when I look at him. We both know we've been had. Not only that, but we're about to get ripped in two.

Seconds later Ren stomps into the room. "You prats never cease to disappoint me with your stupidity!" He stands with his arms crossed and taps his foot angrily. "How many times have you stared at my face? I've even told you how to spot the projected version of me! And still you all fail to detect it!" He slams his fist down on Joseph's desk. "Are you bloody sleepwalking?!" Joseph meets Ren's eyes and holds them. As the fiery redhead speaks spit flies out of his mouth and lands on Joseph's face. "You don't stand a chance against Chase. I'm certain if I throw up a projection and you can't spot it then you're in real trouble when you face someone you don't even know. You all are revolting." Ren picks up the pencil sitting on the desk and begins spinning it through his fingers. "For God's sake, will you all pay attention!"

At his command my eyes hone in on the pencil. With his palm facing up Ren swivels it smoothly through his fingers. It balances easily between his first and middle fingers and thumb. Slowly he rotates his middle finger forward and pushes the pencil making it roll over the top of his thumb. Gently it returns to its original position. He pauses, then spins it again. Each time the pause between rotations shortens until he's whipping the pencil through his fingers in seamless rotations. It's magical and weird all at the same time. I don't want to look away. And then I realize I can't. My vision focuses on the yellow object blurring through Ren's fingers and everything else in the room fades into nothing.

Resist. Look away. He's hypnotizing you! My inner voice is frantic, but I can't follow its direction. I can't look away. Ever. The walls push in, until I'm locked against their smoothness, flashes of yellow are all I see.

Look away! It's not real! Look away!

My fingers scrape against the prison trapping my mind. Again and again the flash assaults my vision. I'm certain I'm about to pass out.

NO! LOOK AWAY, ROYA! NOW!

I grab onto the voice urging me to resist like it's a wild horse. And to my surprise I don't look away; instead my eyelids fall shut. In a matter of seconds my mind clears. The trauma attacking my senses vanishes. When I open my eyes the room spins, my vision blurs briefly before resuming to normal. If I was standing then I would surely have fallen over.

"Well, bravo!" Ren says, continuing to spin the pencil, although I don't look directly at it this time. "Looks like your leader isn't completely useless." He smirks and the pencil halts in his fingers. Everyone in the room is entranced, the same way I had been. Their eyes are still locked on the pencil in Ren's hand. "So, Roya, you were eventually able to resist my hypnosis. However, you were still under for a good bit. Bet it slowed down your reflexes," he says, shooting the pencil at me like it's a paper airplane. In one movement I lean to the left and throw my right arm up to block. It connects with the side of the pencil and knocks it to the ground flatly. If I hadn't been fast enough then it would have stabbed me in the face.

131

Ren narrows his eyes, looking smugly impressed. The team is showing signs of regaining their mental faculties. Joseph keeps shaking his head, like a dog drying off after a bath. Pearl eyes the pencil lying on the floor.

"Chase will do something like that to you until you pass out," Ren says, perched on the corner of his desk. "You all probably would have been comatose after about another minute. Once you're out you can go ahead and bet he'll remove your charm and the next time you awake you'll be doing something incredibly uncharacteristic of your typical behavior—and most likely deadly."

Although I can tell Ren would have preferred not to, he spends the rest of the time divulging how we can resist being hypnotized. I'm sure this is a valuable skill that he enjoys using against people like me. It's probably his favorite bullying strategy. He'd hypnotized me over a month ago by covering a piece of paper with penciled cubes. Then I hadn't been able to resist and I probably would have passed out if Aiden hadn't rescued me. The hollow feeling returns to my belly. Now it's my turn to rescue him. It's my turn to save his life.

Chapter Twenty-Six

Training with Shuman is a welcome break after the torture Ren put us through. The stoic Native American is never happy and rarely encouraging, but she doesn't criticize us. At this point, in comparison to the redheaded Brit, she's as cheerful as a field of tulips. We spend the entire training working on shields. Everyone on the team except for Joseph is successful with this now. He's not been able to shield himself for more than a few seconds.

"You have to focus," Shuman urges him.

"I am," Joseph says.

"If you were then your shield would hold. Being honest with yourself is the first step," Shuman says.

"Look I'm not an addict and this isn't an intervention," Joseph says with a laugh.

"I fear you are not taking this seriously enough. I cannot authorize your participation on this mission unless you make improvements."

Joseph's face goes slack. "You can't do that. Without me Stark won't be as powerful."

Shuman's cold stare revolves on me, then back to Joseph. "I cannot have a liability on this team, which is what you are. I am confident that Roya is still powerful enough without you to complete the mission."

The idea of not having Joseph with me in the Grotte isn't as disappointing as I thought it would be. Actually half of my concern is regarding keeping him alive, so maybe it's better if he isn't on the team.

His eyes flick up to mine, forehead creasing with surprise and offense. "I'm going on this mission," he says with conviction. "You may not want me there right now, but you will when I save your life."

"I hope you do and I hope you do," I say and pretend to take a new interest in the far side of the room. Pearl and George are over there working together. This elfin healer is so quiet that I usually forget she's around. Maybe her shyness is because she's new to a team which is already closely bonded. It could also be because our last healer, Whitney, died tragically. Other than the fact that Pearl can heal I don't know anything else about her. I should probably make the effort to get to know her before we travel to the Grotte to face death.

George says something that makes her laugh. Her tiny hands cover her face, like she's ashamed of her response. He reaches out and pulls her hands from her face, giving a consoling shake of his head. Pearl turns the shade of a ripe cherry. I've been on the other end of that nod enough times to know how disarming it is. Whatever he's saying to her, he's trying to break through one of her defenses.

"If you're not too busy spying on those two," Trent says, angling his head in the direction of George and Pearl, "then maybe you can help me practice."

I take the Nerf gun he's holding. "If it involves rapidly firing a weapon at you then I'm more than happy."

♦

That afternoon at our last combat practice I approach Joseph.

"I need practice using the escrima sticks," I say, rotating them in my hands. They feel natural to me, like an extension of my own arms. "Will you spar with me?"

Joseph laughs suddenly. "Yeah, whatever, Stark. I'm cute, but that doesn't mean I'm stupid."

I was hoping to do more than practice. We need to talk, but his eyes avert mine too quickly these days for us to have any meaningful conversations.

When no one else volunteers, Mario offers to be my partner. That's fine because I can benefit the most by working with him. The others continue to practice. Trent has decided against choosing a weapon since he can steal a knife from Allouette. And pretty much everyone else has failed to find a weapon that feels natural to them. I'm relieved when between sparring rounds with Mario I spy Samara pick up a short sword and show promise working with it.

I approach her, balancing my escrima sticks on my right palm. "So, maybe between the two of us we can keep the group alive," I say, gesturing to the misfits behind us.

Samara diagonally slices through the air and pivots. I spy the radiant fury on her face before she masks it. "Yeah, I think we can guarantee they don't get wasted in the first few minutes. After that I'm not so sure." She slips her long hair into a rubber band, then continues cutting the air. "If it makes you feel better, Joseph made progress with his shield toward the end of practice this morning," Samara says between measured breaths.

"Progress? Like enough that Shuman will allow him on the mission?"

"Probably. He got determined after he thought he was going to get chopped."

"That's good. Wish he would have been that focused since the start."

"Joseph has to be properly motivated to do anything," Samara says, turning around to face me directly.

"Hey"—I lower my voice like I'm about to say something secretive—"did you spy any information about what sort of activity he's been up to lately? Whatever it is that's responsible for making him look so puny and all?"

Samara sighs. "I wish. I can read his thoughts on everything else but that. And I mean everything," she says bitterly.

"Oh, that sucks." An awkward silence passes.

"Did you know he was putting the moves on any girl who isn't his sister?"

I spin one of the sticks around in my palm, testing the balance. "Or Shuman. I don't think she's his type."

"I don't know, I think given the right circumstances he'd hit on her. Besides, she's stunningly attractive," Samara says, staring at Joseph who's across the room.

"And she's also as affectionate and warm as a marble statue."

"Shuman, like everyone else, has reasons for her nature." There's a beautiful complexity in Samara's eyes, no doubt a result of knowing more than someone her age should.

"What did Joseph say when you dumped him?" I ask.

Her face falls with a look of shame.

"Oh, so you haven't kicked him to the curb yet," I say.

"I should," Samara says, frustrated. "I've tried, but every time he looks at me with those green eyes and pleads with that southern drawl I'm toast."

I shake my head. "Yeah, guys have a way of pulling us in, even when we want to resist. I get it."

"And I have to admit I kind of like a bad boy. It's cliché and stupid, but true."

"Maybe someone will kidnap Joseph so you won't have to worry about resisting his temptations. It's worked well for me," I say sadistically.

The edges of Samara's mouth curl in a small smile. She gets my humor or at least isn't completely repulsed by it.

"Yeah, whatever," she says, rolling her eyes. "We both know your temptations didn't go completely away when Aiden was abducted." She flicks her eyes to George, who's pretending to spar with Pearl.

"Why in the world did I have to make friends with a telepath? Is it too late to have normal friends?"

"I'm afraid so." Samara grins. "You know, you and Joseph have a lot in common. I know you think you're polar opposites, but both of you can't stand to be serious for long."

"Oh, I'm way more serious than him by a long shot."

"Really? Well then *seriously*, how heartbroken is this Aiden situation for you? It can't be easy, although you give the impression that it is."

I take a deep breath. "It isn't easy and it isn't heartbreaking. I have a job to do. That's how I see it. I don't think of it as Aiden we're rescuing, but rather something I'm returning to the Lucidites." I shrug. "I know it sounds like a silly way to think, but it's the only way I can without going crazy."

"Roya, it's not silly. Can I be honest with you?" Samara looks a little uneasy.

I raise a skeptical eyebrow at her, but nod still.

"I don't usually tell people about the nature of their thoughts. It's like looking at your therapist's notes, it drives most people crazy. But I will tell you something because I think it might help."

She pauses.

"Yes," I encourage.

"Well, you don't think like anybody else. You've mastered the art of compartmentalizing your thoughts."

"Oh, well, I do like to keep things tidy."

She half smiles. "Thoughts are rarely organized in people's minds. Most people would be managing this whole thing differently."

"Maybe I should be managing this whole thing differently." I try not to sound as dejected as I feel.

"No, how you've disciplined your thoughts is exactly the reason you can lead a mission to rescue someone you care so much about."

"Thanks for sharing that with me. If nothing else it boosts my confidence a little."

"That's what friends are for."

A sharp pang of guilt shoots through my stomach. I eye Joseph in the corner. He's punching a heavy bag. Each strike is so hard that it picks the hundred-pound bag up off its chains. Although I knew my brother was strong, I didn't realize the ferocity of his attacks before. With an intense burning in his eyes he throws a front kick at the bag. It lands flatly, knocking him off balance and sending his other leg out underneath him.

"Maybe it's about time I was a good friend too," I say to Samara, who's also witnessed Joseph land on his tailbone. "I think *he* could use a confidence boost." I stride across the combat studio toward Joseph, ready to extend an arm out for him. Our eyes meet only once before he scrambles to his feet and strides out of the room, face red with humiliation. I consider running after him, but I know that will only make things worse. How can I expect to lead this team when I can't even provide the proper support to my brother? A team is only as strong as its leadership. After everything I've seen today I have enough evidence to confirm that I'm incompetent in this role. So much so I almost feel I deserve a long diatribe from Ren on the subject.

Sweaty and dejected, I take aim at the heavy bag, ready to assault it with all I have left. If everything is going to weigh on my shoulders then I need to be stronger. Not leading this team isn't an option. I've complained and cried about this burden, but not for all the riches in the world would I unload it. Because sometimes our greatest challenges hold our greatest treasures and secretly I'm hoping that at the bottom of this mission there's something buried for me. That there's something I've been searching for and been unable to obtain.

The bag echoes its complaints from my attacks, but doesn't waver the way it did when Joseph struck it. Again and again I crouch, lunge, strike, until sweat rolls down into my eyes blurring my vision.

"You might want to leave something for the Grotte," he says behind me.

I turn to find the combat studio empty, save for George. "Where'd everyone go?" I push sweat out of my eyes, wondering how gross I must look. George has changed into jeans and a T-shirt.

"Dinner…a while ago."

How did I miss that?

"Oh," I say, steadying my ragged breaths.

"You're trying too hard. You're better at this than you think."

"Better at what? At kicking ass?"

"Leading. You don't realize that you naturally lead us. You're always the first to move, to leave, to attempt whatever it is we're doing."

I drop the sticks and roll out my wrists. "No, George, I'm a loner. Not a leader."

"That's interesting because I think it's exactly this loner quality that makes a leader successful."

"How do you figure?"

"Well, the moment a leader wants to be liked or to conform is when they compromise their integrity. How can you make clear decisions if you're seeking approval?"

"Maybe you're right," I say, turning my back on him and toweling off. He's so quiet behind me. George is unbelievably predictable, to the extent I know he's waiting for my emotions to boil to the surface. I consider storming away from him and not saying what we both know I'm feeling. I turn and face him. "Well then, as your leader I want to know why you're wasting yours and Pearl's time by pretending to spar."

He gives me a cautious stare. "I didn't want to hit her."

"Then maybe you should have chosen another partner," I say too loud, sweat still beading my forehead.

"I don't want to hit anyone. Fighting doesn't feel natural," George says, blocking my way to the exit. "And how could I hit Pearl when I'd feel her pain afterward?"

"Well, if you're going to hit anyone then it might as well be someone who can heal themselves." I laugh. George doesn't.

"We were all built to negotiate life differently. You're a fighter, Roya, in every sense of the word and I support that."

"And I should support that you're not, is that right? Well then, I will, but here's the deal. As the leader of this group I expect everyone to find a way to defend themselves in the Grotte."

"And I do have ways, ones that work better for me than fighting."

"Then I expect you to use them not only to protect yourself, but also anyone on this team who needs help. I expect you to train wisely, and the next time I catch you goofing off I'm going to use you as target practice."

I'm livid at George, Joseph, and strangely at Pearl. But despite all my anger and threats, George actually smiles at me, his adorable dimple surfacing on his left cheek.

"Why are you smiling?"

"Because I'm right."

Silence. I refuse to be goaded.

"You're a born leader. You won't let me or even your brother get away with slacking. You hold us accountable, as you should."

"Look, George, I really don't need a pep talk. Actually all I really need right now is a shower."

"This isn't a pep talk. It's my observations. There's a million more I wish you'd let me share with you."

Chapter Twenty-Seven

Who exactly is this scientist that six people are about to risk their life to save? For the past few days I've been telling myself to only focus on the task. Now with this impending doom staring me in the face it's hard to resist the fact that I'm about to endanger my life and many others' to save Aiden. I know how I feel about him, but that *can't* be my only motivation. If the tables were turned would he risk everything to save me or someone on my team? Sure, he'd saved me twice, but always in the safety of one of his labs. And although I know he cares, he's still too much of a coward to make anything between us official.

Why am I risking my life for a guy who won't jeopardize his career for me? With less than twenty-four hours until our rescue mission my heart battles this doubt. With each beat a new emotion pulses through my being: worry, frustration, anxiety, longing, fear, doubt.

I throw myself onto my bed assaulting it with punches until the power of my emotions wanes and I surrender from exhaustion. The ball I curl into is becoming so familiar to my body. I cradle my arms, providing a support I've also grown accustomed to. One only I can offer myself.

Slowly, like waking from a dream, my logical side surfaces. Aiden is the smartest scientist the Lucidites have ever employed, and therefore probably one the greatest assets on the earth. And I've agreed to rescue him because I know I stand a chance of succeeding. My heart wants to tear down every cave the Voyageurs occupy to find him. But my mind knows that if I remain calm and calculated I'll find the path of least resistance to rescue Aiden, and that's what needs to happen because he matters to more than me—he matters to the world.

I see Aiden's eyes clearly in my mind. His smile is only a breath away. He presses his lips against mine. The pulse of electricity so often associated with his touch courses through me. He whispers words in my ear that I can't make out, but my heart feels their comfort. We're two entangled bodies, satisfied by our unrelenting connection to each other.

The next time he speaks I hear his words and they imprint on my soul. "I'm alive. As long you can feel me, I'm alive." I reach out to touch his face, my fingers only an eyelash distance from his skin—

"Wake up, Stark! Wake up!"

I jerk upright. Joseph stands over me, arms crossed. Rapid blinks bring the room into clearer focus. Bed sheets are tangled around me, my heart beating fast.

"What in the hell are you doing in my room!?"

"You wouldn't answer your door. I was worried about you," Joseph says, sitting down next to me on the bed. "Are you all right?"

I run my fingers through my tousled hair. "I'm fine. Just having a strange dream."

He peers at me skeptically. "Want to share? You know I'm a master at interpretation."

"That's all right; I think I've figured this one out on my own."

"I brought you something to eat since you missed dinner." He hands me a white container and a bag of utensils.

My stomach growls with anticipation. "Thanks, I'm starving." I prop myself up and pry the container open so fast, I fling dressing on my bed sheets. "So you decided to start feeding me again?"

Joseph settles back on the pillow beside me, tucking his arms behind his head. "I'm a bit messed up, aren't I? Cold one minute, warm the next, huh?"

I peer at him warily. "How strange, that's exactly what I was going to say."

"I apologize for storming off earlier. I know you were intendin' to help me. My ego is a bit bruised right now."

"I'm not going to ask why and you're not going to give me a real explanation, so why don't we skip to the part where we get past all this?"

"And here I thought you were gonna want another apology or promise from me that I'd act right," Joseph says, staring up at the ceiling.

"I only want what you can give me."

"Do you want me with you in the Grotte?"

"Not really," I say, throwing my fork down into my unfinished food.

Joseph's eyes jerk to mine, a look of disappointment on his face.

"I don't want anything to happen to you." I shrug.

"*And* you're worried I'm not good enough," he says, an edge of hurt in his voice.

"Joseph, I know if you're focused then you're better than anyone on the team. Hell, there's no one I'd rather have by my side. But I know the danger we're facing and I want to shield you from it."

"That's a big fat ditto."

"All right, so then we can both agree that we need to stop worrying and getting distracted and focus on keeping each other alive, right?"

"Yes, we can agree to that, but…" Shame surfaces in his eyes, like a window being briefly opened. "I'm not on drugs, but I'm like an addict. I'm gonna tell you what you want to hear one minute, but the next I'll do somethin' contrary to it. I keep telling myself not to, but then I turn around and realize I've disappointed you again. And that's worse than anything, worse than all the looks of disapproval I keep gettin' from everyone at the Institute."

"Joseph, what has you so mixed up?"

"Everythin' and nothin'. I make it all more complicated than it needs to be. I break my own heart. Torture myself with no-win situations." He sits up and faces me, a mischievous grin plastered on his face. "You wouldn't know what that's like, would ya?"

"Nope, haven't got a clue. And it's impossible to help you when you keep speaking in riddles."

"I never said I wanted help. Let me be a screw-up and love me just the same," he says matter-of-factly.

He hasn't really left me any room to negotiate here.

"Of course," I finally say.

"All right, well, if you hurry up and get ready then we can make it to the party before it's completely lame."

"What party?" I ask, wondering how everything shifted so quickly.

"Trent's. He didn't invite you because he was pretty certain you'd shut it down, but I'm invitin' you because, well, we're building bridges, aren't we?" He gives me the trademark persuasive smile which has won over most of the hearts in this Institute.

"It's the night before the mission. I don't think we need to be partying."

"And that's exactly why Trent didn't invite you. And also because he themed the party 'In Case There's No Afterlife.'"

"Classy."

"I say you prove him and everyone else wrong by showing up and having a good time."

"Are you trying to convince me to go because then you'll have my permission?"

"Oh, Stark, I think we both know I don't need your permission. I'm convincing you to go because it will be good for you." He pauses, and a sly smile unfolds. "And I can't wait to see Trent's face when I prance you through that door."

"You're cunning aren't you?"

"As well as many other things. Now go ahead and fix yourself up so we can get out of here. Currently you look like someone put you through the clothes dryer."

♦

Music pours through Trent's open door. It isn't comparable to the tunes on my iPod. It's under the category of "noise that makes my ears hemorrhage."

The lights are low and an iridescent glow shimmers from the overhead disco ball. Joseph abandons me the moment we arrive to talk to Samara.

Pearl sits on the edge of Trent's bed, looking especially pale. She's masking her nervousness by clumsily moving her head to the rhythm of the music.

"Hey there," I say loud enough to be heard.

"Hey." I see her mouth move.

"How are you?" My voice again bordering on shouting.

She nods.

"I hope you know I'm really grateful you're on this team."

She blinks quickly; it reeks of a lack of confidence.

"Thanks," Pearl finally says.

"How have you liked your time at the Institute so far?" I ask, desperately searching for anything to warrant more than a one-word answer.

A baffled look falls on her face. "I love it. It's my home."

That seems like an awfully sudden adoption of the place. She must have come into the Institute under different circumstances than me, ones that garnered trust and respect.

"Yeah, it's a nice place," I lie.

To say Pearl is socially awkward is an understatement. Her shyness is so painful it paralyzes me, making it impossible to come up with another topic of small talk. She's gone back to gracelessly swaying her head from side to side off the beat of the music.

Joseph and Samara are now dancing. He's doing that ridiculous robot dance. I point at him and laugh. Pearl covers her mouth and laughs too. With a small wave I charge off to get a drink, instantly feeling better when not in Pearl's tense presence.

There's close to two dozen people in Trent's room. How has he managed that? Then the man himself saunters up next to me.

"So tell me, Roya, when you going to be honest with yourself and profess your love for me?"

I smile into my drink. "I think I'd like to keep you waiting in suspense a bit longer."

He laughs loudly, then points at my cup. "Keep drinking that and I won't have to wait long."

I freeze and thrust the drink at his chest. He takes it with a wink.

"So did my invitation to this party get lost in the mail, because if so, I'll totally petition to get Patrick fired."

"Didn't think you'd come, and I'm certain you probably don't think this celebration is a good idea."

"You know, Trent, you're not as dumb as you look."

"And I assure you I'm every bit as seductive as I look."

I laugh, a genuine one. "Well, I didn't think this was a good idea at first, but I can see the importance of letting off some steam before the big event. Will you promise to send everybody back to their room at a decent time?"

"Yes, mom."

I tuck my head down and slide through dancing people. Light grows brighter as I edge closer to the hallway. Snaking my way through the tight crowd of bodies, I have a brief moment of claustrophobia. Only once I reach the threshold does my breath return. I'm not certain how hanging out in an overcrowded room is fun, but more power to the rest of them. The corridor feels double its normal size as I head back to my safe haven.

"Not so fast."

I freeze. He's talking to me.

Chapter Twenty-Eight

Rigid, I straighten before turning around to face George. He continues to stride forward until he's only two feet from me. "Don't leave," he says, a chastised tone to his voice.

The light in the hallway is bright, still messing with my eyes after the disco ball. "I've had a long day, that's all," I say. "I need to get some rest for tomorrow."

"So you're not dream traveling later then." His tone is not questioning, but rather bitter.

"Probably not," I say.

"Okay, well then that settles it." George strides around me, blocking my room.

"Settles what?" I ask, worried he's about to do something stupid.

"Well, it's pretty much my last chance." His eyes bore into me with a new intensity. "It's my last chance before everything comes to a head. And after that it will all change."

What does he mean? "George..." I plead. "Please—"

"Roya, give me a chance. I promise I'm not here to hurt or pressure you. I only want to take advantage of the precious time we have left." His ominous words carry an urgent awakening through my being. He holds out his arm for me. "Would you accompany me? I have something I want to show you."

I hesitate, staring at his arm, then his eyes. We *don't* know what dangers we'll face tomorrow. I've tried not to think about it and honestly, I don't want to spend the rest of the night consumed with thoughts of the unknown. Wrapping my arm around his I allow him to lead me off. With a sturdy force, George guides me to the elevator. His finger presses the 5 with an excited hesitation. Nervous tension mounts within me as I search my brain for what could be on that level that he'd want to show me.

Once we arrive he escorts me out of the elevator without a single glance. His grip around my arm is both gentle and commanding, which I don't just permit, but relish. Right past the Panther room he stops at a doorway labeled "Shhh." I've been by it a million times. George pauses, seems to waver, about to say something, then hits the button with his elbow. The door slides back.

A soothing musk of leather and fresh polished wood hits my nostrils. George drops his grip on me and I step forward. Compared to the cold hallway, the space I enter is rich with mahogany and warm with soft sconce lighting. Marble greets my feet oddly. Most places in the Institute are covered in the iridescent blue carpet. Here black and cream marble spiral together until they disappear into each other in the center of a great atrium. The design is the same as the amulet Trey wears. A yin yang of sorts. My feet bring me to the center of the spiral, but my eyes continue to scan the area. Five open stories tower above me, all uniform in design with shelves lining their spaces. Only one type of item occupies the mahogany shelves: Books. Hundreds of thousands of books. Millions of pages cloaked in dust and inspiration and wisdom.

Once. Twice. Three times I rotate, taking in the vast richness around me. Just when I think the Institute can't surprise me I learn inside its stainless steel walls is the most incredible warmth of intelligence I could have imagined. A library. It looks to be modeled straight from the Library of Congress with its arches, marble columns, and vibrant murals blanketing the walls. This place is the antithesis of the modern design found everywhere else in the Institute. It's perfect.

Two sets of majestic staircases stand on either side of me, both zigzagging from level to level. Balconies stretch off each floor, with a view of the marble display under our feet. The immediate area is devoid of people, but in places like this anyone can hide in alcoves and behind shelves of books. One of the many reasons I love libraries. Everyone is lost and not wanting to be found in a library.

I rush forward to the shelves, touching the first set of books I come to. They're real under my fingertips. As real as flesh and dirt and water. Running my fingers along the shelf of books, I pace forward, sucking in the velvety dust immediately unleashed by my touch upon these unused volumes.

"What do you think?" George asks in a hush a few feet behind me.

That's the most appropriate question I've ever heard him ask. Without turning to face him, I say, "I think this place is incredible." Hungry to suck in everything, I scan, trying to delineate the different sections. Fiction is on the first floor. Does it just compose the first or could more volumes be housed on the second and third floor too? And still that leaves so many possibilities, all waiting to be explored. At once I long to know this place intimately, but then also relish the mystery and opportunity to discover each new volume when the time is right.

Strolling footsteps snake me through the aisles. Fingertips still greet a row of books, welcoming them into my life. Anticipation builds in me until I realize I'm breezing through the aisles, laughing. It's only once I'm deep within the catacombs of the first level that I double over, delirious with excitement. This library is majestically secretive and quiet and lonely. I love it.

Excited to share my overpowering joy, I turn to George, who's trailing behind me. An awe-inspiring look is upon his eyes as he stares directly at me.

"Thank you," I say, as he catches up to me. "I had no idea this was here. It's incredible. It's…" I can find no words to express how overwhelmed I feel right now. The expression of understanding on George's face tells me he's already privy to my true emotions.

"Roya, how you feel about this place right now is how I feel about you all of the time."

The smile etched upon my lips falters. I step back. George makes up the distance quickly though. "I'm not trying to scare you. But Roya, don't you want to know? Wouldn't it be nice to know how you make other people feel, for once?"

His words jolt me like I'm free falling. Simultaneously I'm paralyzed by their allure and also fearful of their true meaning. "George, you promised. You said you weren't going to pressure me again."

"And I'm not. I knew you'd love it here, but I had no idea how much. When I felt your emotions, such brazen affection, I knew I had to say something. I'll never get another opportunity to express the equivalence of my emotion for you."

I stare at him, down the long dark aisle. His brown eyes are hooded by blond hair, but I can still see the softness around them.

"It's different than last time, Roya," he continues. "I'm not urging you to tell me how you feel. I won't ever ask that of you again. I promised you that, but it's unfair of you to silence me. And still, whatever you feel for me I'm not begging for more. I won't do that either. All I want is the opportunity to make sure my case is clear to you."

The space between us is simultaneously too small and too large. Everything escapes me, words, actions, emotions. I let them bound out of me, unshielded—all messy and untamed. George's eyes shift back and forth between mine, and I'm frozen between two solid rows of pages. Frozen by his searching gaze.

Finally the floodgate of my emotions dissipates. Abruptly he turns, striding for the exit. "It's late. I should get you back."

It takes me a moment to realize I'm no longer entranced in his emotional net. I shake my head, recapturing my wits, and stride behind him.

"George," I say, trying to locate my suddenly missing breath.

"It's all right, Roya. I'm not asking for anything. I just wanted you to enjoy this place. I knew you would." He picks up his pace, intent on leaving me behind.

"Stop, please," I say, sounding small. Gently he halts, pauses, and turns, facing me with a masked expression.

"Thank you for showing me this place. It's..." Anything I say will be indicative of how he feels for me. Do I want to vocalize that?

"You're welcome," George says, sounding defeated. "I really didn't come here to confess anything to you."

"I believe you," I say, hoping the pages swallow our words.

A quiet complaint falls out of his mouth. "You have so much emotion inside. Why won't you let it out? Why do you bottle your feelings?"

"Because..." I stare at him, then search the rows for an answer. "Because I need them for battle," I say without making eye contact.

"That will probably work as an answer... until you have no more battles left to fight," he says in a tight whisper and turns to leave.

We exit the library and board the elevator without a word. Inside the silver confines I feel George's tension. It's palpable in this small space. The stainless steel walls seem to ensure that emotions and thoughts are revealed instead of absorbed. Instantly I yearn for the porous marble and wood of the library.

Again George has confessed himself to me, and again I've offered him nothing in return. I'm not sure why I continue to push him away, especially since his whispered words in my ear the other

149

night brought down walls I'd guarded to the point of exhaustion for too long. *Leaning on someone doesn't make you weak.* I feel safe with George, but I also don't want anything to ever ruin that. And every time we erase another obstacle between us I fear my refuge is disintegrating. Maybe he was right when he said the night of the party that I was playing games with him. But I'm stupid, because this isn't a game I know how to win.

He holds the elevator open while I disembark. I walk ahead of him, then pause at my door, the first room on this side of the rooming corridor. George turns after a few paces and searches me. "Goodnight, Roya," he says, his voice catching on my name.

"No, wait," I say, stepping forward. "George, the night of the party you asked me how I specifically felt about you. Do you still want to know?"

Whatever he was expecting, it wasn't this. His expression is a mix of consternation and anticipation. "Yes. But you don't have to."

"And I don't want to. I'm not ready right now, but I also don't want that to be your last appeal."

"I don't need you to prove anything to me, if that's what you're implying. I know how you feel. But for once, it would be nice to hear it from your own lips."

"Is that what you need?"

"Yes, but not yet. If you're going to tell me, do it after tomorrow," he says, tone morose, and adds, "if it's still the way you feel."

"Nothing is going to change the way I feel about you." The cynical look in his eyes fractures my heart, sending me into a quiet frenzy to convince us both that we belong in each other's arms right now. "George." I tip my head back to look at him. Words are stuck in the hollow of my throat. Obviously I've hurt him by not saying enough, but I can't…not right now.

I step, the movement so small, it could hardly be classified as one. Still, I find myself closer to George. His true expression is plastered behind a stone face. The beat of the music from Trent's room echoes down the corridor, but I'm a million miles from there. George and I are chained to each other through our silent, staring eyes, alone inside a bubble. One in which there's only room for his arms to hold me like before. Tomorrow we face danger and death and who knows what other evils. Tonight I need his arms around me, erasing my pain—or at least attempting to.

Reaching out, he cups my shoulder, yanking me forward until I'm pressed up against him. "Oh, Roya, what am I going to do with you?" he says, wrapping his arms around me, wrenching me in tightly. I bury my face in his chest, like the other night. In the flesh he smells of jasmine and wood; it must be his cologne. It's seductive.

My focus remains on his steady breath, the only thing I'm sure I can count on in this moment. I wrap my arms around his torso and press every inch of me against him. I never want to leave this moment. Not even the idea of people spilling out of Trent's room deters me from wanting to stay safe in my refuge.

"You know," George says, breathing into my hair, "I'll stay like this as long as you want me to."

I slide back and look into his tranquil, brown eyes. "I know you will."

With everything that weighs on my shoulders right now all I can think about is my own curiosities: What does his lips feel like pressed against mine? Does he know how long and hard to kiss me? Or will his desire overwhelm the moment?

An inviting smile stretches across George's face, reaching all the way up to his eyes. I'm not masking my emotions and he's picking them up like pansies from an open field. His next moves are not as graceful as the expression he's just adorned. He fumbles several times to find a path to my face, not always tilting the right direction at the right time and retreating when meeting an obstacle. But when he finds my lips he seizes them and lays claim in a way I've yet to imagine possible. And every curiosity I had is put to rest. Of course I should have known: George kisses me exactly as long and hard as I desire. His kiss is elegantly perfect.

Chapter Twenty-Nine

The lecture hall is quiet except for the soft buzzing of the overhead lights. Words blur on the page in front of me. I must have already read through my notes thirty times in the last hour. The door at my back slides open. Half of me hopes it's George and the other half prays it's not. Being alone with him right now is probably not a good idea.

I'm not the least bit relieved to learn its Joseph. His bloodshot eyes barely make contact with me when he sits down.

"You're hungover?!" I say in offensive disbelief.

Joseph grimaces in pain. "Yes. Can you keep it down?"

"I can't believe this!" I pound my fist on the desk. "This is ridiculous!"

"Warned you I was gonna screw up again and again."

I narrow my eyes at him. "This is not the time for screwing up."

"Joseph doesn't care if we have a vital mission," Samara says behind me. I turn to find she's taken a seat three rows back and appears as angry as I feel. "He only cares about himself, isn't that right?"

"You'd know better than anyone how I think, Samara," Joseph says, a cold animosity in his tone.

The door to the lecture hall slides back. I turn around as soon as I spy George. Hopefully there's enough emotion in this room to occupy his attention. He slips into the seat beside me. All night I tormented myself with guilt for kissing him on the eve of this mission. Now that he's close, I yearn to reach out and kiss him again, using passion as an outlet from my fears. Just his presence changes the way my heart beats.

My eyes lead my chin up until they find their target. The look on his face undoes something in me I'm certain was fastened tightly in place. Unsurprisingly he's chewing on his lip. *Damn those lips.* I'm too accustomed to his probe that I know right now he's dissecting me from the inside out. George leans forward, a stern expression on his face. I clench my eyes shut, so afraid he's going to reprimand me for my guilt.

"Good morning, Roya," he whispers, his breath brushing my ear.

I peel open my eyes, looking at him sideways. He's all stone. "Good morning, George." Gracefully he leans back in his seat, never taking his firm gaze off me. The knot in my throat is preventing me from speaking, which is good because I'd probably regret anything I'd let spill from my mouth right now.

"The Grotte!" Ren says, charging to the front of the room. "That's where you'll be vacationing tonight." His laugh is cold. "Everyone loves a good holiday in the south of France, but I'm here to tell you that it's no picnic. The service at the Grotte is awful, the rooms are dark and cold, and the locals make you want to stab yourself...literally."

"Why are we just now covering the Grotte? Seems like something we should have gone over before the day of the mission," Joseph says, lacking decorum. Is he *still* drunk?

"I wanted the information to be fresh." Ren places his fingertip on the surface of the desk in the center of the platform and traces along it as he walks. "It's charming you think knowing about the Grotte sooner than today was going to benefit you. Judging by your appearance, Joseph, I don't think it matters much what you know about the Grotte, except that it will be your final resting place." Ren flashes his eyes on Pearl. "Don't waste your efforts healing Joseph. He's not worth it."

"If that time comes," I say, ripping Ren's attention in my direction, "that will not be your call. It will be mine."

"Brav-freaking-o," Ren says. "You've decided to start acting like a leader, Roya. Way to wait until the last possible moment to rise to the challenge."

I taper my eyes, not taking them off Ren. "The Grotte. Tell us what we need to know. Now."

"Well, since you've got your knickers in a wad already, I suppose I should," Ren says, his calm superiority blistering the room with irritation. He gives a bored sigh. "The Grotte is a network of caves that have been crudely constructed into the Voyageurs' headquarters. The lighting is awful, but there's some. The layout is a confusing mess, but oddly has some logic. And the security is absolutely laughable."

Over the next hour we learn how to navigate the Grotte. Ren has a series of slides that outline the various routes we'll take to the central rooms. I pay special attention to where the GAD-C is located and other rooms that will possibly be where Aiden is imprisoned. When we have completed this portion of the lesson Ren lays a blue and white map on my desk and retreats.

"It will probably be too dark to read it, but that's a rough sketch of the Grotte," he says with zero emotion.

"If it's so dark," Trent says, "then why don't we bring flashlights?"

Ren's pretending to clean his nails with his pocket knife. I know from just spying his nails when he placed the map on my desk that they're perfectly clean. He does this little act to make us feel small and to belittle the current topic. "Well, wise one," Ren says, "the reason you shouldn't outfit yourself with this battery-operated technology is because the Voyageurs don't use it. They're going to have a hard time explaining to themselves why people using technology they refuse are skipping around on their turf. You'll remember that I said they're primitive. They believe that electricity and battery-operated devices leech their mental powers. For this reason the only electricity in the entire joint is in the GAD-C room. The rest of the place is lit by fire, warmed using coal, and secured using mental prowess. So no, I'd recommend that you not carry a torch, your iPod, or any other trendy device that will make you stand out in their evil minds. Bring a match, how about that?"

Once Ren has completely beaten us down he launches into the strategy we'll follow. It's quite simple, but I know all too well how one little hitch can unravel it. We each have a specific mission and purpose at all times, which changes as we enter each new phase of the plan. Furthermore, we're divided up into sub-teams in case we need to separate. My team member is of course Joseph, which should have been a good thing but under the present circumstances makes me feel like a sluggish target.

◆

Knowing I need the sustenance, I eat, although each bite threatens to come back up. Joseph sits at the table with the white coats, while Samara steams next to me. Trent and George talk over strategy, but continuously I feel George's eager gaze on me. After a few minutes I turn to Pearl and ask, "So, I've been meaning to ask you where you're from."

She looks startled, like a bunny who's been cornered. Pushing her hair behind her ear she says, "I grew up here. My mom is Mae, the Head of the Healing Department."

"Here? At the Institute?" I say a bit louder than I intended.

"Yes," she says meekly.

After Trey told me that Joseph and I were separated at birth for our own protection I questioned why we weren't raised here. He made that seem like an impossibility. He said that the Institute wasn't the right place to raise a child. It seemed to be good enough for Pearl and Aiden. *Why?*

"But I thought children couldn't be raised here at the Institute. Aiden said he was an exception."

George's eyes flick to mine at the mention of Aiden's name. I focus on Pearl.

She shrugs. "He's right. And so was I. We actually spent a lot of time together growing up, since we were the only kids here."

A knot tightens in my throat. "Oh, you two must be close."

Regret marks her eyes when she nods her head. "We were, but after his parents died he became really involved with his work and we drifted apart. Still, I've always felt a special bond to him, since we grew up together."

"I'm sorry, this mission must be difficult for you." *Maybe you shouldn't go.*

"It is, but I couldn't imagine not being on this team. I want to be there when we rescue Aiden. I have to see him with my own eyes before I'll stop worrying. And I'm grateful that I've honed my healing abilities enough that I'll be able to help him if he's hurt."

My breaths are shallow and unfulfilling. George isn't hiding his curiosity anymore. He pinches the corner of his mouth together and stares at me, then Pearl. I'd give a million dollars right now to know what emotions he's picking up in Pearl. Is she in love with Aiden? The idea is infuriating.

"Trey said Aiden's parents were killed by Voyageurs. What happened?"

Pearl looks down suddenly. "I don't think it's my place to tell that story. Aiden may not want me to…" Her eyes glaze over a bit as she trails off.

I want to yell at her, tell her no one is closer to him than me. But it's not true. At least I can't confirm it. Apparently I hardly know the guy I'm about to risk my life to save.

I push away my irritation with a fake smile. "Well, tell me about growing up in the Institute. What was that like?"

"About how you'd imagine, I'm sure."

"How would you know what I'd imagine?" I say, irritation edging into my tone.

She blanches. "I meant that it was different than a normal childhood, I've gathered that much from reading books. If it wasn't for Aiden then I would have spent most of those years alone in this place, since all the adults were always busy working. But unlike Aiden I didn't come into my ability to dream travel until recently. He at least was able to escape."

"Yes, I understand he started dream traveling very young," I say as casually as I can muster.

She eyes me skeptically. "Yes, that's true. Once he became obsessed with dream traveling I spent my free time reading religious texts."

"A hobby of yours?"

"Religion isn't a hobby," she revolts.

Inside I smile, knowing I've irritated her. Tit for tat.

"So were you the one who showed George the library?" I ask.

"Yes," she says with a nod. "It's a really wonderful place. My favorite place."

"Yes, it's great," I say, looking at him as he stares back at me. "It's your favorite place too, isn't it, George?"

He gives me a calculated look, one that admonishes my catty behavior and also my jealously.

"Well, thanks for the chat, Pearl. Now I must go study the map." I push off from the table feeling like the most awful leader in the world. To resent one of the greatest assets on my team right at the eleventh hour is the worst possible thing I can do. Still, the look in her eyes when she spoke about Aiden and her obvious closeness with George make an irresistible rage flow through me. I wish I'd never asked Pearl any questions. Ten minutes ago, before I knew

156

anything that she told me, I was only bordering on insanity over two guys. Now I'm a hundred miles past the brink.

♦

From Bob

Bob and Steve <bobandsteveharvey@gmail.com>
to Roya Stark

Dear Roya,

I have something I've been meaning to share with you and the timing is finally right now, although I don't know why. It's an intuition.

I've always known we were supposed to find you. Then Trey asked us to seek you out. But when we did, a puzzle piece fell into place for me. I'd been searching for that piece for a long time and had no idea it would be you.

Over a decade ago I had a dream. In this dream I saw a child floating in water. She was beautiful and radiant. The energy from her pulsed through the lake until it built up a current. The child rode easily on these rapids. Then in an instant she was a girl and swam through these waters, allowing it to propel her to a nearby beach. Once there she stood up and the earth buckled under her as if there had been a small earthquake. She wasn't unnerved by this experience. Instead she stood steady, looking down upon the beach and the water. The lake raged angrily as it rocked the beach. Another quake hit the shore, causing the waters to stir and grow higher. The girl stayed firm, watching as the ground and the waters battled each other. Finally she spoke, "In the end, you'll thank me for this!" Then the girl became a gust of wind and barreled through the water, breaking all its currents down to nothing. She shot back at the beach, sending the bits of earth that were about to vibrate into a quake into a million bits of nothing. The wind dissipated the storm until the area stood calm and still and at peace.

At the time I didn't know what the dream meant, only that the girl was of importance. When I met you I was in awe of you for many reasons, but mostly because without a doubt I knew you were the girl from my dream. You're the wind. I don't know why and I don't know how this will aid you, but for a person who knows nothing about where she came from, I hope this helps.

Love,
Bob

I'm the wind?! What could that possibly mean? Is that the element I should align with, like some Native American tradition? I close my email without replying and head back to my room. I know Bob is trying to help, but why right before the mission did he send me an email with some cryptic meaning? And did he mean I looked like the woman in the dream or that he supposed it was me based on his gut? I round the corner, stuck in my current confusion.

"You're a selfish asshole," Samara screams, tears in her eyes.

"That's an easy position for you to take," Joseph says. "If I knew what was in everyone's head I'd be passin' a lot of judgments too."

"I wish I'd never met you," she says, taking a step forward, and for a second I think she's going to push him.

I think he knows this too and backs away. "The feeling is one hundred percent mutual."

"Why?" she says, tears racing down her face. "Why are you doing this?"

"I'm doin' what I choose," Joseph says. "You're choosing how you feel about it. Don't you see, we all have choices and that's all we've got in life."

"You're an—"

158

"Stop!" I interrupt.

Both of them turn to me, surprised and slightly horrified.

"That's quite enough," I say. "It's obvious Joseph isn't making good decisions," I say to Samara. "And it's obvious that Samara doesn't agree with how you're conducting yourself." I look at Joseph and hold his gaze. "If you survive tonight then you can battle this out for the rest of your lives. However"—I round on the both of them, angrier than I've felt in a long time—"do not be so selfish that you choose to put all your energy into this fight when there are better and greater ones. I'm sorry you two are at odds, but find a way to put it aside, if only for a little while, so that we can operate as a team tonight. Look at each other and find that one thing you respect about the other person and focus on just that. Forget the cheating and the rest of it."

I pause and look at them. They stare blankly at me.

"Do. It. Now!"

Joseph turns and looks at Samara as she stares at him, and for several seconds they're mostly silent, besides some residual whimpering from Samara. I don't give them any privacy, but instead watch to ensure they're doing what I asked them to. After a minute, Samara turns to me with a pained expression. I nod at her. She charges off, leaving Joseph staring at the place where she stood moments prior.

"What is your damn problem?" I finally say. "Are you going to get me killed?"

"Nah," he says, still not looking at me.

"Well, you should know that if you don't get your ass handed to you in the Grotte, then I'll be delivering it in person because I've had about as much as I can take."

"Copy," he says.

I turn and stride off, knowing I need to take my own advice. I *need* to respect the people on my team.

Chapter Thirty

The Kevlar uniform fits about like I'd expect a wet suit to feel. Two long pockets have been made along my shoulders for the escrima sticks. Three times I practice reaching and pulling them from their hiding place. Each time the transition feels smoother. My hair cascades down my back and safely covers the weapons. I turn my protective charm on my wrist. The tiny spark shoots from it and up my arm. With a brief glimpse in the mirror I turn and head for the infirmary. I'm ready for battle. Ready to bring Aiden home.

George glances up at me when I enter the infirmary. Everyone from my team is already gathered. Trey and Mae are talking in the corner; both give me a speculative glance. I ignore them.

"I want to say something before we leave," I say to my team. Joseph's face is propped in his hand, resting on his other arm. He could put a great deal more effort into looking alive, but that would probably wound his pride.

"Up until recently I thought Aiden's life meant more than the rest of ours and that's why Trey put us on this mission." The Head Official's eyes urgently dart to mine, a worried look on his face. "It isn't true though. No one's life weighs more than another. Trey would send another group if it was you, Samara, or you, Trent, who were abducted. We protect. That's what it means to be a Lucidite. If something happened to one of you, I'd willingly walk through fire and suffer torment to bring you back. We don't leave each other behind and we don't turn our backs when someone needs us most." Joseph stares at me, remorse swarming in his eyes. "You already realize you're about to risk danger in order to bring back a valued Lucidite. However, I want each and every one of you to know that I will risk my life to keep you alive until the end of this mission. In return all I ask is that you use your talents to the best of your ability, focus at all times, and support each other. Watch each other's back as if it were your own. We're a team and the only way we're getting through this successfully is together."

Hardened faces stare back at me. No one says a word for several seconds. Behind them I spy Trey letting out a giant exhale, one reeking of relief.

"Amen, sister," Trent finally says, breaking the silence. "Even if you won't get in my bed, I'd still follow you to the end of the earth."

A smile cracks my serious expression. "Thanks, Trent," I say, putting my hand out. He covers mine with his own, his dark skin contrasting brilliantly against mine. Joseph's covers Trent's. Then Samara's. And George's. And finally Pearl's tiny hand reaches into the center. "Let's do this. Quickly, efficiently, and successfully. All right?"

"Let's do this!" the group chants collectively.

♦

I close my eyes, withdrawing my attention from the outside world. For a good three minutes all I think about is the air flowing in and out of my body effortlessly, constantly. It's Joseph's voice that brings me out of this meditation.

"I'm sorry, sis." I open my eyes and turn my resting head to the side. He's lying on the bed next to mine. "I do love you. I really hope I don't disappoint you."

"Me too," I say. Then I focus on my destination and within seconds I'm shooting through the silver tunnel like a rocket. The air blasts through my hair. It feels good to move and have the freedom that dream travel offers. Instinctively I take a series of right turns and push forward. Then, like a hatch opening I fall out of the tunnel and land softly.

The ground is cold and hard under my feet. I expected this. The air is moist. I expected this. A high-pitched screeching noise splinters the air unexpectedly. I remain stock-still, watching as, one by one, each group member joins me.

We've landed in the right room. It's hard to make out much with only the small fire torches on the wall to illuminate our surroundings. My eyes have nearly adjusted and I'm disappointed to learn Ren is absolutely right, this place is dark. However, it's early morning and the sun will rise soon. Some rooms in the Grotte have holes where light streams in, providing help. We aren't to one of these rooms yet though.

I move forward, the slick rock under my feet threatening my balance with each step. Using my hand to guide me I grope along the surface of the wall. The cold limestone is rough and smooth at the same time. I'm the first to autogenerate my body, which takes longer than usual since their model of the GAD-C isn't as efficient as ours.

While the others generate, I pull the modifier out of my pocket. My conscience wrested with the decision of whether to use the modifier. In the end my sheer desire to live and complete the mission triumphed any moral hesitation. The modifier shines ceremoniously in the darkened cave. First I input the group to be targeted. Each push of the keys feels strange, but I urge my emotions to remain neutral. When the group is accepted I input the message:

The new people in the Grotte belong here.

I've never experienced the modifier working. Nothing James said could have prepared me for this moment, I'm certain of that. When I hit the last button the modifier levitates a few inches above my palm, sending radiant warmth in all directions. The space around the modifier glows, then an almost imperceptible charge ripples the air. It sends a shudder down my spine, making every hair on my body stand on end. Without notice the modifier grows dark, then falls back into my palm with a gentle thud, cold and unsuspecting. My eyes jerk up to find George's. We both share looks of disbelief and astonishment.

I don't need to pull out the map to know where we need to head next. All five of my team members stand in front of me looking solid, the firelight flickering off their faces.

"Ready?" I say in a low whisper. They all return silent nods. I look at Joseph for a long moment. His sad eyes are trying extra hard to convince me I can believe in him. My faith wavers as I spin around, feeling the slick rock slide easily under my shoe. I brace myself on the wall in time to secure my balance and not wind up on my tailbone.

Right before I start off, I turn back again and face the group. "Shields up." I concentrate for a brief second, visualizing the greenish gauze net drape over me, ensuring that no one can get to my thoughts or emotions.

Clean, cool air drifts by me as I move into the narrow cave hallway. Torches line the wall every ten feet, but still much of the cave is bathed in darkness. The draft makes the flames dance, creating eerie shadows across the walls. Thankfully the screeching sound has stopped. All I hear now is moving water and Joseph's heavy breathing. He's doing the same as me, scanning the upcoming cave area.

Taking a few tentative steps I feel the team move behind me, keeping pace. Wherever I go, they'll follow. Whatever I say, they'll do. A bubble rises in my throat.

Ahead the cave splits in a Y. I listen, hearing the sound of dripping water off to the left. *Drip. Drip. Drip.* That's the direction we must go. I head off to the left, feeling Joseph at my heels. We keep moving in the dark and cold, my anxiety building as we progress deeper into the network of caves.

I take each step with deliberate force, praying not to slip on the slick limestone. Joseph gasps a second before a figure materializes. I didn't notice her until she was only a few torches away. A woman of about fifty is approaching quite fast. On her bony frame she wears long ripped fabrics that seem to be tied to each other to construct an interesting ensemble. Her hair looks grayish, maybe mixed with fading red. It's hard to tell in the darkness of the cave. One thing I'm certain of is her eyes are small, set back in her sunken face. She almost runs into us as we pass in the cave-way.

"*Que faites-vous tous ici?*" she says, looking flustered. Something flickers on her face and her expression changes to one of understanding instead of confusion. "*Oui*, zats right. I remember now." I stare at her, trying not to look scared or lost or any of the other emotions I feel. Her initial look of worry fades instantly as she scans our faces. "Oh vell, it makes sense you'd be 'ere early. We're grateful for zee delivery."

I smile. Nod at the woman. And continue past her, hoping she can't hear my pulse racing.

"But you should know," the woman says, causing us to halt, "zee infirmary is zee ozer way. You should 'ave taken a right at zee fork."

A new tension surges into my chest. Behind me, George presses close. Samara grips the hilt of her sword, carefully hidden under a long cape. Joseph steps forward and smiles. "Yeah, we've only got to get a quick signature first. Believe the offices are this way, right?" He points in the direction we're headed. My hand twitches at my side, ready to reach for my weapons. Quickly I scan our surroundings looking for options, not knowing what this woman's special ability is.

"Vell, of course," the woman says in a higher pitch than moments before. She flips her matted hair over her shoulder and smiles. Her teeth are black in places, jagged. "*Oui*, keep heading south and you'll find zem."

A gigantic pressure dissipates in my chest. Still my hand presses back until it finds George's. I squeeze it briefly before continuing to move forward, keeping pace with Joseph on my right.

"That's the first time," Joseph whispers so only I can hear.

"First time for what?" I say, moving at a steady speed.

"The first time you're going to be grateful I'm here. I assure you there will be more."

"Seriously, right now is not the time to keep score. Teamwork, remember?"

"Can't fault a guy for gunning for MVP."

The torches illuminate two stone doors flanking each other up ahead. If I've memorized my map well enough then both rooms are offices. One's Pierre's. A tentative glance at Joseph strips the arrogant expression from his face. Step by step we close the distance between us and the offices. The glow from the fire paints the space into something sinister. *It's just stone and dirt.* And if anyone is behind those doors then facing them brings us one step closer to freeing Aiden.

We don't pause at the doors, but rather move stealthily past them. Quickly we're approaching the library up on our right. This marks a huge milestone. Ren wagered that we'd never make it this far undetected. The offices behind us remain sealed and our upcoming path clear. With each step the confidence in me builds. After a week of feeling inevitable doom, it's a relief for things to go smoothly. My pace quickens and I ignore the slick rock under my feet, managing each step with a new grace. I can already see Aiden's face when I stroll into his holding chamber and release him from his chains. He'll be grateful, relieved. And once we return to the Institute we can figure out everything. *I'm almost there, Aiden. Hold on.*

An urgent hand clasps my wrist. I know instantly whose it is. Freezing in place I say, "Yes, George?" He leans down over my shoulder and whispers, "Allouette is in the library. Waiting for you."

My blood pauses in my veins. "Me? What?" I say, facing him directly. Even in this cool, damp cave he looks warm. "How?"

"Roya, she's familiar with your energy. Felt you as soon as you arrived."

"Why didn't you tell me?" I ask, exasperated.

"I didn't know for sure, but Samara has confirmed it."

"Shit," I say in a hush. "It's probably because I spied on her while news reporting. Ren said it wasn't possible, but—"

"No," George cuts me off, looking sideways at Joseph. "She's familiar with Joseph's energy too. Somehow she knows you two. The familiarity is very faint, but still there."

"That's impossible," Joseph says, stepping closer. The library door looms fifteen feet away. I turn back to George.

"Are you and Samara sure? We've never met Allouette. I'm certain of that."

"I'm certain that you have," George says, his words sounding like a curse. "And Samara says that the resounding message in her mind is that *this* time she'll kill you."

Joseph and I connect, sharing a morbid bond of fates. We mirror each other's confused expressions.

"Does she know why we're here?" I ask, returning my sturdy gaze to George.

"There would only be one reason."

"All right," I say, calculating our options. "Trent." I motion for him to join me and he takes George's position as he shuffles back. I whisper my orders in his ear. A second later his white teeth materialize, contrasting against his dark complexion. He nods once. "All right, team." I round on the rest of the group. "We're going to move fast now. Follow my lead and do not turn back. Let's go."

One of my tentative steps forward is followed by five more quick ones. Then the noise begins. A barrage of echoes inside the library. Ones that sound like hundreds of objects assaulting a space. I don't tense from the noise since I know Allouette is the one being attacked by hordes of books all at once.

Seizing our one chance to get ahead I encourage the team to bolt forward, staying back until I'm the only person between Trent and the group. Suddenly the ground begins to slip out from under my feet. I've just passed the door to the library when the ground buckles. I leap over the disturbed earth, pushing forward. The loud thunder from the hundreds of books ricocheting off the walls of the adjacent room grows less frequent, like popcorn popping in a microwave. The dark corridor and slick floor heightens my adrenaline with each step. The main room is only ten feet away, which is one room away from where we believe Aiden's being held. We're so close now.

The earth below my feet rumbles. Through the flickering firelight, a curtain of rocks rains down in front of us only a few feet away. The rocks pour from the ceiling overhead, walling off the main room. Everyone halts, watching the rocks shower down, sending dust and debris in all directions. "Cover your faces," I urge the group. The storm is short and within seconds a solid barrier stands before us. Allouette has done this. Blocked our path. Behind us the library door is only ten feet away. Sounds still echo from inside and Trent, who's stationed beside me, is deeply entranced.

"Joseph, George, and Pearl, clear an opening in this." I motion to the stone. "I want all of you through there as soon as possible. Samara, you stay by Trent's side until the last possible moment to protect him. When I command, I want you all to get through the opening and to the other side."

"What are you gonna do?" Joseph says, moving to my side.

I take three calculated steps toward the library. "I'm going to buy you some time. Now get to work moving those rocks."

"No, Roya, you—"

His words are drowned out by the sound of stone grinding against stone. The boulder-like door of the library slides back and before I can blink, Allouette's obsidian eyes seize mine. She's cold, battered, and wickedly beautiful.

Chapter Thirty-One

Long, black hair frames Allouette's heart-shaped face. It flows over her shoulders like seaweed, stopping at her lower back. Her doll-like eyes are both mesmerizing and terrifying. I know I shouldn't look at them, like they're part of Medusa, but still I'm compelled. Everything about her is all wrong, like her features aren't her own, her body a fabrication of magic and potions.

The firelight behind her illuminates the broomstick skirt she's wearing. It moves like it's caught in a breeze, one I don't feel. Books still move haphazardly around in the distance behind her. A quick glance at Trent tells me he hasn't stopped trying to knock her out. Allouette is less than ten feet away, but the darkness makes her seem farther.

"Welcome," she sings and then giggles. "Ve've been expecting you. Vell, ve've been expecting someone, and how fortunate zat it vas you zey sent. My job keeps getting easier and easier." Allouette throws her head back, shrieking with laughter. "You've grown so much since zee last time ve met."

"We've never met," I say through clenched teeth. "You must be mistaken."

She clicks her tongue three times. Tilts her head sideways. "I'm a Voyageur. I never forget an energy."

Allouette's dark eyes skip to my team and then back to me. "You didn't plan on leaving?" she says, sounding hurt. "Ve've only just been reunited."

"When is it that you think we've met?"

She smiles at me in a pleasant yet sadistic way. A book slams into her back. It knocks her off balance, but not as much as I would have hoped.

Regaining her composure she quickly masks her irritation behind a toxic smile. "I've allowed too many of you to live for too long. Any. Many. Miny. Mo. Vich. One. Of. You. Vill. Go...First," she sings, pointing at a different person behind me with each word.

Without a hesitation I take a step forward. Joseph's fingers pinch my wrist. I tug free easily. "Get to work, Joseph. I've got this."

The hate I feel for Allouette is unnatural. I watched her torture Ren. I know she's behind Aiden's abduction. And that's she's a ruthless killer. For an instant I have a surreal moment where I can hardly believe I'm here with the opportunity to kill her. The idea doesn't sound wrong. Nothing feels more right than to end her life, which I instinctively know has caused such torment and malice to the world.

"It's cute zat you zink you stand a chance against me," she purrs, looking amused. "Maybe you should allow your brozer to assist you?"

How does she know Joseph is my brother?

"I didn't need his help when I killed Zhuang," I say, taking a step forward.

Confused outrage riffles Allouette's face. "Zat is impossible. He's unstoppable."

"No, he was an overconfident madman who allowed me to get too close," I say, shooting forward at a speed only owed to me because of Joseph's proximity. Horror lines Allouette's face as I feint low with my left hand, then punch her in the jaw with my right. Again my left hand comes around, assaulting her in the chest this time. I half expect my bracelet to have a similar effect on her as it did with Zhuang, but no electricity radiates between us.

She stumbles back, clutching her ribcage. With a pained face she rubs her side. *That's not where I hit her though.* The glint of metal barely registers before I unleash the escrima sticks from behind my back. I whip them around in time to knock down the first knife speeding toward my face. My left arm spins around, blocking another knife as it barrels at my side. In quick succession I stop the path of three fast-moving blades. They clatter to the floor, where they instantly rise back into the air and continue toward their target.

Sweat pours down my face, my adrenaline working overtime as I deter blade after blade. I can't afford for my reflexes to slip up even a tiny degree, but I'm not certain how much longer I can keep this up. And Allouette hasn't even broken a sweat, only looks slightly irritated that none of her attempts have worked yet.

Out of the corner of my focused vision I spy a book rise up behind her. It's about the size of *War and Peace*. She doesn't notice it until it crashes down on top of her head, sending her to the ground, the pages spraying as the book tumbles. I knock down the only remaining blade and make a rush. She rolls to her feet faster than I'd expected. Both of us are crouched low. A standoff. Gazes leveled at one another. From a far off crevice a knife floats up, gliding into her hand. A lethal smile unfolds on her mouth right before she lunges at me. The knife grazes my chin as I simultaneously step back, sending an escrima stick into her torso, knocking the wind out of her. A quick step places me behind her, and with my opposite arm I pull the escrima stick down on her throat until she buckles backwards and down. I step back as she falls. A crack accompanies her landing.

Without a moment to spare I sprint toward the hole my team has made in the cave wall. Everyone but George has crawled through the opening to the other side. He's waiting for me at the top of the pile of rubble, arm outstretched. "Come on, Roya. Hurry." I glance back at Allouette, who appears incapacitated. My feet slip several times, but I maintain traction and reach George easily. His hand is firm when he catches mine, his grip urgent. In one swift moment he wrenches me up the pile of rock and propels me toward the hole. I should be the last to go through, but George is forcing me through with such power I don't have a moment to argue. I slither through the hole, feeling jagged pieces of rock poke me but unable to penetrate my armor.

A flash assaults my vision. Quick and vivid. Regret fills my being. In the vision Allouette stands with a long, wavy dagger—her focus directly on George. Only fifteen feet separate them. He squares his shoulders at her, a look of resilient determination on his face. With her free hand she pets her scalp, then a fresh wave of anger flashes across her face as she looks at the blood oozing off her fingertips.

Released from the flash I reach through the hole grasping George with a newly inspired strength. I consider breaking away parts of the wall with my fist to get him through quicker. "Help me," I call to my team at my back. Joseph runs forward, trying to help maneuver George's broad shoulders through the narrow hole. "Push, with your feet on the count of three," I order. His face is red, pressure exerting in every ounce of his body. I reinforce my grip on his arm, making sure it's tight. "One. Two—"

"Oh good, zey left me someone to play wiz," Allouette's voice squeals with evil delight. My eyes widen. I fight harder to get

George through, but he's resisting. He pushes me off him and slithers back the other way.

"No," I mouth. He shakes his head at me once before standing up to face Allouette. I stick my head through the hole and past George I see her paper-white arm as it extends. A curvy dagger soars through the air and lands lightly in her hand. I already know what's coming next, and I have to act fast.

"Trent, get over here," I call urgently.

Without hesitation he takes up the spot next to me, our heads pressed close together as we peer through the hole. "You have to help him. Don't let him get hurt."

"I'm on it, boss," Trent says, narrowing his eyes at Allouette.

She holds up her hand dripping with blood, eyeing it with disgust. "Someone vill pay for zis, of zat I'm sure," she says and wipes the blood from her head injury down both her cheeks.

Trent gives a shiver beside me. "Damn, that girl is f-ing loony."

The next surprise happens when George speaks. His voice is oddly calm and low. "What if I told you I could help you? Help you extinguish the raging fire within you?" The rocks slide under George's feet.

She quirks an eyebrow. "I'm listening like a good girl."

"Within you there's a battle going on, but you can stop it." There's a painfully long silence as Trent and I stare through the hole, watching.

"And you're going to 'elp me, is zat right, pretty boy? How?"

"I can illuminate a path for you."

"Oh, zat sounds very tedious. Maybe you should take off your shirt vile I zink about it? Zat will make target practice more interesting." Allouette spins the dagger around in her hand, then points the tip at George.

"Wait!" he urges. "I feel the anger and know how much pain it causes you. It's what makes you squeeze that handle so tight your fingers hurt. Your fury consumes you, making you feel out of control. You feel you're burning alive. You feel you're carrying an ax in your chest."

Allouette lowers the blade a few inches, her black eyes bearing a sudden heaviness.

"I would agree that this level of emotions would make anyone crazy," George continues, sounding more confident. "But to cause pain just so you don't feel it anymore isn't the way. No one misunderstands you better than you. Each time you hurt someone you create more traumas within yourself, which perpetuates this vicious cycle."

Trent and I exchange confused expressions. Then Allouette puts her blood-covered hands to her face and begins to sob. Again I look at Trent and his expression shows that he's just as bewildered. From behind her hands, Allouette gives a long moan, followed by another loud wail. Then she lowers her hands and unveils a venomous smile. Her teeth are thin and long.

"Nice try, Freud. Did you really zink you'd use words to zave yourself? Zat's charming, and devastatingly naïve," she squeals in her girly voice. "Unfortunately, all your babbling bored me. I vas going to do zomething really naughty, but now I'm just going to kill you." She winks, then pulls back her arm and throws the dagger at George. It races through the air and when it's five feet from him, it freezes. I turn to find Trent deep in concentration.

"George, get through here now," I whisper through clenched teeth.

He turns and moves for the opening. When his foot takes the second step the rocks underneath him give way and he slides to the bottom of the pile.

Oh shit.

Trent tries to turn the dagger around in the air, but Allouette resists. Watching the curvy blade hover in midair chills my core. It turns a quarter of an inch, then swivels back. The blade launches forward a foot and my heart leaps. I'm about to dive through the hole to help George up the pile when Joseph's voice accosts my attention.

"Sis," he says with an edge, "we've got company."

Chapter Thirty-Two

Joseph stands a few feet away, a worried glare directed at a hole in the ceiling of the cave. Streaming through it is morning light and little black dots. I narrow my eyes, forcing them to focus. This room is easily the size of a cathedral and reminds me of one too. The hole is maybe a hundred feet high and to my horror I realize these creatures are not little. One flies down in the stream of sunlight. It's an enormous black bird, double the size of a normal crow.

Urgently I turn back to Trent, who's deep in concentration battling against Allouette. George has made some progress, but is still ten feet down the slippery slope. Torn between my urge to help him and my instinct to investigate the newly arrived birds, I stand motionless. George pins a quick look on me, fingers digging into the broken rock. "Go, Roya. I'm almost out. Trent's got my back."

"Okay. Be fast," I encourage and turn at once, directing my attention to the bright room behind me. Several aquamarine ponds are scattered throughout the space. Stone paths snake between the various pools. They appear to be worn down the same way ancient staircases are. On the opposite side is another entrance. "Joseph." I nod my head in that direction.

"Yep, I've got that one covered," he says, carefully negotiating his way through the stone path toward the entrance.

"What do you make of those things?" Samara asks at my side, pointing towards the birds.

"I'm not certain, but my instinct tells me to keep my eye on them," I say. On my other side Pearl gasps when one of the gigantic birds lands and is soon joined by five others. They fight amongst themselves, pecking each other savagely with curved beaks. With a loud squawk one of the black birds takes flight again, soaring smoothly through the air. It circles above our heads, beady eyes fixed on us. I alternate my eyes between it and its companions on the ground, unsure where the real threat lies.

Behind me Allouette laughs shrilly. It's a long cackle, full of delight. Panicked, I race back in George's direction. I'm halfway there when I hear the scream behind me. Dread freezes me in place and sheer nerve forces me to turn around. The large bird dives overhead, shooting at Pearl like a missile, a menacing look in its eyes. Pearl drops to her knees, tucking her head into her chest and covering herself with shaking arms. The gleam of the chain around her neck peeks out behind her hair. All at once I realize what the birds are after.

"NO!" I scream, lunging forward and simultaneously whipping out my escrima sticks. The bird is too fast, too close. Its beak clips the shiny chain lying on the back of Pearl's neck. Measured wing beats propel the black bird away. It's already too high for me to reach. The sight of the long, silver chain dangling from its beak thins my blood. The possessed creature flies higher and higher, becoming smaller and smaller.

I clutch Pearl by the arm. "Come on, you've got to get up."

Her hands rub her neck, which is already bleeding from the bird's beak. Tears race down her face, a violent moan escaping her mouth. "My charm! It's gone. Chase will get in my head now. I'm dead. I'm already dead," she says in a tortured whisper.

"No, he won't," I say, gripping both her arms. "You have to return to the Institute. Do it now!"

"But—"

"Don't argue. You've got to get out of here."

She nods. "Okay, you're right," she says through ragged breaths.

"Can I get a little help over here?!" Trent's voice calls frantically. He's perched over a blood-drenched George. My heart twists tightly, restricting my breath. Every single part of him appears to be injured somehow.

As I sprint for him, everything speeds up. Pulse. Breath. Movements. "George," I murmur, cradling his blood-covered face in my hands. His eyes flutter open only briefly. Consciousness is a luxury for him right now.

"I couldn't stop it," Trent says. I've never seen a more serious expression on his face.

"You got him here. That's what counts now," I say, running my eyes over the multiple cuts along George's face.

Pearl drags up George's armor. Breath hitches in my throat. Head swims. I almost lose it. There, lodged in his side, is the curved blade. Metal protruding from his flesh doesn't compute. I continue to stare, disbelieving what I'm seeing until blood seeps from the wound and oozes down. This is bad. Extremely bad.

"Trent, give me your bandana," I demand, extending out my hand, not taking my eyes off George's knife wound. The soft fabric of the bandana which was wrapped around Trent's head greets my hand. "Thanks, now move the largest boulder you can to cover that hole." It won't stop her, but it will slow her down.

George's hand in mine is cold and wet with blood. I hover by his side. He drifts in and out of consciousness. Pushing away all the pain churning in this moment, I focus on Pearl. "Can you fix him?"

For the first time I witness her face turn confident. Steadily she places her tiny hands on the hilt of the knife. "Yes."

"Good," I say, the tears rising up in my throat. "As soon as you do then you must travel to the Institute. Okay, on the count of three remove the blade. While I minimize the blood loss you get right to work healing. One. Two. Three."

Pearl's knuckles go white as she grips the blade, trying to free it from George's body. He seizes my hand with an unearthly force, attempting to sit up. My free arm pins his chest down. Gurgled sobs, loud and terrifying, echo out of him and through the cave. And still his eyes don't open. Still he remains locked in a fit of unconscious twitches. "Come on, George. You fight," I whisper.

The blade springs from his body, and Pearl falters back a foot from the release. Immediately, my hands press the bandana into the wound, which is quickly spilling with more blood than I thought possible. All the jerks and flaying have left George's body. He's officially passed out. Lost in shock. "Hurry, Pearl!" I scream, pressing every ounce of pressure I own into George. The crimson-covered knife clatters to the ground as Pearl moves back into position.

Trent has returned, his face three shades paler than it was moments ago. "Hole is secure."

"Good." I regret the order before I give it, but still I force the words out of my mouth. "Take my place here. Help Pearl bring him back."

Trent nods, covering my hands with his own and pressing down as I slip mine away. George's blood drenches my hands like gloves. It's unreal and wrong. My stomach lurches with the sudden urge to spill its contents. Swallowing the bile, I wipe George's blood on my suit and turn my attention to the battle I know is ensuing behind us.

The other five birds. They're attacking Joseph and Samara, diving at their heads. They're trained to go after our charms. It wouldn't take much to slip Samara's earrings off or pinch Joseph's bracelet in half.

Samara parries one bird with her elbow, then pivots and slices another with her sword. It falls to the ground in a heap and convulses. Joseph is seemingly doing pretty well using his fists to batter any of the birds that get too close.

One of the birds dives for me. I shoot forward, spin around, and send my front leg into the air with my back leg tucked. The flying kick successfully collides with the bird, sending him to the ground. Instantly, before he takes flight, I whip my escrima stick down and smash his head against the rock ground.

The three of us form a triangle, our backs to each other. We continue to fight the three remaining birds. They circle us, taking turns diving at our heads. Their loud cries pierce my eardrums.

Then all at once they disappear into the dark cave walls. I take a step back, feeling Samara and Joseph behind me, but not daring to turn around. My bracelet is tight on my wrist and although I know it would be tough to get it off, it wouldn't be impossible. Only one pin needs to be pushed, then it will split in two and be gone, soaring through the air.

Everything's eerily silent. All I hear is a dripping noise. *Drip. Drip. Drip.* All three birds bolt at us from different directions. I make an effort to block, while also not striking my team members behind me. Lunging forward, I attack one of the deranged crow-like birds.

Samara catches her breath, while Joseph defends himself against two birds at once. His knuckles and hands are red and bloody. "Hey!" I shout at him. He looks up in time to catch the stick I tossed in his direction. Reenergized by the new weapon, Joseph unleashes a series of swift strikes, knocking both birds down to the stone ground.

"Get the last one," I say. "I'm going to check on the others."

Relief doesn't even begin to describe how satisfying it feels to see George sitting up. It's hard to believe moments ago he was unconscious. I want to run to him, press my hands against his skin to ensure his heart still beats. Morning light cuts across the distance that separates us, casting everything in a hazy glow. Moving as quickly as I can without slipping on the slick stone I trace a path to him.

The three of them sit by the edge of a pond. George must be washing off the blood. As I get closer I realize he's not moving. Neither is Pearl or Trent. They sit stock-still, eyes focused to the middle of the pond. I follow their gaze to find something so bizarre I quickly blink to clear my vision. A droplet materializes six feet above the pond, suspends momentarily, then drops onto the water's surface, casting ripples. Then in the same spot as the last one another drop materializes and falls. And again. And again. And again.

Even the knowledge that I'm being hypnotized doesn't allow me to look away. Another droplet materializes in thin air and falls on the water's surface, creating the most uniquely beautiful ripples. Again my eyes rise up just as a new droplet forms and again I follow it down. Although entranced by the mysterious display, my eyes still blink, my mind still thinks. I admit to the compulsive allure, but deep inside I know I'm in control. The force I need to look away is within me, a locked box only I can access. The key is a thought, which unlocks an indomitable spirit, one that rages forward causing my head to shake suddenly. It's enough to disrupt my attention from the hypnosis. My eyes jerk away and although I'm queasy and drained, I'm also relieved to have fought back. I'm grounded firmly in myself.

My relief is short-lived when I spin around and focus on the other three. They're fully entranced. Their faces slackened, eyes devoid of emotion. *How long has this been going on?*

Placing myself between them and the hypnotic spectacle I wave my arms wildly. "Hey! Hey! It's me! Roya! Look away now!" No eyes flicker from their focal point. Nothing changes. Assaulted by a new fear I clasp George's shoulders with both my hands, shake him. "Look at me! Fight this! Please!" He moves. My pulse quickens. To my horror George only leans three inches so he can continue staring at the water.

From the corner of my vision I see Samara and Joseph have been victorious against the birds and are rushing over to join us. "Stay there," I order. "Watch the door." The last thing I need is those two spellbound.

How am I going to break this hypnosis? I can't reach the droplet. The rippling water, though—it's a part of the equation. Turning around I ram my hand into the pond, bent on disturbing the effect. Scorching fire attacks. Immediately I retract my hand, which is already blistering from the burn. The water is boiling hot.

"No! No! No!" I scream, almost cry. I clap in their faces, my burned hand smarting instantly. But I don't care; I've got to stop this. "You're being hypnotized!" I scream louder than before.

Pearl cocks her head at me sharply, her eyes lost somehow. A sudden robotic smile. "No, not all of us are being hypnotized," she says, in a voice that isn't hers. "Just these two."

My heart races. Oh, God! Chase is controlling her now. Devastation rips through me, a wild beast. Now I have an android and two zombies. Heat rises in my head as I stare between George and Trent and Pearl. Ren said only one option was left once Chase controlled someone. But I can't do that. Won't.

A spot of red appears beneath Trent's nose. Then the blood begins to ooze from both nostrils.

"Looks like he's ready to be undressed," Pearl says, standing up like a robot and teetering over to Trent.

Chapter Thirty-Three

"Joseph! Samara!" I yell, never taking my eyes off Pearl. She's two feet from Trent. "Get over here now!"

One foot away. Not seeing any other options I lunge forward, sending the escrima stick into Pearl's abdomen. I knew she was tiny, but not until I assaulted her with a deadly weapon did I realize how unbelievably fragile she is. Her knees buckle and she doubles over, gasping for breath. Strange that even a possessed body knows how to react to pain.

"Stark!" Joseph bellows, halting beside me, a stunned expression on his face. "What are you doing?" His eyes flick down to my bracelet, tightly clasped on my wrist.

"I'm not the one who lost my protective charm. It's Pearl. She's under Chase's control." My words are cold and distant. "Restrain her."

Joseph and Samara each seize one of her rail-thin arms. Pearl tugs wildly between the two of them, her movements doing little to free her. "Please let me go," she says with a persuasive whine. "I'm fine. Seriously. He's gone now." Her voice still doesn't sound like her own, it's more pinched, more deliberate.

Joseph and Samara exchange uneasy looks. "Hold on to her. Don't let her go, no matter what," I say firmly. "I have to help these guys. They've been hypnotized."

A chill runs down my spine when I turn my attention back to George and Trent. Blood now pours out of both of their noses. It's leaked down past Trent's chin, snaking its way to his neck. George, who doesn't have much blood left to lose, is the color of copy paper.

This isn't good. Are they going to die in front of me? Is there nothing I can do? Ren said that to break the hypnosis the illusion had to be stopped. But that's impossible. The droplet is out of reach and the pond boiling hot.

Drip. Drip. Drip. The silence between the drips makes it impossible to think. Watching Trent and George slowly sink further into a comatose state arrests any focus I have left. *Drip. Drip. Drip.*

"Damn it! We have to find a way to stop this." I turn, seeking refuge from Joseph and Samara. Doom plummets to the bottom of my stomach. They can't help me. In unison Joseph's and Samara's eyes rise up, watch the droplet form, and then trail it down, like a cat following a string in the air. They're entranced. Pearl stands free, her hands by her side, like a soldier robot.

Drip. Drip. Drip. It's the leak from a faucet in a sleeping house. I'm the only one awake and it's driving me mad!

"Joseph," I say, a scared hiccup in my throat. "Wake up." As I suspected his attention doesn't waver from the illusion. Moment by moment I know he's sinking deeper away. His vibrant eyes are empty, stuck in another world. One I don't know how to pull him back from. One that's quickly sucking the life out of the people I love.

"NOOOOO!" I roar, a new rage taking shape inside me. The Voyageurs abducted Aiden, mutilated George, possessed Pearl, and now are going to suck every bit of consciousness from the people in this room.

"No," I say again, a cold firmness in my voice. Hot winds battle inside me, burning everything until I can't take the pain any longer. I stare at the pond, the object that will destroy everyone around me. "No," I say in a clipped whisper. Maybe I didn't understand Bob's words before. Maybe I don't believe them now. But engulfed by my powerful rage this idea feels right: *I am the wind.*

With everything I have left I push an energy, raw and ancient, out of me. It stirs a gentle breeze, one that rustles my hair. I encourage it, feeding it every emotion within me: hate, fear, desire, love. A force the size of a gale unleashes inside me, pulling my chest skyward like something is being sucked out. For a second I believe my toes will come off the ground as the last bit of power barrels out of me. Blinding white light explodes in front of my vision.

Around me the wind howls. Angry. Vengeful. Using my emotional turmoil I ignite it to greater speeds, urging it to rip apart this cave if that's what it takes. *Yes, blast everything, sweet wind. Destroy everything, even if that means destroying me.* My vision clears to a storm of dust and water spinning horizontally around me, but my hair and clothes remain still. A cursory glance around confirms what I instinctively knew: I'm in the eye of the storm. I am the storm.

I thrust the storm forward. As it moves, it sweeps my hair around my face, stroking me like soft sandpaper. I cover my face

179

from the debris unleashed by the powerful winds. When its gusts fade I open my eyes to the most stunning sight.

There in front of me, at exactly my height, is a cyclone. It hovers in place for a moment before ripping through the pond, spraying water all over the walls of the cave and the nearby banks. The illusion of the droplet can't be seen through all of the wind's disruptions. Still furious, I roar so loud that my chest vibrates. My cyclone shoots forward and bursts into a pile of rocks sending it in all directions. The pond doesn't exist anymore. Its water has exploded onto the nearby stones and walls. The hypnotic illusion is gone. Destroyed.

Chapter Thirty-Four

All at once exhaustion crashes down on me. My legs give way, sending me to the stone ground where I can barely hold myself up on all fours. The power it took to harness the wind drained every last bit of energy I have left. Ironically the breath I need so much to survive is almost too taxing a chore for my lungs to perform. I close my eyes to an inky-black darkness. It's vast. Swallows me. Traps me in a blind prison. Seeps the tiny bit of energy I have left.

And then a spark. So small. Again it flickers across my vision, like fire. With a sudden renewed energy I raise my head. My eyes burst open to the one sight I never thought I'd see again. Crouched before me is Joseph, a tired look of concern on his face. His hand reaches out, touches my forehead. And warmth, like sunlight, flows into me, revitalizing my depleted reserves. A trace of a smile tugs on his lips. "Thanks," I say, my voice shredded.

"My energy is yours," Joseph says, an earnest generosity in his eyes.

The rest of my team is soaking wet and moving, albeit slowly. They look disoriented and slightly burned from the water, but they've been released. All of them but Pearl, who's back in frozen robot mode.

Rising, I move to George's side. He's rubbing his eyes, smearing blood all over his already battered face. I begin pushing away some of the blood from his eyes with my fingertips. A quiet, intimate moment passes where I communicate something deep, not caring if his ability has returned yet. This emotion isn't for him. It's one I need to feel. Not taking my eyes off George I say, "Hey, Joseph." He doesn't respond, but I sense my brother at my shoulder. "Watch Pearl at all times."

"K," he says, shuffling behind me.

"Are you all right?" I ask George, a tenderness tightening around my heart.

He shakes his head, looking at me but seeming blind. "I don't know."

I cup his face. He's fragile somehow. "You will be all right."

I spy Trent over his shoulder, looking not as far off, but still confused.

George grimaces, his hand grasping his side. "Pearl fixed you, right?" I ask.

"Kind of," Trent answers for him.

I don't ask permission, but instead pull up George's torn armor. The wound is mostly sealed, but still bleeding.

"She was half done when we got pulled away," Trent explains, joining me. "She'd sealed up his leg and some of the more serious lacerations on his neck, but she didn't finish with that one." Trent shoots George a faint smile. "I'd take it easy if I were you."

"I'll try," he says, breathing through the pain.

"I want you out of here," I demand.

"No," he says, gritting his teeth.

"Our healer is gone. You need attention now."

"I'm not leaving you."

"Don't argue with me," I whisper two inches from his face.

"How will you find Aiden without me?" he says.

My mind dead-ends in frustration. He's right. We don't know exactly where Aiden is and without George's empathesis I'm not sure we can locate him quickly enough. I ease back on my heels, my heart thundering. There has to be an alternative other than risking George's life to save Aiden's.

"You've lost a lot of blood. There's only one cure for that," I say.

He pushes himself up with great effort. "But I'm still fine."

"Trent." I turn to him.

"Yeah, boss," he says, looking a million times better than he did five minutes ago.

"Keep an eye on this one." I motion at George.

Samara and Joseph stand rigidly beside Pearl. Thankfully they hadn't been under the hypnosis for long. Still, Joseph gave some of his energy to me, meaning we're both weak. With over half the team injured and depleted we need to find Aiden and get out of here…before it's too late. My eyes flick to Pearl. In her present state I'm not sure I can send her back to the Institute. Nothing from my training covered this. With Chase controlling her I'm uncertain what risks she poses once inside the walls of the Institute. And once he knows how to enter our walls, will we ever be safe again? I'm not sure if I can allow her to return. The idea scorches my heart with instant guilt. How can I banish her here? Is that better than what Ren would have me do?

From the other side of the room echoes a weak cough. All our heads snap in that direction. A short young man limps along the stone floor, a contorted hand pinned at his chest. He wobbles through the sunlight portion of the room and toward us. His jawline is uneven and the hair on his head grows in patches. I assemble the group behind me, although I'm not sure why. I don't feel the least bit of fear from this weak and feeble creature.

Only a few feet from us, he stops. Wheezes. "Since nothing I have done appears to stop you, Roya, then I think we only have one more option." The man looks at me with crossed brown eyes. Strangely, he doesn't have a French accent. Doesn't have an accent at all. Each word is pronounced with an odd precision. "Let us try talking."

I have a hard time believing this tiny man is Chase. Somehow I pictured him differently. Strong. Healthy. Older.

"I don't want anyone to die," Chase says, forehead wrinkling. "You must know that. We both have goals and maybe if we sit down and discuss them we can find an option that pleases both parties."

I study him, watching every mannerism, dissecting his sincerity. "Aiden is fine," Chase offers. "You know it was his choice to come here? He has discovered a happy life as a Voyageur."

Something is wrong about this, but I can't figure it out. What's the trick here?

"You don't believe me, your face tells me that much. The Lucidites have brainwashed you to fight us, but is that really what you want to do? I truly don't want to fight," the man says in his strange voice. "The Lucidites always want to battle us, when all we want is to work together. Don't be like them."

His words strum a note, one I resist to label persuasive. Still, what if I've perceived everything wrong? This is the complete opposite of what I've been taught. But I've been taught by the Lucidites. What if it's true? Studiously apprising Chase, I realize I don't fear him. What's more, something compels me to believe him. As he tries to focus his crossed eyes on me I realize I pity him, like a lonely, elderly man in a mental hospital.

"Come and sit and we'll talk," he says, gesturing to a set of rocks. "It's time we acted civilized, don't you think?"

Uncertainty squirms around my mind. Not letting him out of my sight I gauge my group. Their uniform faces tell me they harbor the same hesitation. "Joseph," I call, standing at my back, "keep a guard on Pearl?"

"There's no need for that," Chase chimes. "I've released her."

I turn to Pearl. "It's true, he has. I'm fine." She pushes her hair back behind her ear and squints.

I give Joseph a look and he seems to understand. He nods. Turning back I make note of Samara standing on one side of me, seeming to be on guard of the entrance where Chase had come from. Trent is on my other side and he's mostly steady, although at times he kind of wavers a bit, still recovering from the hypnosis.

Chase motions with his good arm. "Won't you join me over here for a private chat? We can resolve this all, I'm sure."

A clairvoyant flash bursts across my vision: A different man stands before me. He's spookily similar to Chase. His mannerisms. His teeth. His voice. But the man in my vision is tall, with black hair, pale skin, and electric blue eyes. His eyes pierce me, trying to cut from the inside out. The vision fades and I know exactly what I have to do.

At lightning speed I whip the sword out of Samara's sheath and raise it in the air. The crippled man doesn't run, flinch, or fight. The sword is heavy in my weakened arms. Still I drive it down cleanly, slicing the projection in two. It explodes into a cloud of dust and smoke. Incensed breaths pound my chest up and down. Not Chase. Just another trick.

Stunned expressions stare back at me from my team members. I shrug, at a loss for words. Flipping the sword around I hand it back to Samara, feeling a huge weight lifted when she takes it.

Clapping reverberates from the entrance. A sharp, steady sound. A figure enters, taking the same path that the crippled man had just taken. However, he glides across the space, his movements too graceful, too seamless. It's the man from my vision and he's no doubt the most attractive person I've ever laid eyes on. His jet black hair is smooth and pushed away from his intoxicatingly flawless face. Stark white skin makes his pink lips stand out more than any mouth I'd ever noticed. He floats closer, still clapping.

184

Unnerved by his perfection, I gasp. I can't believe he elicits this response from me. Pausing a few feet from me, he drops his hands by his side. Unnaturally drawn to him, I take two steps closer. A smile curls from his mouth and he stares at me ravenously. I'm not afraid in this moment. I'm absolutely trembling inside, but it's from the adrenaline produced when this man strode into the room.

Taking off to my left he makes a tight circle around me, like a wolf. Solid, straight-backed, I listen to each of his footsteps. "Congratulations, Roya." It's the same voice from the projection, but now it does something different to me. Undoes my restraints. Entices hedonism. "You," he says, lingering on the word. "*You* resisted my hypnosis. *You* destroyed my illusion. *You* spotted my projection. And *you* control the wind. Ms. Stark, pardon me if this sounds forward, but I think you're my soul mate."

Chapter Thirty-Five

Chase completes a full circle around me. I remain frozen, completely petrified as he stares, and I can tell he's restraining a smile. I don't even blink when he leans down and whispers in my ear, "Together, you and I would be amazing."

His voice penetrates a part of my core. There's something really wrong about this situation. I figured my skin would be crawling right now, but it isn't. Arousal prickles down my neck, unleashed by his whispered breath.

Chase's eyes lift, evaluating the group behind me with a threatening glare. Like shaking off his last hypnosis, I force myself back from this weird place he's sent me. Two steps backwards put me flush up against George. Joseph steps forward, directly on my right. His presence reassures me I'm not dreaming.

Now focusing solely on me, Chase snakes his electric blue eyes up and down my body. When he meets my eyes, he tilts his head, a lusciously satisfied expression on his face. "You obviously want to protect them," he says, gracefully gesturing at the group. "How about I let them go? Hell, I'll even release Aiden." His lips purse seductively. "But I want to keep you."

"How about," I say, testing my voice, "you let Aiden go, let us all go, and I won't kill you." I'm bluffing. I don't have a clue how to kill Chase. And strangely I don't want to right now. The last thing I want to do is harm him.

He grabs his chest and pretends to look hurt. "Oh, Roya," he says in a hushed voice. "Your threats disappoint me so. I was dearly hoping we could be more than *just* enemies." His eyes pierce me like I saw in my vision, cutting open my essence. Damn it if he isn't the most striking person who ever lived.

A scream shatters the air. High-pitched. Assaulting. Instantly I spin around to the source. Pearl stands, mouth open, blood curdling at her throat. Wide eyes stare at nothing. Horror rips through me as I try to compute what's happening. The blood-drenched dagger slips from her hand as she drops to her knees and falls straight on her face. Samara stands directly behind her, a traumatized look of disbelief on her long face. Plunged into Pearl's back is Samara's silver sword.

The same scream as before bursts from Samara's mouth. Gripping her cheeks in the oddest of ways she shakes her head erratically. "NO! NO! NO! NO!" she screams, staring at Pearl's dead body. Samara makes to reach for her but then retreats, now on the brink of hyperventilating. "I didn't...I...I...I..." A loud wail makes her lips tremble.

Poised and ready with my escrima stick in hand, I approach Samara, careful to keep Chase in my line of vision. "What happened?" I ask, keeping my voice neutral.

A torrent of tears floods her red cheeks. "I...I...I...I..." she says, only focusing on the blood oozing around the sword in Pearl's back.

"Samara," I say. "It's okay. Tell us what happened."

Her gray eyes flick to mine, confused, like she just realized I was here. Again her head shakes, like a dog's after a bath, but with no joy. Whitish blonde hair tangles around her face when she lifts her chin and this time fastens her eyes on Joseph.

"Pearl," she says to Joseph, her voice tattered from tears. "She was about to cut your throat. You *have* to believe me. You *have* to believe me."

Joseph's face couldn't be any whiter, but his expression darkens.

"We believe you, Samara," I say cautiously.

She nods her head, a strange confidence returning from my endorsement. "She was behind you, Joseph. I heard her think, *cut his throat*. I had to stop her."

Pearl's dead body lies face down on the ground, Allouette's curved dagger a few inches from her fingers.

Oh God, this just got to a new level of sick.

Samara's words are hysterical, a rush of emotion. "Him! It was him! He was never going to let her go. He was making her do it!" A long finger points directly at Chase. "It was your voice in her head, controlling her thoughts."

A self-satisfied arrogance exudes from Chase's eyes. The edges of his mouth twitch into a poised smile.

Joseph turns at once and puts his arms around Samara. She explodes into a fresh batch of tears, her chest convulsing from the explosive emotion.

"You," I say, like it's a disgusting word.

"Guilty as charged," he coos, stepping closer to me.

With only a foot separating us I should be on the defensive against him. I'm disgusted, my stomach a raw pit of fury, but I don't feel endangered. "Look at what you've done. An innocent girl is dead." A throbbing veil of rage blankets my vision.

"Oh, but I'm not the one who killed her, am I?" he says wickedly.

Every fiber of my being says I should attack this psychopath. Overpower him using strength, then resume this mission. But I'm not yet ready to strike his chiseled face.

"How can you be so horrible? So evil?" My words sound strangely disappointed. "How can you stand yourself? How can you even stand to look in the mirror? You're the devil!" My anger from before starts to build again and I half expect to feel the wind on my back.

Chase smiles broadly, showing elegantly sharp canines. "Looking in the mirror is quite enjoyable. And in case you're wondering, I sleep just fine too." He reaches out and runs his hand along my cheek. His fingers are like ice. "You're more than welcome to sleep beside me."

Why don't I move? Why don't I take this close-range chance to attack him? Why can't I move? I'm frozen. Again.

"It's easy, Roya." Chase drops his hand and leans in so he's only an inch from my face. "No one else has to die." His breath smells sweet. Too sweet. "Stay with me and your friends will be safe. I assure you."

A bird's wings beat overhead in a rush. Chase turns first to look, freeing me from his hypnosis. Diving through the air at me is an enormous bird. The crows are back. *Not again!* I grip my bracelet with my other hand, this time worried I'll actually lose it. And then I'll be lost forever, like Pearl.

Oddly, Chase's eyes go wide, a look of alarm on his face. *Isn't that his bird?* Scrambled footsteps send him backwards, nothing graceful in his movements now. The bird chirps, a high-pitched musical sound that's almost inviting. Then it dives feet first like it's about to pluck a fish out of the water. Through the morning sunshine I realize it doesn't resemble a crow at all. And more importantly it isn't diving at me. Its sharp talons aim for Chase's dark hair. He throws up his arms, thrashing the bird away. The beating of the bird's wings sends wind against my face. This is no ordinary animal. It's huge. Majestic. Powerful flaps of its wings send it back in the air. Then it dives, this time beak first, going after Chase again.

Joseph grips my arm, pulling me tenaciously toward the exit. "Come on, sis, let's get out of here." A tentative glance over my shoulder. The bird of prey swoops down again, scratching wildly at the devastatingly gorgeous psychopath of a man. An urgent tug from Joseph propels me forward at a sprint, my feet splashing through puddles, leaving Pearl's dead body behind.

The rest of the group is already at the exit, staring at me, bewildered. How long have they been here? How long was I entranced in the battle?

"Trent," I say, my head clearing the farther I get from Chase. "Can you block this entrance?"

He nods his chin. "Sure, thing, hon."

From the archway I watch a nearby boulder levitate off the ground. It's roughly five feet in diameter. Easily weighs several tons. It soars through the air like it's made of cotton rather than limestone. "I'd move out of the way," Trent warns, stepping backwards as he directs the path of the boulder. With a crunching groan it fits like a perfect puzzle piece into the archway, shutting out the sunlight and leaving us bathed in darkness once more.

Firelight casts a daunting glow on everyone's faces. I know they want to double over from emotional and physical exhaustion, but they stand staring at me, waiting for direction.

"Joseph, will you scout the area to ensure we're safe here for now?"

"I'm on it," he says, heading at once down the dark cave-way.

"The rest of you take a few minutes to rest. We're going to have to keep moving soon."

George slumps against a wall at once. I want to go to him, but Samara cuts me off.

"I didn't want to be the one to do it. You know that, right?" she says, a pleading in her voice.

"I know," I say.

"But she was so close to killing Joseph and I had no choice. And…and…and…Ren told us that we'd have to…that if Chase got inside someone that…"

"That they were gone for good," I say, knowing she doesn't want to say it. "I know once he was done using her that Pearl's life would be over, that he'd kill her. But I kept thinking there was a way to save her." A shaky breath spills out of my lips. "I wasn't ready yet to accept Ren's advice." And it was only advice, not the only way to manage the situation. Because how could I accept that the only option left was to kill her ourselves? Without a direct threat how was I going to murder Pearl to save her the suffering Chase would cause? And what if it had been anyone else on my team? The idea of killing Joseph instantly coats my tongue with bile.

"So you think I did the right thing?" Samara asks, doubt in her voice.

"You did what had to be done. And you saved Joseph's life. I can never express how grateful I am for that."

"Neither can I," Joseph says, taking the position beside me. A warm, silent exchange transpires between Samara and him before he turns. "All is clear for fifty yards."

"Okay, thanks. Let's move in one minute," I say. Adrenaline still pounds through my veins, not allowing any real emotions to seep too deep. For now that's keeping me alive, but soon everything is going to soak in and then…well, I'll think about that later. "Does anybody have any clue where that bird came from?" I ask in a conspiratorial whisper.

"Osprey. That's what that was," Joseph says, a proud expression on his face. "You didn't think you were the only one between us who had a spirit animal, did you?" He winks.

"What? That was you? You summoned that bird?"

"Well, I was pretty certain if something didn't happen quickly then you were gonna become Frankenstein's bride back there," he says with a smirk.

Heat rises to my head. "Yeah, well, thanks."

"Told ya you'd be glad you brought me along," Joseph sings too loudly.

"Quiet down. And seriously, right now isn't the time for gloating." I push him aside so I can move closer to George. He's still slumped against a wall, eyes closed.

"How are you feeling?"

"I'm great. Feeling better actually," he lies.

I put my hands on his cheeks and rest them there for a second. He's burning up, but I can't be sure that this isn't because he's just witnessed a brutal murder and the acts of a psychopath. As we have so many times before, we communicate through nonverbal ways. Me reading his eyes. Him reading my emotions. It only lasts a moment, but it's enough.

Turning back to the group I say, "All right, let's move. Joseph and I are going to take the front. George, you're in the middle. Trent and Samara bring up the rear." Everyone gives a silent nod.

Similar to the first cave-way, this one is lined with torches every ten feet. This prevents me from ramming my head on low-hanging arches. The only thing I hear, besides our footsteps, is a quieter version of the awful screeching noise I heard when we first arrived. It isn't like nails on a chalkboard; it's like metal scraping metal.

If the map is correct then one of the next set of rooms is the most likely place Aiden is being held. The problem is there are now doors every few feet. We've already passed a dozen. Each one I come to fills me with anticipation and anxiety. Each shuffle of footsteps makes me jerk, thinking Allouette is going to spring out and assault us. I should be vigilant, but the apprehension is doing my adrenal gland no good at this point. And still I worry that when we reach Aiden I'll be unable to help him. Ren thinks that most obstacles to Aiden will be Voyageurs. But what if he's wrong? What if he's behind a locked door I can't enter? What if there's something chaining him to the Grotte and I can't rescue him? Will this all be for nothing?

Joseph and I move several yards before I realize the team is not behind us. I freeze. Pivot. And spy George immobile, staring at a door. A few quick strides bring me back to him. "He's in there," he says, pointing at the door, not taking his eyes off it.

His words hollow out my chest. "Are you sure?"

He's already nodding before I finish my question. "Yes." George looks at me and gives a wounded smile although I know he's in a lot of pain. Why is he smiling? Because it's over for him? Because we found Aiden?

"George, I need you to be sure because before we enter that room I'm sending you back. You need medical attention now. If Aiden isn't in there then we're lost without you. So are you certain this is the right room?"

"Yes, I'm sure. Unless there's another prisoner here who's starving, scared, and tortured."

A raw ache attacks my core, gnawing at it, seeking substance which I can't give.

"I'm sorry, I—" George says through a measured breath, clutching his side.

"Don't be," I cut him off. "It's all right. We're here now."

"He's fine, Roya," George says in a half-heartbroken voice. "And yes, it's him. I'm sure of it." Reluctance I've seen too many times in his eyes surfaces. "His passion, even under these circumstances, is distinct. Through that door lies Dr. Livingston."

I should be relieved, but something real feels about to end, and with it another beginning is sprouting. Still, I'm not ready to move forward, but backwards was never an option. Swallowing down my fear, I nod.

"Thanks. Now it's time for you to go home," I say, and for the first time all day I feel a little relief. To know George is safe gives me comfort. Now I just need to make it happen. I'm careful not to touch any of his wounds as I place both hands on either side of his face, directing his attention at nothing but me. "Return to the Institute and have Mae fix you, because I need you whole. Okay?" I look at him for a long moment. He doesn't waver.

"Okay," is all he says, pain a precursor and punctuation to his word. His weight slips to the floor. Trent helps me lower him to the ground. He's so much weaker now that he's quit pretending. It makes my insides burn with disgust. I'll kill Allouette if I see her again.

I cradle George's head in my lap. The cold stone floor is hard and sharp under my legs. "I'll stay here until you generate your body," I say, brushing hair out of his face.

He squeezes my hand. "Thanks. And Roya, get out of here soon. I need you whole too."

"I won't keep you waiting long," I say and kiss his brow.

A smile greets his lips before his eyes close. For this night only the security measures requiring bodies to be submerged in water to dream travel to the Institute have been suspended. My hands hold his head for less than a minute when the minuscule sparks begin flecking away from his body at an increasing rate. The sight is perfectly poetic. Second by second it increases until his body is only a few sparks that are soon whisked away into darkness. My heart falters between beaming and sinking. Now my hands hold nothing. George is gone.

Chapter Thirty-Six

One stone door stands between Aiden and me. After the longest week of my life everything is going to shift. I wished I could say it was going to get better, but I don't know exactly what lies on the other side of that door. And there's still so much that lies between the guy inside that room and me. Will he still know me? Care for me? And will I still love him?

"Are you ready?" Joseph says at my side. His eyes are pinned on the door the same as mine, but he's not worried about the same things as me.

"Yeah," I whisper, pressing the side of my face against the cold stone. Nothing greets my ear. Stepping back I gauge the door. "What's the trick?" I ask without looking at Joseph.

"Maybe nothing," he says, scanning the rollers along the door. "Appears about like the other doors in here."

"Let's hope appearances aren't deceiving."

I push against the stone, and it engages in its track where it groans before allowing me to guide it backward. Like the doors in the Institute it glides into a recess inside the cave walls. The light from the connecting room flickers across my vision; it's more brightly lit than the cave-way. An almost bare room stands before me, save for the slumped figure in a metal chair.

A thousand years could pass and I would still recognize him. Feet I forgot I possessed rush forward, magnetized to the guy before me. I hear the door glide back shut. That's not all I hear. Aiden's breath, a quiet rasp. Each one's trying to hold him to the earth, but I feel the drain he's suffering from. For too long I stare at his wilting figure, metal-encased head slumped over his lap, arms pulling him down by an unnatural weight. Aiden sits, bony and mostly naked in his boxer shorts. My eyes have a hard time resisting exploring the parts of him which have always made me curious. I shake this off and step closer.

The dream blocker makes his face look absurdly small. His arms look too long as they trail beside him. That's when I notice his hands are encased in silver boxes locked around his wrist. He looks like half man, half robot. But the bruises and cuts scattered all over his chest and arms remind me that he's no machine. Under all that metal is Aiden. My Aiden.

Longing in my heart breaks out of the cage where I banished it, charging forward. All at once I realize Aiden makes me human. Before him I thought I was a freak. And since my life started with the Lucidites I've felt supernatural. But Aiden makes me weak and vulnerable and absolutely perfect in all of my flaws. He makes me feel human.

Too long I soak in his lonely figure. I know my team is watching behind me, questioning my paralysis. With his eyes still closed he rubs his metal-encased hands against his metal-encased head, causing the worst screeching sound imaginable. It's the one I heard when I entered the Grotte.

My body is a surreal distance from him. In all my recent dreams I've imagined closing this space a hundred times. In each one he vaporizes within my arms. Too afraid to lose him again I hang back, not touching him. My words a cautious whisper. "Aiden, it's me. It's Roya. I'm here. I'm going to take you home."

His clunky metal hands fall, loosely swinging by his side. A baffled look on his face.

"Aiden, can you hear me?" I ask, looking closely for a response in his expression.

Nothing.

With steady hands I jerk the helmet that has been holding him captive off his head. My attention is on him before I even place the dream blocker on the ground. One of his eyes is almost swollen shut, blackened. Long cuts line one of his cheeks. "Oh, what have they done to you?" I shudder.

Blue eyes jerk open, sincere disbelief in them. I halt my words, my actions. I'm petrified, but not like with Chase. I can still move if I want to, but I don't want to. I'm suspended in time, and forever and ever I want to live in this moment where all my nightmares have been put to rest. In this place where Aiden is whole and safe and next to me. But this reality must be short-lived, because the only way to rescue Aiden is to let him go.

"It's time to get you out of here," I say, all business. "You're free. Go home now," I tell him, my eyes barely meeting his as I turn back to watch my team shuffle uncomfortably behind me.

"Roya," he says, his voice a coarse whisper. "This isn't real. You aren't here, are you?" His hand comes up to touch my face, but fear surges through him before he makes contact, sending his metal-covered hand back to his body.

The torment he's experienced is all too apparent on his lined face. It echoes through my heart like an off-key broken instrument. All my restraint wavers in that moment. My eyes sweep across Trent, Samara, and finally Joseph. I've traveled and lost so much for this guy who's valuable to the Institute. But to me he's priceless. "To hell with pretenses," I say, and throw hungry arms around him. "It's me, Aiden. I'm here to take you home."

A jolt rocks his chest, one so brief and sudden I question whether I actually felt it. Still he hesitates before sinking his chin down into my shoulder, burying his face in my hair. He takes great care to keep his metal enclosed hands off me, but still his arms slide across my back, tugging me into him with an intensity I've dreamed about too many times.

"Oh, God, Roya," he says in a hush, one only I can hear. "This can't be real. Please tell me it is."

I ease back, pressing my forehead against his, which is coated in sweat. Just as much as him, I need to know this is real, because I still don't believe it. Not until his cracked lips graze mine, a thoughtful purity behind them, do I believe he's real. Nothing feels like Aiden. Nothing ever could.

I pull back, knowing we have to act before we lose our chance. Samara, Trent, and Joseph pretend to be studying the room, but I spy the awkwardness in their actions. *Oh well.* If we all live then I'll deal with this then. I'll face their questions proudly. Hopefully Aiden will too.

Composing myself, I stare down at Aiden. "We don't have much time. You need to travel to the Institute. Now."

A deranged look sprints across his face. "Are you coming?"

"Yes," I say, looking into his eyes, the ones I've missed so much. "But you have to go first."

He nods, looking weak and frail, but still amazing. Remembering something, I reach down and pick up the dream blocker. His body repulses at once. "You have to take it back. It's yours. None of us can do it," I say, hurt by the look in his scared eyes. The hesitation subsides and he puts his metal encased hands on it, pressing it into his lap. "Yes, of course," he says in a voice so strong it captures my heart.

"Go now," I say again, pushing the hair out of his face. He nods and closes his eyes, bowing his head down so it almost meets the dream blocker in his lap. My hand stays on his cold shoulder until his body disappears, like dust being swept away by a soft wind. When the last bit of him vanishes, I straighten. My job is done. Aiden is safe. He's at the Institute.

The space feels quieter without Aiden. Empty. Glancing up to the team, I already know what I'll see. Nervous tension. "Yeah, well, if you didn't know, now you do. Keep your traps shut about it and get the hell out of this place," I say, knotting my arms across my chest.

"Guess that explains why you keep brushing me off. Thought I was beginning to lose my charm. And your secret is safe with me," Trent says with a salute. "Beam me up, Scotty." He closes his eyes and disappears faster than either George or Aiden. I know he's happy to be going home.

"Ditto to what Trent said," Samara says. Her eyelids gracefully close off her pained, gray eyes. I know her battle isn't over, but I hope her agony will subside when she returns to the Institute.

Both their bodies disappear within a minute, leaving Joseph and me anxiously staring at each other.

"Your turn," I say.

He squints through the darkness. "I don't want to leave you. Let's go together."

"No, we have to take turns generating. And I'm the leader. I need to make sure your body remains safe until the process is complete," I argue. "You go first and I'll meet you there. I'm safe in here. Just go."

"What about your body? Who watches over you?"

"God, I guess," I say with a smirk.

"Not funny, sis."

"We're wasting time. Will you please get out of here?"

Reluctantly he closes his eyes. "I'm only doing this because I know if I don't you'll kick my ass," he says, half laughing.

"Get out of here already," I say.

"I'm already gone," he says. And a few seconds later I see the first particles of his body begin to sweep away.

197

Completed. I actually completed this impossible mission. A quiet victory constricts my throat with tears I didn't realize lived within my body. I haven't cried...since he was abducted. Since I stood up to this challenge. But now my tears mean something new. They mean I persevered. I'm a human who can do things I shouldn't be able to and still live to tell about them. My eyes close, my mind ready to transport me, and then the wheels on the track screech.

Chapter Thirty-Seven

Jerking away from my travels, I focus on the door in front of me. It slowly glides back to reveal an enemy. I consider ignoring the intrusion and escaping, but that would only put me in the blind position of having my body ransacked by whatever demon enters this space. It's too late to dream travel. I have to face whatever appears on the other side of that door. And I have to do it alone. I wait for the person to materialize. It takes an eternity for the stone door to inch back on its track. Is it Chase? Will I be banished to live out the rest of my days as his concubine? A part of me thinks there are worse fates. I shake my head. *What am I thinking?*

The face that stares back at me from the doorway takes a moment to compute in my mind. I should have expected it. Of course I should have, but my mind isn't working in a logical manner anymore. Her brown eyes stare back at me, an evil in them I was never acquainted with before this moment. It was always there, lurking beneath the surface, a hidden part of her she disguised. I should have seen it. We all should have seen it. Then none of this would have happened.

"Well, I guess you've saved him," Amber says without much effort.

Vengeance courses through me, so pure and satisfying. I'm glad I stayed until this moment just so I can break her pinched little nose. "Yeah, I guess I have," I say.

"No real loss for us though," she says evenly. "He was kind of useless. I was hoping he'd be a bit more compliant."

I scrunch up my nose. "Sounds like you didn't know him well."

She narrows her eyes and lunges at me, her braid sweeping over her shoulder. I stand, not moving from my position. Her fist rises into the air, stopping a breath away from my face. I still don't flinch. She steps back, anger flashing in her eyes.

"You're too weak to hit someone. We both know that," I say.

"Shut up," she says, a ridiculous frustration in her voice. Now would be a good time to punch her in the face, but I want to wait until I've thoroughly pissed her off. Then I'll knock her out and head home.

"So you were hoping for a promotion out of this whole thing?" I say, remembering what Samara had said.

"I always knew you'd be a problem," Amber says, staring down at me from her high vantage point. "Since that first task, I knew you'd get in my way. Should have done away with you then. The Lucidites might treasure you, others might be confused about your usefulness, but I'm not deceived. You're trash."

Hungry for this battle I step forward, cutting the space between us short. "Oh, please don't think you need to tell me this. I've never wanted anything. But the real question is what you want. What are you after? Since you abducted Aiden I think the least you owe me is an explanation."

She laughs. It's insincere, like everything about her. "You care about him. I see it in the way you look at him. We both know Aiden won't compromise his career for anything, especially you. You're nothing more than the girl who died to save him. And what I wanted is useless at this point, because you've ruined it." From her back waistband she whips a gun out and holds it steadily in front of my face. Ice runs through my veins, freezing me in place.

"Whoa!" I say, taking several steps back, mind-blocking fear assaulting me suddenly. "Come on, it doesn't have to be this way."

"Is this where you beg for your life?" Amber says, arms straight, shoulders down. Sadly, she looks quite comfortable holding the gun, like she actually knows how to use it.

"This is where I beg you to stop acting like a lunatic. Whatever you're after, it isn't worth this." I sidestep to the left, taking my body out of the path of the gun. She mirrors my action, aiming again at me.

"You have no idea what 'what I want' is worth."

"Then tell me what it is. Maybe I can help you." Another sidestep.

"You don't get it. I already did what I was supposed to do. I suffered at the Institute, captured Aiden, completed my end of the bargain and did it matter? No. Maybe if I had psychic powers I would have known it was never going to work out. Do you know how incredibly demoralizing it is to risk everything for something and still not get it?"

"The promotion? Is that what you mean?" Another sidestep. We've now made a half circle, but none of my attempts to move have worked. Amber stands as rigid as ever, the barrel of her gun pointed at my heart.

She laughs, a cold and sad sound. "Promotion? You keep saying that. Where did you get such a stupid idea? Yes, what I wanted was a position, but not a professional one. But I was led on, deceived to believe if I did all this..." Her eyes flash with a new hostility. "None of that matters now and it sure as hell isn't your business. All that matters is that if I can't have what I want then no one will have what they want." She pulls back the hammer on the gun until it locks in place.

I can't battle a gun. Wind can't get me out of this. The escrima stick in my hand is a sad joke now. How strange it is that this vermin of a person will be the one to kill me. After all the danger I've faced in the last few hours I'm about to meet death by a bullet. It's absurd and stupid.

"Look, I'm not a part of this feud. I'm only doing a job, so why don't you lower your gun and let me go?"

"You're more a part of this than you can ever imagine. Unfortunately for you, you're not going to live long enough to figure that out."

A flash momentarily takes over my vision. Never before has a premonition carried such critical information. Slowly I turn my head, looking at the empty doorway behind me.

"Don't think about running," Amber says, amusement in her tone. "I *will* shoot you in the back."

I meet her eyes with a calculated gaze, careful not to look at the weapon in her hands, which robs me of my remaining courage. A breath later the countdown sounds off in my head. *One.* I take one deliberate step, aligning myself perfectly with the doorway. *Two.* Amber mirrors my step so she's standing directly in front of me. *Three.* I drop my body to the cold limestone. Amber doesn't have a chance to react. Allouette's knife, targeted at my back, speeds overhead, striking Amber in the chest. Confused horror rips across her face. The gun slips from her hands, clattering to the stone ground. Her shaking hands clutch the knife, and for an instant I think she's going to pull it out. Then quite suddenly she slumps to the ground, leaning her back against the chair where Aiden had been. A convulsion rakes her body and again she grips the knife in her chest, tangible pain streaking her face.

Still face down on the ground I allow myself to finally take a breath. Amber isn't dead yet, but she will be soon. I don't have a second to spare. Instantly, I'm on the stone door, pushing it closed. I only have one more option to get me out of here. Allouette is close. She'll be in here soon if I don't stop her. Quickly I pull out the modifier and open it. My fingers shake as I type in Allouette's name. When that has been accepted I put in a message:

Roya is dead.

The modifier rises into the air, glows like it's about to catch on fire, and just before it bursts into flames, recedes back into my palm where it lies cold as stone. Hopefully Allouette pauses to celebrate. Hopefully this will buy me some time. Soon she'll be here and I don't need to waste time.

Amber's eyes are now closed, her chest no longer rising and falling with urgent breaths. She's dead. Dead bodies don't look right, especially when the instrument that killed them still protrudes from their flesh.

Closing my eyes I focus my attention on the Institute. Each passing second is accompanied by a loud pulse in my head. The task of dream traveling to the Institute should be easy, but the anxiety robs me of the necessary concentration. Finally the silver tunnel opens, sucking me in with one giant breath. Too tired to enjoy the ride I fade into oblivion.

The blinding lights of Aiden's lab greet me. A dozen people stand in the space. James is already setting the dials on the GAD-C and within seconds my body is set for auto-generation. Glad not to have had to do the process myself, I close my eyes and wait for the now familiar reunion of body and spirit to happen. A jolt assaults my core, more painful than any time before when I've generated my body.

Anxious to rejoin my team I bolt into an upright position. Everything is wrong about the sensation, like my body isn't meant for that. *Did something go wrong with the GAD-C? Is my body deformed?*

Joseph's and Trey's faces are the first to swim into my line of vision, only a step away. Their eyes are wide. Horror written in them. Everything slows painfully down. Each movement takes an excruciatingly long time in my mind to process. Joseph's hands rise to his face, covering his mouth which has dropped in sudden disbelief. But I can't understand what he doesn't believe or why Trey looks terribly shocked. And my ears have quit working. All I hear is ringing. Persistent, aching ringing. Attempting to sit up more I'm met with a violent stabbing in my core. It's a blinding pain, so intense my head spins. Confused, my eyes travel down and everything becomes devastatingly clear. I've been shot.

Chapter Thirty-Eight

Strong fingers grip my hand. I want to open my eyes, but each attempt is met with defeat. Still I hear his breathing, know his head is slumped next to me. Footsteps patter by. That person's wearing soft-soled shoes. On my other side someone rustles, not as close though. Antiseptics lace the air. I can sense all this, but I can't force my eyes open. *Why?*

Another set of footsteps, these firm and approaching. They stop a few feet away.

"Has she awoken yet?" Trey's voice sounds tired.

Joseph stirs at my side. "No, not yet."

"She will, give her time," Trey says, a strange consoling tone to his voice. "I spoke with Dr. Dunham and Mae. They're both hopeful she'll make a full recovery."

Joseph doesn't respond verbally, but I sense he nods. His grip tightens on my hand.

"Why don't you go get some rest," Trey says. "You haven't left her."

"I have been resting. Haven't ya noticed I'm sittin' next to a bed," Joseph says, humor in his tone. "And they bring me meals when they feed these guys. So actually I'm stayin' fairly comfortable. But I could use some entertainment. Staring at Stark is excruciatingly boring."

"I'll have someone round you up some books and magazines," Trey says, his familiar unemotional tone returning. "And how are you feeling?" he says, his voice directed not at Joseph.

"You should have George answer that for me," Aiden says with a shaky laugh. "I can barely tell you what my last name is, let alone describe how I feel."

"The drugs they gave you will be out of your system soon enough according to Dr. Dunham. Once they are then your body can start repairing the damage. Try to let yourself rest for now."

"Thanks, I will. I look forward to having a clear thought again," Aiden says, his voice foggy.

"And George, how about you? Are you feeling better?"

Sheets rustle in the bed on the other side of me. "Yes, sir," he says. "Thanks for asking."

"Well, if any of you need anything please let me know," Trey says, and then his footsteps retreat.

Joseph squeezes my hand and lays his head down again beside me. "Come on, Stark, wake up already," he whispers. "There's so much I haven't told you. And I really need to. If you wake up I'll tell you everything. I should have before anyway. Please open your eyes."

I want to, Joseph. I want to. Sleep crashes down on me, sucking my consciousness away.

♦

"You're finally awake." The voice is smooth, deliberate. Cold fingers grip my arm. I open my eyes to a mass of blurry shapes. Gradually lines begin to define the figure beside me. Chase's stunning face stares back, a content coolness in his eyes. Dark cave walls lurk behind him.

I gasp, shooting into a painful sitting position. "What am I doing here?!"

"What do you mean? You're finally home. Safe. With me. And I'm never going to let you go. Ever." He traces his pointer finger down my cheek, neck, shoulder, and arm, his attention locked on the skin under his finger.

"No, I'm supposed to be at the Institute. That's where I was. How did I get here? Where's Joseph?"

"Shhhh." A cold finger presses against my lips. I'm stone under his touch. A statue which can never move, only be molded into a different position. And Chase holds the chisel.

"Now it's time we sealed our engagement."

Engagement? What happened while I slept?

Chase leans into me, tilting my chin with a firm grip. His lips an inch away. I shudder.

"Stop!" I scream. My eyes burst open. Breath trembles in my chest. Sweat drips down my brow. From across the infirmary Mae rushes, an urgent concern on her face.

"You're awake," she says, arriving at my bed, breathless.

Pain shoots through my abdomen. It throws me into an instant state of paralysis. My breath pants but the rest of me clenches, waiting for the searing agony to subside.

"Seriously, I go to take a leak and that's when ya decide to wake up?" Joseph says, striding up beside Mae.

"She had a nightmare. That's what awoke her," Mae says, giving Joseph a strange look.

"What was it about?" Joseph asks.

The dream. Chase's eyes swim into my head, so clear and real. Like a pond freezing over in winter, I harden suddenly—frozen.

"She can answer that in a minute. Right now I need to check her injury."

Joseph stares at me, an odd sentiment in his eyes.

"I need to check Roya's injury," Mae repeats.

"Go ahead," he says, not taking his eyes off me.

Mae pulls a curtain from beside the wall, pushing Joseph back out of its path. "Unless you want to see your sister topless then I'm going to ask you to leave."

"It's not like she has anything to see."

My face flushes, knowing both Aiden and George are listening. "I'm sure the same is true of you down there," I say, pointing at his pants.

He smirks. "Fine. I'll go harass Livingston."

Mae pulls the curtain on its track around my bed, creating a private space. She unfastens the hospital gown and begins unraveling my bandages.

"Mae," I say in a hush.

"Yes, honey," she says, preoccupied by my wound.

"I'm sorry."

She pauses, bringing her eyes to meet mine. "About Pearl," I say. Grief contorts her face, a dozen wrinkles materializing. I hadn't noticed until now how red and puffy her usually creamy skin is.

"Thank you," she says, busying herself tending to my wound. I have zero desire to see what lies beneath the white gauze so I keep my chin up, eyes on the ceiling.

"As I suspected when you jerked awake, you reopened the wound," Mae says. Her hand presses against my skin and warmth exudes from her fingertips, soaking deep within me. A tingling sensation spreads along with the warmth. "You were lucky," Mae says wrapping new bandages around me.

"When is getting shot considered lucky?"

"When the bullet goes through your side. More central and it could have been fatal."

"I'll remember that the next time I get shot."

She gives me a tired look. "All right, I don't want you out of this bed. You call me if you need anything," she says, dragging the sheet back to reveal George lying in the bed on my right. Before I'd been too groggy to properly notice him sitting there. He's tucked under his blankets, which are neatly folded over his lap. The expression on his face is poetic, like the look of a warrior after he's returned home from a near defeat. It's heartening. Encompassing.

"Roya," he says, "how are—"

"I don't think so, Anders," Joseph says as soon as Mae clears the curtain on the other side. He springs off Aiden's bed and takes a seat at the edge of mine. "I'm the first one to get an audience with Stark, so there." He pokes his tongue out at George.

"Joseph, do you always have to be such a child?" I say squeezing the hand he's placed in mine.

"Of course I do," he says with a wink.

"How long was I asleep?"

"Thirty. Six. Hours."

"I can't believe you haven't left my side."

"How do you know that?"

I shrug. "I could hear things."

A book slips from Aiden's bed. It snaps my attention in his direction. Our eyes meet. Tears instantly constrict my throat, hot and tight. Aiden looks different somehow, although nothing obvious has changed about him. His eyes smile brightly when we connect, but the rest of him remains neutral. "Welcome back," he says, pulling a knife out of my heart.

"You too," I say, trying to disguise the gasping rawness with exhaustion.

Joseph claps in front of my face. "Back over here, Stark. I want your undivided attention."

Rolling my eyes I say, "It's all yours."

"Good. So you got shot?" Joseph says, irritation flaring in his voice.

207

"It would appear so," I say.

"I knew I shouldn't have left you." Regret streaks Joseph's face, making him look older.

"There's no changing what happened."

"What did happen?" Aiden says, standing up, taking the seat next to my bed. He's so much skinnier. I see it mostly in his face, but also his arms and shoulders.

On the other side of me George leans forward, curious. I flick my eyes to his. "I'd be over there too if I could get out of bed," he says. "Mae won't allow it though." I gulp, nodding.

Returning my attention to Joseph I say, "It must have been Amber who shot me. I thought she was dead, but I guess not."

"Did you kill her?" Joseph asks.

"Yes, but not directly. Right after you left Amber showed up and pointed a gun at me. I thought I was going to die, but then I had a vision of the future. It was of Allouette sending a knife through the Grotte and into the room where they held Aiden. I guess she knew I was still in there. Or maybe the knife was meant for Aiden. Anyway, I ducked at precisely the right moment and Amber took the knife in the chest."

"Trey probably wants to hear this," Joseph says, starting to stand.

I throw my hand over his. "No, don't go. I'll recount it to him later."

"What happened next?" Aiden asks.

"Well, I closed the door and dream traveled back here. Apparently Amber wasn't dead. Hopefully the bitch is dead now. I actually hope her chest wound wasn't fatal. I hope she could have been saved, but the energy she used to retrieve the gun and shoot me killed her."

Joseph snorts with laughter. "Damn, Stark, you're dark."

"Well, would you send well wishes to someone who shot you?"

He pretends to think about it, scratching his stubbled chin. "Yeah, probably, but I'm a better person than you."

"Don't make me laugh," I say, gripping my side.

"Could it have been Allouette who shot you?" George asks.

"No," Aiden says abruptly, leaning more on my bed. "Voyageurs—real ones, not wannabes like Amber—wouldn't use an automatic weapon."

"Doesn't really matter who shot me. It's already been done," I say.

"I thought I was gonna have a heart attack when you arrived profusely bleeding," Joseph says. "Don't you ever scare me like that again."

"Oh, I'm terribly sorry this has been so traumatic on you. I didn't even know I was shot until after I arrived and saw your face. That's a hell of a way to find out such a thing, don't you think?"

"She's been awake for all of ten minutes and you boys are already pestering her?" Mae says, bustling into the room. "Joseph, now that Roya has awoken you don't need to keep watch. I order you to go take a shower and get some proper rest. And as for you two"—she motions to Aiden and George—"let Roya have a chance to relax before you begin with too many questions. And Dr. Livingston, if you don't get back in your bed then I'll move you six beds down. Is that clear?"

Aiden cracks a smile at me before retreating back to his bed, which is crumpled with blankets.

"All right, I'll do as I'm told," Joseph says. "But I'll be back after a bit." He kisses my forehead and gives me a sweet smile. "See you later."

"Later," I say, sinking down in my bed, feeling a wave of exhaustion.

Chapter Thirty-Nine

Although I'd been expecting them, I'm still startled when the Head Officials and my team walk into the infirmary. A mind-numbing stab rips through my side when I try to sit up.

"Dude, Stark, you're really milking that scratch for everything it's worth." Joseph laughs, taking the seat next to my bed.

"Well, without it, I'm just not sure how to get attention," I say.

Trey rolls his eyes at me, a grin on his face. It's almost a playful gesture, which throws me off. When has Trey ever been playful? He clears his throat. "I think what Joseph means to say is that we're all glad to see you're feeling better. We were shocked when you returned shot."

"I prefer to always enter the Institute half dead and in need of saving," I say. From my peripheral I spy Aiden flash a smile.

Trent pulls up a seat between George and me. Ren leans against the opposite wall. And Shuman is stationed beside a timid Samara. Stringy hair lies around her pale face. Her clothes hang loosely off her frame. To my relief it looks like Mae isn't around.

"Now that Roya is strong enough," Trey begins, "I want to be debriefed on what happened in the Grotte. However, Dr. Dunham has urged us to keep this meeting short since all three of you"—he inclines his head at Aiden, George, and me—"need as much rest as possible."

"They're already lying in bed," Joseph complains. "Wish I could attend a meeting in my pj's."

"Get shot," I say.

"Ah, the bullet barely nicked you," Joseph says.

"I'll nick you," I say, holding up a fist.

"If you two are quite done, I'd like to resume this meeting," Trey says.

Joseph dramatically waves his arm, gesturing he's turned the stage over to Trey.

A few quiet seconds pass and Trey's appearance shifts. He's suddenly uncomfortable. "This mission was a success. For that I'm grateful. However, it's never easy to celebrate a victory when a life has been lost. Let's all take this time to honor Pearl."

Everyone instinctively bows their heads. Silence follows, interrupted only by Samara's quiet whimpering.

Trey clears his throat again bringing all our attention up. "Before we begin I want to express my gratitude to the rescue team. Thank you for fighting so bravely and for bringing Aiden back safely. I knew I was risking your lives by sending you to the Grotte, but I also knew if Aiden wasn't rescued, along with the dream blocker, all our lives would be endangered. With the dream blocker the Voyageurs could have abducted any of us. It was not an easy decision to ask you to risk your lives for this mission, but it was one I knew was right. Thank you again for serving the Institute." He looks at me sharply, his turquoise eyes draped with new wrinkles. "And Roya, thank you for leading this mission. Again you've demonstrated great honor and sacrificed yourself for others." He drops his head at me in a show of respect.

"Now at this point I'd like a full report of what happened in the Grotte. It's important that we have a thorough understanding of what the Voyageurs are doing, thinking, and feeling so that we can prepare ourselves if necessary." Trey looks at each us in turn. Finally he extends his arm at Aiden and says, "I'd like you to start by telling us specifically why you were abducted."

Even though his bed is right next to mine, I've still tried to avoid looking directly at Aiden. It's difficult, especially when I've sensed him attempting to capture my attention. Maybe it's the painkillers or the need to process the events from the Grotte, but everything is raw between us right now. A surreal tenderness surges through my heart when I look up at him now.

"All right, I'll do my best to string coherent words together, but I apologize if certain things I say don't make sense. I'm still trying to regain my faculties." For a guy who's been starved, tortured, and drugged he sounds amazingly lucid. Even his energy, though still less than usual, flits around each of his words. "I wouldn't be here right now, I wouldn't even still be alive, if it wasn't for everyone in this room. Thank you," he says, scanning faces, avoiding mine. "As you already know, Amber was sent here to spy on the Lucidites. When Chase learned about a recent project of mine, he ordered her to steal the device once it was completed."

"Chase?" Trey interrupts. "Why Chase?"

"Pierre is no longer first in command. It's Chase."

"Oh," Trey says, astonishment written on his face.

"Anyway, Amber's plans were foiled when I fired her before the project was complete. So taking orders from Allouette, she abducted me instead."

"How did you find out about all of these events that preceded your abduction?" Trey asks.

"Amber is—should I say was—an easy person to incite. During interrogations I used my own strategies to draw information out of her. I needed to understand how I'd been fooled into hiring her. And even more critical was if there was a play I could make to turn Voyageurs against each other."

"And besides what you've told us, did you learn anything else?" Trey asks, tipping forward with interest.

"Oh yeah, a ton. And once I found Amber's buttons I was able to create all sorts of mischief. Thanks to me, she and Allouette had more than one altercation."

"Is that the position Amber was after, second in command?" I ask, the heated conversation from the Grotte rushing back to me. "She told me that she'd been deceived into believing she'd be rewarded, but it was a lie."

"No," Aiden says, not looking at me. "Allouette and Amber were after the same thing: Chase. From what I figured out they were both competing for his affection and I also gather he was more than willing to lead both of them on to get what he really wanted."

"And did you determine what he was after?" Trey asks.

"Yep," Aiden says, popping his lips together. "Since it hadn't been built yet, he wanted the blueprints to the emotional modifier I'd been working on."

I flash on George. His bottom lip is firmly pressed between his teeth. He sucks in a long breath, a slight shake of his head.

"What? Why would he want that?" Trey asks, a crease indenting the space between his eyes.

Sighing, Aiden says, "Unfortunately, I failed to discover that reason. It was the most guarded of any information I came close to."

"You hadn't completed the blueprints for the emotional modifier before you were abducted, correct?" Trey asks.

"I had, but they weren't perfected and Amber was well aware of the status of the project."

"You didn't give them anything, did you?" Trey asks, worry in his voice.

"Well, I withstood the torture both mentally and physically, but wasn't able to resist the powerful drugs they gave me. It made me a slave to their will."

Color drains out of Trey's face. "So they have the blueprints for the emotional modifier," he says. It isn't a question.

"They have *flawed* blueprints." Aiden smiles mischievously. "The drug forced me to do as they commanded, but I was able to resist enough to botch up a few critical pieces."

"Do you think they will be able to build it and fix the errors?"

"Honestly, I'm not certain," Aiden says.

"Why did they have to resort to the drug? Didn't they try to remove your protective charm?" Ren asks, irritated skepticism narrowing his eyes.

"They did, well, they thought they did." Aiden peers down at his chest, remorse marking his features briefly. "They took my father's dog tags which used to be my protective charm. But thanks to something I did a month ago I thwarted their plans. I had recently tested a new technology on myself, as many scientists tend to do." He flashes us the underside of his forearm. "You see, I'd perfected an internal charm that's embedded under the skin. I thought it was going to be pretty funny when Chase removed my dog tags and still couldn't get into my head. Boy was I wrong." Aiden laughs darkly. "It wasn't funny at all. Whatever Chase wants the emotional modifier for, he wants it desperately." Anguish wisps between Aiden's words and echos in his breath, despite his attempts to hide it. A long burn runs down the length of his arm. It's deep, like a branding mark made from red-hot iron.

It's Trey who pulls my attention away from the dull aching in my chest. "I realize you faced excruciating circumstances to protect all of us. Thank you."

Aiden waves him off. "I didn't do anything anyone here wouldn't have done. And I realize now that if Chase wants the emotional modifier that much then...well, whatever he wants it for can't be good. I should have never started the project. Emotions are sacred." For the first time all morning his eyes meet mine, a sad smile on his face. I'm suddenly short of breath, like I've just sprinted a long distance. *Can everyone in the room hear the pulsing in my head?*

"What's done is done," Shuman says from the back of the room, her voice so quiet it startles me. All eyes jerk in her direction. "Regret swallows broken men whole. Acceptance builds them anew."

Trey nods before turning back to Aiden. "She's right. We made the decisions we thought were right at the time."

Aiden shrugs. "That's really all that happened. The rest is blurry at best and not of much interest."

"Thank you. It's good to have you back. Now let's give Dr. Livingston a chance to relax while the team tells us about their experiences in the Grotte."

I start off the recap telling everything until after we encountered Allouette. "Trent is probably in a better position to recount this part."

Trent revolves his gaze around the room as he describes what happened. He makes it sound more like a ghost story than a battle. "If it wasn't for me George would be dead," he informs us with zero humility.

I narrate our battle with the birds and how they stole Pearl's protective charm. "I had ordered her to return, but then George came through the hole severely wounded. The plan was she would heal him and then return. I realize now that I should have sent them both back."

"Don't." George cuts me off, a reassuring glint in his eyes. "Don't doubt those decisions. I wouldn't have been strong enough to dream travel. I was already experiencing shock."

"So Chase now has trained birds to go after our charms?" Trey rubs his chin, thinking. "That's bizarre and terrifying."

"Try being in the same room with one," I say. Then I explain the hypnosis. "When blood began seeping out of Trent's and George's noses I knew time was running out. And then Samara and Joseph were lost too and I was alone." My voice falters as the memory rushes back to me, a tender knot cutting off my air supply. "I-I-I—"

"How?" Ren interrupts, sounding especially hateful. He looks at me for a long minute, then tightens his eyes. "How could you so easily look at Chase's illusion and resist?"

"It was difficult, but still I did. I don't know how or why," I say.

"Hmmm." He looks at me suspiciously.

"Yeah, well, if you don't believe that part then leave now, because you sure as hell won't believe what I'm going to tell you next," I say, throwing him a vile look. Then I launch into the shortest explanation I can manage regarding the crazy wind that saved us all.

"Wow," Joseph says. "When were you going to tell me you could control the wind?"

"Bob just told me right before we left for the Grotte. I didn't believe him though, but when all of you were lost in that hypnotic state I didn't really have any other options. And still, thinking back about it, maybe I can't really control wind. Maybe it only appeared like I could," I say, looking at the far wall. "No, it must have been another illusion," I decide at once. "I just thought I could control the wind. I can't. There's—"

"It was you, Roya," Trey interrupts. "You were the one controlling the wind." He fingers his blue and yellow amulet, looking down at the ground in intense concentration. His turquoise eyes rise and meet mine. Somehow he looks older than even a moment ago. "Go ahead. Continue."

I shake my head and point at Joseph. He describes the projection of Chase. "Honestly, I was kind of feeling sorry for the guy," Joseph says at last.

"That was the point, you prat," Ren says.

"Whatever." Joseph dismisses his insult with a wave. "Anyway, Stark sliced him in two and then the real Chase showed up; at least we think he was the real one."

"How about I help you figure it out?" Ren tilts his head to the side, the overhead light reflecting off his slick red hair. "Was he so attractive, Joseph, that you started to question your own sexuality?"

Joseph laughs. "Well, yeah. He was 'bout the dreamiest man I've ever laid eyes on."

"Yes, that's Chase," Ren says, leaning back on the wall again. "Sorry, forgot to mention that bit in training."

Joseph rolls his eyes. "So Chase was all trying to seduce Stark, and from the looks of it he was kind of succeeding."

"He did what?!" Trey stands suddenly, pushing his chair back with a screech.

I shoot Joseph a scowl. "He's exaggerating."

"I'm not. I have witnesses." He gestures to the team.

"Joseph, this isn't the time for jokes," Trey says, pursing his lips, folding his arms.

"It's not a joke. Chase actually offered to let us all go if Stark stayed." Joseph turns and grins at me. "For a moment there I thought you were gonna take Casanova up on his offer."

"Joseph!" I scold. "What are you talking about?" Mortification burns my cheeks.

"Don't worry, you're not the first gal to get tricked by a dashing, young guy."

"It wasn't a trick," Samara speaks for the first time, her gaze not leaving the floor. "He thinks they're soul mates."

I sink into my bed, pulling my covers up over my chest, which is suddenly cold.

"Samara, are you sure?" Trey asks. "Maybe he was feeding you what he wanted you to know. Maybe—"

"She got it right," George interrupts, bitterness lacing his tone. "Chase wants Roya. Intensely."

What?! It can't be true. The dream which shouldn't be fresh anymore suddenly washes over me, Chase's electric blue eyes swimming in my head. A shiver zips down my spine. When I look up from my fidgeting hands I find every eye on me.

"How long has Chase had blueprints for the emotional modifier?" Ren says to Aiden.

"A few days."

"Is it possible that Amber could have built the emotional modifier by the time the team rescued you?"

"She could have had a prototype. It wouldn't have worked very well."

"And would the protective charms guard against it?" Trey asks.

"No, they wouldn't," Aiden says.

"What? What's going on?" I ask, past the verge of disturbed.

"Roya, your team makes it sounds like Chase was trying to seduce you. This doesn't reflect on you at all—but honestly, was it difficult to resist his advances?" Trey asks.

Heat rises in my head. Anything is better than staring at these faces and answering this question. "Maybe." I gulp. "But I was tired and pressured and worried and still I was able to…resist." The word sounds wrong in my mouth, like I don't mean it.

"Like you were resisting something programmed in your emotions?" Aiden asks.

This conversation can't be happening. Not like this, in front of everyone. "I don't know."

"Roya," Trey says, "specifically, when you were in the Grotte how did you feel about Chase?"

My eyes flick up to Joseph's. He's stone, relentless to the persuasion issuing from my gaze. I need to be rescued from this line of questioning. I need help.

To my horror George says, "Roya, why don't you tell everyone how you feel about Chase? The truth." Embarrassment crashes down on me like a thousand bricks.

"George!" I scold.

"Just tell them. Maybe it will help," he says.

Focusing only on my fingertips, gripped tightly around my covers, I say, "It was peculiar. I felt a strange draw to him, one I still can't explain."

"What?" Aiden says in an exasperated hush. "Can you describe it?"

"I just tried," I say through clenched teeth, my eyes still fixed on the tan wool of my blanket.

"Maybe it would be more helpful if you didn't describe the emotions," Trey says. "Maybe it would be easier to determine whether they seemed abrupt and foreign to you."

"I don't know. It was all so confusing. I was trying to protect the team, guard them and I…"

"Were you possessed by an emotion?" Trey asks.

"No," I say. "How I felt was within me."

"And how did you feel?" Aiden asks.

I ignore him. "I wasn't under hypnosis. I know that much."

"I believe you," Trey says gently. "Just tell me anything that you think will help. Anything that was odd, against your usual way."

"Well..." I say slowly. "I was aware of the draw. Felt petrified in a weird way. I knew Chase was dangerous and also when my best opportunities were to attack him."

"Did you attack him?" Trey asks.

"No."

"Why?"

"Because I didn't want to hurt him," I say too fast.

"Why didn't you want to hurt him?" Trey asks, sensitivity in his voice, one I suddenly trust.

"Because I love him." With a force that sends my head back my hand slams over my mouth. Astonishment stretches my eyes wide. I can't believe the words I've just said. Meant. Faces mirror mine. A sea of surprise. *Bang. Bang. Bang.* A hammer beats in my chest, driving a sharp nail into my heart. "Wait, no!" I say, shaking my head forcefully. "I don't feel that way. I don't know where that came from."

"Oh, fuck!" Aiden buries his head in his hands, clawing at his hair. "Fuck. Fuck. Fuck," he says, slapping his hands against his head with each profanity. "*Now* we know why Chase wanted the emotional embedder."

Chapter Forty

"No! I'm not in love with Chase! I misspoke. I didn't mean what I said. I don't love him," I say.

"Of course you don't," Trey says, stepping closer to me, the delicate therapist tone back in his voice. "You've been embedded. None of this is your fault. Chase is just trying to use you."

A trespassing I never thought possible rips through my consciousness. Nothing I know feels real anymore. "No. No. No," I say between hyperventilated breaths.

"Relax," Trey says, pressing his hands down, like he's trying to suppress my hysteria. "Chase wants you for some reason, but it's all right. Calm down. We'll figure it out."

"No, this isn't all right," I say, stifling tears. *Did I just profess love I didn't know I had for a psychopath? In front of everyone in this room?* "This isn't happening. This has to be a mistake. He must have been testing the emotional modifier on me. I'm not the reason he wanted it." The words I've threaded together out of desperation actually melt away some of the fear. *Yes, I'm a part of the experiment. Not the reason. Again, just a pawn.*

Trey shakes his head. "After everything the team has told me I must disagree. Chase is calculated. He doesn't experiment."

I hadn't said the word *experiment* out loud. Masking my paranoia I study Trey, who's regarding me with a new intensity. *Did he read my thoughts?* Damn, nothing is sacred anymore.

"It still doesn't make sense," Joseph says, breaking the staring contest between Trey and me. "Why would Chase go to all this trouble to make Stark love him?"

"Exactly. Thank you, Joseph." I exhale, relieved to finally have an ally. "Chase didn't even know about me until I entered the Grotte. There's no way I'm a part of whatever evil plan he's working toward."

Trey's already shaking his head before I'm done speaking. "He's known about you for quite some time." His hands glide through his hair once. Twice. Three times. It looks as though he's trying to comb something foreign out of the silver strands. "I never saw this coming, but maybe I should have."

"What?!" I say, bolting upright, a stitch assaulting my side. Joseph lays a cautious hand on me, but I swat it away. "What does that mean? How could he...And why should you have seen—"

Trey holds up his hand, cutting me off. He swings around to Ren. "I want you on this right now and full-time. Find out as much as you can and report back immediately."

Ren stretches his arms overhead, letting out a giant yawn. "Right-o," he says with zero enthusiasm before trotting out of the infirmary.

"What are you keeping from me?!" I demand. "Tell me what's going on!"

"Roya," Trey says, his voice five octaves under mine. "I'm sure this is nothing for you to be concerned with. We really need to find out more information and once we do you'll be the first to know." He sounds like he's trying to talk me off of the ledge of a building. "This probably is a misunderstanding. Let's have Ren look into it before we worry unnecessarily." Everything about his demeanor has shifted, going from erratic to suddenly collected. My guess is he's in cover-up mode. Telling lies must put him at ease. "Now go ahead and finish telling me what else happened in the Grotte."

I regard him for a long minute, unconcerned for the nervous shuffling around the room. It grows with intensity as each silent second ticks by. Trey stays locked on my narrowed eyes. One minute he says he's certain Chase is after me and the next he says it's probably all a misunderstanding. Maybe Trey doesn't think I'm coherent enough to keep up with his incongruities, but he's wrong. Joseph prods me, but I don't take my angry eyes off Trey. I want him to know I can't be fooled. I want the room to know he's hiding something.

"What happened next is that I stabbed Pearl," Samara says in a tortured voice.

Shuman places a large hand on her shoulder. "You did the right thing. It was not the easy choice, but it was the right one. Soon you will see this."

"Do not blame yourself for what you had to do," Trey says, the artificial smoothness back in his voice. "Samara, the Head Officials, including Mae, support the decision you made. If you hadn't taken Pearl's life then I'm one hundred percent sure that you all would be dead, with the exception of Roya."

When it's been quiet for a little while I finally nod at Joseph. He describes when the osprey swooped in and attacked Chase.

Shuman tilts her head, a new curiosity in her eyes. "When did you learn you had a spirit animal?"

"I've known for a while now," he says nonchalantly. "In the Grotte, Chase was about to turn Roya into a vampire and much like she described her emotions takin' over to create the wind, well, that's what happened to me. When the osprey soared into the cave I knew he was there to do my bidding. I told him to attack Chase and peck his pretty little eyes out."

"Thanks," I say, looking at Joseph.

He fires his finger at me like a gun. "Hey, I was afraid that I wasn't pulling my weight in this fight. I'm glad I could save the day."

"After that there isn't much left to tell," I say. "We rescued Aiden, sent the team back and then Amber showed up. I guess I killed her, but it was kill or be killed and so…" I shrug indifferently, exchanging a quick look with Samara. "Then I used the modifier to throw off Allouette, who was approaching and—"

"*You* used the modifier?" Aiden asks in disbelief.

I scowl at him. "Yes, I was trying to buy some time."

"Interesting," he says, repressing a smile.

"I also used it when we got to the Grotte…so we could save you. Is that interesting too?"

"Oh, yes, terribly," he says, a perfect example of professionalism. "And thank you."

"What was the message you embedded in Allouette?" Trey asks.

"That I was dead," I say coldly, finally lifting my eyes from Aiden's. "It was just supposed to buy me some time to dream travel. I knew as soon as she arrived that she'd figure out it was a lie."

Trey actually smiles. "That's perfect! It might have worked!"

"What?" I look at him, confused.

"Yeah, Allouette might believe you're dead now," Aiden says, a new enthusiasm in his words.

I shake my head. "But once she got to the room she'd find out I wasn't there and it was untrue."

Aiden sits up a bit straighter. "Not necessarily. You might have traveled at the time of death, which was almost what happened."

"Well, I don't see much why it matters what she thinks now," I say.

"Because she'll tell Chase and this could buy us some time before he figures out that it's false," Trey says. "If he's instigated this whole thing so he can use the emotional modifier on you then we need as much time as possible to prepare."

"He hasn't," I say, frustration overloaded in my tone.

"I believe he has, Roya," Trey says decisively. "And your denial will only prevent you from battling anything he's attempting to do to you. The sooner you come to terms with what has happened to your emotions the sooner you can take back control, which is especially important before he has the emotional modifier perfected." He turns his attention to Aiden. "Are there strategies Roya could use to resist the programming from the emotional modifier?"

Aiden still looks half crazed. He pulls his hand from his hair, which is more chaotic than usual. "Quite possibly. Without knowing how competent his device is I'm uncertain of the effectiveness of any strategies."

"It's better than nothing," Trey says, rounding back in my direction. "I want you working with Aiden on this."

Yes, of course I should have seen *that* coming. Nothing would be more humiliating than having Aiden help me identify ways to resist loving a madman.

"Sir," George says. "Since I was involved with the creation of the project I might be able to help as well."

*Wait...*Now *that's* more humiliating.

"Thanks, George," Trey says. "Roya, until we get to the bottom of this Chase situation I don't want you to dream travel alone. The Institute has been released once more to dream travel freely, but I only want you to do this when you're with someone else." He hesitates, remorse briefly flicking through his eyes. "This is merely a cautionary measure for the time being. I'm sure it won't last."

I nod reluctantly.

"Thank you all for sharing these events with me," Trey says to the group, and then he trudges out of the infirmary without another word.

"Well, that was uncomfortable," Joseph says, nudging me over in my bed so he can lie down next to me. Everyone's filing out of the room or turning their attention to smaller conversations. "You couldn't make your disdain for Trey any more apparent unless you actually called him an asshole in front of everyone."

"I would never call him that. Maybe a tyrannical, deceptive jerk."

"What's your deal? Why you hate him so much?"

"I don't hate him. I just don't like liars and people who get into my head without my permission."

"It seems to me he's probably hiding somethin', but I don't sense that he's lying about Chase."

"He's one of those who lies through omission. That's still considered deceptive in my opinion." I stare at the exit, thinking over the last few minutes. "I'm glad that you sensed he was withholding information too. I want to know why."

"Maybe he was right and he doesn't wanna worry until there's somethin' more concrete."

"Hmmm...maybe," I ruminate. "You know, Joseph, this bed really isn't built for two." I try to recapture some of the blankets he's tugged in his direction.

"Oh, I bet Anders would disagree," Joseph says, giving George a sly grin.

George pretends not to hear him as he marches back to the showers.

"If I wasn't afraid of pulling another stitch I'd punch you in the face again," I say, suppressing a laugh.

"Sad that you can say 'again.' It's rude to hit your family. Didn't anyone ever teach you that, Stark?"

"Yeah, well, didn't anyone ever tell you that it's rude to not tell someone they're your long-lost twin?"

"You know, oddly enough, that one never came up during bible study," Joseph says, edging me farther over on the bed.

"Seriously, if you push me over any more, I'm gonna fall out of this bed." I elbow him in the ribs. "You're going to feel awful then."

"I won't feel that bad."

"I'll make sure you do," I say, the threat laden in my tone.

"So how's it being stuck between these two?" He motions to the empty beds on either side of mine. Aiden's on the far side of the infirmary, deep in conversation with Shuman.

"They're fine, I guess. I've mostly been sleeping."

He rolls his eyes. "I didn't mean your current sleeping arrangements. You forget so soon that I witnessed the whole sending George back to the Institute followed by the steamy reunion with Aiden."

I avert his eyes. "Things are complicated."

"To say the very least." He whistles through his teeth. "You got some luck, don't cha? Having to be stationed between your two secret love interests for the next week, that's brutal."

"Yeah, I'm fairly certain my whole life is just comedic entertainment for God."

"If it makes you feel better you do a fantastic job of pretending you don't care about either of them when others are around."

"Honestly, I don't think anything makes me feel better right now. I'm in love with three different guys. One I want. One I don't. And another I can't have." For the first time since I arrived back at the Institute I let the regret and heartbreak billow out of me. A single tear peeks from the corner of my eye. I press it away with a fingertip. "I'm grateful Aiden is back and George will recover, but now…"

"You have to make a decision," Joseph says, leaning his head on my shoulder. "Kind of sad that you thought one of you wouldn't survive to this point and therefore the decision wouldn't have to be made."

224

I squeeze my eyes shut, pressing against a pain this conversation has uncorked. As long as I'm imprisoned between these two beds I can't feel these emotions. They'll have to wait.

"So how come my spirit animal is a freaking peacock and you get the majestic osprey?"

"Whatever," Joseph says, snuggling in closer to me. "You control the wind, and can resist being hypnotized literally to death, and also fight like Bruce Lee. I think even with my majestic osprey, I still got the short end of the genetic stick."

I smile, enjoying the moment. It feels so good to know that Joseph is safe and acting like his old self. I lay there snuggled up with him and realize that he's the only person in the world who I think I feel this comfortable with.

Joseph squeezes me into him. "Yeah, me too."

"Stop doing that," I say with a puckered brow.

He laughs. "Don't worry. I can't do it all the time. It's usually only when we're in close proximity."

I sigh. "Hey, will you dream travel with me tonight? Since I need a chaperone and all?"

"Sorry, I wish I could but I've got plans. Actually now that you're doing better, I'm gonna start working on that project again."

"So you're going to pretty much disappear, aren't you?"

"I'll come around, but not as much. The project is demandin'."

"Joseph, you said when I was sleeping that there were things you needed to tell me. You said that if I woke up you'd share them."

Joseph closes his eyes, a sudden strain on his face. "It's true I said that, but I was desperate and…well, I do need to tell you some things, but there's one I'd rather show you. It's the project I'm working on and I don't think it will take me much longer."

"And the other things you need to tell me?"

George limps back over to his bed, sliding under the covers.

"Not now. Later," Joseph says, pushing me over a bit more. "Why don't you scrunch over?"

"Cause it's my bed. Go get your own wound, you dork." I almost laugh.

"Na-uh, been there, done that. I've got the stained T-shirt and nightmares to prove it."

Chapter Forty-One

Sleep is still heavy in my head when I awake that evening. Probably cold by now, my dinner plate sits on the tray next to my bed. The idea of food makes my insides churn with unease. Water, on the other hand, I crave. Too soon the bottom on the glass stares back at me, empty besides a few drops.

"Thirsty?" Aiden says, walking over to my bed holding a pitcher.

I nod and he refills my glass. "Thanks," I say my voice still raspy from sleep.

He sets the pitcher on the tray and sits beside me on my bed, his leg pressing up against me. "I feel like everything is my fault," Aiden says. The bruise around his eye has turned green and yellow. "If I hadn't created the emotional modifier," Aiden continues, "then you wouldn't…"

"Then I wouldn't be in love with a madman," I finish his sentence. "Yeah, I think you can own some of the blame for this one."

"That's not exactly what I was going to say," Aiden says, pressing his lips together, restraining a smile.

"You're not really in love with him," George interrupts on the other side of me. He swings his legs over the side of his bed, looking as tired as I feel.

"I know," I say, wishing Aiden wasn't sitting so close to me right now. "It's just that at times I feel like I am." My fingertips press firmly into my eye sockets. *This can't be a real conversation.* I keep pressing until the white sparks shoot through my vision.

"But it's an artificial love," George says. The springs of his bed squeak when he moves forward. I withdraw my hands from my eyes, my vision taking several seconds to focus properly on George. "Roya, when you love someone it feels much different than how you're feeling about Chase."

"I don't think what she needs is a lesson on how love feels," Aiden says over his shoulder to George.

"I'm not giving her one. I'm also not speaking generally about love." George scrutinizes Aiden with a cold stare before turning his

226

gaze to me. "What I was referring to was the way *you* specifically feel when you love someone. I'm acquainted enough with your emotions, Roya, to know your love for Chase is different, it's shallow and weak, like an imposter emotion—which is exactly what it is."

I hold my breath and George's eyes, wishing he wouldn't have done this. He's making a play right in front of Aiden. Maybe I was being too unrealistic to think he'd pretend nothing had evolved between us in the last week.

"You said you could help me," I say to Aiden. "That there were strategies I could use against Chase's attempts."

"Yes," he says, still watching George. "I need more time to figure them all out though, but there's one that I think might be especially helpful."

"Oh?" I say, nudging him once with my leg.

He finally turns his head to look at me. "Yes," he says, a jealous heat in his eyes. "The good news is I think I can alter your protective charm to fight against Chase's emotional modifier."

"No one ever says there's good news without having bad news to follow," I say.

"You're almost too astute for your own good, Ms. Stark," Aiden says. "Yes, it's true there's not so good news. It will take me some time to have the specs for your protective charm mod ready. First of all I can't start work until I'm out of here. Second of all I have to finish the blueprints for the emotional modifier and then—"

"Why is that necessary?"

"Because a patch to your charm isn't going to work seamlessly until I know exactly how the emotional modifier works." He sighs. "Sadly, it will probably take me a month or more to have something."

"Great." I give a similar sigh of frustration. "Maybe it would be easier to create a device that changes Chase—makes him not a deranged murderer." I laugh morbidly.

Aiden gives me a punishing look. "Then would you allow the embedding?" he asks.

"Oh yeah, and we'd ride off into the sunset."

"I don't think you mean that," he says, a sharp edge in his voice.

"Of course I don't," I say. "I'm simply trying to make light of my incredibly ridiculous life. Maybe when someone starts manipulating your emotions you'll sympathize more."

"I do sympathize and I'm trying to help. It's killing me inside what's happened to you." An uncomfortable tenderness echoes in his words. I see his desire for me erupt in his eyes like a curse. I guess we're both in devastating positions.

"Doesn't the reason Chase is after you consume your thoughts?" George says, pulling my attention from Aiden.

"It does," I say to the floor. "But not as much as it should. I guess I'm used to unanswered questions. I don't know who my parents were. Have a twin I didn't know I had. And recently discovered I can harness wind. So if a lunatic wants me to be infatuated with him, it's just another mystery to this farce called my life. What consumes my thoughts is how I'm going to stop Chase."

"Maybe I can help you with that," George says, dragging a seat over beside my bed and sitting. "I came up with a tactic that might help—until Aiden has a more permanent fix."

"Thanks, George." I exhale, one of relief. "I'll try anything at this point."

He smiles, his lovable dimple surfacing on his left cheek. "Okay, first I want you to close your eyes."

I do.

"Now focus on your heart's center. Really try to feel your heart. Can you sense its intensity?"

I nod, knowing his eyes are on me.

"Good. Now think about Chase. I want you to answer with the first thing that comes to your heart. All right?"

I nod again.

"How do you feel about him?"

"I love him," I say automatically.

Aiden slips off my bed with an exasperated groan and begins pacing, his footsteps impatient.

"Okay." George's voice is even, calm. "Now think about Joseph." He pauses. "Are you doing that?"

I nod.

"Good. How do you feel about him?"

"I love him," I say again. These words sound altered somehow.

Aiden's pacing halts.

228

"Now is there a difference between the love you feel for Chase and Joseph?" George asks.

My focus hones in on the distinct, separate emotions. One is within me, an ingrained part of my soul—so deep and pure it opens my heart. It feels like a magical force, one I'd fight to protect, one I'd die to keep. And the other…it's inside me too. A deep-rooted emotion, but it isn't in my heart, rather attached to it like…a disease. It's a self-serving emotion which doesn't inspire any magic within me, only fear that if I don't feel it I'll die. If I don't love Chase then this cancer will spread through my heart.

My eyes bolt open to find both guys staring intently at me. "I feel the difference," I say, breathless.

A relieved smile spreads along Aiden's face.

"So how do you really feel about Chase?" George asks.

"I hate him," I say confidently. "I really, really hate him."

Aiden leans over my bed and high fives with George. "Nice going, Mr. Anders. That was genius."

"Thank you. I'm glad it worked," George says with a subtle smile. "So Roya, you can use this anytime you need to reset your emotions, anytime you think Chase has tampered with them."

I'm about to thank him when we're interrupted by James wheeling a flat-screen TV into the infirmary. He tosses a remote at Aiden and says, "As you requested."

"Thanks, lad," he says, tipping his invisible hat at him.

Without a word Aiden plugs in the TV and turns it on. He's wearing an endearing smirk and humming excitedly.

I pluck one of my grape tomatoes off my dinner plate and toss it at his head. "When are you planning on telling us what you're up to?"

Spinning around, a look of mock offense on his face. "Well, I didn't much plan on telling you, actually. The way I figure it is you have no choice but to lie there. And since I'm the one with the television remote, it looks like I'll be choosing the feature."

"Oh, come on now," George says, tossing a pillow at Aiden's head.

"Hey, you could have messed up my hair," he says, patting the elegantly disordered mess atop his head.

Aiden pushes a couple of buttons on the remote. "Well, it was supposed to be a surprise, but, all right. Have either of you ever watched any of the *Star Wars* movies?"

George and I both shake our heads.

Aiden gives a look of disappointment. "That's what I feared. So we've got roughly five more days left in this joint. If my calculations are correct, and they always are, then if we start watching right now we can get through the entire series."

"You've got to be kidding. There's like what, four movies?"

"Six," he corrects me. "Don't worry, very soon you'll be thanking me."

"That's going to take forever for us to watch all of them," I say.

"Not forever. Actually it will take exactly thirteen hours and fourteen minutes."

"It's not really my genre," George says, trying to sound diplomatic.

"George, that's inherently false. *Star Wars* is everyone's genre. Now you all pipe down. The movie's starting." Aiden turns to me with a smile before settling down on his stomach and resting his chin on his hands. The words begin scrolling through the stars. I turn and shrug at George. He frowns.

♦

Lucky for me, I'm not asleep when the movie is over, although I am dead tired. George is, which earns him a punishing look from Aiden.

"You're obviously too overwhelmed by the awesomeness that is *Star Wars* to accurately express the myriad of thoughts this film has inspired in you. This is typical," Aiden says, sitting down on his own bed. "I'll let you deliberate on it and you can unload on me first thing tomorrow morning."

I let out a long yawn and nod in agreement. Although I'm thoroughly exhausted I'm still somewhat aware when he plants a soft kiss on my cheek. Aiden hovers over me, a mesmerized expression in his eyes. My hand finds his face and caresses his skin. Still only semiconscious I think I imagine his hand taking mine, but then he pulls it to his lips and I open my eyes wider. With a calm wanting he kisses each of my knuckles, pausing on the last one.

"Goodnight, Roya," he whispers against my skin.

Goodnight, I think, too tired to actually say anything.

Chapter Forty-Two

"Stop resisting." His cool voice slips through my mind like music.

My eyes open to find his, too close. He's leaning over me, arms pinning me to the cold stone.

"I don't love you," I whisper.

Chase clucks three times, shaking his head. "That's not what I want to hear." He slides one hand behind my lower back, drawing me nearer to him. Our hips are closely pressed together now. "Let's try this again," he says into my ear, his free hand flat up against the wall by my face, trapping me. "Roya, how do you feel about me?"

The word *hate* flashes through my mind. Echoes. But I don't say it. Instead I repeat myself. "I don't love you."

With unnatural quickness Chase grips my chin between his icy fingers, pinching my skin. "If you don't love me," he hisses through clenched teeth, "then how about I kill everyone you *do* love. How does that sound?"

Fumbling for space I shove my hand into his chest, forcing him back, gaining precious inches. "This isn't real," I say with conviction.

"You're right. And it's unfortunate because if it was I'd do something incredibly satisfying to you right now." Chase steps forward again, tipping my chin up so I meet his crystal blue eyes. I'm stone once more. Frightened by his allure, by my own draw to him. "Soon though." Leaning down he hovers his lips an inch away from my jaw, a selfish wanting pulsing from his too cold breath. I shiver. "And although this isn't real, my message is." His teeth crush down on my earlobe. It hurts and then it doesn't—at all. Again he grips my chin, rocking me back so I'm staring straight into his soulless eyes. "If you keep resisting me then I'll kill everyone you love. Is that clear?"

I don't answer.

Chase leans down, whispering right against my mouth, his lips colder than his fingertips. "And I'm going to start by killing the one you love most. I'll enjoy watching him slit his own throat. Dying the same way your mother did."

A scream tears through my dry throat. Violent shivers rake my body. Teeth chattering, I clutch my shaking arms. Shudders palpitate my chest. And although my consciousness knows where my body lies, I keep my eyelids tightly pressed together, willing my breath to slow before I meet my reality.

Warmth so real it almost makes me cry wraps around my arm in the form of a strong hand. "It's all right," George whispers.

He's crouched down next to my bed, the soft night lighting of the infirmary illuminating only his figure, not his features. I'm curled into a tight ball, hands cradling my shivering arms. George turns to leave, but I swiftly clap my hand over his. "Don't go," I say in a quick hush.

"I'm only getting your blankets," he says, carefully kneeling down to retrieve the crumpled mess on the ground. I push myself into a seated position, willing my eyes to adjust to the darkness. "Here," George says, draping the blankets over my lap and wrapping another one around my shoulders. "You're trembling."

"I know," I say, wishing my teeth would stop chattering so aggressively. "I've never felt so cold."

George places a hand on each of my arms and rubs gently, urging my thickened blood to circulate again.

"Thanks," I say, looking up at his devoted eyes

"It was only a dream," George says, pushing my hair back from my face.

I shake my head forcibly. "No, it wasn't."

"Of course it was, Roya. It just feels real."

"Before I came to the Institute, the Lucidites sent me messages through my dreams. Told me things. Prepared me," I say, recalling those vivid dreams like I had them yesterday. "This dream feels the same way as those."

"It's Chase, isn't it?" George asks, a strict protectiveness in his tone.

I nod, staring off into the dark infirmary.

"He can't hurt you though. He might be trying to scare you, but he can't hurt you," George whispers, gently caressing the top of my still frozen hand.

"He can though. Chase knows exactly how he can hurt me most," I say, my voice sounding haunted. How does he know how my mother was killed? Maybe he's lying. Maybe I'm imaging the whole thing. Maybe I'm losing my mind.

George folds me into his arms. They're so warm, they instantly melt away the block of ice around my core. I bury my face into his shoulder, breathing slowly though his shirt. Something stirs in my peripheral and I raise my head only an inch. Aiden stares back at me, a quiet wariness on his face.

Easing back a few inches I turn my attention to George. "Thanks."

"You need to tell Trey about these dreams," he says emphatically.

"What dreams?" Aiden asks, fumbling for his glasses on the bedside table.

"Roya, if Chase is trying to threaten you—"

"Don't worry, George, I'm not going to give in to him. And I also won't be threatened. I can still think in my own brain at least. I just have to take back control."

He nods, chewing on his lip. "Aiden," George says, not taking his eyes off me, "can Chase invade people's dreams?"

"Oh yeah," he says, a dark memory briefly surfacing on his face. "It's called dream invasion. He's a master at it. Taught me a thing or two."

"And is there any way to stop him?" I ask, grateful that it's dark and hopeful Aiden can't see my hand pressed between George's.

"Is he in your dreams?"

I nod.

"But it could just be your subconscious," George says.

"It's not. I know the difference," I say, slipping my hand from his and gripping the blanket around my shoulders, making it tighter.

"I'd go with your instinct on this," Aiden says in his clinical voice. "If Chase is in your dreams then you could try shielding. It works the same on emotions, thoughts, and dreams. It's harder during dreaming because you have to remain completely lucid the entire time, but it can be done. Honestly, your best defense is dream traveling."

"Yeah, well, besides from the fact that I need to be supervised to do that, I also don't think the painkillers I'm on will allow it. They're too disorienting for me to focus."

"I know what you mean," Aiden says.

"I'm not taking them anymore," I suddenly decide. "I'd rather have coherent thoughts and be in pain, rather than the reverse."

"If I didn't know any better then I'd swear your gift was telepathy and you were just in my head," Aiden says. I lift my gaze up from my bed and our eyes collide. Not the way he looks, but specifically the way he looks at me threatens my inhibitions. It's all greedy yearning. The blankets fall from my grasp. I'm suddenly roasting.

"Since we both can't dream travel and you're probably in no mood to attempt another dream right now, can I make a recommendation?" Aiden says, suppressing the heat in my chest with his casual tone.

"Sure."

"Episode two?" he says, picking up the remote.

I turn to appraise George. He shrugs, looking slightly defeated and definitely exhausted. "You look like you could use some rest," I say. "I don't want the show to keep you up."

George squeezes my shoulder before returning to his bed. "Oh, don't worry about me. Sci-fi actually puts me to sleep."

Aiden huffs. "Mr. Anders, you scorn me with your insults. You don't hear me criticizing…" He pauses, tilts his head. "What sort of things *are* you into?"

"Classic literature."

Aiden arches an eyebrow. "Well, I'd never say something like reading classic literature is a flamboyant interest and best reserved for those still developing their masculinity."

"Are we going to watch the movie or what?" I say, leaning forward to block George from Aiden's direct field of vision.

"As you wish, my dear," Aiden says, turning on the television.

"Good night, George," I say. "Thanks for everything."

"Anytime, Roya," he says, rolling over in his bed, back toward me.

"Might I suggest," Aiden says, wheeling the television directly in front of my bed, "we'll be able to see better if we're both in front of the television."

"How are we going to do that?" I say, straightening my blankets.

"Scoot over," he says, all brazen, the heated look returning to his eyes.

235

"There's not much room," I say, flushing red.

"Oh, I saw you and Joseph sharing the bed and since my diet at the Grotte I think I'll fit."

An overly dramatic sigh, reeking of pretense, falls out of my mouth.

"Don't worry, I promise to give you plenty of space," he says, resting his hand an inch from mine on the bed.

Chapter Forty-Three

Warmth so perfect, like filtered sunlight, covers me. His heartbeat under my ear gently wakes me from sleep unspoiled by dreams. Lifting my chin I look directly into Aiden's eyes. Although the infirmary is still dark, I see the smile in them.

"You're awake," he whispers, wrapping his arms tighter around me.

"How did we end up this way?"

"These kinds of things just happen."

I twist around too fast. George is still asleep, back facing us.

"He hasn't stirred," Aiden says, pulling the covers up higher on my shoulder.

"Didn't you sleep?"

"No, but this is more peaceful anyway."

I slide my arm around him, feeling the bones too easily through his shirt. Still our bodies lie against each other's seamlessly.

"It's torture being stationed so close to you every day and having to hide my affection," he whispers into my hair.

"Torture? Are you sure *that's* the right word?"

He smiles against my head. "Well, maybe not," he says. "It's still causing me a great deal of stress though."

It's hard to accept that he's here. Beside me. I half expect to wake up from this dream to find myself alone in bed. Silence fills the air, save for his gentle breathing and steady heartbeat. Those two sounds unearth the fear I'd buried since Aiden was abducted.

"I thought you were dead," I whisper against his chest. "I thought I'd never see you again."

"The dream was supposed to reassure you."

"The dream?" I ask, instantly confused.

"You had one of me, right? Where I told you if you could feel me that—"

"That was you?" I ask, dumbfounded.

"Dream invasion," he whispers, a smile in his voice.

I lift my chin again to stare at him. In the darkened room the bruises on his face appear harsher. A new heaviness invades my heart when I think about fists hurting him. The Voyageurs torturing him. My fingers trace along one of the bruises marking his face. "I'm sorry they did this to you."

His mask falls away. A pain as ingrained as DNA surfaces. It makes him look stronger than I remember. "Are you ever going to tell me what they did to you?" I ask.

No answer. Just a wounded smile.

"Well, you can if you ever want to."

"I don't dwell in the past," he says, rubbing his face into my hand. "It's behind me now."

"Did you think you were going to die?"

"No," he murmurs. "Somehow I knew *you* were coming."

"I didn't want to at first," I admit, tucking my head back down under his chin. "I didn't want to be the one responsible for you because what if I failed?"

"I'm glad you came around, because after a week in the Grotte there was no one's face I needed to see more," he says, squeezing me into him, then stops, going suddenly rigid. "I'm sorry, I didn't hurt you, did I?"

"Not at all." I suppress a giggle and slide my leg along his. "You can even hold me tighter if you want to."

His chest rocks with a silent laugh. "I don't think you should push it, Ms. Stark."

"I know what I can handle," I say, slipping my hand under his shirt, sliding it up his torso. Suddenly remembering the multiple cuts and burns I'd seen on his chest in the Grotte, I halt. "Wait, I'm not hurting *you* now, am I?" Our injuries make us both seem fragile in each other's arms, but also perfectly paired.

"No," he growls low in my ear. "Just the opposite."

I dip down lower, tracing S's along his side. His skin seems to hum under my fingertips.

"If you keep that up, I'm not going to be able to remove myself from this bed."

"I'm not sure I see the problem there." I slip my hand from under his shirt, wiggling upward so my face is against his neck. The bed creaks from my movement. I should be worried about waking George, but I'm not. Right now all I want is this. It's so clear to me suddenly. Aiden stole my heart when he first saved me, and I'm never whole without him. Not like I am right now.

Enticing him to turn his head and kiss me, I slide my nose along the space between his jaw and his neck. He shudders but doesn't turn.

"You're going to get me in so much trouble." The sternness in his voice surprises me.

"Me?" I say, teasingly outraged. "You're the one in *my* bed."

"And believe me when I say I don't want to leave it. But Mae is going to be here soon. It's almost morning."

"Don't go," I say, cinching on to him with a new tenacity.

"I can't have Mae seeing us like this," he says in a firm whisper.

"I'll tell her you're making me feel better."

"Roya," he pleads, prying my hand off of him. "You know I can't. We can't."

His fragmented sentence is completed in my breaking heart: *We can't really be together.* That's what he means to say, but doesn't have the guts to. Like the assistant in a magician's act, I'm cut in half. He may be tortured, but I'm broken.

He retracts his arms out from around me, making me instantly cooler.

"Why?" I ask as he stands up.

"You know why." He puts back on his glasses.

"No, why are you crawling into my bed at night and abandoning me in the morning? It's…frustrating."

His response is a guilty shrug.

"Get some more rest, Roya. I'll be right here."

Chapter Forty-Four

"I'd hoped you hadn't run off and gotten yourself killed yet," Patrick says, his face shining brightly.

He dumps a huge box on my bed, looking unsympathetic about almost crushing my leg with it.

"I'm not going to be able run at all if you break one of my limbs," I say, eyeing the box.

"We both know I wouldn't hurt you," he says as he steers his hand truck back to the exit. "And don't have such little faith in my unloading abilities. I'm not too bashful to say I'm the best courier out there."

"I'd never argue that point."

Patrick's mustache twitches with a smile. "Until we meet again, Roya," he says with a slight bow.

"What about me, Patrick?" Aiden says from his bed, shutting his laptop.

"What about you?"

"Although you don't have a package for me, aren't you at least going to say hi?"

"Hi," he says indifferently.

"That's the greeting I get after getting abducted?"

"Were you? Oh, that's right," Patrick says looking amused before turning around and leaving.

"Some people." He sighs before flipping back open his laptop.

I haven't graced Aiden with a single look all morning. Actually, I'm proud to say I've gone out of my way to stare at random objects when addressing him. I can tell it's starting to grate on him, but since he likes pretending so much he can pretend it doesn't bother him.

Of course the package is from Bob and Steve. I don't know anyone else outside the Institute. Not really. Deranged psychopaths don't count.

My greedy fingers sling the tape off the top of the box before digging into it. A card sits on the first layer of tissue paper. Inside it I recognize Steve's handwriting.

Dear Roya,

Words hardly express how grateful we feel that you're returned from the Grotte safely. However, Trey has informed us that your injury is still pretty severe. Since you'll be laid up for a while we decided to make sure you have the proper supplies. Enjoy!

Love,
Bob & Steve

I set the note on my bedside table and pull out my presents. George and Aiden are now eagerly watching from their beds. There's a multitude of snacks, everything from Moose Munch to dried banana chips. I throw a bag of jelly beans at George and keep digging. Next I unearth a book of vintage world maps. The book is large and heavy and the maps are all in pristine condition with vibrant colors. Lastly, I pull out an iPad.

"Who's the secret admirer?" Aiden asks.

"Admirers," I correct him, turning on the iPad.

"That's so your style." He laughs.

"Ha-ha," I say without enthusiasm. "It's from my pseudo parents, Bob and Steve. They kind of adopted me after I learned my entire life was a lie. Don't you already know all this stuff though? Doesn't it show up when you secretly record and track my energy levels?"

"Glad to know you're feeling better," he says, sitting on the far edge of my bed, fingering the snacks with curiosity. I snatch a bag of gummy bears from his grasp without a look, putting it on my bedside table. "Your sassy attitude seems to have recovered anyway," he says, leaning forward.

I ignore him as I focus on the screen loading in front of my face.

"You ever call them Steve and Bob, or does Bob's name always come first?" he asks, grabbing the book of maps and thumbing through it.

"Sometimes I call them Beve, but that's only when I'm not thinking quite clearly," I say, taking the book from him and pinning it next to my side. From my peripheral I catch his disheartened expression. *Good.*

I'm grateful to find that my iPad automatically connects to the internet. The first thing I do is send Bob and Steve an email. They ping me back immediately, which fills me with an excited anticipation.

"So is anyone up for episode three?" Aiden asks, returning to his bed.

When I don't answer, George says, "I think I'm good, but thanks."

I feel Aiden boring into me, willing me to connect with him, but I refuse. Right now I could crawl into George's bed and he would hold me and accept me and declare our love to the Institute. But Aiden can't do that. A part of me wants to do just that, fling myself into George's willing arms. Then maybe Aiden would realize what's at stake.

"Roya?" George asks, tearing my attention from my attempts to ignore Aiden.

"Yeah," I say, swiveling in his direction.

"Are you still planning on leaving the Institute? Now that the mission is over? I know it was the only reason you stayed."

I sense Aiden on the other side of me, soaking up this information and hungry for more.

"I'm not certain," I say, arranging the presents back in the box. "Joseph thinks he needs me to stay, but I'm not convinced. So many things about the Institute don't feel natural to me. My life here is shrouded in secrets and I'm to my limit with that."

George nods, a thoughtful look of understanding. "I know, but I still hope you plan to stay."

"And I want to stay for you, and Samara, and Trent and…" I pause, pretending to think. "And…news reporting. But I still don't know. I'm torn."

"Those are all good reasons," he says, a smile in his voice.

"What will you do?" I ask, pretending I don't see Aiden shuffling uncomfortably in my periphery.

"I'll stay," George says. "At least for a little while. I'm going to check into a few departments to see if I might be a good fit."

"George, any department here would be lucky to have you."

His eyes smile at me before they slide to my right, I'm guessing finding Aiden's.

♦

The silver tunnel greets me like an old friend. My body howls with intoxicated gratification. I've never enjoyed the experience of dream traveling this much. Near death makes every part of life sweeter. And also like an old friend, the trustworthy tunnel deposits me safely in exactly the right place.

My eyes instantly squint, unaccustomed to such brightness. Sunlight. It warms me and the cobbled street under my feet. It's been too long since I've felt it glow on my skin. Even one day without sunlight is too much, and I've almost gone four.

Bob waves to me from a café on the other side of the street. A smile breaks across my face as I hurry in his direction. Just as I'm about to cross the street, I notice something out of the corner of my vision. Chase's unmistakable face. It stares back at me from the darkened alleyway. Not love, but fear washes over me. I spin back around and sprint across the street, ready to protect Bob and Steve if necessary. I throw my back up against them, searching the space where Chase was a moment ago. He's gone. Ragged breaths whistle through my chest as I scan the street occupied only by busy Middlings jostling by.

"Roya," Steve says cautiously. "Is everything all right?"

"No," I say, turning to face him. "I mean yes. It's fine. I thought I saw…never mind." I run my fingers through my hair. It wasn't real. There's no way Chase would be able to find me so quickly. I'm imagining things.

"You're as white as a ghost," Bob says, peering at me sideways.

I feign a smile. "Well, you know dream traveling washes people out."

He gives me a skeptical look.

"Blood loss will also do it." I laugh, enjoying the freedom to do so while dream traveling. "Thanks for meeting me here," I say, hugging both of them. "I know it's simple and plain, but I needed that right now."

"Roya, you've come a long way if you think a café in the center of Verona is plain." Bob grins.

"Can we walk?" I say, looking over my shoulder. "I've been locked in a bed for too long."

Bob presents me his arm. Steve does the same. I hook mine into theirs and we set off for a causal walk. *How's it I always have a guy on either side of me lately?*

In detail I tell them about most of the Grotte, with the exception of Chase. It's bad enough that most of the Institute knows about that mortifying situation. Not telling them preserves my ego a tiny bit. And besides, it would only make them worry, and that's not necessary.

"I have a question for you," I say, taking in the smell of fresh bread wafting from a corner bakery. "That note about the dream you had, Bob, did you know I could control the wind? Was that what it was about?"

"Yes and no," he says, earnestly. "I knew that the dream meant you were powerful."

"But how? We hadn't even met yet when you had the dream," I say.

Bob shrugs. "How does anyone know anything?"

I stop and stare at him, confused.

"The universal source must have placed the information in my brain. I didn't know at the time I had the dream or even when I wrote the letter to you that it was literally true. I thought that you would provide some balance to this tumultuous battle between the Lucidites and the Voyageurs. It has been going on for too long," he says, irritated.

"Really, how long?" I ask.

"Since the beginning," Steve chimes in.

"Why, what's the rub?"

"I don't know," Bob says, scratching his head. "I've never met a Lucidite who knew."

"Hmmm…sounds like another Institute secret."

Bob shrugs again. "Whatever the cause for the rivalry, it's produced extra strain on our society. We're loyal to the Lucidites, but I wish that the hatchet could be buried so we didn't always have that extra threat hanging over our heads. I was hoping you'd be a part of that change."

"And she still might be," Steve says.

"If anyone can then it will be the girl who defeated Zhuang," Bob says with a smile.

"And can control the wind," Steve adds.

The Lucidites still believe I defeated Zhuang, although Trey hasn't been able to confirm this. Now's not the time to burst their bubble so I simply say, "Thanks for the vote of confidence."

We continue walking until we come to the riverbank. There we find a stone bench and sit, listening to the waves gently rap against the shore.

"Are you getting lonely being held up in the infirmary?" Steve asks.

"No, I could actually use a little less attention."

He arches a curious eyebrow. "Oh?"

"Aiden and George are also current residents of the infirmary. And relations between the three of us are...tense."

"Ahhh," Bob says, like he's realized something suddenly. "Tense like in a romantic way?" My eyes slide to the right, avoiding Bob's impish grin. "Yep, I guessed it!" He turns to Steve and beams.

Steve shakes his head at Bob, looking irritated. "Wait, you're all sleeping in the same room? The three of you?"

Bob slaps Steve on the arm. "Stop being such a prude, would you?"

He gawks. "Bob, they could try something with her."

"Oh, I'm sure they probably will." He winks at me. "If they haven't already."

I flush and slide down an inch. Why did I even bring this up? Talking about Chase's programming would be way less humiliating than this.

"So let me get this straight," Steve says, sitting forward, blocking Bob from my view. "The Head Scientist has a crush on you?"

"Crush? Really, Steve?" Bob slaps him again on the arm. "They're not kids on a playground."

I'm fairly certain I've lost the ability to speak. My voice is buried under the loads of embarrassment piling higher in my chest.

"And there's George too?" Bob says, giddy, his voice dripping with curiosity. "Oh, that must be tense." Steve flashes him a look of disapproval. "Oh, come on, Steve, she's a girl. Let her be one."

"I know, it's just, look at her," he says, waving his hand at me like I'm a mannequin in a display case. "And she's saved the Lucidites twice, who wouldn't be in love with her? I don't want her getting hurt. That's all."

Bob waves his hand at Steve, dismissing him. "She's probably going to get hurt. We all do and we manage to get along fine. It's life, don't you remember? And it can be kind of fun too." He gestures with his thumb at Steve. "He's worried that they're going to break your heart, but he forgets that's part of the game of love."

Steve clears his throat. "And Bob forgets that you're young and although wiser than most, still naïve."

"Well," I say, finally finding my voice, "I appreciate the concern and the enthusiasm. Sadly, I'm actually in love with both of them, but I really don't think I have the option of being with either. So in a way my heart has already been broken."

Bob takes my hand, pulling it across Steve's lap, and pouts his bottom lip. "Oh, Roya, I'm sorry. Love is complicated and rarely is there a straightforward path to it."

I nod.

"Maybe what you need is a break from them and all the demands at the Institute," Steve says. "I know staying with two middle-aged men doesn't sound exciting, but the offer still stands if you want to live with us."

"I've had just about enough excitement to last me awhile." My mind flashes to Chase and my heart sputters suddenly. *Yes, no excitement would be good.* But then there's his threat, which I believe. Am I safe at Bob and Steve's? Would I be putting them in danger? Am I putting them in danger already by having contact with them? And what's the alternative, cut off everyone in my life because I fear Chase will harm them? I spent the last sixteen years in a vacuum, devoid of real love. I'm not about to withhold my affection for the people in my life now because of some threat.

"Well, you think about it and let us know," Steve says, finally breaking the silence. "Bob could teach you to play the harp and I could teach you the piano, if you wanted to."

"That would be incredible," I say, but my voice doesn't reflect my excitement. Living with Bob and Steve feels like a good solution to my complicated life, but again I find myself torn. It's becoming the overarching theme to my life. "Thank you. I'll think about it."

We spend the rest of the morning bathing in the Italian sun, walking the streets, and exchanging tales. Being with them is wholesome. I imagine this is how most people feel in the company of their parents. They approve of me, validate my emotions, and make me ridiculously sentimental.

Chapter Forty-Five

To my relief Mae discharges me early from the infirmary. She still orders me to take it easy, but I no longer need observation. If I hadn't dream traveled last night then I'm uncertain how I would have slept. To spend another night imprisoned between George and Aiden would probably kill me. And the cold shoulder I've been giving to Aiden is slowly starting to warm. If I don't get away from him now then I'll be back in the act, ready to be sawed in half again.

"You done with that box, missy?" Patrick says, wheeling a cart behind him. "I've been asked to deliver it to your room. Apparently, you're still too feeble to lift a finger."

"You know how I do." I fold up the box and push it toward him on the bed.

"Yeah, you got the rest of the Institute fooled, but believe me when I say I've got you figured out," he says as he loads up the box and pushes it out of the infirmary.

George and Aiden have also been released. As we all prepare to leave I sense the ever-present tension increase. I wish I could grab my stuff and go, but I feel obligated to say goodbye.

"Roya," George says approaching me, "are you almost done? I'll walk with you."

"Not quite. I need to make sure I didn't leave anything else behind. Can you wait?"

He turns and appraises the clock. "I've got a meeting in a few minutes."

"Go ahead then," I say. "I'll see you soon."

Aiden's fumbling with the cord for the television, failing multiple times to get it wound to his liking. George glances at him over his shoulder and then back to me. "I wanted to tell you that spending this time together, recovering, has been meaningful. We've been through so much. And more than anything—"

A sudden crash interrupts George's speech. I peer around him to spy Aiden retrieving the *Star Wars* box set of DVDs from the floor.

"Sorry," he says with an embarrassed wave.

George nods and then turns back to me.

"Anyway, I want to say more, but later," he says, seizing my hands.

"Okay." I squeeze them once and pull him forward, hugging him, arms gripped around his neck. "Thanks for everything, George."

His hands glide up and down the length of my back, pressing me against him. When we separate there's something different in his eyes. A warning, maybe? Worry?

He leans forward and whispers in my ear. "You deserve the best. And I want that for you, no matter what."

I ease back and nod. "Thanks."

What does that mean? Does that mean him? Or Aiden? Or neither? Or does it even refer to my love life at all? I search George's eyes, which always feel strangely like home to me. It's his warmth and acceptance, like a fire on a winter's night.

George leans down and grazes my cheek with a kiss. "I'll be around if you need to talk about anything."

"Thank you," I whisper. He evaluates me once more, a solid look in his eyes, and then turns to leave. There's a brief exchange of handshakes with Aiden. Neither of them looks at the other. Then George walks to the exit faster than I could manage in my current state.

I retrieve my iPad from the bedside table. The infirmary door hasn't even swung completely shut before Aiden throws the cables to the ground and marches over to me. "Roya, please stop being angry with me," he says, taking the iPad out of my hands and tossing it on the bed.

"I'm not angry at you, Aiden," I say, staring at the letters on his T-shirt.

"So look at me already."

I lift my gaze up to his. The bruises I touched a day ago have already dissolved a bit. "Happy now?"

"No, not at all," he says, stepping forward again until less than a foot separates us.

"Aiden, I'm tired of being your secret. I don't want to sneak around. It feels wrong and like I said the other night, it frustrates me that we can't just be together."

"It frustrates me too," he says, staring down at me.

I step back, needing some space to clear my thoughts and bolster my confidence. "Well, this is your situation. I keep wondering why I'm subjecting myself to these restrictions. I don't have a job where I have to hide my relationship. I can be with anyone I want—openly."

"Like George?"

I gulp. *Should have seen that coming.*

"Yes, like George." His eyes flare with red-hot anger. "But that's not the point I'm trying to make here," I say, brushing past him to clear the candy wrappers which have accumulated on my tray. More than anything I need to do something with my hands which are threatening to shake. "The point is that I can't keep this up much longer. And I shouldn't have to."

Aiden places his hand on mine, bringing my attention directly to him. I let the cellophane wrappers fall back on the table. "Roya, it's not like I want to either. I wish I could broadcast how I feel about you on the Lucidite newsfeed."

"That would no doubt be deemed an inappropriate use of the technology."

An almost imperceptible grin reaches his eyes.

"I'm not asking you to publicize anything about us. I'm tired of sneaking around. It cheapens this," I say, motioning between us.

His expression darkens. "Look, life apparently has a vendetta against me, 'cause if you were anyone else and I felt the way I do then this would be easy, we could make our relationship public. But with you, it's not that simple."

"How's this suddenly about me?"

He laughs. He actually laughs. If I didn't want to kiss him so badly, I might actually clock him.

"Roya, this has always been about you."

I close my eyes, shake my head.

"It's true. When you were elected to challenge Zhuang it was made clear to everyone working at the Institute that we needed to support you in every way possible."

"Well, that mission is over."

"It doesn't matter. Even after the Day of the Duel I've been required to make daily reports regarding your frequency changes."

"How are you doing that?"

"I installed a recorder device in there." He points to the frequency adjuster around my neck. I forget I'm wearing it most of the time. "It sends me your readings every half hour."

"Why are you measuring my frequency changes?"

"Trey worries that the adjuster could have long-term effects on your natural frequency vibrations. Since he isn't about to kick George out of the Institute, he's asked me to innovate another device that will fix the problem without changing your frequency. And until then he wants me to keep an eye on the changes."

"That's so weird," I say, stretching out the last word. *Not to mention totally perplexing.*

"And now there's this whole Chase situation to deal with. I'm certain once I leave here I'll be working nonstop to find a patch for your protective charm."

"Aiden, what does this have to do with you and me?"

He snatches my hands. His grip makes my eyes widen. I have yet to feel such urgency in him. Maybe he's desperate to express his point. Maybe he's still off because of the drugs from the Grotte. I listen regardless.

"Can't you see that you're not just some girl? You're the one that my work is often centered around. Exposing our relationship would give the other Head Officials ammunition to say I'm not taking my job seriously. They'd think I was taking advantage of my position."

Suddenly he's haunted by something so real, and without knowing what it is I'm still assaulted by the chill it leaves in his eyes. "Since I was promoted I've had to prove myself. I've had to watch my behavior more than any of the other Head Officials. They're all conservative. Close-minded. Old-school. That's one of the reasons Flynn promoted me, he wanted innovation. He said he'd persuade the others to accept my ideas, but he died before he could fulfill that promise. Since I've been in this position I've only met resistance from every one of the Head Officials. I feel like they're all looking for a reason to discredit me now that Flynn isn't here to vouch for my worth. I already have to regularly churn out new technology in order to keep them off my back."

"But you do," I say. "Mind-blowing technology constantly comes out of your lab."

"You think my technology is mind-blowing?"

"Of course, don't you?"

A provocative glint lights up his eyes. "The only thing that has ever blown my mind is you."

"That's a great line." I laugh.

"It's not a line. It's how I feel." His penetrating gazes are becoming increasingly difficult to ignore.

"Well, excuse my skepticism. It's hard to believe anything you feel is real when it's a big fat secret. I get your reasons, but that doesn't make it easy to accept them."

"No, and I fear you're going to continue to doubt how much I care for you. I can see why though. I know secrets make you uncomfortable. I get that."

"So what are we going to do about it?"

"How about we take it one day at a time?"

"That sounds like an awful idea."

He exhales, dragging his hand through his hair. "To be honest, I don't have any solutions. Right now I can't risk my job. I'm sorry."

My teeth crush down on my lower lip. Am I really willing to ask him to expose himself for us and risk losing everything he's worked for? What if I do screw up everything for him? Without his job, this passion he loves so much, he isn't the same guy. He isn't the guy I love.

"Why does this have to be so complicated?" I mumble mostly to myself.

"Most things of any worth are," he sings, a mysterious expression covering his face.

I slump slightly. *Why does he have to be so damn cute?*

Aiden steps forward, lifts his hand to my face but pauses before moving any closer. When I don't move away he closes the rest of the distance, brushing his hand against my cheek. A tiny spark radiates under his touch. "Did you miss me?"

I close my eyes, wishing I didn't have to answer this question. But Aiden doesn't need a device to steal my heart. "Yes," I breathe. "Like crazy."

He slides his hand down until it's gently resting along my neck. "Crazy doesn't even begin to cover it for me. I didn't have food for a week and still you're what I thought about most." I rise to my tippy toes, glide my arms around his back, and tilt my head, ready to meet his lips. He leans into me, but pauses an inch from my mouth. "You know I'm not worried about George," he whispers.

Whipping my arms off him, I step back with an exasperated groan. "Seriously, Aiden? You're bringing that up again? Right now? Are you insane?"

He pushes his way into my line of vision until I have no choice but to look at him. "Do you want to know why I'm not worried about George?"

"No doubt you're going to tell me regardless."

"Well," he says slowly, "if I knew everything you felt then you wouldn't be surprised when I fulfilled your desires, right? However, *I* don't know how you feel, and so I have the element of surprise when I give you exactly what you want."

"How long have you been working on *that* line, Dr. Livingston?" I finger a lock of my hair, feigning nonchalance.

"Honestly, it just came to me. When you're around I'm frequently graced with spontaneous inspirations."

"Oh?" I say, gnawing on a smile.

"Imagine how much better my work would be if you could lounge around my lab all day," he says, staring off like pondering the details of this scenario.

"I'm not sure you'd get any work done at all."

His eyes return to mine, a wolfish grin on his face. "No, I suspect you're right." His pronounced chin tips sideways, like he's trying to study me from a new angle. "Now would you kindly get over here, there's something I need to tell you."

"Aren't I close enough?" I gesture at the three feet of space separating us.

"Absolutely not."

I take one step forward. "How about now?"

He shakes his head again, a ghost of a smile on his lips.

I take another step, which I'm quickly chastised for with a glare.

"Well, if you wanted me right up against you, why didn't you just say that?" I say, taking the last step, feeling his warmth immediately.

"Roya, I want you right up against me." He strokes my hair away from my face and leans his forehead on mine.

"You had something to tell me?"

His smile disorients me, causing sudden lightheadedness. "I wanted to thank you. You risked your life to save me and if it wasn't for you then I'd be dead."

Automatically my hands slide around his waist. "Just doing my job."

Aiden tilts his head and closes in on my mouth. I lean into him, but when our lips are just about to connect he cocks his head back. I follow his action, seeking his lips. Again he angles away, darting an inch to the left, a playful expression present in his eyes. His toying is about to drive me mad. I drop my head in an act of defeat. "If you don't want to kiss me then you don't have to," I say.

"Oh, is that what you think?"

I look up at him, pinching the sides of my mouth together.

He takes my face in both his hands and pulls me into him with a hungry fervor. His lips smash into mine. His determination to prove his passion for me tightens my heart. Something uncaged escapes from within me. All my pent-up emotions, the ones I've harbored, are unleashed in this moment. Tears ache in my throat and each time his lips caress mine I'm closer to the dam within me bursting open. He's undoing me, tearing out my demons with burning strokes of his lips and the salty taste of his mouth. In his arms I'm changing, becoming anew.

Breathless, I break away, but only a few inches. My fingers interlock behind his back, bolting him in close. His forehead lowers and rests on my shoulder. He pants softly beside my ear.

"I would gladly spend another week with the Voyageurs for another kiss like that," Aiden says, straightening.

"You don't have to get abducted for me to kiss you."

"Thank God."

He smiles and dips down to kiss me again, this time slowly, treasuring each time our lips touch and we inhale each other. All I want is to feel this. Against my mouth I feel him smile again. It makes me smile too and I slide my head down until it's resting in the crook of his neck.

"I guess we're even," I say, my words muffled against his skin.

"How do you figure?" he says, a smile in his voice.

I raise my head. "Well, I saved your life. We're even now."

He doesn't take those sapphire eyes off me, just shakes his head. "Oh no, Roya, I believe I'm still one up on you. I've saved your life *twice*." He snickers and kisses me again. "Nice try, though."

Chapter Forty-Six

While the kitchen staff is still prepping food in the main hall I slip into my normal seat like I've done since I was discharged from the infirmary. Joseph has to eat at some point. I've beaten on his door for minutes at a time. I've even considered charging in to find out what he's up to. Instead, I always sulk away. He said he'd be gone a lot, but it feels like he's disappeared. And what if he has? When would I know for certain? Samara and Trent haven't seen him since the meeting in the infirmary. My instinct tells me he's dream traveling, but how can he be gone for so long? When I consented to him going back to this project I forgot about how the last time it turned him into a different person, one I couldn't reach.

My routine mealtime vigilance has earned me certain knowledge. I know which staff members prep the fastest, who dawdles while socializing, and that at exactly thirty-eight seconds before meals are scheduled to start the last food runner darts back into the kitchen. Usually the main hall remains quiet, save for the sound of the Sterno-heated pans sizzling in their water baths, until the first few people file in for food. A group of white coats always marches in a minute past the hour. Then George, followed by a horde of people I don't know.

"Here, I brought you your usual," George says, laying down a bed of wilted greens and a mound of marinated veggies nestled next to them.

"Thanks." I meet his gaze and instantly regret it. His eyes say a whole host of things that trip wires around my heart.

"Still nothing?" he asks, pushing his roasted potatoes around with his fork.

I shake my head. "At what point do I turn in a missing person's report?"

"I don't know. Are you attuned to the connection you have with him?"

"Yes, and I know he's somewhere close. Not more than a layer away. But still…" I trail off, catching sight of Aiden as he strolls by, two full plates in his hands. As he has on every occasion, he pretends I don't exist while passing, taking a seat at the table beside ours.

256

Actually I thought it was an act until he almost ran into me the other day in the hallway. He was deep in conversation with the new scientist he hired to replace Amber. Her name is Mia and she's tall, slender, and her long black hair drapes down to her perfectly toned butt. I thought when Aiden jostled by me, knocking my shoulder so I dropped the books I'd borrowed from the library, I'd get an apology, but I hardly got a second glance.

"How are you feeling?" George asks, taking a sip of water.

"*You* should be forbidden from asking that question," I say between bites.

Behind his glass I spy the slightest of grins. "I've been trying to give you privacy. I thought it was what you wanted."

"Thanks," I say, stabbing my broccoli with a force it doesn't deserve.

"Specifically, I was wondering how you're feeling about Chase?"

"I hate him still," I say, acid in my voice.

"Good," George says evenly.

What I don't say is that the hate constantly morphs into unadulterated lust bordering on heart-aching love, one that if I don't have I'll die. I don't tell anyone this. Since these emotions aren't real I know I can battle them alone.

"How are you recovering?" George ask.

"Still sore, but mostly fine," I say, staring at a mushroom I've over-abused with my fork.

"Amazing, the skill Mae has."

Scanning the hall, I linger a second too long in Aiden's direction. He's in an animate conversation with a white coat. For all the attention he's given me I could cease to exist and he wouldn't notice. Instead of using all those cheesy lines Aiden should have been real with me, told me it was all just a fun game. He was probably afraid I'd blacken his other eye. The idea runs through my head constantly lately. Every time I see him in the main hall and he grazes past me like we've never met, I fantasize about sending a roundhouse kick to his head.

"I'm sorry, George, I'm totally inconsiderate." I turn to him, lay a hand on his. "How are you feeling? How's the knife wound?"

A tamed smile touches his lips. "I'm at around eighty-five percent."

"Wow, that's impressive, considering it was just over a week ago that you were stabbed."

His hand grips my fingers, tugs them closer to him. "When we're both better I say we celebrate. There's a place I want to take you."

How is George always here, never wavering? Always offering comfort I don't deserve, company I'm unworthy of, and sympathetic looks which break my heart. He's not stupid though. He watches me, sees the disappointment that flares across my face every time Aiden strolls by high-fiving Trent, asking Samara if she's feeling better, and ignoring me completely. And he feels the ache that erupts afterwards. George is brilliant actually, because he knows by just being available, he's giving me the one thing Aiden refuses.

"I'm not sure I'm recovering as quickly as you," I say, my hand suddenly perspiring in his. "But I agree to a celebration once I'm up for it."

George swivels, a cautious look in his eyes. "Roya," he says, facing me, "I feel that someone you've been looking for is approaching."

My eyes go wide. The chair rubs the carpet, catching its fibers as it slides back. Ambling through the crowd, now only a table away, is Joseph. All breath leaves my chest as disbelief invades my head. His ghostly white hands tremble as they seek to hold onto the plate between them. Hollow eyes flick up to mine, a look of complete apathy on his nearly transparent face. His skin reminds me of that of an elderly person's, smooth, lacking its usual elasticity and color.

"Joseph," I choke out.

He nods his chin at me before taking a seat.

"Where have you been?!" All eyes in the main hall flick to me.

"Around," he says, his voice croaky.

"I've been looking for you. Worried," I say quieter, leaning across the table.

"I told you I'd be busy." Eyelids rimmed with spider web veins close. For an instant I think he's fallen asleep at the table. He rocks forward, catching himself right before he smashes his face into his ham sandwich.

I want to run around the table to him, but there's already too much attention on us. Trent takes the seat next to him, steadying Joseph's shoulder with his hand. I sit.

258

"Dude," Trent says, "you don't look so hot. Maybe you should have Mae check you out."

"I'm fine," he says, his drawl more pronounced. "Just hungry and tired, that's all."

From the concaved appearance of his cheeks, he doesn't look like he's eaten in days. And I know for a fact that he hasn't had one meal in the main hall since I was released from the infirmary.

Joseph brushes Trent off and then pins his hands on either side of his plate, like he's trying to stabilize his equilibrium.

"What are you doing?" I ask. "What's causing you to act like this?"

"What do you mean?" He reaches out for his sandwich but misses it by a couple of inches. A grimace falls over his face until his hand haphazardly bumps into his sandwich. Satisfied, he grips it, brings it up to his mouth like it weighs a ton, and takes a large chomp.

"Joseph, I haven't seen you for a week. You..." I hesitate, embarrassed to say what I'm about to. My eyes find George's and he offers a reassuring nod. "Whatever you're doing looks like it's robbing you of your senses and your life. Don't you see that? You can hardly keep your head up."

"I don't know what you mean, Stark," he says, straightening, menace in his eyes.

"You don't know what I'm talking about? You look like a pitiful street beggar who's experienced a particularly awful winter under the bridges. Tell me why you look like you're on the verge of death."

"I already told you I'm working on something. It's draining, but I can handle it."

"Tell me what it is," I say in a hush, sensing curious eyes from other tables spying.

"No." He lulls his head forward like it's suddenly weighted. "Give me a bit longer. It's wonderful and it will be worth the wait."

"It doesn't look like you have much longer," I say through clenched teeth.

"You're overreacting." He pushes his food away.

"I'm not. Either tell me what you're working on or stop it."

"No."

"Remember our deal before, Joseph?" I say threading my arms across my chest. "Before when you were working on this project I said if you didn't tell me what it was then I was going to leave the Institute, prevent you from pulling on my energy. Remember that?"

He nods, a coldness in his eyes. A standoff in his gaze.

"Well, the deal still stands. Tell me what's killing you slowly or I'm going to stop you by leaving the Institute, cutting off your extra energy supply." It's a split-moment decision, but I know as soon as it spills out of my mouth that it's the right one. I can't stay here allowing Joseph to pull on my energy for secretive reasons, ones that are turning him into a zombie. I'll deal with Chase. I'll keep Bob and Steve protected. And somehow by leaving Joseph, maybe I'll save him.

Beside me I sense George stiffen. I stay locked on Joseph.

"Seriously, Stark?" Joseph says, an ounce of his casual manner surfacing. "You're doing that one again?"

"I was planning on leaving before and would have if Trey hadn't stuck me on a project," I say.

"We both know you don't want to leave," he says shredding his bread into tiny bits like he's going to use it to feed ducks.

"We both know that I don't want to watch you kill yourself."

Bloodshot eyes ram into mine. Red embarrassment flares in his cheeks. I'm willing to stay locked in an intense stare-off with him for as long as it takes, but then Aiden materializes over Joseph's shoulder, breaking my attention. From the corner of my vision I spy him wave at me. My eyes rise to him and again he points in my direction and waves, looking impatient. "Yes, you, Mr. Anders. Join me over here, would you?"

Heat rushes to my head as I pin my eyes to the table. After a moment of deliberation, George stands and joins Aiden. The Head Scientist leans over, whispering something in George's ear. Then George nods and turns to leave.

Aiden is halfway back to his seat when Joseph calls out loudly, still not taking his eyes off me. "Hey, Livingston!"

Aiden pauses, turns. "Yes," he says in a much quieter voice.

"Get over here!" Joseph says, his face burning. As his twin I feel certain parts of him and right now his anger seeks to set me on fire. I take a drink of ice water.

"What can I do for you?" Aiden says, clapping Joseph on the back, not seeming to notice that a gesture like that could fracture my brother's weakened frame. Heat rises in my head.

"You can tell my sister that she can't move out of the Institute to some boondock town. Maybe she'll listen to you."

A smirk unfolds on Aiden's face, but it stays facing Joseph. "You're right, Joseph, she can't."

"See there!" Joseph says, pointing at me. "Now tell her that leaving here is stupid."

The Head Scientist can't look at me. Won't. I led the mission that rescued him and I'm not even worth a casual glance. "I don't have to and you don't need to worry any further. Roya isn't going anywhere."

How dare he speak about me like I'm not even here? Treat me like I'm not sitting a few feet away?

"If that's all I'll take my leave," Aiden says, standing tall, eyes still not finding mine.

"Yeah, you're dismissed," Joseph says, a satisfied grin on his face.

When Aiden and I parted in the infirmary, I was still unclear on our arrangement. Now I realize there wasn't one and that I was being used. Maybe he was making up all those excuses about why we can't be together. Maybe the real reason is he doesn't want to. I don't want to believe it, but my ego can only take this neglect for so long before it decides that he never really wanted me at all. Aiden loves games and unfortunately I think I just got played.

"Well, there you are, Stark. How do you like that?"

"You've lost your mind," I say in an undertone, watching Aiden's retreating back. "You think that because some stupid scientist says I can't leave it makes it true? I can do whatever I want. Campaign all you like, but the fact still remains that I'm not staying here." I stand up from the table, press my palms down on its surface. "While I'm off enjoying the country air, try not to kill yourself, would you?!"

Chapter Forty-Seven

When the knock sounds at my door I answer it, hoping it's Joseph. Hoping he's changed his attitude.

"Don't leave," George says when the door slides back, a penalizing tone in his voice.

"Please, not right now, George," I say, wringing my hands. "I don't want to argue with you about this."

"Then don't," he says, stepping into my room and sending the door closed behind him. "Just talk to me. Let me help you," he pleads.

I know how that feels: to plead. I know how it feels to wish someone would give you a chance to help them. "You don't understand, George," I say, looking off. "Being here—"

"Hurts," he finishes my sentence. "Watching him abuse himself plagues you. And you feel like leaving will erase the pain, since you can't erase the problems."

He does understand. Perfectly. Simultaneously I want to rush into his arms and also shield myself from his prying. Instead I wrap my arms across my chest.

A stricken expression marks his face. "Even after you leave here you'll still worry. The torment won't go away."

"I know. I'm cursed to carry this emotion no matter where I go. But if I'm not here then Joseph can't pull on my energy and maybe he'll be forced to quit this secret project. Maybe—" The smile that flickers to his lips interrupts me. "What? What are you smiling about?"

"I love the way you think."

"Think? What?" My brow knits with confusion.

"It's exactly the same way your heart feels: selflessly. You would remove yourself from the Institute when you really don't want to just to protect him." He looks impressed, although the smile has faded.

"Well, now that you understand my flawless reasoning behind leaving maybe you'll give me a break."

His determined look feels to be anchored by a deep motivation. "Roya, how can I not fight you on this? How can I support this decision when it takes you away from me?"

Takes you away from me. His heavy words stick in my core. I don't belong to George, but do I want to?

"You may not know what you want, but I do," he says, a secret desperation written on his face. My eyes clench shut, frustrated that I can't have a normal conversation with him. One where he isn't one emotional step ahead of me.

"I know what you want," I say, opening my eyes to find him chewing on his lip. "You want me to stay and I appreciate—"

"No, Roya, let me be clear. I want you with me," he says, a careful conviction in his words. "I want to fulfill the desires you've buried inside you, the ones for love you don't feel you deserve. And I can't do that if you leave."

"Why?" I ask, my voice just above a hush. "Why are you so devoted to me?" What I don't ask is why he's still loyal to me after everything with Aiden.

George dips his chin, studies my face. "Roya, you bring me clarity. I've lived my life in a cloud of emotions, but when I'm with you the way I feel is so intense that *my* feelings take center stage. They become the rare priority."

A knot settles in my throat, followed by a raw aching. He makes it sound like he needs me, like I'm the antidote to the disease he's suffered from his entire life. How can I not give him that? Be his antidote?

Deranged by my confusion and constant heartache I impulsively spring forward. In one movement my fist knots in his shirt, pulling him into me. Our lips meet in a rush and his startled reaction only lasts for an instant and then he's kissing me back. Lust joins my other tangled emotions rolling around inside my chest. Then in all my furious passion, I'm interrupted by an angry shame. It roars through my head like an incensed monster.

I firmly press my hand flat against his chest, shoving him a few inches. "I'm sorry. I shouldn't have done that." Guilt shivers out of my voice. "I'm sorry," I repeat. "Something just took over me."

The light in his eyes dims. "Don't be sorry," he says.

"I don't know how I feel or what I want right now, George. I really don't want to hurt you." I close my eyes, not able to bear seeing his disappointment. "I'm sorry."

"You don't have to know what you want right now. And you have my permission to hurt me. Break my heart into a thousand pieces, just don't be sorry you kissed me."

He tilts my head up so I meet his brown eyes. "I know what I want though. You know what I want. Hell, the whole Institute knows. It isn't a *secret*." The insinuation hangs in the air like a cloud of dust.

His hand drops, but I stay locked on his eyes. Anger blazes across his face. "You deserve to be loved openly."

And once again he's done it. He's dipped into the deepest reservoirs of my emotions and found the hollowed out part of me and filled it.

"You do too, George."

"Then this kind of seems like a no-brainer to me," he says, a smile in his voice.

A nervous laugh escapes my mouth.

"Before we left for the Grotte you said you'd tell me how you feel about me. I told you to wait. Will you tell me now?" He's encased behind his normal hardened exterior. With all its intimidation it still begs to be broken.

"Well, you already know."

"But I want to hear it from *you*."

"Okay," I say to the carpet. "I feel like you sincerely care about me. I feel like your loyalty is unconditional."

"Never mind." Anger flares in his words.

"George," I say, astonished.

"Roya, I already know how I feel about you. That's not what I asked."

"I'm sorry. I'm a coward."

"No you're not." He runs his thumb along my jawline. "You're the most stunning person I've ever met."

"I feel…" I stop, studying the pulsing in my heart. "I feel like I don't deserve you."

A question rises in his eyes, but he doesn't speak.

"I keep trying to convince myself that it doesn't matter, but I fear one day you'll wake up and see me for who I really am, and not the idolized version that I think you see right now. When that happens then I'm going to be destroyed inside because I'll have convinced myself that my love for you was enough even with all its flaws."

He shakes his head, a knowing look in his eyes. "What you don't know is an ounce of your love is greater than most people feel in a lifetime. I felt that you could control the wind before you knew it, because you carry its power in your love."

In that moment he must know he owns me. I could look away and break the spell, but I don't. Rising to my tiptoes I wrap my arms around his neck, pulling him down to me. "George, I have no idea what I'm doing anymore. I'm so confused," I say, my words brushing against his skin.

His hands grip my hips, drawing me into him. "Stop thinking so much and just do what feels right."

I rub my nose against his and our lips graze. I take in the shape and firmness of his mouth. With each soft kiss I study him more, absorbing the way his hands clutch my hips, his thumbs caressing my hip bones. George's kisses are hungry, and resonate in my lips even after he pulls away.

♦

"You did what?" Samara looks at me in disbelief.

I kick the sand a bit, feeling the weight of my bad decision in my heart. Even the brilliant blue-Gatorade-colored water on the beaches of Bora Bora aren't making me feel better right now.

"I know, it was the stupidest thing I've ever done," I say, chewing on the inside of my cheek. "I feel so guilty kissing both Aiden and then George. I feel dirty."

Samara twists her long hair up on her head and pins it there with a few bobby pins. "Ummm...I disagree. It was the smartest thing you've ever done."

The gentle water splashes up on my feet and ankles before receding again. "I'm sure you have some incredibly flawed reasoning that's supporting that opinion," I say, staring off at Mount Otemanu.

"No offense, but you're about as affectionate as a great white shark."

"Ha," I laugh. "None taken."

"But George changes you," Samara says. "When before George did you ever make the first move?"

"Never," I say after a little deliberation.

"If you ask me, George is good for you."

I hadn't asked her, but I should have realized the moment I told her about last night that she was going to offer unsolicited advice.

"If I had the choice between Aiden and George I'd pick George for sure. Those shoulders and that chest," she says, staring off like she's imagining him right now in her head.

I slap her playfully across the arm. "Would you stop picturing George naked for a second so we can have a productive conversation?"

She smiles slyly.

"Honestly, I don't have a choice between the two," I say. "There's only George. Aiden has made it pretty clear that whatever we had was a joke and I'm dead to him. More than anything I want to confront him, but I can't muster the nerve."

A sudden laugh rolls out of her. "You faced Zhuang and you can't get up the courage to find out why some guy is giving you the cold shoulder? You're ridiculous."

"Samara, please don't make me break your nose again."

She gives me a mock look of horror and covers her nose like she's trying to protect it.

"Anyway, I'm not sure if I should be with George. Being with him is complicated since he's always invading my heart. I want to believe it could work, but... And I still have feelings for Aiden. I need to purge those from my system before I commit to anything. That's what makes me feel so guilty. I wish I would have done that before kissing George. Now I feel shameful."

"Yeah, apparently playing hearts runs in your blood," Samara half jokes.

"That's low," I say, kicking up water on her.

She jumps back and laughs. Just then I notice a strange man leaning on the railing of his over-the-water hut. It's odd because he's staring straight at us, but I know he's in the physical reality and can't see us while we're dream traveling. It must be a coincidence that his eyes follow us all the way down the beach.

When we tire of walking, which takes a long while, we peel down to our bathing suits and swim. The water is soothing as I slice through the waves.

"So, I'm going to go back to investigative reporting," Samara says as she wades.

"Oh, that's great!" I say, moving freely with the current.

"Yeah, I had to be cleared by my therapist. Apparently I was suffering from post-traumatic stress disorder. After a week's sabbatical in the psych ward I've been downgraded to therapy only twice a week," she says, wiggling her nose.

"Or you told them what they wanted to hear so they'd release you."

"Well, if I told them that I was still having nightmares of stabbing Pearl then I'm fairly certain they would have made me keep up the three-therapy-sessions-a-day routine. It's impossible to get anything done with that kind of schedule."

"How are you feeling now?" I look at her and add, "Honestly?"

"Good," she chirps. "Mostly. I mean, I get it. I know I had to kill her. The logical part of my brain accepts this and has already moved on. However, there's the emotional part of my brain that still can't come to terms with the actions that made Pearl dead. I replay it in my head on a regular basis and it never computes. The good news is that with each passing day I replay it fewer times than the day before." She looks at me hopefully. "I think that's a good sign."

I consent with a nod.

"You know who I spent my afternoons with?" Samara asks.

I shake my head.

"Misty. Can you believe it? She's like a vegetable. She can still move and all, but she hardly ever does. Seriously, she's like a stone statue. Nothing seems to be going on beneath the surface. She's this shell of a person. It's odd. Anyway, we played a lot of Chinese checkers and shockingly I won every single game."

The idea of Misty imprisoned in a mind that hardly functions, all because Zhuang was using her to destroy me, makes my stomach churn. Yes, she got under my skin and I could hardly stand to be in the same room with her, but I didn't want her to become some catatonic, permanent resident of the Institute's psych ward. What I really wanted was for her to fight Zhuang, but now I know that was never meant to happen.

"So when do you start investigative reporting?" I ask, trying to shake off the remorse.

"Tomorrow. Shuman said I can move into the Institute permanently and do it full-time."

"Wow! What about your other life?" I ask.

"Actually I emancipated myself from my mom right before coming to the Institute. I'd been living with friends on and off for a few months prior to that. My mom and I never really got along and my stepfather pretty much hates my guts. I always told my friends that when I'd saved up enough money I was going to New York to be a model. They probably all assume that's what I've done," she says, now lying on her back, staring off at the ultramarine blue sky.

I smile, rolling over to my back too. "Well, it sounds like you have a home now."

"Yeah, it feels nice."

◆

About Leaving the Institute

Bob and Steve <bobandsteveharvey@gmail.com>
to Roya Stark

Dear Roya,

You didn't tell us about Chase? Why? From how Trey described it, that was an important part of the events at the Grotte. He informed us that Chase has an unhealthy fascination with you. Furthermore, he thinks, and we both agree, that you would be safer if you remained at the Institute. This disappoints us greatly, but your safety comes first. Here, at our place, we can't offer the same protection that the Institute provides. Chase is dangerous and it makes us nervous that he could want you for some reason.

We can already sense you rebelling against the message in this email, but also know that if Trey has a concern about Chase then we must

268

take this extremely seriously. Trey is logical and his instincts on these things are never wrong. If he thinks there's a danger then he's probably right. Please stay vigilant and guard yourself. Also, write as often as you like. We want to know everything that's going on with you.

Love,
Bob and Steve

This is Trey's doing. This is due to his influence. His interference. He does control me more than I thought or was willing to admit. Angry tears well up in my eyes. I push them back with everything I have.

Chapter Forty-Eight

Unconcerned for the early hour I knock on his door. I assume he's in his office. Sure enough a rustling greets my knock seconds later. Then the door slides back and Trey stands staring at me, bleary-eyed, tired.

"Hello, Roya." He looks around behind me like he assumed I wasn't alone. "Do you want to talk to me?"

"Briefly."

"You can have as much of my time as you like." He stands back and welcomes me into his office.

I must have been too panicked when last here. That time I didn't notice his large wooden desk. I'm not sure how I missed it with its turrets on each side and all the exquisitely engraved details. For some reason it feels like the sturdiest piece of furniture I've ever seen. If there was an earthquake, I'd want to be under that thing. It looks indestructible, and also beautifully elegant.

"It was Flynn's," Trey says.

My head jerks up, wondering if he's read my thoughts again. His eyes are resting on my hand, which I now realize is tracing along the intricate detail work on the front of the desk.

"It's not my style. A bit too ornate, but I wanted to keep it." A fond nostalgia wrinkles his eyes. He must have respected Flynn very much. Everyone seems to have.

Apparently I've been off in thought and have somehow ended up in the leather chair stationed in front of Trey's desk. He's scanning the contents of a shelf, moving objects around. "Here it is," he says, plucking something from the back. "I'm glad you stopped by. I have something for you." He places the object on the desk in front of me. It's a copper and bronze statue of a Buddhist-type figure sitting on a horse. The features of the person and horse are painted in animated blues, reds, and golds.

Trey walks around his desk and sits. "I picked this up the other day because when I saw it I thought of you."

I gauge him and then study the statue.

"The figure," he says pointing at it, "is Achi Chokyi Drolma. A full history on her would take quite a while, but—"

"She's the mother of the Buddhas," I interrupt him.

He looks surprised. "Yes, that's correct. She also protects an ancient lineage as well as Buddha's teachings. She's an extremely symbolic figure and is thought to offer protection from obstacles and difficulties." I chew on my lip, staring at the statue. "Later, I can fill you in on more of the details surrounding her. They're fascinating. I was actually raised by Tibetan Buddhist monks and although I don't practice that religion anymore, it's still close to my heart."

Is Trey sharing with me? Why? That's odd. It's probably a trust-gathering technique so he can cover up more secrets and lies.

"Do you follow the Buddhist religion?" he asks, looking curious.

"No. Why?"

"Well, many people wouldn't know who Achi Chokyi Drolma is."

"I read," I say. "Honestly, I don't know what I believe in."

He nods his head, a conspiratorial look. "I think because we're Dream Travelers it's difficult for us to choose merely one religion. We see so much more and with that comes an overwhelming burden. For me, one religion isn't enough. I need all of them to make sense of my world. And even then, sometimes I still don't feel like it's enough."

Disbelief clouds my head. Trey doesn't even sound like himself right now. Or at least he doesn't sound like the persona that he's modeled since we've met. And even though anything he says I want to reject, what he's shared is one hundred percent the way I've felt for too long. Undeniably I need to be connected to the spiritual realm, but some days it's difficult to know what I should believe. Sometimes I fail to find a philosophy or religion or inspiration that helps me navigate my life. And that's when I feel as alone as the coldness in Trey's eyes right now.

"I hope it's all right that I've given this to you," Trey says, bringing me out of my reverie. "I thought you could use a good luck charm of sorts."

"Why? Are you sending me on another deadly mission?"

Something passes in his eyes. Amusement maybe? "Not currently. I was referring to the protection I thought you could use against Chase and whatever he has planned for you."

"Well, thanks."

271

"You're welcome."

A silence fills the space between us. It doesn't seem to make him uncomfortable. I allow another long few seconds to roll by as I study him.

"Now are you here because I've ruined your chances of escaping the Institute for a second time?" he says, leaning back in his chair, threading his fingers together.

"You'd think so, but actually no."

Trey gives a curious expression, mixed with relief.

"I just figured that maybe you could exert some of that influence that seems to work on everybody else to do *me* a favor."

He looks at me blankly for a second and I just let him sit and wonder.

Finally I say, "It's Joseph."

A sudden look of concern crosses Trey's face, but it quickly passes. He remains quiet. I explain Joseph's strange behavior before the Grotte and then how he got better. "Now he's slipping away again. Hardly anyone ever sees him. I don't think he's eating much and I'm really worried." A thought occurs to me. I narrow my eyes. "You don't have him working on something, do you?" I ask, accusing.

Trey shakes his head, looking off deep in thought, contemplating the information I've given him. The look of concern has returned to his eyes. He runs his fingers though his silver hair. "I apologize for not seeing this earlier. I figured he was having trouble adjusting to the Institute." Trey focuses his turquoise eyes on me. "I wish you would have brought this to my attention before now," he says, a harshness in his tone.

Oh, so now this is my fault. I won't be shamed. "Whatever. You know about it now," I say, copying his tone. "I want you to intervene. Find out what he's into and stop him. It can't be good. He's not himself. And you owe me this. If I'm going to be forced to stay here, then I want you to make Joseph stop doing whatever it is that's causing him to be..." I stop, searching for the right word. When I'm unable to find it I finally say, "*this* way."

Trey studies his hands lying on his desk. He presses his lips together and shakes his head. Then he rubs his head, seemingly on edge. "Roya, I'll do everything in my power to bring Joseph back." When Trey finally looks up at me his eyes are red, exhausted. "I fear that whatever he's mixed up in isn't good. If it's what I think, then it's… lethal."

I blink as those words sink in to my brain. My heart races. Mouth parched. Fingers tense around the arms of the chair. That one word strips me of any remaining peace. "What?!" I say.

"Let me do some checking and I'll get back with you as soon as possible. In the meantime find your brother. Don't let him leave the Institute again." Trey stands and hurries around the desk. He picks up the statue and hands it to me. It's surprisingly heavy for its size. The cold metals remind me of my bracelet. Taking Trey's not so subtle hint I make my way to the door.

"I'll be in touch with you soon," he says, hitting the button for the door.

I don't look back or acknowledge him as I exit his office. Worry sprints through my mind like a zebra trying to escape a hungry lion.

Chapter Forty-Nine

For five solid minutes I beat against Joseph's door, barking threats which quickly turn into pleas. Trey's word echoes through my mind again, disrupting my rational side. *Lethal.* Joseph could be mixed up in something lethal. Instinctively I knew it, but to hear it spoken out loud makes the impending doom feel inevitable. I slam my palm down on the button for his door. But it remains locked in place. How's that possible? I didn't think these doors locked. Mine doesn't. Or does it? Again my hand taps the button, this time repeatedly. I remain staring at a solid mass of door.

Sliding down I nestle up next to his door. I wait. I try to read to pass the time, the waiting, but my brain won't focus on words. I lose track of the hours that tick by. And in that time fear slowly morphs into anger. How could Joseph be so dumb to get himself mixed up in something dangerous? How can he make me worry like this? I want to think I would never put him through this torment.

The elevator announces its arrival. I look up, praying that this time Joseph is the one about to step off. The groan that escapes my lips is automatic when I clamber to my feet. I've been hunched over for too long on the hard ground. My wound is not pleased with me.

"You all right?" Aiden asks, peeking his head around the corner.

My head swivels, certain he must be talking to someone behind me. We're alone in the hallway. I stretch, testing my limbs.

"No," I say, shaking my head. "If you remember, I was shot." I scowl at him as he saunters toward me. "Saving you," I add.

He peers at me sideways, obviously caught off guard by my belligerent attitude.

"I'm glad I ran into you. I was just about to send you a mess—"

"It was you, wasn't it?" I cut him off.

Aiden raises a curious eyebrow. "Do tell me what I'm being convicted of this time."

"You told Trey I was leaving."

"Actually I didn't. But I was right, wasn't I? Under the current circumstances he wasn't going to let you leave."

"If it wasn't you, then who told him?"

"I'm guessing it was someone else interested in keeping you here. I know a certain empath who perfectly fits that criterion."

I scowl again. If I keep it up, my face is probably going to stick like that. "George wouldn't do that. He wouldn't go behind my back."

"People who are obsessed with you will go to all sorts of lengths to keep you here."

"That's ridiculous. George isn't obsessed with me."

"Appearances suggest otherwise," Aiden says, not disguising the bitterness in his voice.

Two can play this game. "Well, it would *appear* that you're ignoring me."

A sigh flees his mouth. "God, Roya, I'm not ignoring you."

"Then why haven't you given me even the slightest look all week?"

"You seem to think I can be around you and contain my feelings," he says, a morbid laugh in his voice. "The only reason I'm talking to you now is because we're alone."

"That's absurd. You're the king of pretenses."

"Do I have a stupid grin plastered on my face right now?"

The question takes me by surprise. "What?" I say, scrunching up my brow. "Yes."

"That's because I'm looking at you," he says like I've done something wrong by existing. "Since I've returned from the Grotte I've had a hard time putting on the mask."

I don't want to believe anything he's says. It's another trick...but why? Why is he playing this game with me? "Did you really have to refuse to apologize when you ran into me in the hallway or not look at me once in the main hall all week?"

"I'm sorry, but yes. After the infirmary I kept trying to pretend, hide how I felt, but I can't do it, not like I used to. I found I could hardly look at you without..." He pauses. Swallows. Sighs. "Almost dying, heightening everything. And you almost died too. And now every time I'm close to you something irresistible takes over and I'm battling to resist it, but it's getting more difficult. That's why I've been pretending to ignore you, but I can promise you I'm not. I'm all too aware of your presence, all too aware." My pulse gallops in my head. I steal a giant breath. "I watch everything you do." He says it like it's a curse. "Every look. Every movement. Every word. My attention is always hinged on you. Every ounce of it."

"That hasn't been my observation," I say.

"That's because it's complicated. You know that already." He rubs his forehead, obviously aggravated. "The truth is I can't take my eyes off you, personally or professionally. It's part of my job to watch you."

"How romantic."

"Look, Roya, Trey's ordered me to keep a very close eye on you. He's incredibly concerned that Chase is going to attempt to do something to you soon."

"He's overreacting,"

"No he's not. Chase abducted me." A chill runs through his eyes. "I'm certain he'd take you if he had the dream blocker."

"You know what? I can't keep up these pretenses with you. I understand why you have to, but it's hurting me. Every time you pass me without a single glance my heart aches. Let's *just* be friends. Then you can focus on your job and I won't feel used."

"Used? That's the furthest thing from the truth, Roya. I genuinely care. I want you, but Trey—"

"I'm so tired of Trey dictating my life. I can't live where I want, do what I want, love who I wa—" *Shit.* I clench my eyes shut. Those words didn't just come out of my mouth. *They didn't. They didn't. They didn't.* My eyes open to find a satisfied grin covering Aiden's face. *I guess they did.*

"Trey does exert his influence on everyone's lives," Aiden says. "I believe his intentions are good though."

I can't find a single person at this Institute to take my side against Trey. "I want to control the parts of my life that I'm allowed to, Aiden. I get that you can't afford to risk your career and I'm not asking you to. But I'm not putting myself in this position anymore. I won't be your secret any longer." I can't believe what I've just said. Affirmed. I'm fairly certain that my heart has fallen on the ground and is slowly taking its last throbbing beats before it dies.

His blue eyes drop to his shoes, but not before I catch the disappointment emblazed in them. "I'm sorry, Roya. I haven't put you in a fair position."

"It's not about what's fair, it's about what's smart. It's foolish to want something I can't really have. I'm tired of pretending this works." I motion between him and me. "It doesn't," I say, smothering the approaching tears with a blanket of threats.

His eyes are still pinned on his black Converse shoes. I expect him to dissuade me or launch into a speech. Instead he only nods. It's almost worse than any words because even from his hooded face I know it's over. One nod ended it all.

"I have to go." *I don't.* "I have something I need to do." *I don't.* Another nod.

Brushing past him, I start for my room. I might be imagining it, but I feel like I'm limping, wounded physically by the last few minutes. My legs are warm jelly. Still I will them forward with excruciating effort. Tears are winning the battle against my determination and soon they'll erupt, but not here. *Please not here. Not in the hallway.* I don't turn back when I reach my room. Can't. I know Aiden hasn't moved from the spot where I left him, but looking at him now will undo me.

Once in the sanctity of my room I slide down against the wall and cradle myself with my arms. Suddenly the tears which had been waging war on my insides have disappeared, replaced by numbness. I'm too shocked to cry now. It's impossible to believe what I've done. The last few minutes are a surreal nightmare.

All I wanted was Aiden back. Safe. And I deluded myself into believing that he'd choose me when he returned. How couldn't he? And when he held me in the infirmary I convinced myself we belonged together. He was the one. But love is a two-way street. And he doesn't... George was right. I deserve to be loved by someone who can give me what I want.

The knock makes me jump, because it is both unexpected and loud. Pressing myself up to a standing position I steady my breath and stare at the stainless steel door in front of me. Who knocked? What if it's Joseph? My finger glides against the button. I freeze. What if it's George? I can't face him right now.

"Roya, please open up." Aiden's voice is scratchy and low, like he's speaking right into the crack between the door and the wall.

The button clicks gently under my fingertips. His hands drop from his face. Undeniable grief cloaks his features.

"I lied before." Ache is tangible in his words. "When you asked me in the infirmary if I thought I was going to die at the Grotte, I lied. I did think I was going to die and my mind was filled with regret. It wasn't the same regret that I always thought would haunt me in a deadly situation. It wasn't about the things I hadn't discovered or created scientifically. My solitary regret was that the only girl I've ever loved didn't know it." He pauses, assessing my reaction. I'm stone on the outside, but inside every crazy emotion he elicits is squirming around, trying to find a way out. "I regretted that I'd been too much of a chicken to risk my career to be with her. And then I was rescued and once in the safety of the Institute I buried the regret, hoping to figure out a strategy later. I told myself that we had time to be together when things weren't so complicated. I convinced myself that the timing was wrong, but all my rationalizing was flawed. Because if my time at the Grotte taught me anything it's that life is unpredictable and I'm not promised a future, only a here and now."

"Aiden." My voice catches. "I'm not asking for you to risk your career—"

He holds up a hand to silence me. Then it drops but he doesn't say anything; his eyes just shift back and forth between mine. Tense seconds pass. Something similar to music fills my being. Jerks on my heart. Erases boundaries. Each moment he stands stoically assessing me the louder this silent music grows. "And I realize now that since I've returned the only thing I've risked is losing you. And that's unacceptable."

"Aiden, you still don't have to—"

"Roya, I love you." His words send rampant joy rushing through my veins. He steps forward and brushes his hand against my cheek. "I've loved you since the first moment your green eyes opened on the GAD-C. I may not have your gift to see the future, but I know you *have* to be in mine. I need you in my life."

I lay my hand over his against my cheek. His warmth fills the spaces between my heartbeats. I don't know what it is about him, but he lures me in so effortlessly and tangles my heart in a net. Can I really let him risk his career for me though?

He loves me. He freaking loves me! And all I want is to love him back. To shout my adoration for him through the Institute. To hold his hand publicly. But what if I ruin it all for him? What if he's ridiculed? What if that starts a domino effect that leads to a demotion or worse…termination? How can my heart feel heavy and elated at the same time?

278

"Do I have your permission to talk to Trey about this tomorrow?"

My eyes widen with disbelief. "Aiden—"

"I'll explain to him about our relationship," Aiden cuts me off. "I'll convince him it won't affect my work—that it will encourage it. Would that be okay?"

"You would do that for me?"

He shakes his head. "I would do it for us."

"But what about the other Head Officials? Won't they give you hell?"

He shrugs. "Fuck 'em. All I need is Trey to sign off, then I'm golden," he says, almost sings.

Before I know it his lips are on mine. They burn with a new intensity. Fire melts me into a million pieces. And if I can be put back together I want it to be with his hands which are pinned against my back, urging me nearer. I'm so close to him that his heart thumps against my chest and still I beg for more, wishing to erase the atoms I know that buffer us, that keep us from really touching. Threading my fingers through his gorgeously disordered hair I gently bite his bottom lip. He growls low in his throat. It sends a shiver down my back. Twice more he kisses me before peeling himself away.

Breathless, Aiden stares down at me. "Is my plan all right with you?"

I yank him back and laugh into his chest. Giddy.

"I'll take that as a yes." He laughs. "All right, tomorrow we'll go public. Tonight though, I need you to come down to my lab. I have something to show you. Will you meet me there in an hour?"

I nod, then pull him down toward me again, this time until we're only separated by a breath. "I love you, Dr. Livingston."

Chapter Fifty

A few minutes to six o'clock, I board the elevator and hit the button for the fifth level. Just when the doors are about to close an arm shoots through, halting them. They spring open again. Joseph's pale and sunken face floats into the elevator. Knees responsible for holding me upright give slightly. I steady myself on the steel wall. The cold hardly registers under my fingertips because all I feel is his intense pain, like a vise grip around my chest. All day I've been looking for this face and now I stand speechless, gawking at it. His features are wrong. Hollowed cheeks make his green eyes seem oversized. Lips so chapped they've split open in multiple places. "Hey, Stark," he says, in a guttural voice that shouldn't be his.

"Joseph?" I say, sounding wounded. "Are you okay?" The urge to wrap my arms around him, to hold him up because I sense he needs it, courses through me.

"I'm fine."

Instinctively I know he's lying. I reach out for his forearm, needing to know his skin is warm and his pulse is beating. He bats me off. "Leave me alone," he says, staring straight ahead.

"Trey says you might be mixed up in something lethal."

His eyes go wide with shock. He turns and looks at me for the first time. "You talked to him about me!? How dare you."

"I'm worried, and can you blame me? Look at you!"

"You may not understand what's goin' on with me right now, but that doesn't make it wrong."

"Joseph—"

"I don't know why you won't trust me." He twitches slightly.

"Have you lost your mind? Why would I trust you? Look at yourself. I can't be the only person who's telling you something is seriously wrong with you."

"Damn it, Stark!" Joseph roars, stepping into my face. "You're not the only one who can save the world. I might just have something to offer the Institute, if given half the f-ing chance."

I don't stand down or wipe his spit off my face. "Is that what this is about?"

"No." He shakes his head. "Well, yes, but it's not like that. I want you to give me a chance to prove that what I'm workin' on is worthy."

When the elevator doors spring open, I stalk off for Aiden's lab. Joseph follows. "I don't understand why it has to be a secret. Trey said...and it makes me worry."

"Sometimes you worry too much." His voice is bitter.

"Sometimes you're too flippant."

"Well, sometimes you act like you know it all," he fumes at me as we walk briskly.

"Well, sometimes you act like a selfish asshole!" I shoot back at him.

"Well, sometimes you can be a real bitch!" he yells as we round the corner into Aiden's lab.

A dozen puzzled faces stare back at us. "Surprise!" they say after a moment, not quite in unison. The intended enthusiasm is muffled by embarrassment.

Joseph and I freeze next to each other. Nerves hum in my chest as I take in the faces in front of me. Most mask the awkwardness behind a fake smile. I take a step backward and think about running away. But then the singing starts. "Happy birthday to you! Happy birthday to you! Happy birthday, dear Joseph and Roya. Happy birthday to you!"

Birthday? Oh, that's right.

I can't believe my friends threw a birthday party for us. That they remembered...when I didn't. Sentimental warmth radiates around my heart. Still I haven't moved, only let a smile form on my face. Joseph is better at this kind of thing. He holds up his arms, covered by his large leather jacket, and rocks his head back and forth.

"Yeah!" he says, pumping his fist in the air. "Thank you!"

The group goes wild. The party officially starts. Friends rush at us taking turns giving us hugs. First Samara, then an awkward one from George, then Trent, then Patrick, and then my arms almost wrap around Aiden but I pause. A nervous bubble rises in my throat when he looks at me.

Most of the group has swarmed into the center of the lab, which has a long buffet set up in the middle. Peacock and osprey feathers arranged in blue vases are sprinkled around the lab. Dozens of strands of Christmas lights hang vertically from floor to ceiling around the perimeter of the room. Overhead plays a song I don't recognize but instantly love. And playing on the TV over Aiden's main workstation is a Bruce Lee movie. The work that must have been put into this...and all before our conversation earlier. Aiden really wasn't ignoring me. How long had he been working on this? And with everything else he has going on? This explains why his eyes are rimmed red, although still carrying their usual excitement. *God, I love this guy.* For everything he's done and everything he's willing to do. And because a single look from him uncages the crazy monster inside me. I love when that monster roams free, sending flurries to my stomach and tightening my chest with excitement.

"Did you do this?" I point to him.

"Well...I had help," he says, taking my hand and spinning me around.

"Doesn't this kind of gesture expose us before you've talked to Trey?" I say, looking at him sideways.

"Not really. I believe this is a party for a girl *and* a boy," he says, with a half-smile.

I watch from the corner of my vision as Joseph chats with a white coat. Even with Aiden soaking up my attention right now I'm reluctant to take my eyes off my brother. He can't disappear again.

"Of course, we still need to be careful until after my meeting tomorrow," Aiden says, turning, following my line of vision. "I probably shouldn't have kissed you in the hallway earlier. I couldn't help myself. This is a delicate situation and I need to handle it that way. I don't want Trey to find out from anyone else but me since I suspect he'll have concerns."

"It's stupid that he'd have concerns about something that isn't his business."

"The Institute is his business, and we both work for it. So, Roya," Aiden says, in a different tone, "I've got a question I've been dying to ask you."

I pull my attention away from watching Joseph and look at him directly.

"The modifier. *You* used it," he taunts.

The sigh is automatic. "Are you serious?"

"Well, I think you know the conversation had to come up sooner or later." His hand reaches out for mine, but halfway to me he catches himself and drops it back to his side.

"I had no choice but to use the modifier. It was the only way to survive long enough at the Grotte. And then later it was the only way to survive long enough to get home."

"Hmm," Aiden says, rocking on his toes and then his heels, looking cunning.

"Dr. Livingston, gloating doesn't suit you."

"Whether it does or doesn't, I'm still relishing this one. You should expect no less after you chastised me for working on the device and now..." He lets the sentence hang in the air, a mischievous grin on his face.

"So you're saying I can't count on you to be the bigger person in these situations?"

He huffs. "Absolutely not. Physically I'll be the bigger person in our relationship. You'll have to be it in all other senses of the word."

Our relationship. Those words wrap around my heart like vines.

"Oh, you're going to try my patience, aren't you?"

"Every chance I get," he retorts.

"Well," I say, a little defeated, "I realize now the moral issues surrounding the modifier aren't black and white." A triumphant smile lights up his face. "Try and contain yourself until I'm done," I warn.

He holds up his hands like surrendering. "Continue."

"I'm not saying that I condone the modifier entirely, but I understand certain times warrant its use. I realize now that I'd cast a hasty judgment on you and for that I apologize."

"You continue to amaze me. If I could, I'd kiss you right now." I hold his gaze and smile politely, like he's just told a bad knock-knock joke. "Speaking of kissing you," he says casually. "I've already set up my meeting with Trey for tomorrow. I'll come and find you afterward and let you know how it went."

"Are you sure you still want to do this?"

He pauses for too long. If he says no right now it will be like being shot all over again, but this time I won't make a full recovery. "Sometimes we don't want to do something," he says, punctuating each word with a stroke of his hand, "but it's the only way to get us to where we want to be. And life is too short for regrets."

He holds out his hand. I shake it. Our last secret gesture. It fills me with desire and anticipation of what our life will look like tomorrow.

"To no regrets," I say.

Trent throws his arm around my shoulder. "Have I told you two how incredibly talented I am?"

"It's being published in all the Lucidite newsfeeds," Aiden tells him.

"As. It. Should," Trent says. "Seriously though, after only a little while working in the Strategic department, I've already been promoted."

"Wow!" Aiden says. "That's really incredible." His eyes stay focused on me.

"How's it working with Ren?" I ask Trent.

"About like you'd imagine. He inspires with fear, bullies us, and never offers praise. But hey, the pay is worth it," Trent says.

"There's not enough money in the world," I say.

Aiden winks at me. "Good to know you can't be bought."

"Yeah, Roya might have integrity, but that don't buy you a mansion in the Hollywood Hills." Trent chuckles.

"Well, if you'll excuse me I need to go grab something." Aiden bows low to both of us before leaving.

"So you and Aiden, huh?" Trent says, watching him stroll away. "Or is it you and George? I'm confused."

Blood rushes to my face. "Well…" How can one word be laced with so much guilt?

"Girl, I'm not judging. Just asking."

"Maybe I should get rid of both of them and take you up on all your offers."

"That's probably a poor decision on your part. I like to flirt but if I'm honest you're not my type."

"I can change," I say, a laugh in my voice. "What's your type?"

"Shorter hair for starters."

"Hair can be cut."

"And I like 'em taller too."

I snap my fingers and swing them through the air. "Oh well, I can't do anything about that. Maybe Samara's your match, if she chops her hair that is."

"And switches her gender," Trent says, poking me in the ribs with his elbow.

"What?" I gasp. "I had no idea. You're always flirting with the ladies."

"Yeah, well I'm thinking about coming out. Tired of living a lie," he says, seeming distracted as he scans the room, looking for someone maybe?

"I know exactly what you mean," I say, a new pride in my voice.

An angry growl rumbles in my stomach. "Hey, I'll see you around, Trent. I haven't eaten all day."

The spread is incredible, far better than the offerings in the main hall, which is impressive. Trays of Thai, Greek, Lebanese, Persian, and Mexican food line the table. A satisfied grin spreads across my face. No meat in sight. Aiden must have known that just its presence might upset my taste buds. *God, I love that guy.*

The Styrofoam plate threatens to break from the contents I've loaded onto it. I slip another plate underneath for reinforcement. Creamy hummus on a soft pita slice has just greeted my tongue when Joseph hoarsely whispers in my ear. "Hey, Trey wants us in his office at seven."

I turn to look at him. "Yeah?"

"Yeah." There's a bite to the word. "He sent a message down here along with his best wishes."

I cram an olive in my mouth and shrug, unable to hide my satisfaction. Trey's going to put a stop to Joseph's project. Everything is going to work out.

"Try not to look so smug, would you? It's pissing me off."

"You'll be pissed off no matter what," I say in between bites of food.

"And would you eat like a lady, Stark? You've got tzatziki sauce dripping down your chin."

"I'm starving. Spent my whole day looking for you," I say, running the napkin across my face.

"Well, you found me," he says, storming off.

From the far corner of the room I feel George's eyes watching me. His penetrating gaze is unmistakable. Must be part of his gift. He maneuvers around Samara and Trent, his path no doubt headed for me. Suddenly I'm not hungry at all. Actually the contents of my stomach churn with dread. I drop my plate on a table. George is six feet away when the lights dim in the lab and two cakes blazing with candles roll out on carts pushed by kitchen staff.

Unabashed glee rips through the tension that was mounting. Again the crowd serenades us with another round of "Happy Birthday" and by the time the song is over I'm in front of the first cake. It's in the shape of a peacock. Joseph is beside me standing in front of his cake, an osprey. I chance a glance at him, but as I suspected he's not looking at me. He's already blowing out his candles. Leaning forward I suck in a breath and release it with my wish. Seventeen candles are extinguished immediately, their wax splattering onto the blue and green frosting. Again I steal a look at Joseph. I feel like we should say something, make a speech maybe. Thankfully, Aiden interrupts any of these plans forming in my head.

"Thank you all for joining us to celebrate Joseph and Roya's seventeenth birthday. I owe these two people so much. For that matter I owe the whole rescue team my life. They're not getting it, but regardless I owe it to them. Please join me on center stage, Samara, George, and Trent. I have something I'd like to give all of you who risked your life to save mine."

When we're all gathered around Aiden, he lays a small box, about an inch and half in diameter, in each of our hands. "These gifts are to show my appreciation for your efforts. It's not much, but it is a token of my gratitude."

The velvet-lined box makes a popping sound when I open it. Inside sits a silver ring with a small round black disk.

"You've heard of mood rings, right?" Aiden says. "Well, those work off of body temperature. Here in your hands you have what could actually be considered a real mood ring. Thanks to George I've been able to accurately detect real moods using an advanced technology. With this ring you will know your own mood and be able to warn those around you. Won't that be fun!?" he sings. Everyone laughs.

I pluck the ring from its box and place it on my finger. It automatically turns gray. Pasted to the bottom of the box is a legend. I scan it. Gray means anxious. That's about right.

"Thanks, Aiden," Trent says, looking at his ring, which is currently purple. "I've never ever wanted something like this and I think it's completely useless."

Aiden smiles. His blue eyes dazzle. "You're absolutely welcome."

Pulling off the ring I stuff it into my pocket and flinch when George leans over my shoulder. "Rumor is you can't leave the Institute as planned."

I scrutinize him for a second. "Yeah, Trey won't let me leave. Not sure how he found out about it though."

"You've been avoiding me," George says, ignoring the accusation overloading my tone.

I bristle. "No I haven't." Thankfully the others have moved off to cut and distribute the cakes.

"Roya," he says, a warning in his voice. His eyes are sharp, like they were cut from stone.

"Look, I'm sorry, George, I'm preoccupied at the moment." I scan the room until I find Joseph in a corner talking to a girl with red hair. That figures.

"At the moment?" he challenges.

My gaze falls to the ground and as it does I catch notice of George's ring on his finger. It's black. Stressed.

"Fine, all the time, but especially right now." I look straight at him. "The truth is I have been avoiding you. I was really confused when I kissed you. I'm sorry."

"I'm not sorry. I just wished you'd do it when you weren't so confused."

"Well, maybe at some point life will stop being so confusing for once and then maybe I'll get everything all figured out."

"Yeah, maybe," he says coldly.

Over his shoulder I check the clock. It's almost time to meet Trey. "Look, we need to talk, but I have to go right now."

George scans my eyes. I haven't wanted to hide anything from him recently and so I'm slow to throw up my shield. His eyes narrow. "Roya, when I gave you permission to hurt me, I didn't mean right now. I meant after we'd been together for a long time. Like years."

Why does he have to make this so pathetically painful?

"George, I'm not going to hurt you." *That's a lie.* "We just need to talk about something. It's no big deal." *Another lie.* "But I can't get into right now. I've got to go." *Truth.*

I search for Joseph. It's like my new hobby. Surprisingly he's actually already waiting by the doorway for me. I'm halfway down the corridor when I hear footsteps racing behind me. I turn around just as Aiden pulls up.

"Hey," he says, panting softly.

"Hey."

"I wanted to say happy birthday, Roya."

"Thanks," I say. That's not all he wanted to say, but with Joseph around he's being careful. His smile speaks volumes though. His eyes flick to Joseph behind me. I suspect my brother is giving him a dirty look. "Happy birthday to you, Joseph."

"I'm sorry," I say, gaining back Aiden's attention. "We have to head out early. Trey's orders. Thank you for the party."

"My pleasure. I'll save you both some cake. See you tomorrow."

"Can't wait."

"Me either." There's a promise in his voice. I seize it for all it's worth.

Joseph tugs my arm and I turn and stride off.

Chapter Fifty-One

Trey stares at us across his desk with burdened eyes. After a minute he sucks in a long breath. "For almost a month now I've been traveling the globe, trying to figure something out. I kept thinking it was outside the Institute. I thought it was far away. And so that's where I searched." Trey shakes his head, looking absolutely revolted, like he's about to be sick. "I combed the world and it was here all along." Quite predictably Trey runs his hand through his silver hair. Joseph's knees jitter wildly under his hands.

Trey focuses on me, eyes heavy with concern. "My sources say that Zhuang is gaining power. Turning thousands of Middlings into hallucinators again. "

"What?" My voice comes out as a croak. "You're just now telling me this?"

He dismisses me with a shift of his eyes. "At first we thought— we hoped—he was dead, but then our reports indicated that he was alive, but only barely. And recently I've been informed that he's regaining strength."

"Trey, you—"

His hand flips up from his desk, a small movement but it still commands my silence. "I've searched, trying to determine how he could be recharging. My reports indicated that someone with significant ESP had been giving their power to restore him. That's why I've been away so much. I've been trying to find this person. You see, the only power that can heal Zhuang is clairvoyance. It's pure. It's everything that he needs to regain his strength and skills." Trey snaps his attention on Joseph. "You, Joseph, have unknowingly given your power to Zhuang."

Shock and repulsion flash across Joseph's face. "No, I haven't!"

"You have," Trey argues. "You have somehow brought him back from the depths of darkness which Roya had sent him to."

What Trey says is fathomless. Bob and Steve said he's never wrong. This has to be his first time. Has to be.

"I'm working on something else," Joseph says looking from me to Trey, his eyes growing more desperate each second. I want to believe his pleas, but it's difficult as I stare into his cold, hollow eyes. Could he have done what Trey is accusing? I knew he needed help, but I never imagined...

"It may appear as something else, but Zhuang has tricked you." Tragic disappointment brims from Trey's eyes. "Whatever you think you're doing is wrong. Look at what he's done to you! He's drained you!" Trey's usual even voice has elevated to a level I've never heard him use before. He loosens a breath and when he continues his voice is more restrained. "I should have seen this. I'm so sorry I let it happen." Again his hands sweep through his hair. "I should have—"

"Look," Joseph interrupts him, "you don't get it. I've been working on somethin' important and it has nothing to do with Zhuang. Your reports are wrong."

I turn and look at Trey, who's looking at Joseph, who's focused on Trey. I look back and forth between them again and again. "What is it then?!" I yell, the anxiety hammering my heart. "Tell me! Now!"

Joseph pivots so he faces me. Leans forward. "I didn't wanna tell you until I was closer to being done. It was supposed to be a surprise. I haven't been bringin' Zhuang back." He says it like it's the stupidest thing he's ever heard. A small smile pulls at his lips, a subtle triumph in his eyes. "I've found our father. I've been bringing *him* back."

Wading through disbelief and shock, I choke out a single word. "What?"

Joseph nods, victory spreading his face into a wide smile. "Yep, I've found our father. You're welcome."

"No you haven't!" Trey explodes, a thick vein popping on his beet red forehead. "It's Zhuang!"

Not only have I never seen Trey so livid, but Joseph's anger matches his. "He's not Zhuang! It's Stark's and my father!" Joseph turns to me, frantic. "I've seen him. You have to believe me. He's not Zhuang. He's old and gray-haired. And *not* Asian." He fires the last sentence at Trey.

"It's Zhuang." Trey's voice is steadier when he repeats himself.

"No he's not," Joseph hisses. Then he turns again and focuses on me. "Look, he loved us. He was wiped of all his power when our mother died. He's been ill this whole time, withering away in an awful slum." From the corner of my vision I see Trey shaking his head, his lips pressed into a thin line. "But he can draw power, like life force, from people, but only if they're willing. I've been givin' someone my power, but it's not Zhuang. It's our father."

A tenderness I haven't seen since I found out Joseph was my brother visits his eyes. Hope, that's what it is. And I know him enough to know he believes this, whether it's true or not. My heart palpitates like a snare drum. I want it to be true too.

Joseph reaches out, grabbing my hand. His fingers, frigid and bony. "He's much stronger now and I believe he'll survive. Stark, I can't wait for you to meet him."

"It's Zhuang!" Trey stands, pushing his chair back with a screech that assaults my ears. "He's used a projection to fool you. During the Day of the Duel he must have read your thoughts. Later he knew how he could lure you to him. And you have brought him back and almost killed yourself in the process," Trey's voice drips with disgust. "He's right too. He does need permission to leach energy out of someone and he has yours. Zhuang was too weak to steal life force. The only way he could recover is if someone willingly gave him theirs, but not just anyone. He needed a clairvoyant. He needed you. And he read your thoughts and knew he could manipulate you."

Trey puts his hand to his head like he's in pain. When he speaks his voice sounds a million miles away. In a hushed tone he says, "He's not only stronger now, he also has clairvoyance. You've restored this part of him. If my findings are correct, which I believe them to be, then Zhuang is more dangerous than ever before."

"But how do you know all this?" I ask.

"It's a part of my gift," Trey says, not taking his eyes off my brother. "I know for certain Zhuang has been revived and now I know it was Joseph."

Joseph stands. He's shaking his head furiously. "NO! NO! You're wrong! This isn't true! I didn't bring Zhuang back! The person I brought back is our father!" Tears well up instantly in his red eyes and race down his face. Raw ache envelops me immediately. I want to fold him in my arms, erase this pain and Trey's accusations. But I don't. I remain planted in the leather seat, unable to move.

"No, Joseph! It's Zhuang!" Trey erupts again. "You've brought him back and now he's going to come after Middlings, and Dream Travelers, and..."

Without him finishing his sentence I know what he's going to say. If Zhuang is alive he'll come after me. He'll finish the fight. He's wanted my consciousness for so long and only death would stop him.

Trey's anger, the yelling, this heart-wrenching news, and Joseph's desperation all combine to create an intense pressure in the back of my eyes. My head feels like it's going to detonate from the force.

Joseph throws his head in his hands. Shakes side to side. Over and over again. Crying. Moaning. Gasping. "No, no, no. You're wrong. You're so wrong."

"I'm not," Trey says through clenched teeth.

Joseph looks up, his face red. Frightened. "How can you be so sure?"

"Because I know. I'm one hundred percent sure you've brought Zhuang back," Trey says in a cool, but irate tone.

"But how!? How do you know the man I recovered isn't our father?!"

"Because I know who your father is!" Trey fires back.

Stunned, I whip my hand to my mouth, and a startled gasp breaks through it.

"What?" My voice comes out like a shiver. "Who is it?"

Trey's eyes close for a half beat. It's enough to make me crazy. When he opens them he doesn't look at us. "It's me."

The End.

Flip to the end of this book to continue your journey with the Lucidites and read the first chapter of the last installment: *Revived.*

Acknowledgements

While I was writing this book I kept calling it a "Monster." I'm 1126% sure I'd never have tamed it if it wasn't for the numerous people who supported me and my work. The first thank you for this one goes out to my husband, Luke Noffke. His unwavering support stuns me at times (yep, I just said that). I've abandoned him many a night when writing and editing this book. Too many mornings he's awoken (yeah, I did it again) to an empty bed. And every day he's expressed his encouragement to me for the efforts I put into this project. It's so much easier to write a book when you know the ones you love support your crazy routine and neurotic behavior.

Speaking of neurotic behavior, I want to thank Colleen Maliski for indulging my neurosis. I think I'm to blame for making you a little crazier. Yeah, I said it. You're crazy. Even more so now. I know that without you to bounce ideas off of I would have delivered a much lesser book.

Thank you to my daughter, Lydia. You're stronger than Roya, smarter than Aiden, sweeter than George, and funnier than Joseph. Again, my muse.

Thank you to my beta readers: Dane Maliski, Jennifer Wilkerson, Fay White, Heidi Magner, and Meghan Toledo. I seriously have the smartest, most insightful beta readers in the world.

Thank you to my friends and family. When I came out of the writer's closet I was embraced by such love and encouragement. It's intimidating to be a writer, but you all make it so much easier. Thank you to my father, Kathy, and Bea. Thank you to Randy and Edie Noffke. Thank you to my Anne, Chelsey, Cathryn, and Jason for all your support and to all the other family members who have shown me support throughout the years. I'm blessed with such a wonderful family.

Thank you to my editor, Christine LePorte. You did an even more spectacular job on this book than the last. Is that possible? And you're encouraging words made my heart sing. Yes, I used that corny phrase. Sue me…no, please don't.

Thank you to my cover designer, Andrei Bat. I know I really wore you out with the changes on this one, but you knocked out a truly amazing cover in the end.

Thank you to the musicians who inspired the playlist for this book: Cary Brothers, Counting Crows, Fiona Apple, Josh Doyle, Philip Philips, Christina Perri, The Fray, and Linkin Park. Fight scenes don't write themselves, they're only born by the angst in music. That's what I believe anyway after completing this book.

And lastly, thank you to my readers. I've always written because I was driven to. Then I took the next step and shared with you and my heart never knew how large it could grow. Your feedback and excitement over the books has been a true encouragement. I used to write just for me, but now I do it for you too.

Thank you to all!

Love,

Sarah

About the Author:

Sarah is the author of the Lucidites and the Reverians series. She's been everything from a corporate manager to a hippie. Her taste for adventure has taken her all over the world. If you can't find her at the gym, then she's probably at the frozen yogurt shop. If you can't find her there then she probably doesn't want to be found. She is a self-proclaimed hermit, with spontaneous urges to socialize during full moons and when Mercury is in retrograde. Sarah lives in Central California with her family. To learn more about Sarah please visit: http://www.sarahnoffke.com

Check out other work by this author:

The Reverians Series:
Defects, #1:

In the happy, clean community of Austin Valley, everything appears to be perfect. Seventeen-year-old Em Fuller, however, fears something is askew. Em is one of the new generation of Dream Travelers. For some reason, the gods have not seen fit to gift all of them with their expected special abilities. Em is a Defect—one of the unfortunate Dream Travelers not gifted with a psychic power. Desperate to do whatever it takes to earn her gift, she endures painful daily injections along with commands from her overbearing, loveless father. One of the few bright spots in her life is the return of a friend she had thought dead—but with his return comes the knowledge of a shocking, unforgivable truth. The society Em thought was protecting her has actually been betraying her, but she has no idea how to break away from its authority without hurting everyone she loves.

Rebels, #2
Warriors, #3

Spanish version of *Awoken*: *Despertada*

Turn the page for a preview of *Revived*, Book Three in The Lucidites Series.

Chapter One

If there were any windows in the Institute, I'd shatter them all. Assaulting stainless steel walls isn't just unsatisfying, it's ridiculously stupid. As evidenced by my bruised knuckles, steel is unrelenting to attacks. When glass shatters, it releases pain, numbs ache, dissipates anger. Steel mirrors me, amplifying the negative emotions. Encouraging them. I loathe metal. I'd tear my silver and copper bracelet off and chuck it across the Institute except it's the only thing keeping Zhuang from boring into my head and making me insane.

For the rest of my life, I will never forget the moments that followed Trey telling my brother and me that he was our lost father. Joseph's face paled; there was this weird mix of hope and pain in his eyes. Silence filled the room. I imagined a sound like sandpaper on tile as Trey's eyes shifted between Joseph and me. His fingers flexed as he braced himself, waiting for a response. Trey was already accustomed to my bad temper and tendency to explode, like when I learned that Joseph and I were twins. This time, I remained silent. Stunned.

Now I'm sitting in a remote corner of the Institute's five-story library. I have surrounded myself with fifty-eight books like a shield-wall. Hopefully this serves well enough to tell anyone who happens to find me that I want to be left alone. If it doesn't, then I'll rip pages out of the books and make a banner that reads "Stay Away!" I'm hoping it doesn't come to that. I love books and these are all of my favorites. Having them around me brings an ounce of comfort as I review the conversation from the night before.

Trey's words were like jagged pieces of stale bread that I was forced to swallow. After his confession, he explained in broken sentences that he had to split Joseph and me apart and have us raised by strangers. To protect us from Zhuang, he insisted. If we'd spent our childhood at the Institute, there would have been other problems. His eyes didn't look directly at us when he said, "It was difficult to make that decision, but that's the one I made. I know you're already wondering why I've kept this secret from you. I don't see what benefit you'll gain by knowing I'm your father. You'll just be consumed with resentment and frustration now—exactly what I wanted to avoid. The moment I split you up and sent you away from the Institute, I made the decision that you'd never know the truth. In light of the severity of our current situation, however, honesty is the only remedy."

He was deflecting his mistakes onto Joseph. Also, he'd already played that "difficult decision" card on me in the past. This was manipulation and I wasn't buying it.

Surprisingly, it was Joseph who asked the first question as I sat frozen. "Who was our mother?"

"Her name was Eloise. She was a Middling," he said, meaning that she couldn't dream travel. Even the description of our mother as a Middling stuck in my throat. I thought that soon I'd be gagging from all the new information.

"What happened to her?" Joseph asked, not meeting Trey's eyes.

"There was an accident on a ship with no way to save her." His voice was cold, businesslike, and it made me hate him even more.

When I finally spoke there was nothing "businesslike" in my tone. I had questions and I wanted answers. No more deceptions. "Who else knows?"

"Only Ren," Trey said, staring directly at me. "No one else knows I'm your father."

"Why him?" I asked, disgusted immediately.

"That's not relevant," Trey answered.

"You realize this is complete bullshit!" I yelled.

"I figured you'd see it that way," he said flatly.

"Roya," Joseph tried to caution me.

"Shut up, Joseph!" I roared, feeling heavy and motivated. "You know whose fault it is that Zhuang has been revived? It's yours!" I said, pointing a shaking finger at Trey. "If you hadn't kept everything from us then this never would have happened."

"Roya, I really wish I could take the blame for Joseph's mistakes, but I can't," Trey said, staring at me, eyes red.

"Well, Trey, I really *wish* you'd take your lies and Institute and shove them all up your ass!"

Needless to say, that was the end of that conversation.

♦

300

Somehow, by breakfast the next day, most of the Institute knew about the latest scandal. Sitting at my table, I stirred my oatmeal until it turned to sludge. I tried to make sense of something that was never going to compute, even if I owned all the greatest minds in the entire world—like my father.

"You don't have to be a mind reader to know you're about to murder someone of high status," Samara said, easing into the seat next to me.

"Oh, well, I'll work on altering my thoughts a bit. I don't want to get arrested." I gave a ridiculously fake laugh, then added, "Do the Lucidites have a police force?"

Samara shook her head.

"So do you know?" I asked, letting the question hang in the air like smoke after a fire.

She nodded and stared at my oatmeal, unable to make eye contact with me.

"And is it because the information is sitting on the top of my head?" I asked.

"Well, yes, and also because Patrick told me when I was having my omelet made."

"Oh, that's fabulous," I said without a hint of enthusiasm. "Just how you want your closest friends to find out the news." The Institute suddenly felt small, although it was huge and went on for miles. Everyone would know within the hour. No one would hear the news from me.

I looked up right then to find George framed in the entryway to the main hall. He scanned the room, then his eyes seized mine, a whirl of concern in them. Hurried steps brought him over to me. He blinked, like trying to clear suddenly blurred vision. "Roya, what is it?" he asked, taking the seat on the other side of me.

Undulant pressure rose to the surface at the sound of his voice. I shrugged in response to his question. It wasn't a good response, but it was the only one I could manage without turning into a blubbering idiot, which wasn't an option. His presence piqued every emotion—making them impossible to easily handle. Unable to meet his eyes, which were no doubt leaking with desperate concern, I shot Samara a look and nodded. She returned the gesture.

"Roya and Joseph just learned Trey is their father," she said too loudly, an excitement in her voice she failed to suppress. "As you can probably tell by scanning the main hall, most of the Institute has just learned this too. I found out in the breakfast line," she added in a conspiratorial whisper.

George turned to me, went to grab for my hand, but paused an inch away. "Oh, Roya, I'm sorry. This is so unfair."

Unfair. George overuses that word the same way people overuse the word *awesome.* Most things aren't awesome. The Milky Way is awesome. Niagara Falls is awesome. But a pair of shoes isn't awesome. A side of fries isn't awesome. Neither is a new hairdo or most other things that are described using *that* word. And most things aren't unfair. Fairness isn't something that even exists in the world I live in. Things just are. Trying to equate them using a scale of justice is ridiculous and only leads to frustration and defeat.

"It's okay, George," I said, sounding oddly like I was trying to console him in this awkward situation. "I'm not fine, but I will be. Just need time to process."

He leaned down low, his breath smelling minty. "I'm here if you need anything."

"You didn't know, did you?" I accused, suddenly gripped by the idea. "You didn't know Trey was my father, the way you knew Joseph was my brother? You said you could feel the connection between us and that's how you knew before I did."

He shook his head, a roughness in his eyes like he was appalled that I'd even consider the notion. "No. I hardly feel any emotions from Trey," he said.

"I'm not sure he has any," I said, looking up from the table and immediately regretting it. Most people in the main hall were staring at me like I was wearing a plate of spaghetti on my head. And one person's expression in particular was enough to snap my sanity like a twig. Aiden's eyes grew wide as the white coat next to him leaned over and whispered the news in his ear. His chin jerked to the side and down, repulsion written on his face.

I expected him to bring his eyes back up to find mine, to offer me comfort in a look. I expected him to raise his head and finish his toast. I even half expected him to come over to me and say something, anything. But he didn't. Aiden stayed, eyes pinned on the table, stress furrowing his brow, for too long. I lost track of how long he stayed frozen. Then I left, unable to bear how his paralysis threw my heart into a fit of wild tics.

Now I'm cuddled up on a couch in the library surrounded by books and not able to make sense of any of this. Volumes written by Poe, Emerson, Thoreau and their contemporaries aren't doing their jobs anymore. I'm starting to feel the doom push in on me.

Joseph strides up to my fortress of books and swiftly knocks it down with a single kick. "Enough!"

I turn over on my side, pull a book up next to me, and pretend to read it.

"Stark, this is worthless behavior," he reprimands.

"Who says?" I say, stretching out my feet on the coffee table in front of me.

"Face this *with* me," Joseph says, looking defenseless.

"Why'd you blab to everyone?" I ask, not hiding my disdain.

"It was an accident actually," Joseph says, pushing his hands through his short blond hair. "I told Trent when we were standin' in line at the buffet table this morning. I guess one of the kitchen people overheard it. By the time I'd gotten through the line and sat down it appeared a fair amount of people already knew. People love a scandal, what can I say."

"It shouldn't have come out," I say bitterly. "You were sloppy."

"Well, it's too late now, so get over it."

"That's what I was trying to do. You're interrupting my 'get-over-it' ritual."

"No I'm not. You're just using this as another excuse to sulk."

"I don't really need any more excuses, thank you very much." I pull a few of the closest books to me, hoping they'll provide the comfort and salvation I'm seeking through osmosis.

"I just need you to wake up," Joseph pleads with an exasperated tone. "You think I can face this without you right now?" Apparently he forgot how much he made me face alone while he was off resurrecting Zhuang, but this is probably not the right time to throw it in his face.

Joseph ignores my obvious body language that warns him to stay away, shoves a dozen books on the ground loudly, and sits down on the sofa next to me. "Please, just this once don't run away. I need your help. This isn't somethin' I want to deal with on my own."

Suddenly something new enters my heart; it isn't my own self-pity, it's Joseph's suffering. I pull at the string attached to his emotion and a series of thoughts follow. They aren't my thoughts though, they're his. For some reason now I can pick up on his thoughts and emotions the way he's always done with me. I stay silent as I listen to him. *Why does she have to be so difficult? She's so selfish.*

I swiftly punch him in the arm.

"Ow!" he yelps. "What was that for?" he says, rubbing his arm.

"Selfish? Really? Well, you haven't seen anything yet."

Realization falls on his face after a brief moment of confusion. "Oh, well it's about time, Stark. Welcome to the sibling mind reading club."

Joseph has been able to pick up my thoughts since the beginning. However, I've had more difficulty with it. I suspect this is because I was too overwhelmed with facing Zhuang and dying. After that whole mess was over, Zhuang was apparently in Joseph's head, blocking our connection. Now is the first time I'm able to truly feel and know his thoughts. The experience is foreign, like I've just put on a pair of gloves that are too big but soon conform to my hands. It feels all wrong and also, completely right. And it creates an obligation to him I haven't felt before.

"All right," I finally say, "you're not alone in this, Joseph. We're a team. I'm here for you."

"Thank you," he say. "It hurts, doesn't it? It hurts to know that whatever his reasons were, he let us go. He put us each in a stranger's home believing that was somehow better for us than being here…together." Joseph stares off in the distance at nothing in particular.

"It doesn't make sense," I say.

With a shake of his head he continues, "He's so distanced from this whole thing. There are a million things he should be telling us, but instead he sums up everything in a few words."

"My thoughts exactly," I say.

"Like something about our mother. More than just her name would be nice."

"And why is it that Ren is the only other person who knew?" I ask, the question suddenly occurring to me.

"Yeah, that makes no sense whatsoever," Joseph says, then laughs unexpectedly. "Bet Trey is being bombarded with questions now."

"Good, I hope it's terribly difficult for him." My words feel rough as they come out of my mouth.

"Nah, I doubt it. He appears to be pretty good at deflecting these things."

"Isn't it weird that he's spoken to us so many times and not shown the least bit of sentiment?" I ask, twirling my hair rapidly around my finger.

"You think that's weird?" Joseph gawks at me. "That's you! That's totally your behavior."

I narrow my eyes. "I resent that statement."

"Sorry, but that's the truth."

"That's your opinion," I say, but silently I know there's some truth to what he says.

"Trey is really the least of my problems at this point. I'm actually grateful that people are busy gossiping about this conspiracy." Joseph tugs on his shirtsleeve, yanking it down by his wrist like he's suddenly cold.

"Because it takes the attention off the fact that you brought Zhuang back," I state abruptly.

"Yeah, as I said, sensitivity really isn't your strong suit."

"I can understand the guilt and frustration; however, it could have happened to anyone. Zhuang picked you because you fit the criteria, but it just as easily could have been me or someone else," I say.

"It wouldn't have been you. There's no way you would have fallen for it. If you can spot Chase's projections then you'd spot Zhuang's for sure."

"It was going to happen one way or another. You can probably appreciate Samara's position more than ever. She was in a similar predicament when she killed Pearl. What's done is done. Zhuang is alive because he was never dead. This just means that this time we have to kill him for good." I sound much more triumphant than I feel.

"We?" Joseph looks at me weakly.

"Yeah, this time we're a team," I say. "We have to act that way. For starters, we need to figure out how we're going to confront this whole Trey mess when we face the Institute."

To continue reading, please purchase your copy of
Revived.

Made in the USA
Charleston, SC
24 September 2015